THE FIRST TO

FORGIVE

Book 2 of The Triumvirs

Daniel Dydek

BEORN PUBLISHING, LLC

DEDICATION

For my Alpha Readers, whose tireless anticipation for the next book helps
keep me writing:

Erin, Tyler, Abby, and Jesse

CONTENTS

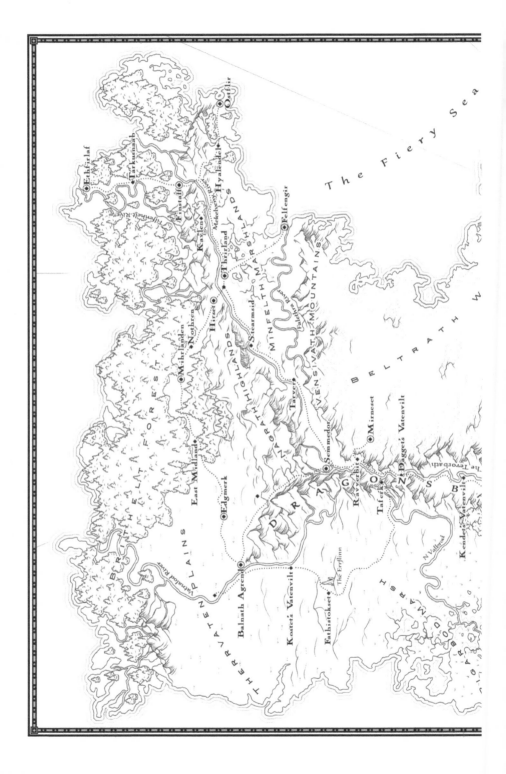

I

Night Visions

"They are making good time."
"It is not necessary for us both to be here."
"I have nothing to do."
"Let us correct that."

33 Haschina 1320[1] — Winter

"Would you tell Roth Kamdellan I need to speak with him?" Catie asked the young guard, trying to sound as though she saw Roth all the time.

But the boy never blinked. "No," he said.

She crossed her arms and shrugged. "It's your fault if this information doesn't come to him."

"What information?"

Catie's mouth twisted. "I can't tell you that," she said. "It's for Roth only."

"I'm sure it is. See, the thing is, we've already asked Roth about you, and he has no idea who you are." His eyebrows flared. "So you can keep coming here day after day, and trying your same ploy with all different guards, but

---

1. See Author's Note on Calendar for explanation of dates

we've already all been told about you."

Catie's arms drooped. "I've only come here three times."

"Five, and I can give you the names of all the guards. Now go away."

Catie turned and moved away. She wiped her face, then paused. "How did you all know about me?" she asked quietly.

"Because we all talk about what happens when we're on duty," the boy replied. "In case anything seems important."

"Is that part of your training?" She sniffled in the cold.

The boy shifted. "No, we just talk about things," he said. "In the barracks."

"Oh, that makes sense," she replied. "I didn't realize you all had barracks here."

"Well, they're not proper barracks. We put up in the west wing of the inn."

"Thanks!" Catie called as she strode off toward the building the boy had indicated.

"Wait, where are you going?" he said, taking a step toward her.

"You're not leaving your post, are you?" she asked in a clear, strong voice, her stride quickening.

"You can't—oh, no... Would you stop and come back—Why are you—would you stop?"

But Catie continued down the street. Five guards knew about her, did they? They obviously didn't know about her resolve.

She stopped by a small bakery—Akervet Brodlek was littered with them—and purchased a few fresh rolls. She didn't have much coin, but if this worked, she would need very little more. She smiled to the baker, wound the rolls tight to keep them warm as a light snow began to fall, and continued on her way.

Though she had only been in Akervet for a week, she knew the town well enough, knew which inn would have a wing, and be comfortable enough for Roth to keep his soldiers. They did like to stay warm, and they didn't only rely on beds and blankets to do so. Catie slid one side of her cloak off her shoulder, and undid a lace from her buckskin jacket—but just one: it was still cold, and she valued herself too highly to give *too* much away.

She approached the inn, glimpsing a soldier as he exited the west wing. She smiled as she passed, saw his eyes drop below her chin and linger. She resisted the urge to close the jacket until he had passed, then gave heed to a chill that was not only from the air. Resolve. That's what she needed.

She could almost feel the heat of the roaring hearths inside as she knocked on the door. It cracked open, and a balding head with squirrelly eyes peered out at her. "Who are you?" he asked.

"I thought you might like some warm bread," she said sweetly.

The door opened wider, and three more pairs of eyes squinted in the sudden sunlight. "That would be very nice," the squirrel-eyed one said, not yet taking the offered gift. He didn't seem to want to risk her leaving as soon as her errand was done. "Would you like to come inside and get warm?"

"Oh, thank you," Catie replied, stepping quickly through the door. It was *very* nice and warm. Once the door was shut, she handed them the loaves, and stood beside the fire as they remained awkwardly quiet behind her. She almost wanted to laugh as she could sense the men working up some sort of courage. But they were taking too long. She swept her cloak behind her, and sighed.

"Truly, I don't know how you stay in so warm a room," she said, taking the cloak off completely. "It seems so uncomfortable." She shook out her hair—which actually made her feel warmer, but men always seemed to like the loose curls. Dannid had.

"Well, there are ways to keep cool," said one—not the squirrel. "And other ways to keep warm besides fire."

She rolled her eyes before fixing her smile and half-turning toward the speaker. "Oh?" she asked. "Could you show me?"

"Well, first, you need to be further from the fire," the same speaker said quickly, trying to be faster than his friends in coming toward her without making it seem like a competition.

She took a step backward. Toward him. "Like, here?"

He managed to laugh. "No, a little further than that. Here, come with me."

Looking sideways at his friends, the tall, broad-shouldered guard led her into a side room, and shut the door. "See how much nicer it is in here?" he asked as he gently slid the bolt closed.

"It isn't so hot, in here," she agreed, glancing around the room. It looked to be a more private quarter, and she wondered whether he had rank, or poor judgment. The latter would serve her nicely. Or both.

"It isn't hot—yet," the guard said, maintaining his cryptic tone. "But you can change that, too, and make it warmer." He pulled a chair up in front of her and sat down. His hands reached out and gripped her hips.

Catie quickly held up a finger. "Not yet," she said, her eyes still casting about for—there it was. She pulled away from him, amazed he let her go, and picked up a chamber pot near the bed. She quickly checked to see that it was empty.

"What—?" was all he said before she struck the pot off the floor, then stomped her feet a few times. He stared at her as a scuffling could be heard outside the room.

"Is everything all right in there?" asked a voice.

Catie looked at him, drawing her arms behind her and pushing her chest forward as she batted her eyelashes and smiled.

"Uh, yes, everything's fine! Go away!" he snapped. His voice lowered. "What in the name of the gods did you do that for?"

Catie smiled, then smashed the pot over his head, stomping her feet a few times as he fell to the floor, unconscious. She darted to the door, pressing her ear against it to listen for anyone approaching.

"What in the bloody Marfey is going on in there?" muttered what sounded like the squirrel-eyed one.

"Marfey's got nothing to do with it, Steth," said another. "Sergeant's up for it, anyway. Did you see her face? I don't think there's a woman made better than brown hair and matching eyes, like that. I'd be up for it too, if it was me."

"You always were for the faces, Korgan," said the third. "I go for the part what strains the laces, if you know what I mean."

"It was chestnut hair," Steth said quietly. "But I think I prefer the part that doesn't matter what clothes they have on."

Korgan glared at him. "What's that, their wits? Gods know you don't know what to do with anything else."

Steth, for his part, put up a loud argument. Catie, still amazed her plan was going better than she hoped, slipped out through a window with a new set of armor, complete with a helmet that would hide a fair portion of her face. As the fight continued inside the inn, she checked her boot for her hunting knife. She took a deep breath and, pulling the helmet over her head, struck off back for the building occupied by Roth Kamdellan, leader of the rebellion against Sheppar, Kinnig of Andelen.

"'Kinnig,'" Roth scoffed. "Do not call him that in front of me. I refuse to call him by that title. Who would think of saying 'no, don't call me king; call me *little* king'?"

"I'm sorry, sir," Rodigger said. "I am sorry. I had called him that for a long time."

"Your whole life, I know," Roth said, gently now. "I am so glad I could save you from that. I know it seems disrespectful to only call him 'Sheppar', but what he has titled himself is even more disrespectful. And if he cannot respect himself, how does he expect the rest of the country to do so?"

"Right, sir," Rodigger said. "But, back to the original point..."

"Oh, yes, of course," Roth said, shaking his head. "Please—"

He was interrupted as the sweat-smell from the helmet finally made Catie sneeze. The force of it echoed back in her helmet, and rang in her ears.

"Ow," she said, then squeezed her eyes shut at how plainly feminine her voice was.

Roth straightened, his eyes going hard. "Seize..." He gestured. "...that." The guard on the other side of the door did himself credit, grasping her swiftly despite his shock. Rodigger was in front of her in two steps and yanked the helmet from her head.

"I have some information for Roth alone?" Catie said hopefully.

"Then by all means, give it," Roth said.

"Your guard is holding down the arm I was going to deliver it with," she replied.

"Sir?" the guard asked.

Roth regarded her for several moments. "Rodigger, check her right boot, would you?"

Rodigger glanced down, and his shoulders stiffened. He bent over and yanked the knife from her boot, then turned and handed it to Roth. "We should throw her deep into a hole somewhere," he whispered.

Roth's gaze never left Catie's face as he took the knife. "She may have a very good reason for what she attempted," he replied. "And considering how far she made it *this* time, I am almost curious to see how far she might make it the next time."

"Sir?" Rodigger said, his brow furrowing.

Roth addressed the guard. "Put her outside the walls, and don't let her back inside," he said, turning away with a backward wave. "If she makes it to the next inn, she deserves to live."

"I need my horse," she said quietly, already knowing the answer. But today had been a day of foolhardy hope.

"I suspect you do," Roth returned lightly. "Rodigger, once she's gone, please show in my other guests."

"Sir, you're not giving her the, um..." Rodigger paused as Roth glared at him, then turned to the guard who still held Catie. "You heard him, get her out! And make sure the guards know her so they won't let her back in."

She went willingly back into the cold, through the streets as people gazed curiously at the strange parade. The snow by now had gathered in corners and on ledges, shading everything else a little whiter as it came down in lazy flakes. Catie stumbled along a little from numbness, a little because the guard who restrained her took his charge very seriously.

Once outside the walls, the doors did not boom shut as she thought they should. But the guards' crossed spears were as unyielding as anything made of oak, and she turned her face resolutely down the road and began to walk. The snow, for spite, fell thicker.

Roth looked up as the doors shut behind the two men he had summoned from Balnath Agrend several weeks ago. He had truly been uncertain that Gabriel would come. The fact that the mercenary would visit the enemy of his friend spoke volumes of his situation. And of course if Gabriel came, Deuel did too. They were a package deal in the mercenary world—and an expensive deal, but worth the coin.

But if they had been two sides of a coin, one side had apparently fared far worse than the other.

"Please, sit," Roth said, gesturing to a couch opposite his own chair. Rodigger stood inconspicuously to one side, observing but not too alert. He was a good lad. He would do fine.

Deuel remained standing, his posture exuding an ability for sudden and decisive movement even as his muscles relaxed. His cloak was thick, and Roth thought briefly that he seemed to wear it a little too carefully. But then, the man was strange entire. From his face, one might think he was twenty to thirty years Gabriel's junior. But a glance in his eyes told a story of ages, older it seemed than the mountains far to the east. It was rumored a glance was usually all one could withstand before looking away. Roth tried quickly, and confirmed the tale. What was it, in those depths?

It did not matter. Gabriel sat down, very nearly slouching, and seemed prepared only to move if buttered biscuits were set before him. But, according to other stories Roth had heard...

"We're here," Gabriel said. "What do you want?"

Roth settled back, his eyes narrowing. "I want to hire you," he said.

Gabriel blinked at him. "No kidding? I thought I was coming down here for tea."

Roth glanced at Deuel, who regarded him with unnatural stillness. Roth's eyes went back to Gabriel as he hurried to regain control of the meeting. "Very well," he said. "No pleasantries, then. Do you know of the Berkarfor?"

"Hidden goblets of legend..." Gabriel trailed off, gazing at him for several moments, then burst suddenly into loud laughter. "That's what you propose?" he asked between gasps. "Pay me now, and I'll give you cups," he said, snapping his fingers.

Roth waited until Gabriel's mirth subsided. "The Berkarfor are real," he said quietly, his gaze level. "The first can be found near Agirbirt Lake."

The humor in Gabriel's eyes was gone but for a faint spark. "How did you find this out?"

"Careful study," Roth replied. He raised a small glass from a nearby table and took a slow drink. "When you find the first, it should lead you to the second—and so on."

"Why us? I'm old," Gabriel said. "I might die before I find them all."

"That is my risk to take," Roth replied. "Besides, I believe your partner will be most helpful to you."

Gabriel betrayed his surprise only by the slightest glance at Deuel. Deuel did not react at all. "He does seem to know things no one else does," the mercenary replied. "But he never mentioned to me knowing where the goblets are."

"I am sure he doesn't. But the riddles to be solved to learn the location of the next one should be less difficult to one with his...experience."

"This gets better and better. And what is the recompense for a mission such as this?"

"Five thousand nerist," Roth replied. Gabriel hid his surprise better, this time. "To start," Roth continued. "Another five when you return successful."

Gabriel slid his palms against his knees, and Roth knew he had him. Normally one would haggle at this point, but one was not normally offered ten thousand nerist for search-and-find. "This is very important to you," Gabriel said.

"It is important for Andelen," Roth corrected smoothly, setting down his cup. "Without the Berkarfor, my work for my country will never be finished."

"And without your pay, my work for myself will never be finished," Gabriel said dryly. "We'll set out tomorrow morning. I assume we have rooms, somewhere?" The mercenary rocked to his feet. Deuel barely shifted, but one glance told Roth his muscles were alert again.

"Would you like to look over what I have concerning the first hiding place?" Roth asked, rising as well.

"Have it put in my saddlebags. It'll be a long journey to Agirbirt."

"Very well, my aide will place them for you. The Rustling Ivy has a room prepared for you, and stall-space," Roth said, extending his hand.

"Are stalls something hard to find?" Gabriel asked, grasping the proffered hand and releasing it quickly.

"I have many horses," Roth replied with a thin smile that held, barely, until the mercenary and his partner exited the room. Then he snatched up the glass and drained the contents. "Rodigger, you are going with them," he snapped. He glanced up just as the young man shut his mouth decisively. "I don't like this man, and I somehow don't trust my offer to keep him faithful. If you must, take over the mission. And bring me those Berkarfor!" he finished, managing to refrain from hurling his empty cup to his protégé.

He made it to the door, hand on the latch, before he stopped. His gaze was down, focused on nothing. Then his eyes slid sideways. "Actually," he said, "I think your missions will be two-fold." His hand left the latch, and he turned. He drew close to Rodigger. "Or perhaps three. Word of our cause needs to spread outside the Fallonvall, and you will be in a unique position to do that. But there's something else—or, some*one* else. I need you to keep alert for a man." Roth's smile grew. "A very particular man. And here's how you will know him..."

If Catie reached the inn by moonset, it would be a miracle. And as far as she was concerned, she had used a lifetime of miracles getting that close to Roth in the first place.

But she still had her cloak, and wrapped it tightly around her. It would serve for now. Roth risked little by letting her keep it. The sun—a vague bright spot on the clouds—was past noon. The day would be long, as the plains here were utterly flat. But there would be little dusk, and the temperature would fall as swiftly as night. And she had small way of making fire: there was precious little fuel adequate to burn, not until she reached the Dragonsback Mountains almost two hundred miles away.

Or the inn that was a tempting, but futile, thirty miles away.

As she considered it, she wasn't sure why she walked. It kept her warmer, which was something. But it could not do so forever, not this time of year. Perhaps because she had rarely stopped moving for the last two months—not until she found out Roth was garrisoned in Akervet. She should have been on her way home. She *had* been, and was passing through Aresmak in the 'Back. She should have continued up the mountains, then east to Agirbirt Lake and home.

When she made the decision to turn west, she hadn't had a plan. She simply went, hoping everything else would fall into place. Some decisions were made that way, it seemed: one step led to an entirely different road, and she walked down it. Her Grandmother had told her that, more than once.

And so she did, without thinking. Even when she'd gotten to Akervet, no real plan had formed. Each step followed another until she sneezed and gave herself away.

She would have died in that room, if she had succeeded. She knew that, and had accepted it. But to die now, in the cold, while Roth lived on in the warmth? It had not seemed like utterly the wrong road until that moment. She had strode confidently along, reaching Akervet, petitioning the guards for entrance, figuring a way to slip inside on her own, and actually standing in the same room as that man while he talked on, oblivious to her presence and the death she had intended to bring. The whole time, it had seemed the right road. But in two moments...could it happen that quick? Had there been no warning signs that she was making a bad decision all the way back in Aresmak?

Sure, there had been small obstacles, but barely more than briars overreaching the verge. Now she was locked in a thicket, no way out, and night and cold were descending like stooping falcons. It did not seem like the same road, at all. More like she had been plucked from one path that was free, and clear, and led precisely where she wanted to go, and set instantly down on a path she had not meant to trod.

Yet here she was, still walking. Why? She glanced backward, and was surprised to see how small the village had gotten behind her. When the snow flurried just right, she almost couldn't see it. She turned forward again, wrapped her fingers around her collar, and twisted her face in frustration, anger, sadness. She wanted to cry, knew it would be a release. But nothing came. Walking was pointless, but she had to do it, knowing it served no purpose. She had made a stupid decision, which got her only this walking sentence, and no justice. Roth, that smug, arrogant, witless catfish didn't have the decency to kill her outright, when Catie had very little will to live, anyway.

Her steps faltered just once, and then resumed their normal cadence. She didn't mind the dying—that was supposed to have happened. But why must she go on with this worthless living for so long before it came? And what did it serve to have so much time to think, when she would meet no one before night, and would die before dawn?

This time tears did come, and froze against the collar of her cloak.

By the time the glow of the sun behind the clouds reached the horizon, her pace had slackened. The snow, blessedly, had stopped. But Catie was already chilled to the marrow. And the waning full moon wouldn't rise for some time yet, so it was about to get very dark as well as very cold. Certainly no conditions in which to walk.

With what little daylight remained, Catie wandered off the road until she found a low area with thick shocks of knee-high grass. Pausing occasionally to blow into her cupped hands, she pulled up the blades and piled them. Perhaps, if she could gather enough, she might make something of a nest. Such things served the birds that stayed for winter.

By the time she had anything of a bed, daylight had gone. She laid down, tried to burrow deep without going so deep as to reach the frozen ground, failed because she hadn't been able to get quite enough of a nest built, and turned over on her back to look up into the sky. She would have liked to see the stars, one more time. But as weariness from cold and shivering clouded her brain to match the sky, she knew she wouldn't. The wind rustling through the grasses, though chill, calmed her.

Sleep came, but she would not stop living yet. In a dream she went far to the south, to Bokessin near the coast, to the square she knew well, that would be emblazoned in her mind eternally. The pool in the middle of the square already ran red. The resistance had failed, and Roth's blades were sharp as his vengeance. A crowd had gathered at spear-point, and Catie was among them. Those terrible swords, flashing in the sunlight. It had been a remarkably beautiful day, and the bloodshed in that square was not enough to dim it. Every detail was captured perfectly: every prisoner, every sword-stroke, every death. One by one, and Dannid in line, working his way toward death step by shuffling step. He was saved for last, and Roth himself performed the act, because Dannid had started it, and led it to what it had become.

Dannid stepped forward, that last step, with the same confidence as he had stepped toward Catie only three days before. Roth did not know she was in the crowd, wouldn't have cared if he did. Because he still wouldn't know that Dannid and Catie had just been married.

She tried to turn away, but this was a demonstration for the people of Bokessin, and a guard was close enough to prick her with a spear until she turned forward again. Dannid's head was at the edge of the pool. Roth's sword—perfectly clean and brilliant in the sun—came down swiftly.

Catie's eyes snapped open. The dream left her, as did the weariness from the cold. There was a sound on the air, like a kitten trying to mew, except the note held and seemed to echo across a vast distance. She looked to the horizon, and her brow furrowed as she slowly sat upright.

Far to the south, beyond the horizon, an orange light—thin as a blade of grass held sideways but immovable as the Dragonsback Mountains—pierced through the night sky. Where it originated, and where it went, was impossible to determine. She sensed somehow that it did not even originate in Andelen.

All at once the light disappeared and the sound ceased, and Catie's breath was ripped from her lungs. She sat gasping, not sure of what she had just seen. And yet she felt at once a terrible anguish and an incomparable joy—and a will to live as she had never known. She felt at that moment as though the Dragonsback Mountains could bury her, and the Fiery Sea could drown her, and she would dig and swim until she found daylight again.

And yet she did not know where to go. There was only a sense of flight, and a vague direction northward. But like a bee drumming against a window, her thoughts knew only *go! go! go!* while her destination was blocked firmly from her mind. Somehow that didn't matter. She knew that nothing would stop her, ever, until she reached wherever it was she was supposed to go.

That was, until she heard hoofbeats rumbling in the distance along the road from Akervet.

In the hotel room, a sudden movement woke Gabriel from his slumber. The darkness was nearly complete, save what washed in from a fading moon. He searched for what had woken him, and saw Deuel sitting upright in his bed.

"Skald?" Gabriel asked, rising to his elbows.

Deuel's head drooped, then turned to gaze at Gabriel. "Paolound is dead," he murmured.

Gabriel levered himself up. "You thought that before."

Deuel shook his head. "He had died then too, but someone revived him. I do not think he will be revived again. He is dead, Gabriel. The Call is strong."

Gabriel sighed quietly. "This is not good timing, *Skalderon*. I will need you now—"

"I know." Deuel lay back down slowly. "I cannot help the call, Gabriel. I felt it, and it woke you, and now you know. I will see how long it will last this time. Good night."

To all appearances, Deuel resumed his slumber. Gabriel knew both their thoughts ran swiftly behind closed eyelids, and mostly together. He did not whisper to the God of All much, at least not formally. But to whom else could his thoughts go as they floated through his mind: *let us find these goblets quickly. Don't make him miss this opportunity again.*

2

STRANGE RESPITES

"I thought you hid those long ago?"
"It seems they seek to find them again."
"You leave now for Andelen?"
"I think it should be yours, Teresh."

34 Haschina 1320 — Winter

C atie turned onto her stomach, eyes searching the thin gloom. The moon had risen, and with snow-shine gave shadows to the landscape. She could see the thin line of the road. And there, not one but two horses, one empty-saddled, coming toward her.

She shuffled on her elbows, craning her neck. It was odd that someone traveled so late at night, and odder that they led a riderless horse. It was still too close to Akervet for something to have gone amiss, so the rider had to have brought the horse riderless from the town. And if they were simply heading for Aresmak, they would have waited and left in the morning, wouldn't they?

As both horses neared, she stood, knowing her brown leather would show up starkly against the snow—which reminded her how cold the night was. Her arms came up reflexively and crossed, her shoulders stooped as she felt the light breeze.

Horses and rider stopped, their breath squirting into the air. The riderless mount squealed and turned toward her. Catie straightened as she recognized the voice: it was Kelsie, her mare.

Leaving her cloak and nest, Catie trotted to Kelsie's head, forgetting the rider for the moment. Her mare ducked as Catie pressed in and curled her fingers in her mane.

Catie backed away, still scratching Kelsie's muzzle as she finally looked up at the rider. Her fingers stopped as she noticed his squirrelly eyes, and could imagine the balding head under his warm cap.

"My name is Steth," he said. "And yours is Catie?"

"It is," she replied, suddenly feeling the gap in her boot where her knife had been.

"You tried to kill Roth, which is why you came to the barracks."

"Yes."

Steth tossed her the reins. "And he didn't kill you outright?"

Catie resumed her scratching, rocking a little as Kelsie pushed into her. "He felt if I could make it to the next inn, I deserved to live."

"Did he say exactly that?"

"Yes."

Steth looked eastward, and adjusted his seat with a creak of leather. "Then I don't feel wrong for helping you. Who deserves life more than one who can win the hearts of her enemies?"

"And how did I do that, exactly?"

Steth turned back to look at her. "By coming closer than anyone else to killing Roth Kamdellan."

Catie's fingers moved up behind an ear. "You're one of his soldiers," she said.

"Who better to know the failings of a leader than one who serves him?"

Catie shrugged. "I've known a few people who knew his failings well enough, who would never serve him."

"Some have that luxury," Steth said. "Others have families."

"Some have that luxury, too," Catie murmured, tracing the star between Kelsie's eyes with her thumb.

"I'm sorry?"

Catie shook her head. "I can't repay you for bringing me my horse," she said with a smile.

"Yes, you can," Steth said, turning his horse toward Akervet. Catie looked up, squinting. Steth smiled. "Come visit Roth again, sometime. If you can. Hopefully better prepared, next time."

"Are you that certain he's wrong?"

Steth cocked his head. "I cannot say about his ideas. But certainly his methods."

Catie watched Steth as he rode off, slower now that his mission was complete. She could agree with that: whether or not Roth was right about Sheppar and how he was handling his rule, Roth's way of fixing it had to be stopped. But how? As Steth said, she needed to be better prepared. Simply going to Akervet and 'seeing what happened' would not work again.

Again. Catie glanced at her nest where her cloak still lay: clearly it hadn't worked the first time. And why should it have? Her father might have taught her much about survival before he left, but that was survival in the absence of others—not survival in dealing with others. As much as Dannid might have influenced her, too, they had only known each other for two years. And little of that time had been spent training in assassination.

Catie sighed, and retrieved her cloak. Part of her just wanted to be home again. Another part wasn't sure how she would tell her story to Grandmother. In the three years since she had run away, she had joined a resistance, gotten married, seen her husband executed, and was herself nearly executed for trying to assassinate someone. What every Grandmother wanted, surely.

She shook the snow from her cloak before wrapping it around her shoulders. Another part of her remembered the light that pierced the sky. That part was still trying to understand what happened, and why she felt an enormous pressure to go home, while also knowing that same pressure would not keep her there. That it would pause for a time, but only a temporary stop before going on to something else. How could she possibly know that? And how did an orange light and a faint keening make her know that? Or did she just dream it?

She glanced toward her departing savior. She should have asked Steth, but he was far down the road now, and the night was cold.

She turned. Kelsie was staring at her. And why *was* she still standing in the cold when a horse waited to take her to a warm fire? Kelsie whinnied and tossed her head as if reading Catie's thoughts, and Catie smiled. They had been through a lot, they two. Maybe the mare *could* read her thoughts, by now. She mounted, and Kelsie turned for the inn without prompting.

Despite the cold, she fairly slept in the saddle as Kelsie made her unerring way. Catie blinked when Kelsie stopped and huffed: the inn was before them. Still in a weary haze, Catie stabled her mare, fed some hay into the trough, and circled to the front of the building. Her hand rose and yanked the rope to ring the bell inside, then stood in front of the door, waiting to be recognized and allowed in.

But no one came. The breeze picked up again, and she shook with chill. Fear crept back, waking her a little. Had it closed? She had never heard of that. The scrapes on stone near the door from goblins and hellhounds trying to get in were all old. Surely...

She returned and rang the bell again. Something brief and likely colorful was muttered inside, and the rope suddenly sped through the hole and disappeared.

"Hey!" she cried, her hand leaping out in reflex alone, as the rope was long gone before she moved. "Let me in!" she shouted, kicking the door.

Miraculously, it opened. It was mostly dark inside, the fire having died to coals, but she could see well enough the spindly old man in thin red cotton night clothes and heavy boots. His white hair grew long to make up for what was no longer there, and still kept in the filthy manner that had probably led to his balding in the first place.

"Why didn't you come in daylight?" he demanded.

"I wasn't here in daylight," Catie responded, twisting sideways past him and into the warmer interior. She went straight to the fire and began tending it.

The old man shut the door, but remained near it as he watched her work. "You're supposed to come in the day," he said. "You could have been a hellhound or something."

"Ringing the bell?" Catie asked, leaning three logs together, and throwing some bits of bark underneath to help them catch.

"Goblin."

"They don't exist anymore." She blew on the coals. They glared, then stuck thin tongues out at her. She continued blowing until the bark caught. Kindly flames greeted her, then, and went to meet the logs.

The keeper harrumphed. "Of course they exist. Why else am I here?"

Catie waited to answer until the logs caught. She sighed, steadying herself as her head lightened. Weariness crept in again. She sat on the hearth, shedding her cloak so the heat would soak into her skin faster, and turned to the old man.

"My name is Catie," she said. "And I'm frozen and hungry."

"I'm Lothan, and I don't much care," he said, remaining steadfast by the door.

"You don't remember me?" Catie asked. "I was through here a few days ago."

"I don't remember people, they die too much. Dinner was hours ago, as was bed time. My inn keeps you safe from big nasties, and that's all I owe you."

"Big nasties are all gone, Lothan," Catie said. "Remember? Sheppar killed them all thirty years ago."

"All by himself?" Lothan asked, crossing his arms.

Catie stared, then turned to make sure the fire was still growing. "I'm sorry I had to wake you in the middle of the night," she said gently. "But I was sent out from Akervet in the middle of the day, on foot."

"You could have been killed!"

"So many different ways," Catie muttered.

"Exactly," Lothan said. "Goblins, hounds, vipers...not vipers, it's too cold, I suppose."

"Lothan, there aren't vipers on the roads anymore," Catie said, rubbing her eyes. She was beginning to warm, and realized she hadn't slept much since—well, for several months now, if she really thought about it. "Sheppar and his soldiers cleared all the wilds. It was a massive campaign."

"Rumors and myths," Lothan replied with a grunt.

"Have you had many attacks, lately?" Catie asked, then yawned.

"Just because I haven't doesn't mean I won't," he said. "Why would I be here if travelers didn't still need my protection? The reason these inns were built was to protect travelers, and that's still what we do."

"Do you please have anything to eat?" Catie asked. "Even something cold."

"Breakfast is at Morning," Lothan said, leaving his post by the door and heading toward his personal chambers, near the kitchen.

"Fine," Catie replied. After the door banged shut behind the keeper, she stared at it for several moments, hoping he was only angry at being disturbed so late. She glanced at the fire and shook with one final chill. The heat had reached most of her bones, by now, and she had to ignore her hunger. That left only her exhaustion. Her upper body pitched forward as that need washed over her. She caught herself, pushed herself upright, and after one brief moment to collect her shambled resolve she got to her feet.

After that was another haze of moving toward the back where the communal sleeping quarters were, to the first of the row of cots. And she woke up *underneath* the blankets, so that happened at some point, too.

Thin, vertical slits in the walls near the ceiling allowed the morning sun to shine through and wake the occupants, alerting them that they would need to be on their way soon to make the next inn. These slits were well-designed, and piercing sunlight fell precisely on Catie's eyelids, waking her instantly despite her every desire not to. The smell of frying bacon hit her nostrils an instant before she understood the sound, and she smiled. He was already making up for his surliness the night before.

After a good breakfast—though a silent one: Lothan served her, then sat behind a game of *feth* and glared at the scattered pairs on the board till she finished—Catie was off properly, whispering to Kelsie of a better night's rest at the next inn. It was a sunny, clear morning, promising more of spring to come than remembering winter past. She had inexplicably survived death yet again, and her soaring spirits dragged the sun into the sky with them.

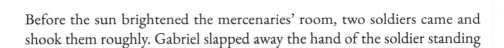

Before the sun brightened the mercenaries' room, two soldiers came and shook them roughly. Gabriel slapped away the hand of the soldier standing over top of him.

"Roth said to wake you," said the man as he folded his arms.

"Even for five thousand, he does not own me," Gabriel retorted. "And you may awaken me more gently, lest you lose your hands."

"I will be sure to kiss you next time," the soldier replied. "And Roth does own you, on pain of death, not promise of money. Get up. Your companion and your horses await."

"Companion?" Deuel said.

"Roth will not leave you to your own devices," the other soldier replied. "He is sending one of his own, whom he trusts, to go with you."

"Oh, splendid," Gabriel replied. "The help will be appreciated."

They rose and gathered their gear, then followed the men into the crisp morning. A thin blanket of snow covered the grass, and the horse's nostrils steamed.

Standing by the horses was a vaguely familiar young man in his early twenties. His red hair scraggled just above his shoulders, and a thin beard covered his chin. He slouched just a little, though his eyes scanned constantly. When Gabriel approached, the young man straightened a little and extended his hand.

"Rodigger Kytes," he said pleasantly, though without smiling. "Aide to Roth Kamdellan, and companion to you."

"You were in the room last night," Gabriel remembered aloud, shaking the proffered hand in passing. He stopped suddenly as he looked at Rodigger's horse. "Is that what you're riding?" he asked.

"Why? Shouldn't I?"

"It's a Therian," Gabriel said. When Rodigger only blinked, he continued: "We're likely spending a lot of time in the mountains, you know."

"Gared and I have been through them before," Rodigger replied. He glanced at the others. "Your horses don't look like that much."

Gabriel glared. "You named him 'Gared'?" he said, his voice rumbling. "Is that supposed to be funny?"

"Roth said it was a good name," Rodigger said, his voice faltering.

"I'm sure he did," Gabriel muttered. He mounted his horse. "Berok and Rodan are Midlands," he said, indicating his and Deuel's geldings. "They'll beat you up the 'Backs, and I don't like waiting for anyone."

"Not even a companion?" Rodigger asked, extended his hand to Deuel. Deuel ignored it and climbed onto his horse.

"Accomplice, perhaps," Gabriel replied, swinging Berok around. "Acquaintance, maybe. But Deuel and I choose our companions. Mount up, if you're going to follow."

The two friends cantered down the road and out into the countryside. Rodigger leapt onto his own horse and spurred after them, setting his chin grimly.

When he caught up to them, he stayed a a few lengths behind. Gabriel noted it: he could be called on if necessary, but they could still speak in private. He begrudgingly admired the tact. He called Rodigger forward.

"Sir?" Rodigger asked when his mount had approached nearer.

"Why does Roth fight this revolution?" Gabriel asked.

"To help the people," Rodigger answered promptly.

Gabriel and Deuel blinked at one another, and Deuel turned his head to the fields. "I assumed that much, Kytes," Gabriel answered with a thin smile. "I was not aware the people needed help."

"They do, sir," Rodigger replied. "I have heard Roth talk about it many times."

Gabriel sighed loudly. "Rodigger, before I allow you to return to your trailing position, would you mind telling me exactly what the problem is that Roth hopes to correct?"

Deuel turned to glance at Rodigger as his back straightened a little. "Sheppar does not want to protect the people," he said. "He does not want to be King, and takes on a debasing diminutive. He wants to hand his power over to city magistrates, and turn control of the countryside over to them."

"Sounds like good news to the city magistrates," Gabriel commented.

"But bad for the farmers," Rodigger countered. "The magistrates will be more concerned with city-folk than the farmers who also rely on the community to sustain their way of life. Their needs will be overlooked, and the heart of Andelen will suffer because of it."

"So why does Sheppar want to give over control?"

"Because he doesn't want to be King."

"Leave us alone, Rodigger," Gabriel said.

The young soldier opened his mouth in hurt retort, but closed it quickly and allowed his mount to drop back.

"He is trained well," Deuel commented when he was out of earshot.

"I doubt he resisted the training," Gabriel replied. "If he was trained well, he would have better answers, not the same answers repeated three times."

"Do you think he lies?"

"Not intentionally," Gabriel said, glancing back at Rodigger and pausing. "And most likely not entirely," he added. "Sheppar's reasons may be a mystery, but his actions are probably not. And we'll probably get the same answers as our young friend's until we are out of Kamdellan-controlled territory."

"Sprativerg, then?"

Gabriel nodded. "More than likely."

The night's snow did not stick, and diminished through the day. As the lowering sun set the grass afire, the travelers' shadows stretched for the fortified inn. The two mercenaries reached it first, Rodigger still trailing behind. By the time he caught up they had dismounted and were unlading their horses.

"You still carry those? Even here?" Rodigger asked as Deuel and Gabriel belted on sheathed daggers.

Gabriel gave him a swift glance, then nodded. "Oh, old habit. I forgot the paradise your benevolent Roth brought to the Fallonvall."

"I'm sorry," Rodigger said, smiling. "I just meant..."

"Forget it," Gabriel said. But he did not take the weapon off as he entered the inn with Deuel close behind him.

Rodigger shook his head, rubbing his Therian's muzzle. "I'll keep going if you do," he whispered. Gared tossed his head and shook it. Rodigger smiled. "Me neither."

Though it was a squat, unadorned building of thick round stone, the sun that washed its face invited Rodigger through the heavy wooden door and into the well-lit and primarily oak interior. With hundreds of these inns scattered across Andelen, they were not much different from one another. Rodigger enjoyed the game of trying to notice the little touches each keeper inevitably brought. In this one, stone columns rose from a wooden floor to support a wooden roof, though Rodigger knew more heavy stone lay above that. Broad antlers decorated the walls and columns, serving as sconces and candleholders. That was not rare, but not standard either. The common room was small, as there were never that many travelers this deep in the Fallonvall. A small archway led back to the cot-room. Across from the bar a fire roared beneath a leering goblin's head. As small as the skull was, it probably came from after Sheppar's almost entirely successful campaign.

Behind the bar was another door that would lead to the kitchens, and next to which sat the inn's keeper. He glanced up from a *feth*board as Rodigger entered, and before the young soldier could ask he jerked his head toward the back, and returned his attention to the game.

Rodigger carried his gear into the cot-room. Gabriel and Deuel had claimed two of the cots, and the great mound of another traveler had clearly claimed a third as he lay with his back to them at the far end of the room. Iron-banded chests sat at the foot of each bed, a key protruding from their locks—definitely standard. Rodigger moved to one across from his companions, checking the lock before opening the chest and placing his tack and bags inside. He pocketed the key and turned to Deuel and Gabriel.

"Who's he?" he whispered with a nod toward the sleeping figure.

Gabriel shook his head and shrugged. "He was like that when we came in. I'm sure he'll be joining us for dinner."

"Dinner?" called a voice, deep and rumbling as the figure turned over and picked up his shaggy head. "Already?"

Rodigger glanced at the face mostly of black hair, then back at his companions.

Gabriel spoke up. "Soon, I imagine. Sun's set."

The man blinked a few times, then smiled. "Of course: no windows. And those slits are little help, after dawn." He pushed himself upright, settling his stocking feet on the floor. "I kept thinking it was no darker in here than when I went to sleep." He rose to an enormous height. His brown rough-spun tunic and trousers must have cost two long-wool sheep apiece to make. He crossed the length of the room in four strides, a meaty hand swallowing Rodigger's whole, but gently, as Rodigger introduced himself.

"Keltan," he replied. He turned to the mercenary.

"I'd say you are. Gabriel."

Keltan laughed as he shook Deuel's hand last, though his mirth faltered a little as he looked the thin man up and down. "Mam tells everyone I was born this big, and she could think of nothing better to call me. Said I came out with this thing, too," he added, burying his hands in his beard with another chuckle.

"What brings you out here?" Gabriel asked.

"Lothan," Keltan said, nodding toward the main common room. "He's the best challenge I can find south of Sprativerg. I always stop in if I'm coming down this way."

"*Feth?*" Rodigger asked, trying to wipe the surprise from his face.

Keltan nodded, then gazed toward the archway. "Wonder if he's made a move yet."

"It looked like he was still studying when I came through," Rodigger said.

Keltan's eyes twinkled. "I left him in quite a bind. I suppose I should check on him."

The big man left. Gabriel shrugged and led them back to the common room. Keltan was looming over the bar, grinning in good-natured malevolence as Lothan's forehead still puckered over the board.

"Your guests want food, Lothan. Make your move."

"You're always in my light, Keltan," Lothan replied with a sharp glance.

Keltan gave a slow nod and a wink at the three companions. "Excuse me, Lothan. Curse of my birth." Long arms and fingers grasped four mugs and filled them from a small cask against the wall. Keltan nodded toward a table, gesturing with the mugs of ale.

Gabriel led the way, and the four sat down while Lothan pondered his next move.

"And what brings you three out this way?" Keltan asked.

"A job," Gabriel replied.

Rodigger coughed and spluttered into his mug. Keltan's hand came down against his back a few times, nearly bashing his teeth into the rim. "I'm alright," he said, holding up a hand to stop the blows. "Took a little too much foam, is all. Gabriel, do you think—?"

"I had you pegged as a soldier as soon as I rolled over," Keltan said. "And these two are not soldiers, but they can handle themselves: mercenaries?" Gabriel gazed hard at Rodigger, who returned to his mug. "You haven't been on the road long, which means you came from Akervet," Keltan continued. "Which means Roth and the rebellion."

"Revolution," Rodigger corrected automatically. "So why did you ask?"

Keltan laughed. "Because if you lied, the job was important. It's the moves that the player tries to make subtly that you have to pay the most attention to. Right Lothan?"

"Aha!" the keeper exulted. "Take that, you wily, elusive, unnoticeable Keltan."

The big man roared laughter and rose. "First I'm always in your light, then I'm unnoticeable. Next you'll tell me I'm only good in the kitchen."

"You are, at that," Lothan replied as he stood. "So I can count on your help, since your deviousness cost these travelers a timely dinner?"

Keltan glanced at the board, grinned, and gestured to door behind the bar. They exited, leaving the other three with only the sound of the rushing fire.

"Probably shouldn't question my methods again," Gabriel said, taking a drink.

"You told him the truth, but completely diverted him from more questions," Rodigger replied, shaking his head.

"Almost like I've done this before."

"I thought maybe you would think we were safe enough in the Fallonvall, or that you didn't care much for the revolution..."

"Me?" Gabriel said with arched eyebrows. "Who still carries a dagger into a fortified inn? Feel safe?"

Rodigger shrugged and smiled.

"But as for your rebellion, you still haven't answered my question," Gabriel continued in lower tones. "Why should the Berkarfor, which were scattered ages ago, be gathered again?"

"Revolution. They were scattered for a reason," Rodigger replied in equally hushed tones, with frequent glances toward the kitchen. "What if that reason is past? What if the reason they were made in the first place has risen again? I actually like the symbolism: Andelians are scattered as well, and must be re-gathered. By gathering on this smaller scale, Roth will be given the power to gather on the larger scale."

"And if Roth's power should harden? If the goblets should need to be scattered again?" Gabriel asked.

"I know him," Rodigger replied. "His rule will be just, because he cares for the people of Andelen."

"I wonder if everyone would agree with you," Gabriel said softly.

"Why shouldn't they?"

"Because many people have died opposing the *revolution*, Rodigger. Those who survive them might not understand why."

If Rodigger caught the understatement, he did not show it.

The road ran straight across the plains, giving the town toward which Catie rode its name: Arrow's Mark. Of course, time and use had eventually made it 'Aresmak'. Only older towns and cities kept their Old Rinc Nain names, like Akervet Brodlek—which, she had probably heard in Stramfath, translated literally to 'Field at Road's End'.

As the sun reached its height that afternoon, the horizon was jagged with the Dragonsback Mountains, but it was three more days before she reached their feet. There had been some travelers at the inns, heading to Akervet. But she mingled little, and they did not seem bothered by it. Roth had not taken her coin, blessedly. But every time she pulled out her purse she double-checked it, hoping for more coins lost in the folds. There never was. She knew what was left would last her a little while, yet, but certainly not all the way home.

The road zig-zagged upward, peeping out here and there where the mountain leaned back, before finally crossing a low saddle. Kelsie plodded slowly, but steadily and predictably—she was a Midland, and had probably been born on a mountainside.

They crossed the first range by After-Noon. On the other side, Aresmak could be seen next to the Balnathva River below. Great fir trees marched up the mountain to greet travelers, sending out advance riders of juniper and sage. Calling out orders faintly behind them was the river itself, swollen here from its long journey through the length of the 'Back and now tripping headlong over a granite cascade. It seemed the noisiest place to put a village. But here the roads met, and where roads meet so do travelers. Travelers here just spoke a little louder.

She lay awake that night, listening to the sound of the river through her pillow and a few layers of blanket. She had asked for a room away from the river, but of course those were already full. With a deep breath she closed her eyes, and now saw again the strange orange light and the distant mewling sound. As she also thought of the feeling afterward, it seemed to stir up inside of her, though not as strong this time. She lay motionless, barely breathing, as something in her spirit willed her to leave Aresmak. But she could not discern what. It was not a feeling of danger, exactly. At least not mortal danger. But through her exhaustion, ideas of travel surfaced more readily and stayed with her longer than they should have. Her eyelids were shut like a portcullis, but her mind ran like a carnival.

Suddenly the feeling disappeared, and she knew nothing until the morning sun spilled into the room.

3

THINGS GAINED

"She will not run?"
"She may."
"But then...?"
"You look too far ahead, Teresh."

2 Mantaver 1320 — Winter

The Dragonsback Mountains loomed ahead of the three riders, the inn on the fourth night lost in their shadow as the sun rose the next morning. Before the sun could clear the peaks, they were on the road up through the first pass. Here Rodigger's Therian became a rockcrab, his hooves skittering and clattering against the stones. Rodigger fell into the motion more easily than his first several trips into the 'Back, but now his jaw set as his companions' horses plodded sure-footedly ahead of him, just as Gabriel said they would. Despite Gabriel's threat, they did wait at switchbacks and curves for him to catch up. Though all three labored in the sudden steeps, Rodigger's was the only one flecked with foam when they stopped at a natural plateau.

The road ran through a low saddle. On the other side it plunged straight into the valley—the mountain walls here were just gentle enough—and Aresmak could be seen slightly brown against the gray rock below. They descended, their path of rock fading below first sand, then into good earth where junipers took root, their winter skeletons rattling and whispering in the wind.

Rodigger knew Aresmak well. The revolution had spent a summer here last year before Roth decided to move west to Akervet, disliking how swiftly the river might bring boats of soldiers to his doorstep. The valley allowed some sheep-farming, and attendant textile production, but a lack of dyeing meant most of the village relied on the traders making their way up and down the peninsula. Small and secluded as it was, there was still much to be had in Aresmak, and Rodigger knew exactly where to find it.

Larens was busy with a customer when Rodigger walked in, so he made his way to another corner and glanced over some of the goods there. A collection of carpenter's tools caught his eye, their iron shafts and wooden handles polished and gleaming. He picked up a hammer, feeling the ash press into the heel of his thumb as his little finger balanced the other end, then swinging forward, the weight pitching against his index finger and catching against the outside of his palm. It was his weight, a hammer he could wield with precision.

"Can I help you—Rodigger!" Larens broke into a wide smile as Rodigger put the hammer down and faced him. The shopkeeper caught him in an embrace, then held him at arm's length. "Are you still growing?" he asked, gazing at the top of his head.

"I think you're shrinking, Larens," Rodigger replied, returning the glance with a smile.

"Hah." Larens waved a dismissing hand, and moved to a chair near the counter. "What brings you back here?" he asked as he eased himself into the chair with a short sigh.

"A job," Rodigger replied.

"And how is Roth? I wish he would come back here. He always has a home in Aresmak."

"He is well, and he knows that. But the river..."

Larens waved him off again. "Too swift," he said. "Any army would be dashed to pieces before they made it halfway from Thinneh. What's the job?"

"Do you remember the legend of the Goblets?"

A smile spread across Larens' face. "My Oldmother told me that story every time I asked. Twice a night, sometimes." The smile disappeared. "Why?"

"Roth thinks they were not just legends, and he sends me with two mercenaries to try and find them."

Larens shifted uncomfortably. "Rodigger, how is the revolution? Really? We haven't heard much lately, and the merchants from up north are certainly believers in Sheppar. Costs have never been so high. And if Roth is turning to this legend for some faint hope..."

"We'll find out in a few weeks, Larens," Rodigger said gently. "The first is supposed to be around Agirbirt. If we can't find it, then the stories he found are just taking the legend too seriously. That's not what I worry about."

"Oh? What do you worry about?"

Rodigger scrubbed his scalp. "A lot of things: some big, and some small ones. The mercenary I'm traveling with, he mentioned something about not everyone understanding why so many have died during the revolution. And, since then...I don't know. I can't help but think he might have agreed to this job just to make sure it fails."

Larens scratched his chin as he studied Rodigger. "What's his name?"

"Gabriel," Rodigger replied. "Gabriel Owens."

Larens' head bobbed. "I know of Gabriel. He served under Sheppar in the last part of the Beast Campaign."

"And that's supposed to make me feel better?" Rodigger exclaimed. "I didn't realize he was that old."

"He served him young. And he's done much since then, for anyone who would hire him. Mercenaries are the same everywhere. They work for money, not anyone or anything else."

"I hope so," Rodigger said. He put his hands on his hips. "It figures Sheppar would allow someone young to serve his ends."

Larens shrugged. "We know that. The trick is getting the rest of the country to see it."

"Don't remind me," Rodigger muttered with a grin.

Larens cocked his head. "Remind you?"

Rodigger took a deep breath. "The other reason I'm going along is to try to get people to believe in the mission of the revolution, so when we finally do break out of the Fallonvall, we'll have some support already." He sighed. "But now, with what I've seen of Gabriel and what you've told me, I think I'm going to have to work for his and Deuel's support first."

Larens' fingers twitched, but he smiled. "Well, you still have some time to work on them while you're in the Fallonvall," he said, then cleared his throat. "You might also start with some of these traders. They've convinced too many of Aresmak to abandon their Andelian traditions and buy from them this Starfall."

Rodigger cast him a condescending glance. "Larens, Starfall is not Andelian, you know that. It's left over from our Rinc Nain oppression, and should have been cast off after we won our freedom centuries ago."

"Oh, you're right, you're right," Larens said, his head bobbing in time. "Perhaps these old bones just wish for some rest."

Rodigger smiled, too, though he thought sadly that rest would not come till he ruled the *feth*board over his companions.

Gabriel also knew Aresmak well, though the goods he sought were not traded for money. At least, not usually.

"Good morning, Eidemon," he said, sitting next to a man whose Rinc Nain eyebrows were beginning to whiten. His hair similarly carried a few struggling braids, though the rest was better kept than Gabriel's. Thick wolf pelts padded a thin frame, and mittens hung from strings to allow gnarled fingers to strip chunks of meat from the goat leg in front of him.

Eidemon took a drink, then glanced sideways at Gabriel. "Hello," he said in a deep, quiet voice. His eyes continued toward the door, then around the room. "No *skalderon*?" he asked.

"He's enjoying the wilderness."

Eidemon grunted. "I bet." He chewed through a few more chunks as Gabriel retrieved a mug of ale for himself. "What brings you here?" he asked.

"What always brings me here?"

Eidemon shook his head, drank, then gazed directly at Gabriel. "Remember when this made a difference, what we said to each other?"

"The world has grown safer, Eid."

"Tell that to the wolves," he replied. "Sheppar forgot to tell everyone what was a dangerous beast and what was natural predators."

"You seem to have figured it out," Gabriel replied, raising an eyebrow at his friend's attire.

"All from wolves I found killed and left to rot," he replied, returning to his plate. "So who is it this time?"

"Roth."

Eidemon's teeth stopped halfway through tearing another morsel as his eyes leapt to Gabriel's. He bit down slowly, and chewed even slower. "Is it that bad?" he asked.

Gabriel took a drink, gazing at nothing behind the bar. He saw the fires of Bokessin, the ruined houses, his wife inside to whom he swore he would never leave... Then he saw the cold winter in Balnath Agrend, the apple he was so tempted to steal, the ghost he followed to Balnath's cemetery, Deuel waiting for him when he returned home, and a messenger from Akervet. He took another drink, and pulled on his lower lip. "Yep."

Eidemon sat back and finished his mug in four long pulls. When it *thunked* back to the table, he looked at Gabriel. "Someone was speaking against Roth, last night," he said. "Badly drunk, I heard. They're maybe a day ahead of you, and not happy about it. So be careful."

"Who?"

"I saw a hood, and heard a voice. I came in late, and he left quickly."

"What kind of hood?"

"A green one, from underneath well-fitting brown deerskin. He looked quick, and quiet." He cast a sideways glance at Gabriel. "Like you, thirty years ago."

"Thanks," Gabriel replied drily. He finished his own drink and dropped a coin next to the empty mug. "See you around."

She rode through fields littered with herds of sheep that morning, giving way to three separate convoys headed deeper into the continent. She had not been this far north since she was going the opposite way two and a half years ago.

After Sprativerg. After meeting Dannid.

Sprativerg was a city full of ideas, so it had surprised her when Dannid wanted to leave. He had said something angrily about being a man of action as well, didn't she know? And he had almost left her there. Now she was not too sure of returning, even to pass through on her way home.

But that was some time away. Her next full stop was Thinneh, high up on a cliff overlooking the valley. As she counted out her coins that night to the innkeeper, she knew it would be more than her usual stop: she would not be continuing past Thinneh until she had some money to get the rest of the way home. The inns between here and there would not charge much—during Sheppar's campaign, he had forbidden it, and came down hard on any keeper who disobeyed. It became a habit they now found hard to break. But lodging was never free.

Eight long days later, she arrived—hungry, for she had not the coin to eat at the last inn, and no food grew in the wilds. As she walked through streets that had changed little from the past, she began to remember bits of what she and Dannid had spoken of on the way south. It seemed he knew a lot about villages and towns, at least in some abstract ways.

In Thinneh, there were vendors stalls everywhere. It was the first town that was both large enough to accommodate longer stays of merchants bringing goods from Burieng, and was not so near a thundering river that every traveler wanted to be on their way as soon as possible. And it was high up on a ridge, so there was little fishing to be done, and no pastures. So the only way Thinneh survived was by convincing those merchants to stay, and offer their goods there to sell. The sale was everything. And Catie had no means to purchase anything.

She stopped in front of an inn. Dusk was settling, and a general clamor inside the inn punctuated as someone went through the door before her. The door closed as she tied up Kelsie, and she followed the patron into the storm.

The tables were nearly all full. Four serving girls were kept busy among patrons ranging from warmly-dressed tradesmen to men whose bulk owed to a life cutting trees, to others—men, mostly, but also a few women—with oiled boots and lower garments spun thicker than upper garments: fishers, if they dressed anything like fishers from Catie's hometown. A few she thought she recognized from the last inn, closer to the water.

Along the wall to Catie's left was a bar, equally full, and one bartender who—at the moment—was not busy. Catie approached, wedging herself between two men whose eyes darted to her, then down and back up. She ignored their grins and got the bartender's attention.

"What can I get you?"

"Is the owner here?" Catie asked.

The two men beside her chuckled as the bartender gazed at her. "No," he said finally. "I left a while ago, and haven't come back yet."

The two men laughed, which she also ignored. "Do you have anyone to sing or play music tonight?" she asked.

"They seem to be staying for the beer," he replied. "And it couldn't get much fuller in here."

Catie turned to glance at the room just as three younger men, tradesmen by the look of them, shuffled past and went out into the night. She watched them go, then turned back. "I guess they didn't get any beer," she said.

"What's your name?" he asked, now the center of attention instead of her.

"Catie."

"I'm Farris," he said. "You do what you want. And if people are staying, you can too."

She paused. "Do you have a Tamis flute?" she asked. Farris stared at her, and she waved him off. "I'll figure it out." She picked her way across the room to the corner the tradesmen had just emptied. She sat down on the table, her feet on the bench, her hands on her legs. She glanced at Farris, who was still watching, then down as she tried to think of an appropriate song.

Her hands started tapping on her legs. The nearest patrons glanced over, their eyes narrowing as they saw she was not sitting like the rest of them. The beat that her fingers found on their own finally reminded her of a song, and as she drummed with greater purpose she began to sing.

It had the lyrical simplicity of a child's song, but that was why she liked it. Her voice did not travel far in the din, but enough that those who heard stopped talking. The silence spread, and more eyes turned from their food and drink to her.

As she finished the first song, another came immediately to mind. Pausing only to swallow, she launched into it. A livelier song, and the people near her began to drum their hands against the table. The lyrics to this one were also simple, and soon they sang along with her.

When she came to the line: "And for all, my lads, drink up!" someone actually handed her a glass. She paused quickly to drink, then hoisted the cup with a smile as the room laughed. She got up onto the table and began a simple dance as she sang. That line repeated often in the shanty, and each time she sang it the room lifted their mugs and drank. By the time the song was over, everyone needed their mugs refilled, and when Catie caught Farris's eye he nodded.

After three more songs, Catie paused and looked around the room with a finger on her lips in thought. "Long ago, deep in the Brithelt Forest," she began. She eyed the patrons as they sat up, curious. "There lived a master craftsman—a blacksmith and whittler named Karan Tamis. Many of the days he worked in an open forge amid the trees, and shafts of sunlight filled the woods. And keeping almost a protective ring around Karan were birds of every sort and color, and they used to sing to him as he worked the bellows, or when he rested.

"But one day a terrible storm tore through the forest where he worked, stripping trees of their boughs and leaving no loft from which the birds could sing. Karan carried on his work as best he could, but soon he could no longer, so much he missed the warbles and wheeps that sang to soften the strike of his hammer. He wept long, and hard he wished for a way to honor his lost friends, and to draw them back, to fill the forest again with their song.

"So Karan laid down his hammer and quenched his forge, and picked up instead his carving knife. And from the shattered remnants of the boughs he began to fashion a peculiar flute—one which played not only quiet notes, or shrill notes, but both equally, as the piper willed.

"When I was a child, my Grandmother taught me to play this Tamis flute. I would like to play it for you now, that the Brithelt Forest full of birds may enter this distant inn."

When she finished, she inclined her head to their applause. She looked up, and smiled hesitantly. "Um, does anyone have a Tamis flute?" She laughed at the absurdity. The room laughed too, and all the harder as a young boy stood up and held one triumphantly aloft. She thanked the boy as she sat back down onto the table, taking a few drinks as she allowed her pulse to slow. When everyone was settled from their latest rounds ordered, she began to play.

Her voice had been enough to keep patrons seated. As she played the flute, it brought them in from outside. Farris' smile—wide already at the evening his inn was having—grew wider as more and more beer flowed from his barrels.

By the end of the evening, though she was still starving, she was warm and full of joy as the patrons enjoyed her singing and playing. They had been a good crowd, humming and drumming and singing along and laughing. When Farris showed her the room for the night he handed her a bag of coin.

"They left this for you," he said. "At least, this is what's left of what they left for you—I gave you the opportunity, after all. I'll have Mareth bring you some food." He turned to go, then paused. "Will you stay long, here?" he asked, innocently enough.

Catie hefted the bag and smiled. "Maybe just one more night. Although you'll have to ask that young man if I can borrow his flute again."

"Oh, I forgot." Farris smiled and reached inside his shirt to pull out the flute she had played. "He left it for you. Said he hated learning it, but loved hearing you play."

"Oh," Catie said, taking the Tamis from him. "I loved playing it," was all she could think to say—but it was true.

Word had apparently spread, and the room was full next evening when she finally came down to begin. She did much as she had the first night, with a few newer songs that she had remembered. She told the same story, this time being able to pull the flute out straight away when the story was over.

By the end of the evening, she had earned almost double what she had made the night before—more than enough to make it home.

"Well," Farris said when she told him, "I'm sorry to see you go. If you wanted to, you could certainly stay on here."

"I know," Catie said. "And I might be fine with that, if things were different. But I need to go back home."

"You wouldn't have to work as hard as you have," Farris said quickly as she turned away. He snatched at her arm to keep her from leaving. "We would make a good partnership, you and me," he continued, his grip softening until only his fingers rested against the back of her arm. "You could make a good life here."

"Farris," she said gently, "you were kind to give me the chance to earn my way. That has not earned you the right to touch me like that." As she said it, and without thinking too hard, the feeling in her heart...*pushed*.

Had he not been gazing into her eyes, he might not have dropped his hand so quickly. "I'm sorry," he said, flexing his fingers. "You're right; I..." He trailed off, then turned quickly and left.

As she shut the door, Catie drew a long sigh. What was it she did? It had not been her words—it never was. And it was a conscious thing, though she sometimes did it without thinking. Whatever 'it' was. It felt as though she projected her emotions tangibly, making them into something physical. Something a person *had* to react to, the same as stepping around an obstacle in their path. It wasn't just rejection, as it had just been with Farris. She could make people love her, pity her, even fear her. If she felt the emotion strongly enough and pushed it outward—that was the only way she could think to describe it—and the person was looking in her eyes, it seemed they felt it too, as if it were their own.

She shook her head, and pulled off her outer garments. She didn't like the ability in the abstract. But when it was useful, she was glad to have it.

She blew out two candles that sat on the desk, then turned to the lantern beside her bed. She gazed at it, blinking as strange dread came to her mind. Was she afraid of the dark now? And yet, her hand shook as she trimmed the wick. She blew out the flame, sinking the room into complete darkness.

Fear slammed into her gut, and she nearly knocked over the lantern in her haste to relight it. But she stopped, the taper near the wick as her mind revolted at the idea of striking too bright a light. She blinked in the darkness. What was *this,* now? It shrank a little as she considered it, but did not go away. A worry? It felt almost familiar, like when she had heard the rebellion was nearing Bokessin.

She blinked a few more times. It was *very* much like that. So, not worry: dread. But not, she thought, like when Roth's soldiers came and took Dannid. It was not that immediate.

She lowered the trembling taper, put it back in its stand. Why ever she felt this, it was not immediate. But it was approaching, and may be immediate by morning.

Faint moonlight streamed through the clouds and into her room, enough to see her clothes, and she dressed again purposefully. Did this terror approach from the north, where she needed to go? Or did it come from where she had been? It was impossible to tell. Perhaps the night would be dark enough that it wouldn't matter.

Her father—and her own curiosity, after he had died—taught her to survive without soft beds and sturdy roofs. She only needed to get outside Thinneh. Nothing should follow her. Everyone traveled during the day.

Unless this was some strange return of the creatures Sheppar had wiped out. Many people thought they would. A few even thought that they should.

Catie exited the room. The inn was dark, and no light from the common room warmed the wooden staircase. If such a thing occurred as all the creatures returning—what, from the dead?—it made sense it would begin with some strange orange light in the night sky and a faint keening sound.

So much was possible, but very little was practical. She blunted the fear by focusing on her escape.

Kelsie was already looking toward the door when Catie entered the stables, tossing her head without vocalizing her impatience. Catie cocked an eyebrow at her mare's prescience.

As silently as possible, she saddled Kelsie and led her outside. Catie had not yet decided to turn north, though it was the way she needed to go anyway, but as soon as her right foot was in the stirrup Kelsie was off without being prompted.

The fear drained from Catie's gut as they reached the edge of town and began down the long path to the valley below. The sky had cleared, and Kelsie was in her element. With nothing else to do, Catie rested in the saddle, letting the road pass beneath her.

4

LOSING FAITH

"I feel like I'm doing nothing."
"You are."
"And I feel like I should be doing something."
"When she arrives at the inn..."

11 Mantaver 1320 — Winter

As the mercenaries approached Thinneh the road climbed away from the river as the valley ahead became a narrow canyon. Countless switchbacks carried them across the face of the mountains and up. At each turn, Gabriel and Deuel waited while Rodigger's Therian struggled again on the rocky slopes. Dusk came and went before the road crested the pass, where a dozen of the lonely huts they had passed on their way up gathered for the warmth, if not the fellowship, of Thinneh.

At the sparsely filled inn, though it doubled as the village tavern, groups of two or three sat silently apart, and many of the tables nearest the fires were empty. As they drank their own ales, Rodigger considered the various patrons. Those men with bits of sawdust still trapped in the hair of their forearms were carpenters. A little further away, they all had oiled boots—fishermen. Still another group, further from the fire, had heavy traveling coats and thick fur hats—traders.

He had been as far north as Thinneh once, delivering a message when this was the front of the revolution. He still recognized some of the men, but despite how small the village was, most were unfamiliar.

As he thought about it, he still could not understand why Thinneh did not support the mission of the revolution. If Roth's vision were mirrored here, these men would all be around the same table, sharing stories, food, and drink. The inn would be alive with music and laughter. There would not be cringing and glancing around with deep frowns when a mug hit the table a little harder. No, this—this was what Sheppar wanted: islands, self-sufficient and selfish. Perhaps the revolution should revisit some of the towns and villages.

But here he was: he *was* the revolution, wasn't he? He was certainly supposed to be, once they went north of Vatenhal. Could he practice here? Should he?

One of the fishermen was glaring at him. Before he could think he smiled and raised his mug in salute. The man's frown deepened, and he returned to his mug. Rodigger's fist tightened on the handle of his ale.

"Are we not both Andelian?" he muttered.

Gabriel and Deuel glanced up, then turned to follow Rodigger's gaze.

"Do you know him?" Gabriel asked, his voice low but clear.

"Your answer lies in the answer to my first question," Rodigger replied.

"I don't understand," Gabriel said. Deuel's eyes glittered as his gaze pried into Rodigger's mind.

"This is exactly what the revolution is about, Gabriel," Rodigger said, gesturing around the room. "Look at these men. Feel this silence. A far cry from Keltan, isn't it? That inn was noisier than this with a third of the patrons. And why are they separated and quiet?" He gestured around again. "Carpenters, fishermen, traders—they see themselves separately, instead of all Andelian."

"People come and go in Thinneh," Gabriel said. "It's a lot easier when you have time to get to know someone."

"But that's why we need to build that commonality, and spread it across all Andelen," Rodigger said, pointing hard at Gabriel. "Then it won't matter where you come from. Everyone you meet will share at least one thing, or even ten things, regardless of their daily life."

"And how do you do that?" Gabriel asked, his hands spread. Deuel sat back, his interest seemingly lost. Rodigger tried to ignore it.

"Traditions," he said.

Gabriel scoffed. "Now you sound like a Cariste, celebrating every full moon."

Rodigger scoffed too. "What does that celebrate? Full moons? All the world has full moons. We need celebrations that honor Andelians, and the work they do. Celebrate fishermen," he said with a nod at their table. "The carpenters, the traders." His gaze lingered on Gabriel a few moments. "The mercenaries. We should honor and remember one another. And we should look to Andelen's history for those traditions, *after* we won our freedom from Rinc Na."

"So which traditions should we practice?" Gabriel asked. "You tell me which ones."

Those words went in Rodigger's ears and swelled in his throat. He swallowed, but it stuck. Roth had never talked about which particular Andelian traditions. He had denounced many, but as Rodigger's mind buzzed with the silence in his ears, he could not remember Roth advocating any.

"Look to your history books," he said, with as best he could muster of Roth's mix of authority and derision. But his voice began to fall away. "Ask your...father, and mother." Something Rodigger had vowed never to do again. "We are all Andelian," he muttered again. His gaze fell to his mug of ale.

"Well my mother and father aren't here," Gabriel said. "Or my history books." Deuel gave the mercenary a glance, and Gabriel gave a short sigh. "Fine. Maybe when we get to Stramfath. You can look it up and let me know." Gabriel gazed at Rodigger for a few moments from underneath his eyebrows, then returned to his drink.

Silence remained the most present guest. Rodigger glanced sideways. A few tables away a young man sat with a group of men who appeared to be his father and father's friends. The young man drew a deep sigh and spoke something. The men around him glanced at him, and their mood seemed to darken. Rodigger returned his gaze to his drink. What had the young man said? *I miss the Tamis flute.* Rodigger wondered if Gabriel would know what that meant. But a swift glance that only made it halfway to the mercenary's face was all he allowed himself.

Though it was cold, the nights were also shorter. Now she should have time to reach the next inn at least a Shift before daybreak—enough time, with a horse that could guide itself, to nap before striking out again at daylight. Whatever was behind her, if it took only one day in Thinneh, would still be a day behind her.

She did not think about how to escape it completely, because she did not know enough about it. It might not even be after her. "It," she muttered. Kelsie's head continued to bob ahead of her. "Talking about my feelings like they're something real." Her mare tossed her head once and squealed. Catie cocked her head, considering. "Don't even pretend you can understand me," she said. "Then I'll really think I've gone..." She cut off as her mare turned a considering eye upon her for several moments. "Fine. Shall we give my fear a name? Pob? How about Pob? Or Vorbet? I never did like Vorbet, he always looked at me...well, too long for a man his age—back to ignoring me, then?"

A waxing moon allowed her to see more clearly, and let her remember the steep road as it switched back and forth. Far below, near the river, the moon gleamed off block walls. It seemed close enough she should reach it by Mid-Night. But then the road crooked, and for the next leg the inn moved further and further away behind her. When they turned again, it felt even further away.

Somehow they reached the door as the sky above the eastern slopes turned indigo, and the weakest of stars began to fade. Smoke curled from the chimney in streams too thick for a fire banked for the night. The keeper was awake.

The stable in back was empty. She loosened the saddle's girth only a little. They wouldn't be staying long, and she could ease Kelsie of the tack once they were further down the road. She left her with soft apologies and oats, and went inside. The keeper—a man barely older than she in shirt and breeches that shined in the firelight—looked up with a confused smile when she entered.

"You're not here the normal time," he said, though he rose in preparation for her request.

"Um, you're right," she said. She hadn't thought of a way to explain that. She was still deep in the peninsula, wasn't she? "Message from Roth for the front lines, and he wants it there quickly. I'll only be here a few hours. Do you have anything prepared?"

"Some fish," was the reply. "Trout, actually, pulled from the Balnathva yestereve."

Trout was all she had in Thinneh, just about. "Perhaps just a few rolls?" she asked hopefully.

The young man was looking at her intently, while trying to seem like he wasn't. "It's really good fish," he said.

Be careful.

Catie smiled. "Why not?" she said. "As fresh as that—and I'm sure you can prepare it just right. Living this close to the river you probably make fish all the time."

His smile was broad. "Oh, all the time," he echoed. "I'll run to the back and fetch some for you."

He exited into the kitchens. Catie paused only briefly to look at the fire: it would have been nice to warm herself for a few minutes, at least.

Instead she went tiptoed out, then ran to Kelsie. She knew she should be angry or at least shocked, but maybe she was too tired. Maybe she was over-reacting. But when she saw her mare again she knew she wasn't. If only he hadn't been so keen on feeding her fish. And trout, no less! He could probably put ten thimbles of sleeping draught in that dish and she wouldn't taste it until she woke up half a day later, at best with a lighter purse, at worst... And with the aftertaste stuck in her teeth for days.

"What a twerp," she said to Kelsie, who only blinked at her. "We won't go far," she promised. "There's sure to be some secluded spot along the river to sleep. After that we'll talk about having strange thoughts pop suddenly into my head." *What next?*

Yet, when Catie mounted, her usually-spirited mount only plodded away from the inn into a light snow that was drifting through the valley.

The weather continued against them. The wind soon howled between the mountains and swirled in among the only rocky nook they could find to build camp, icy off the waters that cascaded through there. Catie managed a small fire, and shared as much of her blanket as she could with the mare lying dutifully beside her. But it was small comfort.

Catie wondered if the—Vorbet—coming behind her would stay at that inn. Of course he would. But she wondered if he might fall prey to a trap she only avoided because of Dannid. Whatever people might say about those who think the world is after them, sometimes fear kept you safe if tempered a little.

The sky brightened as Catie's eyelids grew heavy despite the wind and the cold. "At some point, I'm going to have to try to see what's following me," she said to Kelsie, who nickered shortly. "I can't keep thinking of it as Vorbet. And what if he's more than one?"

Then, her fear might be warranted. She would not stand against two or three. At least, not in a fair fight.

Despite the cold, she finally fell asleep, waking again as the sun reached its zenith and shone over her sheltering rock and into her eyes. She laded Kelsie quickly, with only a few glances up the mountain to see if she could spot anyone following her. She thought maybe she saw a flash of green behind her. Surely Vorbet—she rolled her eyes—was not that close? Closer than when she was in Thinneh, but without the sense of dread?

After several moments of wind and rushing river, but no further glimpse of movement, she shook her head. Early sign of spring, perhaps, but now lost among the rocks. She turned body and horse northward, and rode.

As they rounded a switchback, Deuel suddenly pointed below. "There," he said to Gabriel. "A rider with a green hood."

"What about him?" Rodigger asked, his voice still shattered of confidence.

"He was speaking against the revolution, some time ago," Gabriel replied with a sideways glance. "How far ahead, Deuel?"

"Too far. We might catch up to him in Getakenner, but not find him."

"Outside it though? Still in the 'Back?"

Deuel glanced at Rodigger, then Rodigger's horse. "Probably not."

Gabriel frowned. "Oh, right. Well, hopefully north of Getakenner then, at one of the inns."

They rode without speaking, though Rodigger's thoughts whirled. Gabriel had reminded him of some hope last night: Stramfath, one of the towns Roth wanted most to reach. At the head of Lake Agirbirt, it had managed to collect more books and schools of learning than anywhere else in Andelen. If Stramfath could be turned to the revolution, there would be no stopping Roth's march. His ideas and beliefs would spread to every corner of the country with the power of the scholars of Stramfath.

But Sprativerg still lay between them and the Agirbirt, and Roth would also desperately want that city, for its trade if nothing else. The loss of Sprativerg would be staggering to Sheppar, forcing trade from Burieng north to Ostflir, and clogging the road west of Ostflir to Balnath Agrend.

But Sprativerg was massive, a tree centuries old and broad as a house that would tempt Rodigger to carve a palace for Roth. But to attempt the carving would take his entire life and remain forever unfinished, while hundreds of Andelians would suffer in the cold because he distracted himself from the simpler homes he could build instead. No, Sprativerg would be for the older, wiser, and swifter wood-smiths. But perhaps Rodigger could still make some initial markings. Until he could study in Stramfath, they would be the merest of scratches, and might be mistaken later for woodgrains—

Oh, what was the use. Gabriel and Deuel rode ahead, again, horses close and voices low. Rodigger let Gared drop a little further back. In two weeks of traveling, he could not even convince his companions of Roth's way of thinking. What could he hope to accomplish when they spent only one night at any one place? What could Roth have hoped for him to achieve?

"So, Rodigger," Gabriel said as they tied their horses at the inn on the valley floor that night. "These inns are a Rinc Nain tradition as well. Should we get rid of them?"

"They are not tools of oppression," Rodigger replied absently, his gaze on the light spilling over the far mountain and sparkling in the waters. A shadow was growing from the foot of the mountains, darkening the turbid river and creeping ever nearer as the sun sank.

"Isn't any tradition forced on a nation oppressive?" They entered the inn as a cluster, Gabriel trying to watch Rodigger as he spoke, Rodigger with his eyes on the ground and only trying to move forward, and Deuel trapped somewhere in the middle.

"Only when that tradition has nothing to do with the nation."

"I think people are more individual than you think," Gabriel said as they continued into the cot-room. They each put their effects in the chests. "I don't think you can make everyone—what did you say? Honor everyone else? Why should the farmers around Akervet honor the fishers of Thinneh? They'll never deal with them."

"We've traveled," Rodigger replied. "Why shouldn't they?"

"Maybe they should. But they don't."

"Then it will be good for them not to forget they aren't the only ones in the world. Can we eat? I'm hungry."

"They're going to forget why they follow the traditions," Gabriel said, leading them back out into the common room. "Two or three generations, and they'll be following an Andelian tradition with the same attitude they follow Rinc Nain traditions."

"What's wrong with Rinc Nain traditions?" the keeper asked, approaching as they sat down.

Rodigger's shoulders drooped, but he kept quiet.

Gabriel glanced at the keeper and smiled. "They're oppressive. Your best dinner, please."

"I remember that rebellion leader coming through here," the keeper said, taking Gabriel's proffered coin. "He thought the entertainment he provided should have covered his stay."

Rodigger's head sank lower as Gabriel cocked an eyebrow.

"Entertainment?" he asked.

"All my guests that night thought he was hilarious. They stayed eating and drinking for hours listening to him."

Gabriel grinned broadly as Rodigger's head finally came to rest on his crossed arms.

"I had never heard that story," Gabriel said. Another coin appeared in his fingers. "We're also looking for a friend, in deerskin and a green hood."

The keeper took the coin. "No one has been through here in two days," he said.

Gabriel's smile disappeared. "Then give that back!" he said. Rodigger's head came up as the keeper glanced over the three of them.

"That's still information, isn't it?" he asked, turning swiftly toward the kitchens.

Gabriel's mouth gaped until Deuel shrugged. Gabriel shrugged too. "I guess it is. Why would he avoid the inn though? We saw him this morning too far ahead to not have stopped around here for the night."

"I don't like this," Rodigger said, crossing his arms a little tighter. "He acts like a spy, or worse."

"Perhaps his coin was low," Gabriel said, casting a glare toward the kitchen door. "Or perhaps he knew something about this inn that we don't."

"Like what?" Rodigger asked.

"Like why no one has been through here in two days," Deuel said. "This might not have been his first time down this road."

"Well, didn't you stop here before?" Rodigger asked.

Gabriel shook his head quickly. "We did, but it was packed that night, at least ten other guests. Probably too full to try anything."

"Should we move on?" Rodigger whispered. "Find somewhere else to stay?"

Gabriel shook his head again, slower. "Too late now, probably."

"He might also be pursuing something else," Deuel murmured.

"Well, as long as it's not us," Rodigger said.

The windows were black, candlelight glaring off the obsidian panes. The door to the kitchens opened and the keeper approached, three plates steaming with fish and assorted boiled vegetables.

"Here we are," the keeper announced, setting the plates before them. "And let me refill your mugs, as well." He quickly retrieved a jug, topping off the mugs with foaming ale. "Let me know if you need anything else."

Deuel raised his mug and sniffed it, then tasted it gently. His eyes took on a faraway look, then he shook his head. "It's fine."

Rodigger breathed a sigh of relief, and started on his food. He was not lying when he had said he was hungry. It had been a short day, true, but they had eaten while riding, and just a few rinds of cheese and crusts of bread. This fish was cooked to perfection, and the vegetables seasoned expertly. It was the best meal Rodigger remembered since leaving Akervet.

"Don't eat the fish," Deuel said, scraping the piece off his fork and moving on to the vegetables.

Rodigger choked on a chunk of filet already crawling down his throat, trying in vain to cough it back up.

"Is it poison?" he whispered hoarsely. Gabriel and Deuel regarded him solemnly.

"Why didn't you wait till Deuel had tried all of it?"

"How was I supposed to know?" Rodigger said. "He had tried the ale, that's the easiest thing to poison. How do you know it's in the fish?"

"Deuel has been eating foods for a long time, Rodigger. He knows when something is wrong."

"Well I've been eating all my life, too. But what's in it? Am I going to die?"

Gabriel smiled. "Rod, you're, what, nineteen? Deuel's been eating for hu-aaa—a lot longer than that."

"What's in it!" Rodigger grated, pounding a fist against the table.

"Is everything all right, gentlemen?" the keeper asked, looking over in concern.

"Fine," Gabriel replied as Rodigger's eyes bulged. "Our friend just cut his tongue on his knife."

"It's a sleeping agent," Deuel whispered.

Rodigger glared at them, then pinched his tongue with thumb and fore-finger and managed a rueful shake of his head for the keeper's benefit.

"I hate the boaf of you, wight now," he muttered, then glared at his fingers and wiped them on his pants. "What do we do with the fish? He'll know if we don't eat it, and he might try something more drastic."

Gabriel snorted. "I'm not sure it's his style. There's probably only enough to make you sleep through the night, and soundly enough for him to take your key and some of your gold."

"When we're the only ones here?"

Gabriel shrugged. "How often have we checked our bags after staying at an inn? No one does, because everyone keeps their things locked safely at the foot of their bed."

"Surely someone would have noticed eventually."

"When? After a day? Two days? They'll have traveled through two other inns by then, if they even suspect a..." Gabriel cast a quick glance at their keeper, who occupied himself with a book.

"Deuel," Gabriel said, flicking his eyes toward the man. Deuel's eyes slid to him a moment, then back.

"His eyes aren't moving. He's not reading."

"Finish your fish, Rodigger," Gabriel said. "You've already started, and he probably noticed how quickly you went after it. You can't say you're just not hungry anymore."

"And what if there's more than Deuel suspects in here?"

As one, they replied: "There isn't."

"Oh," Rodigger said, brightening sarcastically. Hesitantly, but finally, he began picking at the fish again. "What about you two?" he asked around the mouthful suddenly too dry but to chew it a hundred times.

"Oh, I'm not that hungry," Gabriel replied. "Neither is Deuel. We'll prob-ably just pick at it, really."

Rodigger glared, helpless, bolting the fish down with two slugs of ale. True to his word, Gabriel and Deuel did eat some of their fish. The keeper showed no surprise as he cleared their plates, only smiled and asked if they enjoyed it and if Rodigger's tongue was not cut too badly. They went to their cots assuring Rodigger that Deuel would be able to keep watch.

Even as he smiled hollowly at them, he plunged headfirst into darkness.

He awoke as someone cried out. His eyes opened sluggishly, and the blear was hesitant to follow. There came a slap, another cry, and faint light flickering against the wooden ceiling. Voices muttered, one calm, the other under duress. Rodigger blinked and stretched his jaw. The voices became clearer.

"This is no way to run a respectable inn, Lindo," Gabriel's voice said. "So tell us the truth: you've seen the green-hooded traveler at some point, haven't you?"

Another slap, and cry, and some babbling. Rodigger turned his head, but the bunks beside him were empty. Finally, with effort, he raised his head.

Gabriel and Deuel had the keeper—Lindo, apparently—tied in a chair against the wall. His face was red, but his eyes were still defiant and his lips were pressed into a thin line. Rodigger tried to lever himself into a sitting position, and it was not until Deuel glanced sharply at him that he realized he was groaning.

Gabriel glanced at him, too, then came and helped him sit up while Lindo glared on. "Are you okay?" the mercenary asked.

Rodigger blinked, then felt his head going up and down. He sensed the wool blanket against his feet and hands. They had taken off his boots but he had still slept otherwise fully clothed. The glow from a nearby torch warmed him a little—at least he could feel the bloom of heat against his cheek. His tongue rolled in his mouth like his mother's ball of dough in a mixing bowl when it needed flouring. And the room smelled wretched, as if someone sicked up and let it harden.

"Did we catch him?" Rodigger mumbled.

"No!" the keeper shot out. "I came in to check and make sure my guests were sleeping soundly when this panther leapt upon me." He drew in a long sniffle, glancing warily at Deuel, who folded his arms. "S'not natural," he muttered, then turned his hard gaze back upon Gabriel.

Nothing about him is natural, Rodigger thought. *He even wears that silly thick cloak in the middle of the night.*

"And do you commonly drug your guests?" Gabriel asked quietly.

Lindo looked truly hurt. "My duty is to give my guests a quiet night's rest. I try to aid them in that, and they assault me in the darkness."

"A quiet night's rest," Gabriel repeated slowly. "And a lighter load for the next day's journey?"

"Did I?" he asked, looking at Gabriel a little too keenly. Gabriel's glance and Deuel's sigh answered enough: they had not caught him in the act of thievery. His gaze lowered. "Exactly. Now untie me before I complain to Roth's soldiers. He'll do you up right."

"Oh, he already did," Rodigger muttered, rubbing his eyes and nearly falling backward in the process. "He sent me with these two."

Lindo swallowed, but said nothing. With a sigh, Gabriel rose and untied the man. "We require your attention no longer," he said lightly. "No need to check on us further."

"I wouldn't think of it," Lindo replied, glaring at Deuel. The thin man uncrossed his arms, and the keeper scuttled out of the cot room.

"Sorry you woke for that, Rodigger," Gabriel said, capping the torch to extinguish it. "Good night."

Rodigger fell backward, knocking his head a little against the stone wall, and slept till the sun shone against the western mountains.

"I still want to report him in Getakenner," Rodigger said the next morning. "He's a menace, and destroys the very foundation of the inns."

"Do as you like," Gabriel replied, swinging onto his Midland. "Though I doubt the lord of Getakenner cares much for an inn three days to his south. Deuel?"

Deuel gazed ahead—though what he expected to see escaped Rodigger. The road wound around giant boulders thrown from the river, or carved from the banks, keeping beside the Balnathva for another day.

Yet, miraculously, the strange, impossible man pointed ahead. "Climbing that rise," he said, then shook his head. "If he doesn't stay two nights in Getakenner, we won't catch him there."

"Ah well," Gabriel said, and they rode out.

Rodigger kicked Gared, and the Therian moved out at a reasonable pace, flicking its ears in irritation. Rodigger's mouth twisted, accepting the rebuke. But that innkeeper! Roth was trying—Rodigger too—to bring Andelian together, building compassion for one another no matter if one hailed from

Satflir and the other from Ethfirlaf. And the inns were the earliest realization of that, even if they were a Rinc Nain idea, older than Roth by almost a century. Yet that man insulted not only Roth's ideas, but the very idea of what he ran, with such tactics. The sun grew warmer, and with it Rodigger's ire as he stewed over the insult.

Before Noon the road sloped upward, climbing the rise upon which Deuel had spotted the stranger in the green hood as it briefly left the river.

It took everything Rodigger had not to turn his horse around and go back—if going to the innkeeper would be in vain, at least back to Thinneh and report him there. But he knew their mission was too pressing.

Roth! As they crested the climb, Rodigger knew Roth would want to hear of this rogue innkeeper who destroyed the revolution's core beliefs in their territory. "I'll send a message to Roth when we get to Getakenner," Rodigger said aloud with a smile.

Gabriel glanced back briefly. "Okay."

Rodigger nodded his head. That would take care of it. He glanced off the side of the road to where the Balnathva coursed below.

The next three inns had seen no one in a green hood, though Deuel managed to pick him out almost every morning, climbing this rise or that rise, or appearing past a switchback when the road climbed out of the 'Back again. This time the road did not stop till it dropped into the pampas of East Fallonvall.

East Fallonvall was a geographical oddity: despite the mild rains that fell east of the mountains and the lush farmland it generated, waterways never seemed to coalesce, leaving no ready supply of water except what could be dug from the earth. After Getakenner had been established, along with the farms that supplied it, settlement of the rest of the East Fallonvall halted. Getakenner grew large enough that it was no bother for the road to divert out of the 'Back, and it remained a renowned center of grapes, especially fermented ones.

Catie looked behind her, back toward the river that now raged silently below, and it was then that she saw them: three men on horseback making their way along the road behind her. She may have paid them little mind—the Fallonvall, and Getakenner lying just inside it, was a common destination—except that one of the three men seemed to be regarding her. It was less that she could see his eyes—they were too far back to tell that—but his face was definitely upward, and she *felt* something inspecting her. Her Grandmother had given her the same feeling as a child when she told a story that may or may not have been true. It was impossible that she should feel that way from the gaze of someone so far behind her. And yet...

The road wound down the slope below her, then flowed across the gently undulating plain between the mountains and Getakenner. Kelsie was winded from the long climb up, but Catie knew there was more in her. And she wouldn't need to push too hard. Those behind her still faced the same ascent, and were probably not pursuing her. Despite that chance, Catie wanted to come to them on her own terms. All the better if, when they crested the ridge, she was nowhere in sight.

Her height above the town played tricks, seeming further away and less attainable than it was—or Kelsie had more energy reserved than even Catie hoped. Either way, Catie rode through the great doors of the west wall before Evening, and a quick but casual glance to the far ridge gave away no hint of movement. It had been enough time for a new suspicion to be recalled, a memory even more distant than her Grandmother, but far more vivid.

As they crested the pass, Rodigger sat a little forward in his saddle, and his horse mimicked his excitement. Getakenner sprawled below, encircled by well-tended earth that reminded Rodigger of the combed and oiled hair of the vintners who tended it. The lines were bare now, the vines pruned back to start afresh in the spring. The dearth outside was balanced, Rodigger knew, by the plenty in the cellars inside. There was always more food and drink than citizens, though they tried hard to reverse it. Roth had found great support here, Rodigger remembered, and he looked forward to returning.

But great dark clouds were building on the horizon and sliding swiftly on a steady east wind. His eye measured the road before them, and he hunched his shoulders.

The snow hit a mile from town, covering roads and fields quicker than even Rodigger had anticipated. He followed Gabriel and Deuel, who seemed to be picking their way along well enough. Their descent out of the mountains would have been impossible in these conditions, Rodigger knew. He also knew, embarrassingly, that difficulty would have been mostly with Gared.

They pressed on in timelessness, as the sun only lent a hazy gray glow to the world. Soon enough, the great doors to the city gaped wide before them. A few hardy merchants in thick furs and grim smiles were only now pulling in their meats, cloths, leathers, tools, ornaments, services, and supplies. A few spared glances at the passing riders, but none asked to trade.

"What are we looking for?" Rodigger asked after they turned right, heading back in the direction they had come.

"A good inn," Gabriel replied.

"It's Getakenner," Rodigger scoffed as he wrapped one arm tight around himself. "We could stop at any home and receive just as warm a welcome as any inn."

"Perhaps," Gabriel replied. Deuel's head was swiveling up and to each side, then twisting back at the way they had come. They had crept to a stop in front of The Therian's Stall as Deuel glanced around, down the street, craning his neck as if to see around a faraway corner. He glanced at Gabriel and nodded.

"Perfect," Gabriel said, dismounting from his horse in front of the inn. Rodigger glanced at the sign of a tall horse pawing the earth, then back at his companions.

"It is?" he asked. "We want to stay at an inn which indicates sleeping on loose hay and horse manure?"

"We've stayed here before," Gabriel replied as if deciding the truth of the statement on the spot. Deuel only gazed at him, and Gabriel shrugged a shoulder.

Rodigger sighed and swung down from his horse. There was no point in arguing. He was, still and regrettably, only there as an aide if needed. Surely there would be patrons enough to talk to, for practice.

Though Catie had not been to Getakenner in years, she had spent enough time there to remember it well. If she was right, she knew to which tavern the three riders would come. She had made her way there, stabled Kelsie quickly, but went into a store down the street and began an interest in the herbs collected in the window.

"Is it a healer?" an old woman crooned as she came out of a light doze, her face bearing a line for every memory of her life.

"No, not today," Catie replied with a smile. She flared an eyebrow. "A spy."

The old woman chuckled. "And who does she hope to catch, then, ay?"

"I don't know," Catie said, a little distantly. "Three, perhaps."

"Those are the best catches: unknown and many." She chuckled again. "Such an adventure! But why does she seek that, ay?"

"Sometimes they come whether you seek them or not."

"Ah." The old woman clicked her tongue. "And to one so young?"

Catie's eyes dropped from the herbs to the floor. "Sometimes."

"Is there a war going on, then, ay?"

Catie's eyes came up to meet the old woman's, then went distant again as she thought back over her journey from Bokessin. She shook her head, and met the woman's gaze. "It's hard to say, sometimes," she answered frankly.

A hesitant smile added a hundred creases to the woman's face. "It sounds wrong," she said, her tone rising in hopeful question.

"Yes, it does," Catie replied simply, looking through the window in time to see the three men who had been pursuing her arrive in front of the inn.

"Will you catch them?" the old woman asked, back in their game, her voice a conspiratorial whisper.

Just then, the strange man whose gaze pierced her from almost three miles away fixed her through the window, through bunches of hanging herbs. Catie's mouth opened, but her voice stuck. Finally the men went inside, and she breathed out a sigh. "I don't think so," she said, glancing at the old woman with troubled eyes.

The old woman only chuckled one last time, and drifted back to sleep. Catie shook her head with a wistful grin: she hoped to be that old one day, and spend her life just so. First, she had to make it through this meeting.

The cold of the streets was quickly rebuffed by the warmth of the inn. Roaring hearths battled each other from across the common-room, and nearly every table was full. Serving girls strode to tables, barely pausing to unlade their trays before scampering to another table, or to the back. One flashed them a smile as she passed, but said nothing as a patron's bawl recalled her attention.

They caught the eye of the keeper, who gestured absently towards the tables before turning and attending some other business. Gabriel nodded.

"Help ourselves," he muttered, turning to his companions and indicating a table against the wall beside the fire.

"Why did you pick this particular inn?" Rodigger asked as they sat.

"Because," Gabriel replied, pausing as a server dropped off three mugs of ale. "Because it wasn't full."

"You didn't know that outside," Rodigger said with a grin.

"Deuel did."

Rodigger's grin slipped. "Deuel did."

"Yeah." Gabriel glanced around as he took a drink, then back at Rodigger's level stare and shrugged.

"How could he know that?" Rodigger asked, screwing up his face.

"He's..." Gabriel shrugged, meeting his friend's emotionless gaze. "He's very good."

"Oh, whatever." Rodigger returned to his drink with a sigh.

She exited the shop silently, then paused briefly before the inn door to take a quick, calming breath. She was more sure about the stranger's identity now. Normally, that would have comforted her, but she still knew nothing about the other two with whom he traveled. Straightening, she pushed through the door and entered the inn.

5

MYSTERIOUS
CONVERSATIONS

"Now?"
"Yes."
"And say what?"
"Teresh..."

16 Mantaver 1320 — Winter

"There he is," Deuel muttered, gesturing toward the door. Rodigger turned, catching sight of the green-hooded man as he stepped into the common room. Surely it was no coincidence that Deuel led them straight here, but how could he have possibly done that? Rodigger glanced at Deuel, and when he turned back, suddenly the man was no longer there. In his place was a woman with a fire in her hair that was surely lit by the spark in her eyes, fueled by her grace as she moved unerringly toward them. Rodigger felt himself stand barely more than he heard his companions do the same.

"I'm Catie," she said, extending a hand to no one in particular. "You've been following me."

Rodigger grinned and stepped forward, but Gabriel had been closer and got to her hand first. "Gabriel," he said. "And you came in after us."

"Deuel." He did not shake her hand, but his gaze was ever-piercing.

Rodigger's hand was still outstretched. She turned and glanced him over, and her smile widened just a little as she shook his hand. "Rodigger," he managed, then left his mouth open for something else to come out, something witty and charming. Nothing did, and it shut.

"I hid across the way," she said, turning back to Gabriel. "I wanted to see who I would be walking in on."

Gabriel arched an eyebrow. "Well done," he said. "I thought Deuel might mention something if he had seen you," he added, casting the same eyebrow upon his friend.

"How would he have known?" finally tumbled from Rodigger's mouth as his gaze tore from Catie.

Catie gestured at Deuel. "Because, he's—"

"He's very good," Gabriel finished. Catie's own sharp gaze searched Gabriel's face, then Deuel's, and turned quickly back to Rodigger.

"Just look at the way he carries himself, and how quiet he is," she said, with further gestures. "It's the quiet, poised ones who always know everything that's going on."

Rodigger nodded once, and his mouth formed a voiceless "oh."

"Shall we sit?" Gabriel asked, glancing around the room. He smiled and placed a hand on Catie's shoulder as if they were old friends. Rodigger swallowed hard as his gaze flailed from Catie, to Gabriel, to Gabriel's hand—though his smile stayed desperately in place.

Catie smiled and nodded, and the four sat down with scraping chairs and rustling clothing. "So why are you following me?" she asked, quietly in the general din of the common room.

"We're just traveling," Gabriel replied, raising his hand for more drinks. "You happened to be in front of us—though, avoiding the inns." He paused and smiled at the barmaid as she refilled their mugs and left. "So one might ask, instead, why you were following us from the front."

Catie's smile faltered, and she gazed at Deuel as though deciding something. "I had a close call with one of the innkeepers," she said finally.

Rodigger's fist came down hard on the table, causing more than just those who sat around it to jump. "I told you I need to report him," Rodigger fumed with a jabbing finger. "It wasn't just us, and it's not going to be just us. We should go back and give him steel—one foot of it for every ounce of draught he put in his patrons' fish!"

"How will you know how much that is?" Catie asked. "I knew better, so don't count me in your tally."

Gabriel's arms folded and his eyebrows raised expectantly at Rodigger.

"Well...at least a foot of it, then," Rodigger said. "That'll still do enough damage for me."

"It only takes a few drops to put someone out," Catie continued. "Who took it?" she asked, her gaze only including Gabriel and Rodigger.

To his credit, Rodigger noticed. "Oh, of course Deuel didn't get any, because he's very good, right?"

"I was being diplomatic," Catie confessed, looking directly at Rodigger. "I knew Gabriel wouldn't have, either. I am sorry. Did you have a headache?"

He did *now*, he thought, his peripheral vision locking onto Gabriel's quivering lips as the mercenary barely contained his laughter. It was a quivering that Rodigger knew from childhood—but one that he did not see in Catie. As his mind refocused on her, he realized she seemed genuinely concerned, and he smiled a little.

"No, not really," he replied, noting how her eyes drifted down to his mouth as he spoke. Again he found himself trying to think of more to say, to keep her gaze on him, but his mind failed once more. She turned back to Gabriel, her departing eyes taking a little of Rodigger's spirit with them. He lifted his mug to drink.

"You're not traveling anywhere near Agirbirt, are you?" she asked.

Rodigger coughed up his beer. Gabriel and Deuel both gave him withering looks. Catie only blinked.

"Would you like to travel together?" she asked, as if the answer had been given to her plainly.

"I fear that would be a bad idea," Gabriel said. "Our purposes otherwise might not mingle."

Catie glanced around the table. "I only said I was going to Agirbirt," she replied. "Is your purpose somehow for me to not go home?"

"You were overheard," Deuel said.

She rubbed her lip. "If I had been serious about that, would I be going north, or south?" she asked.

"It doesn't matter where you're going," Rodigger said heavily, his chest feeling like it had dropped entirely to his waist. She couldn't have denied it? "You oppose the revolution, and you tried to kill Roth once already, and we can't trust you."

She glanced at him, then back around the table. All their countenances were set. Her eyes narrowed and she stood. "I might find you again in Sprativerg," she said. "I think by then you'll find great masses of people who oppose the revolution, who might have even thought about killing Roth if they had the opportunity, that you can trust now." Her gaze lingered on Deuel for a moment. "Good day."

As she turned and left, Rodigger's foot came from behind the table before he stopped himself—or rather, Gabriel's stare stopped him.

"Don't you dare go after her," the mercenary growled. "You started it."

Rodigger's mouth gaped. "You said our purposes might not mingle, as I recall."

"'Might' being the key point, *hetan*," he replied. "But she was absolutely right. If she had been serious, what does she have to gain in Agirbirt, where she is undoubtedly from?"

Rodigger paused, then his eyes widened. "Maybe she knows about the Berkarfor!"

Gabriel drew a long breath. "You know Rod, one day Deuel, myself, and Roth won't be here. Who exactly do you expect to do your thinking for you then?"

Catie exited the inn, stopping just outside the door despite the swirling snow. Across the way, the herb shop was dark, the old lady returned to her home. A voice in Catie's head sighed: she missed her Grandmother. She missed warm beds, and familiar surroundings. She missed Dannid. Her throat hardened as she swallowed, and the winter sting in the wind did not help the water in her eyes. The door behind her opened, and the boisterous noise inside pushed her as firmly aside as the drunken tradesmen who exited. She caught her balance, but stayed, her eyes still upon the frosting panes of the shop where she had taken refuge for only a few moments—but long enough to remember times not so long past when the world was right. She wanted it all back, all that time spent traveling, meeting people, doing things that seemed to make a difference at the time—she would trade all of that, everything she had become, would do over again all the years at her mother's side learning.

If only for the opportunity to choose the right fork instead of the left.

She turned away. She liked this inn: the beds were soft, and gentle on her shoulder blades where a terrible ache had grown a few years ago and never left. Dannid had used to massage there, but stopped when it made the ache worse. And the muscles there never seemed to relax, anyway. It's how she knew the three men would stop here—not that Deuel had aches in his back, but with what did rest upon his back, it made sense.

And Rodigger didn't know. A feeble grin came to her lips, then strengthened at the thought of the moment when he learned. And they would have to travel together for presumably some time longer after that.

Her grin faded as she walked to find another inn. What could their mission be? Agirbirt had little more than historical significance. It was on the road toward the port of Satost, but they did not say they were headed for the port. It was not as though the lake held mystical properties. And her village of Attelek was just that: a village. A fishing village, with perhaps a few more inns than fishing villages normally had as it was on the way inland from Satost. But it didn't attract visitors for itself. At best, the lake was part of a legend of...

Catie stopped, her head bowed. Her grin returned, and her shoulders shook in silent laughter. She traced an eyebrow with her finger: the Berkarfor. This pathetic little man who had killed her husband so ruthlessly was so desperate as to seek such a legend. And he sent a twit of a soldier, an aging mercenary who only by miracle stayed in his saddle on steep pitches in the mountains, and so great a being as Deuel to find them.

Oh, they probably existed. Her feet continued carrying her through drifting snow. Almost assuredly, they did. But, knowing the people of Andelen, those three would probably stop for a few days in Stramfath. A fine place for learning, to be sure, but only about the things that people already agreed were mostly true. Almost no one believed in the Berkarfor.

No, she would see them again. They would need to come to Attelek. They would need to see Catie's Grandmother. And they would probably need Catie to find the rest.

The sun was muted the next morning by a frosty fog, though the rumor of it dazzled against the Dragonsbacks as Rodigger, Gabriel, and Deuel continued on the road northward. After a few moments of straining his eyes forward, hoping to see a rider somewhere up ahead, Rodigger sat back with a sigh. Gabriel shook his head with a grin that Rodigger ignored. He glanced at Deuel. Though the man's eyes pierced toward the mountains as well, nothing in his face betrayed what he might have seen. *Nothing in his face ever betrays anything,* Rodigger thought as he sneered silently. A good illusion of wisdom.

Deuel's eyes turned and fixed upon Rodigger, who swallowed his sneer thickly and watched the back of his horse's head bobbing. Why did he have to *do* that? What kind of man had such abysses for eyes that to look in them seemed instantly as if you had been plopped into a cave with no way out except five thousand passages leading into darkness?

Rodigger glanced again, barely, out of the corner of his eye in time to see Deuel's gaze shift forward. *This is going to be the longest ride, ever. Why did that beautiful woman have to leave without us?* Rodigger's eyes darted to Deuel again, in case the man could read thoughts. But, of course, his expression revealed nothing.

"Why aren't we at the inn?" Rodigger asked, glancing around the docks at Farenglinn's Vatenvilt—another of Andelen's oddities, for those who traveled elsewhere.

"Because I like the smell of the river," Gabriel replied, watching the rushing waters go by down the middle of the course. Here at the docks was a natural eddy, and the reason for the Vatenvilt: boats laden with supplies could slow, and dock.

When Rodigger was silent for too long, Gabriel looked at him, then rolled his eyes. "It's a 'vilt, Rodigger: I'm having something delivered."

"We have everything we need," Rodigger said.

Gabriel glared at him. "Perhaps *you* think you do. I, having stayed alive much longer and under much more pressing circumstances, know I do not." He turned back to the river and crossed his arms.

"So we stand here and wait? For how long?"

"Probably a week."

"Gabriel..." Deuel rumbled, but somehow in a way Rodigger knew was not threatening. That was another thing about Deuel that unseated him.

"Rodigger, find us comfortable lodgings, please?" Gabriel said, not taking his eyes off the river. "It won't be long."

Before Rodigger could open his mouth, Deuel's gaze locked onto him and he scuttled off as if he had never intended to sit there and wait with them.

"You should be nicer to him," Deuel said when Rodigger had gone. "This does not promise to be a short journey."

"I'm cold and I'm tired, *skald*," Gabriel replied, his voice sounding as thin as the air around them. "Do you think they only hid the Berkarfor?"

"No, they are guarded."

Gabriel cocked an eye on his friend, reading in Deuel's tone precisely what the man had put there. "You would have stopped me from having these sent, otherwise," Gabriel confirmed. Deuel did not have to nod, and they both watched the river.

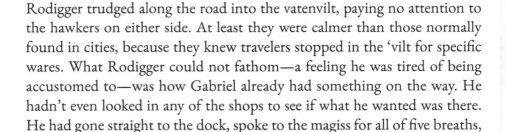

Rodigger trudged along the road into the vatenvilt, paying no attention to the hawkers on either side. At least they were calmer than those normally found in cities, because they knew travelers stopped in the 'vilt for specific wares. What Rodigger could not fathom—a feeling he was tired of being accustomed to—was how Gabriel already had something on the way. He hadn't even looked in any of the shops to see if what he wanted was there. He had gone straight to the dock, spoke to the magiss for all of five breaths, then waited, looking upriver. No hawk had flown upstream with an order, and that's how things were brought into the 'vilt.

He continued, his eyes on the road as the noises of the 'vilt moved around him. Inns were always at the edge of the vatenvilt, and farms beyond that—all according to some law of the 'vilt that permitted only shops within the jurisdiction of the magiss. No telling where that had come from, but probably was not Andelian.

Rodigger reached the crossroad, and gazed at the three identical inns. The one on the far left seemed the quietest. He went in, secured a room for the three of them and a mug of ale for himself, and sat by the fire as he waited to learn what was going on. Hope, it seemed—however malnourished—had not left him yet.

"Why do you carry these?"

The question, asked by one of the guards at Vatenhal, was the spoken echo of Rodigger's silent question that had rang in his head since they left Farenglinn's two weeks ago. Gabriel had never unsheathed them in Rodigger's presence, but they were clearly not normal swords.

"We are heading out of Roth's domain," Gabriel replied smoothly. "We don't know what we might find in the wilds of Sheppar's kingdom."

You mean his kinnigdom, thought Rodigger snidely. *Whatever that even is.*

The guard handed back Gabriel's sheathed weapons, and glanced over the staff Deuel still held. Rodigger had been impressed. The guard had made a valiant effort at almost taking the staff for examination, stopping just short of asking aloud. Rodigger had never even made it that far, and could barely imagine it. And as much as Rodigger had wished it, the guard had not bothered to unsheathe Gabriel's weapons, either. All he knew, still, was what stuck out of the sheath: it almost resembled a sword, except the two-handed grip was bare, the half-guard was wrapped in leather like a grip, and a cuff-like half-moon of metal was attached perpendicularly where a pommel would be. He could also tell by the sheath that the blade was off-center, as if it sat on the opposite side from the cross-guard and cuff. It looked, on the whole, completely lopsided and entirely unusable—and Gabriel had two of them. But given the pitted and rusted appearance of the cuff, it would seem he took care of neither of them.

The dubious expression on the guard's face mirrored Rodigger's thoughts. Weapons had not been used on either side of the front lines in many years. The guard glanced at his companion, who shrugged. "Very well," said the first. "But I don't want to see them drawn within the city. There's no use for them." He made the last sound like a general statement, one which Gabriel clearly ignored as he rode through the gates.

Of all the times of the year to visit Roth's crowning conquest, Rodigger thought, winter was the worst. Vatenhal rested high in the mountains. There were no nearby peaks to disturb the wind that blew almost constantly, and it was near enough the edge of the Dragonsback mountains that storm clouds from the west would not have dropped their snow before arriving at Vatenhal's doorstep.

What had made it such a crowning achievement were some of the same reasons it was detestable to visit in winter: those distant peaks were also too far away from which to launch ballistae, and the single wind-swept road on which they had approached switched up from the valley below twelve times, too exposed and within reach of Vatenhal's own defenses before it arrived at the double-gated entrance. How exactly the castle had been attained was something of a mystery to Rodigger, but he knew it had involved months of building up sympathy within the walls. Despite some contrary comments, Roth's power—Rodigger felt—was always in his ability to persuade others. Rodigger knew, bitterly, that it had not been an army that had taken this castle.

They stopped at the first inn on the thoroughfare, and tied their horses to the post outside. When they entered, the common room was perhaps half-full, though it was the middle of dinner time. Gabriel approached the bar.

"Two Midlands and a Therian outside, for one night," he said.

The keeper looked at him, astonished. "You brought a Therian up here?" he asked.

"He did just fine," Rodigger lied hotly.

The keeper glanced at him, then briefly past him, then back at Gabriel. "I'm afraid we're full tonight, but have a couple ales for whatever ails you," he said with the barest of grins.

Gabriel cocked an eyebrow at the keeper, but Rodigger looked around quickly and spotted two men with black cloaks and hoods pulled back. "Over there," he said quietly, nudging Gabriel. "Three, please," he said, hoping to savor this moment when he finally knew more than his companions. But with one look at Deuel, he knew there was no mystery, and he nearly snarled as he looked away.

They sat, not with the two men, but nearby, drinking for several moments in silence until a bard returned to the small side-stage and began to strum.

"Is it watched?" Rodigger asked quietly, looking sideways at the bard. He turned back to the two men in time to see one rub his nose. Rodigger blinked, and felt his heart teeter on the precipice. "How long?" he asked, looking at his companions. There was motion again as the second man scratched where a ring might have been on his third finger.

Rodigger's heart fell. *Three weeks.* Too long for Catie to have gotten through—at least, not on her own. "Have you helped anyone else through, recently?" he asked.

There was a pause as both men's eyes darted around: that hadn't been part of the script, and in the end the first man simply shook his head.

I bet Gabriel and Deuel are loving this, Rodigger thought, rubbing his forehead. When he glanced up, he saw the amused smirk he had expected to see on Gabriel's face, but for once Deuel wasn't even looking at him.

"What time," he asked flatly, his enjoyment in the secretive conversation now completely gone.

The first man stood, and began walking away. The second spilled a few coins on the table, then picked up four of them: after Mid-Night. Both men paused at the door and pulled up their hoods, then exited.

Gabriel was watching him with a cocked eyebrow. "Do we still stay here, after the keeper said it was full?" he asked.

Rodigger swallowed. "No," he replied. "There's another inn two streets up where we'll have a room already ready."

"I guess you thought of everything," Gabriel said, draining his mug and standing. He tossed a coin on the table and turned, then twisted his head back to look at Rodigger. "Is it okay that I did that? That's not code for anything, is it?"

Without waiting for a response, Gabriel headed for the door. Deuel was looking at Rodigger again, whose knuckles were white around the handle of his mug.

"What?" Rodigger snapped, his eyes boring into Deuel's chest.

"I apologize for my friend," Deuel murmured. As if those words broke something free, Rodigger's gaze came up to meet Deuel's eyes and—for once—he was able to keep from looking away.

But Deuel said nothing else before standing and following the mercenary to the door. Rodigger, after figuring out how to close his mouth, stood and went with them.

Rodigger, Deuel, and Gabriel sat at the edges of their beds, saddlebags packed and tied. Rodigger glanced out the window. It was a new moon tonight, and he had always had trouble telling time of night when that happened. He knew vaguely it had something to do with the stars, but usually he was asleep by this time, or someone told him what time it was. He would not ask, now. He could not even bring himself to look at Deuel, again. Whatever barrier had fallen earlier in the evening was re-erected.

Deuel glanced at Gabriel, and Gabriel at Rodigger. "It's time," the mercenary said, rising with a sigh and a hearty push with his hands against his knees. Deuel rose beside him. Rodigger followed them out, sparing one final glance around the room before closing the door quietly.

They made their way downstairs, and into the dark. No one seemed to be about, though with no moon anything could have been hiding in the dark. Snow sat in thin drifts in the corners of streets and buildings, and the rest of the streets looked wet and dull. It was a perfect night, despite the cold, for moving without being seen.

"How do we get outside the walls?" Gabriel whispered. There was not even a taunt in his voice.

Rodigger said nothing, but took the lead, heading toward the main gate. "The guards are most definitely on our side," Rodigger said finally, whispering only because in such darkness it seemed appropriate. "It's okay if they see us."

For a time as they left the castle and began the descent down into the valley, the only sounds of the night were their horses' hooves. Soon enough the river rushed steadily ahead of them. Here it did not cascade but was a wide, flat ribbon in a broad valley.

The road turned north, and so did they. Rodigger slowed, his eyes darting around the gloom for some sign of their guides. How foolish it would be to pass them by and stumble directly into Sheppar's troops! His blood thrummed in his ears, mocking his attempts to listen. The clouds overhead slid in front of the stars. He tried to slow his breathing, but his intermittent gasps made it worse.

Suddenly they were before him. A short cry left his lips, and the hand he clapped over his mouth echoed even louder. He could almost feel the cold glares coming from the utterly black hoods.

But they said nothing, moving quietly off the side of the road and down a series of boulders arranged nearly into steps. Rodigger, Gabriel, and Deuel followed. The narrow ledge led downward, never switching, till the river flowed hard beside them.

"We will be in the river a few times," whispered the first guide, pointing at the waters. "Try to slide your feet through the water instead of splashing, yes?"

Rodigger nodded as the second man relayed the instructions. They pressed on. The man in the lead glanced upward frequently. Rodigger followed his gaze once, seeing a lip in the rock above where the road had to be. If anyone came to the edge and looked down, surely they would be dark shapes against the river. Rodigger shuddered once, then focused on putting silent feet upon the narrow track.

He was four sliding steps through the water before the iciness hit his feet. He gritted his teeth with a small groan, fighting desperately against the urge to pick them up out of the water. He could feel them growing numb, but could not see where the path rose above the water again—where, hopefully, was some relief.

But when they reached it, that relief did not come. He could feel almost nothing by that point, which was *some* relief. But at the next ford, the water came even higher, numbing him halfway up his calves before the track rose above the river once more.

Twice more they forded. He wondered briefly—since she was rarely far from his mind anyway—if Catie had found this route, and if she had turned back when she hit the water. Or if, by some miracle, she made it through and might still find them on their way to Agirbirt. The warmth of those thoughts did not quite make it to his feet, and after slipping and nearly falling completely into the freezing waters his mind returned fully to the task at hand.

Finally the track went upward. The guides paused near the top, peering backward along the road. The second man hissed quietly, holding up a hand for a few moments. After several breaths he beckoned urgently, and both guides moved at a crouch down the road. The three companions followed, leading their horses in long strides to keep them from picking up a canter.

A few hundred steps down the road the guides ducked behind three large boulders. Rodigger came upon them, his breath hard and thick in the frosty air.

"I'll be glad for spring," he whispered as Gabriel and Deuel squeezed in behind him, and coughed quietly as he placed a hand against his throat.

"You should be fine after this," said the first guide. "You might not want to be seen on the road, or as little as possible, until reaching an inn, or until Onesstritt, so it's less obvious that you came from the south."

"Tradesmen don't move from the south to the north?" Gabriel asked.

"Few enough," Rodigger said, glancing at the mercenary.

"And you aren't tradesmen," the first guide said flatly. "You don't even look like ones."

Gabriel shrugged and grinned. "Thank you," he said.

The two guides glanced at Rodigger. "Good luck," they said.

As they watched the two men slink back down the road, Gabriel took a breath. "Fortunate, isn't it, that small path skirting right where the kinnig's forces put their outpost."

"I don't question good fortune when it smiles on me," Rodigger replied.

Deuel took a shorter grasp on his horse's reins and moved away from the shelter of the boulders.

Gabriel smiled at Rodigger. "Yeah, I—"

"We should head further in," Deuel said, cutting Gabriel off. "And build a fire to dry our boots. Riding now will turn them to ice."

Being reminded of how cold his legs were distracted Rodigger from the shock on Gabriel's face. Rodigger followed Deuel, not even paying attention to the fact that he now walked in between the two friends.

Deuel took them off the road and deep along a canyon for some time, past several turns, before stopping in a small bowl where—almost miraculously—a small pool and shocks of matted grass were surviving the winter.

Later, after Rodigger had dropped to sleep, Gabriel turned and faced Deuel. "Choosing him over me, now?" he whispered. "You know what he's going to say when he finds out what you are."

"And he will still have to travel with us," Deuel replied. "Making him a worse enemy now will not make him a better companion later."

"He's a terrible companion right now," Gabriel grunted. "You know *ked* well there were no soldiers back there. This rebellion is only in Roth's mind—and Rodigger's, because he has no mind except what Roth gave him."

"Then we have little to fear on the road northward," Deuel replied. "And one terrible companion is often made by two people."

Gabriel glared at Deuel's back as the man turned away from him. "You're the worst *skalderon* there is, right now."

"I am the best *right hand* there is, right now," Deuel murmured, "because

I will not allow the body to which I am attached become corrupt and evil."

Gabriel's mouth gaped for a few moments, then muttered several grumbling curses as he turned away and tried to get comfortable against the thin earth.

Rodigger lay with his eyes closed, keeping his breathing deep, feigning sleep. *He has no mind except what Roth gave him.* Was that so terrible? He would have thought it a wonderful thing to mimic so great a mind. But the way Gabriel said it... He managed to avoid sighing. At least Deuel seemed to be on his side. *"When he finds out what you are."* What, *'very good'? He already knew that.*

As he began drifting toward sleep, his thoughts drifted back to Vatenhal, to the code. It excited him, being given that by Roth before he left Akervet, made him feel even more a part of the revolution than he had. Of course, he could not remember that without remembering the other code: one who looked for the man with wings. Was that what it was? Something like that. And no explanation of who would say it, or where, or why he would be looking for a man with wings, or how the man had wings. Nothing but that it was critical that Rodigger help that person however he needed—maybe to the extent of abandoning the Berkarfor.

Rodigger shifted fitfully. That made him worry. How would he know? He thought the Berkarfor were everything. What if he hadn't found them? What if the mercenaries were threatening to stop looking for them? Who would the code-giver be? How...?

6

SEARCHES BEGIN

"Everyone seems to be doing fine on their own..."
"They should be together, right now."
"How do you know?"
"That's the way the God of All would always have it, Teresh."

20 Thriman 1320 — Winter

Two and a half weeks later, they entered the Skaldvath Mountains—a slender arm coming down from the Dragonsbacks and splitting the Fallonvall from the Birnesath. This broad plain was bordered on the north by the Beltrath Wastes, and the south by the Fiery Sea. Agirbirt Lake glimmered in the distance, a sapphire plume spilling from Stramfath and over the horizon.

Rodigger paused when they first caught glimpse of the lake. He had never seen anything like it. As they rode, Gabriel told him it would take more than seven days to ride around the perimeter of Agirbirt—something they might have to do to find where the hidden Berkarfor lay.

"How much do you know about these goblets?" Gabriel asked as they plodded toward Stramfath.

Rodigger shrugged. "Not more than Roth told me," he said, hiccuping when Gabriel snorted. "There are only four, but they're scattered all over

Andelen. They were made during the Age of War, used by the kings of Andelen to gain their freedom from Rinc Na, then hidden for fear that their power would be misused. Now, though, Roth says…"

Rodigger trailed off as Gabriel suddenly turned off the road toward a clump of trees. Stramfath was at least an hour away, and the sun was descending. Rodigger followed silently, knowing any questions were pointless. Gabriel and Deuel dismounted and tied their horses to some branches. Rodigger climbed down hesitantly.

"Check out the lake," Gabriel told Deuel. "See if there's any spot likely for something to be hidden. Don't go swimming just yet." Deuel nodded and stepped away from the grove.

"But I thought you said it would take days…to…"

Rodigger stiffened as Deuel threw back the thick cloak that had been perpetually wound around him. Great, leathery wings reached out from his back and stretched, having been folded for so long. His gaze locked onto Rodigger for a few moments before he leapt, and with three great bursts from his wings he shot into the sky.

Rodigger took a step back as his gaze snapped up to follow the swiftly-receding silhouette of Deuel. "He's—He's…"

"Behamian," Gabriel grunted with a nod. "A dragon-son." His gaze, too, went to the sky where Deuel was now a thin dot gliding over the lake.

"But that's—that's an abomination!"

"You say so," Gabriel said darkly, staring hard at Rodigger before returning upward. "I don't think he can help it, though."

"Catie!" a young man shouted in surprise.

She actually startled, looking around for the source. To her right, standing in mid-step, was Teyor, his smile wide in disbelief. She smiled hesitantly in return, seeing that others in the square were noticing. She had walked almost to the middle of her hometown without being recognized, which was why Teyor's outburst caught her quite by surprise.

"Hi," she said, with a little wave.

And just like that, everyone nearby suddenly streamed toward her with smiles and welcomes, while others near the edges of the square shouted to people unseen and waved them over. She had almost expected this—well, it would either have been this, or everyone running over to throw her out of town. She had not been sure. She had gone back and forth between the possibilities ever more frequently the closer to Attelek she came.

But as they pressed around her, it was all friendly smiles. Names she could not recall on the road sprang to mind as their faces bobbed before her, and hands outstretched to touch her as if to make sure she was real.

"Jayna; Dejor; Friela, hi again. Peyt, how are you? Catie Two!" she said, beaming wide and hugging a girl her own age who had come to Attelek from Satost fifteen years ago and was the only person in the village to share a name with someone else. "Oh, it's so good to see you all again. Velta! I've missed your *piraltas* in the mornings. Oh, they're the best fresh; I'll be by in the morning tomorrow. I know, Dath," she said with a quick laugh, her hand on his bony shoulder—it was bonier now than she remembered. At his well-concealed wince she slid her hand to his shoulder blade and rubbed gently. "I—probably, Sar. Definitely for a while." Her head swiveled around the small crowd. "I'll need to talk to—hi, Tyafor! Do you even realize how big you've gotten? Is Gandreth putting you to work or something?" Those nearest chuckled as she winked at the blacksmith, who stood with arms folded but smiling at the edge of the press.

Heads suddenly turned and the questions went silent. Catie, still smiling, glanced behind her then turned fully. The crowd parted as Grandmother made her way forward, her hand gently on the shoulder of a small girl that Catie didn't recognize. Of course, when Catie had left, the girl would probably have been two or three.

This meeting was still one Catie had feared, for she had defied Grandmother in leaving—at least a little bit. Catie knelt, her head bowed, her heart hammering. Surely if the others had welcomed her back so completely...

A withered but surprisingly still-strong hand cupped her chin and lifted till she was looking in Grandmother's sparkling eyes, and her heart soared.

"It is so good to see you healthy," Grandmother said. "Please stand up and let me look at you, Caytaleane."

Catie stood. Grandmother always used the full old names, and now Catie knew she was home.

Rodigger stood resolutely facing his horse as Deuel returned. His stomach convulsed as he heard leathery appendages flapping and folding—couldn't help but see them in his mind wrinkling and tucking behind a cloak that would no longer hide the truth. He rubbed Gared's forehead.

"You probably have questions," Deuel said quietly, not far enough behind Rodigger.

Rodigger frowned and shook his head. "Surprisingly? No."

Teeth clicked, then clothing ruffled. Gabriel spoke next. "Let's head into town," he said. "We'll look into the libraries tomorrow morning, first thing. Get the goblet from here and move on."

Rodigger took his time getting into the saddle, letting the others mount and move ahead of him. Maybe he could drop far enough back that he wouldn't instantly be associated with them, riding into town.

But the roads were empty, the day drawing late. He sighed, looking forward without trying to look at anything. But Deuel's back still was in view, the cloak draped so carefully.

The man with wings.

Rodigger spurred his Therian. He needed to be in front. Then maybe he could forget about it. Gabriel and Deuel watched him go by without comment. They knew. He knew they knew. That was why Deuel had been nice to him, to try to seem less of a disgusting creature than he was. And Rodigger was far from done with them. How in all of Oren was he supposed to continue this journey, knowing what he knew? His heels dug deeper, as if a swifter wind might clean the filth that seemed to coat his body.

"Why do you come back to us now, Caytaleane?" Grandmother asked, her tone merely happy curiosity.

Catie stood quietly, glancing around Grandmother's kitchen—a place she could not recall before, but now could not remember leaving. Was it the same bread baking in the oven as when she had left? The towels had definitely been folded just so, and even the chair Grandmother gestured to was where she had left it when she had gotten up to leave. Surely she had only walked outside, then turned around and came back in. She sat down, the seat still warm from her body.

There was one difference, and now it seemed to gather all her attention: the little girl. She stood in the same corner, but now grown by some years—or perhaps some magic? Luceldar. That was her name. Brought here to replace Catie as Newmother. Lucie's parents, too, were gone. But hers were most definitely dead, drowned. An accident: not her fault, and not their choice. For a moment Catie couldn't smell warm yeast, didn't really feel the familiar seat beneath her, and didn't notice Grandmother arranging herself in a chair on the opposite side of the table. The whole room was only Luceldar's presence: the smell was her sunburnt hair, the sound was her breathing, the feel was her cotton dress. Catie's mind was Luceldar's mind. Bereft, still, but not guilty, not uncertain. Sorrowful, but not wondering what it was about *her* that made thus, so.

Luceldar's presence shifted, and Grandmother was smiling, welcoming, not caring why thus was so but only glad. Catie blinked into an uncertain smile, a small sigh.

"Because everyone keeps leaving me," Catie said, still smiling through the gasping sob that escaped quite without her permission. Suddenly, months of tears unshed rushed forward, not waiting behind her eyes for their turn. Almost maniacally she tried to hold her smile, until Grandmother's stricken face allowed her to drop that, as well, and she knew only weeping.

———◆○◆———

"...get up. Rodigger, wake up. Rodigger!"

Rodigger swiped the hand from his shoulder frantically and squirmed away. It was Gabriel, though—but still Rodigger had to catch his breath.

"Bad dream?" Gabriel asked without sympathy.

Rodigger stared at him for a few moments. "Yeah, yes, it was." *I thought you were Deuel.*

"We're going to the libraries. Let's go."

"What about breakfast?" Rodigger asked as he swung his legs off the bed and grabbed his boots.

"Grab something from a vendor on the way there."

"You're in a hurry," Rodigger mumbled as he pulled on his shirt.

"You would rather this job take longer than necessary?" Gabriel asked coldly as he headed out of the room, clearly already knowing, and not wanting to hear, Rodigger's response.

Rodigger shrugged. Fair enough.

Most large towns in Andelen—Rodigger had heard—had, as a remnant of their past, the large center spike that was the keep. It was the building that could be seen from nearly every quarter of the rest of the town, unless one was hard up against a taller building. In Stramfath, however, what dominated the view from nearly every direction, was the libraries.

Though the word was plural, the building was singular in every sense: seven stories tall, and long enough to block five through-ways, it was the largest collection of books in Andelen, and probably points across the oceans as well. The keepers of the libraries were known everywhere. Many said that the entire place could go up in flames, but find the keepers and they could recite to you its contents in detail.

Oddly enough, it had not been here that Roth had found his stories of the Berkarfor—but perhaps those who hid them so many centuries ago planned that. Stramfath was known even then as a center for knowledge, and the Berkarfor were supposed to fall outside of knowledge.

But those who hid them had not planned on Roth, Rodigger thought with a boyish grin. Of any man to replace Rodigger's father, he could not have picked better than Roth.

So, even though he could not see Gabriel or Deuel when he exited the inn, he could see where they had likely headed. He wasn't quite ready to face Deuel anyway. He knew he would have to, and would have to continue for perhaps months to come. Before falling asleep last night he had almost settled that within himself. But a few extra hours of preparing to face that reality was fine by him.

He did not dawdle, but he did not rush either. He stopped at a few vendors and looked at what foods they had before finally parting with a few coin for a piping hot *tetan* and chilled goats-milk. He slowed his pace now, if only to keep from slopping his breakfast as he continued toward the libraries.

As he approached the main doors, he licked the last of the cinnamon from his fingers and wiped them on the squirrel-skin now drained of milk. He tossed the empty skin to the gutter, and entered.

There were great windows set to allow in rivers of sunlight, and the stacks glowed where sunbeams struck gold- and silver-embossed books. Thick trunks supported an alarmingly thin lattice of iron, it appeared, that were the floors of the six levels, so that—when Rodigger craned his neck in surprise—he could see all the way to the cedar roof almost one hundred feet overhead. Row upon row of shelves soared upward till it seemed they would have to fall over. In front of him, as he brought his head down dizzily, the shelves ranged to the far wall in an impossible-to-fathom number. He swallowed hard. How were they to find what would surely only be a few books on the Berkarfor among this labyrinth?

"Can I help you find a particular book?" asked a gentle voice beside him.

Rodigger turned swiftly, and again dizzily. A small man, perhaps five feet tall, draped in a thick maroon robe, smiled up at him. The man was nearly bald, and his forehead folded tightly into a few wrinkles as his soft eyebrows arched in polite inquiry.

"Um, I'm looking for something on…" he trailed off. He probably should not talk about their mission specifically. "Actually, I'm meeting two friends here."

"Ah! You seek the Berkarfor as well?" the man asked in rapture. "A most interesting subject. I had not read on them for years, but I soon shall. Follow me, please!"

Rodigger waited to glower until the man had turned away. Those two had no sense of discretion! Rodigger's mouth twisted sideways: truthfully, Gabriel had no sense of discretion. Deuel had probably said nothing. Maybe that was just as bad.

Rodigger quickly set off after the keeper as the swirling maroon robe disappeared up a staircase.

Catie awoke, blinking. A white oak chest of drawers she did not recognize glowed in the slanting morning sunlight, nearly blinding her. She nestled into the pillow a little, stretching her back, and sniffed. The lavender-scented sheets she knew, and some of her clothes hanging behind the chest she knew. After a few more wonderfully thought-free blinks, she raised her head and looked around.

She was in Grandmother's spare room.

No.

It was her room. Hers after her parents had gone, when her home had been too empty for her to stay. But it had never been *hers*. She would not have put the things in there that were there, and certainly not where in the room they were: they made no sense where they were. She had been fitted into the room, loose around the edges and uncomfortable in some places. She utilized it as best she could, but did not have it hemmed. It was not hers. In that sense, it mirrored her life in just about every way.

She glanced again at the white oak, angled her gaze to try to look out the window but could not. Still, if the sun was up, so was Grandmother. Another blink and the scent of maple syrup sprang to life in her nostrils. Memories of last night's exhaustion slipped away as she inhaled deeply, and smiled. After generous helpings of what Grandmother was making, she would be ready to talk, memories buffered now by sugar and love borne by sharing a good meal.

Catie rose and dressed quickly, then made her way to the kitchen. Grandmother was turning from the oven, wooden paddle laded with cakes fresh from the fire. A jar with canted lid sat near the flames, and she knew the source of the warm syrup smell was there. Catie smiled and sat before she noticed Luceldar in the same corner as last night, silent and watching, and Catie's smile wavered.

"Fetch us a few mugs," said Grandmother, to almost no one in particular. Luceldar moved silently and immediately. Grandmother seemed to think that was right, so Catie settled more firmly into her seat.

When all was arranged Grandmother looked to the ceiling. "May we accept this bread from your hands," she said, "and give back at the end of this day the bread of our labor."

Catie bit into her cake quietly. It had been years since she had offered that simple supplication, though she very much liked it. She only hoped—if the God of All took her—she would not go until she had given back equal to what she had taken that day. It seemed only fair.

They ate without speaking. Grandmother's house sat near the edge of the village, and behind it were a dozen large trees. So the birds did not permit the silence to hang heavy. Luceldar cleared the dishes when they had finished, and returned to her corner.

"I met a man in Sprativerg," Catie said. "Named Dannid. He was...bursting with ideas," she said, smiling a little.

Grandmother smiled too. "You always liked the quiet, thoughtful ones."

"Oh, he was not quiet," Catie replied. "The quiet ones still ponder. Dannid had finished pondering and was past ready to speak. I think that's why I liked him more..." Catie's voice lowered. "That's why I loved him."

"But he has gone?"

"He was taken," Catie murmured resolutely. She could no longer be timid about her thoughts, and how she expressed them. "By Roth, personally. In Bokessin."

"That sounds far away."

"Almost on the tip of the Fallonvall, in the Dragonsback," Catie affirmed with a nod.

"You were deep in Roth's territory."

"A week or so from his headquarters," Catie said, with another nod. "Or, where he was supposed to be headquartered. Dannid achieved too much, and Roth came down to put a stop to it. He was very successful."

"You were close to this man?"

"We were married," Catie said, her lower lip quivering a moment before she pressed her lips together. She paused to collect herself with a deep sigh that she released audibly. "For three days, before Roth arrived."

"You're a widow?" Luceldar exclaimed from her corner. When both sets of eyes swung on her, she looked appropriately mortified at speaking those thoughts aloud, though her eyes were still wide with incredulity.

"At twenty-three years old," Catie responded. It was not as if that were the first time the realization crossed her mind. When widowhood in a child's mind is always associated with *old* women, the two are hard to separate. It was only slightly easier for Catie.

"So you came back here," Grandmother said.

"I tried to get revenge on Roth," Catie admitted. "He had a moment of luck, though. I sneezed, and he could hear my voice. It's a longer story," Catie said with a wave of her hand. "But he also had a moment of mercy and only sent me out of the town without my horse, and with only a few hours until sunset." She proceeded to tell the rest of the tale, including meeting Gabriel, Deuel, and Rodigger—but she left out the strange light that pierced the sky that first night. She wanted to contemplate that on her own, for at least a little while longer. She did not normally keep things from Grandmother—why would you, when wisdom sat right in front of you?—but until she could bring her thoughts closer to bear on those events, she would wait.

"I know I could feel him. Deuel," Catie said. "Which was strange. But I know—well, I wondered if he might be a dragon-son. You remember telling me about those..." Her posture affected a question if her inflection did not.

"I would like to see him," Grandmother replied carefully. "You found him in the right spot. And your description of his eyes seems to fit. But they are so hard to find." She wagged her head and smiled. "I haven't seen one since..." Her eyes flashed, and she shook her head again. "What will you do now?" she asked.

Catie ran her finger up and down the side of her empty mug. "I don't know," she murmured. "I'm not sure if I'll stay here, or..." She shrugged, but did not look up. "I don't know."

"You want to try to travel with these men?"

Catie drew a deep sigh. "I don't know," she answered more firmly. "Not yet."

"Thorgiar got it wrong, Jahsonn, I read it in Kuelgar's *Treatise on mid-Ancient Rinc Nain.*"

"You are the only one to have read that ridiculous work, Perator," Jahsonn replied wearily. "Not a single one of Kuelgar's contemporaries agreed with him—and few enough even recognize such a dialect! It simply doesn't exist in any accredited work."

"But it is worth recognizing that, in the absence of practical proof, this explanation is certainly better than none as to why that verse sounds the way it does."

"There isn't enough research!" Jahsonn's voice was rising in strain if not as much volume. "Just because no one has *found* it, does not mean the evidence is wrong. Almost no one is looking for it!"

A third figure in maroon robes walked up. "What is this arguing?" he asked in a deep rumble.

Gabriel rolled his eyes. "I guarantee they could not begin to tell you," he muttered. Rodigger looked on as well, though his eyes were glazed over. Deuel was still among the books.

"Jahsonn is trying to say that *Berkarfor Hidden* is translated absolutely properly, when anyone who has read anything on the work can tell it was shoddily done. Just reading the text in translation, there is so much that doesn't make sense!"

"The translation is the best we have," Jahsonn replied. "Perator is arguing for argument's sake because he fears he isn't valued here."

"These men seek a perfect translation of *Berkarfor Hidden*?"

"Oh," Jahsonn replied as Gabriel fairly growled. "No, Kreath, they seek the Berkarfor."

Kreath's gaze went to Gabriel, then to Rodigger, who still was not paying much attention. Without taking his eyes off the two men, he plucked the book from Perator and tucked it under his arm. "The Berkarfor do not exist," he said quietly, but firmly.

Rodigger's eyes snapped to, then. "Yes they do," he said, just as firmly though much louder.

Kreath ignored him, proceeding to the shelves where he put the thin book back in the thin hole where it had been. "You are not the first to look for them, and you will probably not be the last. Anyone whose dreams rest on such a preposterous idea are made to let them die by chasing a non-existent breeze. As it should be. If you want power and influence, then earn it the same way as everyone else."

Kreath turned on his heel and disappeared among the shelves. Perator and Jahsonn looked everywhere but at Rodigger and Gabriel for a few moments, then with swift glances turned and left as well.

"What—what now?" Rodigger asked, too stupefied to be angry. Gabriel turned to look at the shelves, then down the line at the thousands upon thousands of books in the libraries.

Deuel walked past, his cloak rustling slightly as he moved. "We chase the breeze," he said without hint of concern.

Gabriel squinted, then followed. Rodigger, his mouth propped open, came last.

7

WORDS MISTAKEN

"How is yours doing?"
"He seems to be accepting it. Yours?"
"I think he is accepting it, as well."
"So you do not choose the one I suggested…"

21 Thriman 1320 — Winter

The three men rode through a crisp, clear day. The air was still, and they plodded slowly enough to almost enjoy the day. Perhaps Gabriel and Deuel did. Rodigger did not. That…*behamian*…rode in front, leading them the God only knew where. The lake lay flat and sapphire to their left, broad tan fields lay to their right. In between the heavy hoof-falls of their mounts was the crunch of the short grasses still awaiting spring's birthing—there was no road on this side of the Agirbirt.

Deuel's eyes roved far out across the lake. How far or what he was looking for, Rodigger did not care to guess. The dragon-spawn had not said what he had found in the books, if anything. Rodigger shifted to his right to relieve a twinge in his knee, and sighed as quietly as possible.

He wondered, not for the first time, if Catie would have been able to help them find the Berkarfor. There was no reason she should have, any better than they themselves, but at least they could have passed the time in her company. He sighed again, not worried about muffling it this time. He sensed more than saw Gabriel shift to look at him, and kept his eyes everywhere but on their guide.

Deuel had stopped, completely and unnaturally still. Rodigger scoffed at himself: the entire man was unnatural, anything he did would be unnatural. But this time he exuded as much life as a bit of timber. It made Rodigger shiver, though that might have just been the brief, chill breeze that sprang up from across the lake.

Deuel's eyes returned forward, and their horses resumed their plodding.

"What did you see?" Rodigger asked. "Or think you saw?" he added, not realizing it was going to come out of his mouth until it was entirely too late.

"The breeze," Deuel replied.

"You saw the breeze?" That wasn't too scornful, was it?

"I saw it ruffling the lake," Deuel replied. "I hoped it was something else."

"If I knew what we were looking for, I might be able to help," Rodigger muttered.

Gabriel's disdainful snort carried. Deuel made no such noise. "The first Berkarfor is in the middle of the lake," the dragon-son replied simply.

Rodigger's Therian felt him go still and mimicked, while Gabriel and Deuel rode ahead. "It's *in* the lake?" he asked faintly.

Gabriel twisted to look at him, and reined in his horse. "Well, hopefully it's more *on* it, than in it. Like an island might be in the middle of it."

This made enough sense for Rodigger to continue riding. "But why didn't he see an island when he scouted it, earlier?"

"The most obvious answer would be that it wasn't there to be seen," Gabriel replied patiently.

"It might be sunk," Deuel replied, up ahead. "I could not come too low for fear of being seen, so it may hide well under the waters."

"We won't have to row all over this lake, will we?" Rodigger asked, then wished he hadn't. He might not want the answer.

"Someone probably already has," Gabriel replied. When Rodigger gazed at him silently, he pointed.

It took Rodigger a few moments, against the white horizon, to spot the slowly-moving masts of small fishing boats that had no wind to propel them. He pursed his lips. Villagers from Attelek, of course, would range all over the lake for fish.

"Why didn't we just go straight to the village?" he asked, managing to keep mention of Catie to himself.

"We are," Gabriel replied, his gaze still sweeping the lake.

A few heartbeats passed. "On the road," Rodigger added.

"Because everyone takes the road," Gabriel replied. "It would be a terrible place to hide something like an island."

"We will stop and rest ahead," Deuel said, gesturing forward to where Rodigger could just make out a small hill on the horizon. "I may try to scout again, there."

Rodigger shuddered, and wished he were in Attelek.

Catie walked the familiar streets filled with unfamiliar people.

That wasn't entirely true: everyone over the age of fifteen looked the same, or nearly. Lederor apparently thought he looked better with a full beard, but he changed himself more than Eltsabech changed her dresses, so that was not surprising. What unnerved her were the children, who would stare at her until she finally recognized them, or realized she was supposed to. She almost never remembered them properly, taking them for their older siblings. By lunchtime, she figured she had distanced herself from at least half the village's young people because of it.

The buildings and streets, thankfully, were exactly the same. Wannaker's dress shop was next to Kalador's candles was next to Jutes and Peteyda's stone and iron cookware was next to Hadera's pottery. Geezer Matteuer, for a wonder, still stood griping to Canatheta, who looked just as weary of hearing it as he did every day. Yet somehow they met in front of the forge every morning between errands.

Catie's head tilted as she walked, remembering the day long ago when she suddenly thought that calling Matteuer "Geezer" sounded absurdly disrespectful. Then, as now, she had found him near the forge. The setting was so similar, she found herself reliving the memory.

She walked boldly up to him, barefoot in a linen dress.

Matteuer's scowl softened only a little as she approached. Canatheta looked completely relieved.

"Caytaleane," Matteuer growled.

Catie smiled. She also knew, for Matteuer, this was him at his friendliest, and it pleased her.

"Why," *clang!* "do you let," *clang!* "us call you th—" *clang!* Catie glanced at the forge; so close. "That?"

"Call me what?" he replied, with the appropriate pauses.

"Geezer!" Canatheta said loudly.

"What? One at a time, now."

"And why do you try to hold a conversation right next to the forge?" Catie asked, almost losing the end of her question for how long it took to ask.

"I don't usually have to answer so many—oh for—what was the question? Not supposed to ask so many questions!"

"Why do you let us call you 'Geezer'? It's not very nice, really."

"It's my name," he replied.

"No it isn't."

"It's not, Geezer," Canatheta agreed.

"Then why do you keep calling me that?"

"Well, because..." Catie paused, glancing at Canatheta and flushing a little.

One of Matteuer's great, white, bushy eyebrows rose in anticipation as his gleaming eyes flicked back and forth between the two, but neither was able to answer him. "Because I'm an old geezer?" he asked.

Catie cocked her head a little, and nodded.

"Or because that's what you keep calling me?"

Catie's head straightened, and her brow furrowed. Matteuer bent and placed both his hands on her head, and glared at her. She blinked for several moments. His hands gripped a little tighter—except the skin was soft, not calloused, and held her still rather gently. The eyes that gazed into hers were a crystal blue, shining as the Agirbirt on a clear day. His scowl—no, that was his mustache. Now that she looked this closely, she could see the line of his lips curving upward, slightly, behind it. His eyebrows were thicker at the center, but the tops rose from outside to inside, they were not drawn down in anger.

"You call me that because you have always called me that," Matteuer said quietly. "And you see me that way because you have called me that and did not bother to look closer. When what you see agrees with what you believe, Caytaleane, then you must ask the harder questions."

He released her, and as she stepped back his scowl returned. She blinked a few times, trying to focus. He was still smiling ever so slightly. She shook her head. "You could make a better effort," she said, grinning.

He did, smiling widely, and he looked so absolutely comical that she burst out laughing. "Okay, fine," she said. "You know yourself best, I suppose."

"That is something almost no one believes," Canatheta said, jabbing his finger at her.

"Do you believe it's true?" she asked.

"Not in the least," Matteuer replied. "But it's a better starting point than the opposite. But don't you have better things to do than stand around talking to a couple of old geezers?"

"A couple?" Canatheta said, sounding hurt.

"Yeah, I only see one," Catie said.

Geezer squinted at her, putting on his best, actual scowl. "Be off, with you both!" he said, forgetting to pause for the strike of the hammer.

She smiled and waved as she passed. Geezer's face split into his comical grin, and she laughed. It was good to be home. But almost as quickly as she thought it, her heart stirred northward.

Deuel flew, skimming across the water with his wings flat and wide. Rodigger watched him grow larger and fidgeted. He was going to be able to stop, right?

The wings suddenly showed their broad sides, vein and bone in sharp relief. Deuel hit the ground running, quickly folding them away and steadying to a walk.

"I do not believe there is anything out there," he said. Was it exertion, or did he sound disappointed? Rodigger blinked and looked at Gabriel.

"They wouldn't drop it just into the lake, would they?" the mercenary asked.

"That would hide it," Deuel suggested.

"They were not hidden so that they could never be re-found," Rodigger said firmly. "There has to be a way. Or it's somewhere else."

Deuel said nothing, but returned to the horses. They had hobbled them at the base of the hill. The side facing the lake had fallen away, leaving a short cliff perhaps ten paces high, and would make good shelter in a storm.

"We'll continue around the whole lake, seeing what we see," Gabriel said. "Surely something will stand out."

She had been back in the village for over a week and still had no idea what to do with herself. She had revisited all the old friends, all the old shops, and even a few of the old shores of Agirbirt. Her mind knew she needed to restart her life, find something to do around the village. She would not live with Grandmother forever. But her heart was not attuned. Something told her she would not be staying in the village, though nothing told her why. She recalled a vague sense from so long ago that she would return home, but not stay long. None of the urgency was there. One day, as a test, she tried to fake the urgency, but it refused. And yet neither could she force herself to think of staying at home.

And so she walked, enjoying the sunshine today. It was spring, finally, and winter had the urgency to leave that she lacked. Already tulips raised bright green buds skyward, and the robins dotting the fields wreaked havoc on the earthworm population. The lake was a calm blue, the river running out of its south-eastern end frothing over the rocks. Attelek's full complement of fishers were out, already preparing to stock for next winter. The Agirbirt never quite froze over, but if they could fish on a day like today, and not those of two weeks ago, why wouldn't they?

As a breeze tickled her hair, Catie's smile faded. Before she looked up the road toward Stramfath, she knew what she would see: three riders, one whose eyes could pierce her before she could even make them out. Without fully knowing why, she turned and went back into the village.

"They're here," she said, standing in Grandmother's kitchen doorway.

Grandmother paused only a few moments. "I've just put a pot on," she said gently. "But if you want to bring them by, they would be most welcome."

"I—" *was hoping you would come with me, so I could hide behind your skirts,* Catie didn't say. "I'll see why they're here. They may just be passing through."

Rodigger came in the lead, glancing around the small collection of houses. It was surprisingly well-established. He had expected huts ready to be blown away by the first storm off the lake—but perhaps that had occurred already in the village's history, and they had learned better.

"We'll see if anyone around the village knows anything," Gabriel said behind him. The silence at the end of his sentence caught Rodigger's attention strangely, and he turned to look at the mercenary. Even Deuel was gazing at his friend as Gabriel's eyes roved unhurriedly around the scene before them.

That man was getting too old, Rodigger decided. He was enjoying things too much. Rodigger had fidgeted every moment as they wasted six days circling the lake, another back in the libraries in fruitless search, and three more riding back to Attelek. What could a village like this possibly know that Stramfath didn't?

Stramfath said the Berkarfor didn't exist at all, said a small voice inside Rodigger. It was a good point, and the part that criticized himself the most was surprised he had thought of it. But who to ask?

Catie.

Someone young, perhaps. They were the most learned, usually. Maybe one of them had studied at Stramfath but had returned for any number of reasons. Someone who had traveled.

"I wonder how hard it would be to find Catie?" Rodigger mused aloud.

Deuel and Gabriel reined up short, and he turned. They were staring at him.

"I just thought—she did say to find her if we came out this way, didn't she?"

Gabriel's mouth twitched. "No," he said.

"I thought she did. Either way, we probably want someone traveled, learned, someone who may have actually heard about these things. So I figured..." he trailed off as he suddenly realized they both were looking past him. He turned forward.

And there she was. In a light dress, though what of her legs showed beneath the hem were protected by thick wool leggings and leather shoes. She was striding toward them confidently, her slender arm giving a slight wave, her smile filling Rodigger's vision. Her hair waved and bounced almost joyfully as she walked, though her pert—

Rodigger's Therian shifted, and he gripped the saddle horn tightly, pretending to ease himself in the saddle as he shoved desperately at the thoughts in his mind.

"So, did you find what you were looking for?" she asked, innocently enough.

"Afraid not," was Gabriel's easy reply.

She cast a raised eyebrow around the trio. "What about what I said you would find?"

It must take an angel to say 'I told you so' and make you feel better about yourself for it—and the angels must have come to Catie to learn, Rodigger decided. He grinned with genuine happiness. "I suppose we did," he said. No one outside the Fallonvall thought what Roth did was right, and yet Rodigger had not once felt in danger because of it. He felt in danger for other reasons, but not that one. "Actually, I was thinking you might be able to help us find what we're looking for, or at least get started," Rodigger said. Her smile seemed easy enough, Rodigger thought, and yet...

"And what is that?" she asked.

There it was: the tone Roth took with him when his mentor already knew the answer, and just wanted to hear Rodigger say it. Rodigger glanced at his companions, who looked back at him and made no sign of reply.

So he didn't bother to explain. "The Berkarfor," he replied simply.

Catie's gaze locked onto him. Why couldn't it always be that easy? But then her smile faded as she nodded. "Then you'll need to see Grandmother," she replied. With a final glance at the others, she turned and walked back into the village. The men dismounted and followed.

Catie said nothing, did not even look at them again as they reached a house and tied up their horses outside and then followed her inside.

"Grandmother," she called out as they entered. "I have brought three who need to speak to you."

They entered the kitchen, and there sat an old woman—Catie's grand-mother, apparently—and a young girl of about seven or eight, Rodigger thought. Catie's sister? She seemed too young for that, but too old to be her daughter, surely. Hopefully.

The woman rose, and assessed them all in a glance that would have made Deuel proud. "Welcome," she said. "I'll have fresh bread in a few moments. You must stay."

"That would be wonderful," said Gabriel, bowing his head. "I am Gabriel Owens. This is Rodigger Kytes. And behind him is Deuel."

Rodigger stepped quickly out of the way with a grimace. How had that happened?

"From Burieng?" she asked. Rodigger glanced up, then over at Deuel as the dragon-son gazed at her.

"I am," he said.

"Your name," the old woman said, with a brief wave of her hand and a small smile. "It is not Andelian." Deuel inclined his head briefly.

"And what is your name?" Rodigger asked as politely as he could.

Her smile strengthened as she looked at him. "Grandmother," she replied, as though it settled the matter. Glancing at the others, it seemed she was right. "Do you not have a Grandmother where you are from?" she asked, her gaze directed at Rodigger.

"Well, of course," he said. "Or, I did. Two, but they both—what?"

"An Elder Woman?" she asked gently.

"Oh," Rodigger said flatly. "Yeah, not anymore. No need."

"Ah yes," Grandmother said, lowering herself back into her seat. "Everything is in books, and in the minds of the young, educated people."

It was almost as if she had read his thoughts, so why deny it? He nodded once, gently.

"Yet here you are," Grandmother continued with a sharp glance. "What aren't they teaching you, anymore?"

This time Rodigger did not reply as he steamed under her rebuke, and squirmed for looking the fool in front of Catie.

"The Berkarfor," Gabriel replied for him.

Grandmother sat back, her expression cooling. "Why do you look for those?" she asked.

"Because I am paid to," Gabriel replied.

"It is a sad motivation."

Gabriel snorted. "Then it is because I am hungry," he said.

"Interesting how our ways of life are worn like our skin," Grandmother said, rubbing gently over the backs of her hands. "You do not feel it until someone pokes or prods. For most of us in Attelek, the need for food does not so instantly equal the need for money. Just a bit of work. Those who spend most of their time in Balnath Agrend, I imagine, could not grow and harvest their own food if they wanted to. Can I say to them 'scorn your coin and do a bit of work'?"

Gabriel bowed a little at the waist. "No, Grandmother, you could not."

"What do you know of the first goblet?"

"Beqart el laken zeum finten qa Berkarfor peya on de traschen," Deuel replied. "The first was hidden in Agirbirt Lake."

Grandmother stood, turned to the oven behind her, and pulled out a loaf of black bread that rested near the edge. She cut off a few slices and lay them on a bit of cloth. "These will need to cool a moment, but they should not be too cool, to be enjoyed most."

"Is that to help us, somehow?" Rodigger asked, thinking she still spoke in riddles.

But the corner of her mouth quirked upward. "This will only help Gabriel's hunger a little," she replied. "It would do very little in answering the larger question."

"Can you help us?"

Grandmother seated herself again, her gaze bent upon the table as she sat silently for a long while. Catie stepped forward first to claim a slice of bread. On her cue, the three men did the same, and they ate in silence. Rodigger could feel his shoulders relax as he ate. The warmth of the bread and the silent camaraderie in sharing a simple meal was not lost on him. He was pleased to see Catie did not snap at her bread, or chew unevenly—he could not stand it when a girl ate noisily, or bit down too swiftly. He could see the muscles of her jaw working, the thin, small lines that flashed at the hinge of her jaw as it worked.

He took another bite, then noticed Grandmother was watching him. He blushed, then scratched at his forehead to obscure his face.

As they dusted off their hands of crumbs, Grandmother finally spoke. "The answer lies in your translation. Or, rather, your interpretation. Deuel's translation is perfect, as I would expect," she continued with a respectful nod. She paused, then took a crust of the bread and set it on the table before her. She wadded up a towel, and placed it over the crust.

"Where is the piece of bread?" she asked, glancing around those gathered.

"Under the towel," Rodigger replied first.

"Very good." She grasped the towel and lifted it. The crust was gone. She overturned her hand, showing the bread in the folds of the cloth. "Now where is it?"

"In the towel..."

"It's under the lake," Gabriel said with a nod. "In a cave, under the lake?"

"For your sake, hopefully," Grandmother replied with a smile.

"How exactly will you help us find it?"

Gabriel knew the answer, but enjoyed the animated gestures Rodigger was making behind Catie's back, trying to convince him to let her come along.

"I know this area, and I know the lake certainly better than you do," she replied.

"We've been around it once, already," Gabriel said, though Catie had not quite finished speaking.

"And the fishers will probably talk to me, before you," she finished.

Gabriel considered this for several long moments before slowly nodding. He thought Rodigger might just turn into a puddle of relief. Catie smiled as she turned away, but it was almost a smile that shared in his joke, rather than eased in relief. She knew she was going. This girl was bright, and would probably prove immensely useful.

As Catie fetched and saddled her horse, Gabriel stood physically with his companions while his mind wandered around Attelek. It reminded him of Bokessin. Not because of the surrounding landscape: Bokessin was deep in the mountains, and Attelek, well, Attelek was not. That far south, the mountains around Bokessin had begun their descent toward the sea. But here one could stand at the edge of the village and see, flat outward, to the horizon. The fields nearby offered just enough grains for breads, and probably beer, with a little extra for Sheppar's collectors when that time of year came. Most of the rest of their needs came from Agirbirt's fish or Satost's traders.

But it was more than that, more than the smallness of the village or the simplicity of life: it was the people. It was the culture he knew lived here. He could see it as he glanced around, saw people on paths oblique or at right angles stop, and wave, and talk. It took a lifetime to get to know someone, and that's what they had, here and at Bokessin and dozens of other villages around Andelen: a lifetime. Gabriel was rarely in one place long enough to find all the best spots to eat, let alone get to know anyone. It's what they had at the inns, most times: common-rooms and shared quarters meant that no one meeting at night on the road were strangers for very long. A shared meal was more than just sustenance, it was commonality.

It was, he had to admit, what Roth wanted—commonality on such a grand scale that a villager from deep in the Brithelt could travel to south-eastern Fallonvall and still find it. It was a grand, beautiful, impossible idea. Grandmother had said it best: she could not tell a citizen of Balnath Agrend to grow their own food. She could, perhaps, persuade them to drink Attelek beer. It amused and surprised Gabriel, sometimes, how the slightest of commonalities made for the fastest of friends. But never would one get to know another beyond those little details unless they put down some roots, became part of the forest. Or plain, as the case may be.

He sighed as Catie rode up. Perhaps it *was* the simplicity of life here. He pulled himself into the saddle. Perhaps it was the camaraderie. He had Deuel, sure, but he no longer wondered what commonality they had. There was none. Circumstance, at one time, perhaps. But Gabriel was past getting old. Deuel had a few centuries, hopefully, before he would start to think he might be approaching old age. Of course, by that time, Gabriel would still be a human, and Deuel, hopefully, would not.

"Why did Grandmother look at you like that?" Gabriel asked Deuel as they began their route out of the village.

Deuel's eyes glittered. "I do not know."

"What did she do?" Rodigger asked, riding up beside them and scattering a few villagers in his wake.

Gabriel looked straight ahead for a few moments, then shook his head and looked at Rodigger. "Didn't know you missed that. When she asked if he was from Burieng, it wasn't just because his name isn't Andelian."

"Grandmother knows about *behamien,* or at least a little," Catie said from behind them.

"Everyone knows a little about them," Rodigger muttered, though his gaze was carefully away from Deuel.

"Well, a little more than most," Catie responded. "She knew at least one before, personally."

Deuel's posture shifted. "Did she say his name?" he asked.

"Who said it was a he?"

Gabriel and Rodigger both took a quick glance. Deuel's silence felt like he acceded the point.

"She never told me, actually," Catie said. "It might be a he. She doesn't *say* much. But you can tell she knows."

"This was a common topic?" Deuel asked.

"Sometimes," Catie said slowly. "I find them—you—or whatever...fascinating."

"That's a word for it," Rodigger said. All eyes shifted to him, but his gaze remained resolutely toward the lake now coming into view.

"When did you find out what he was?" Catie asked.

Rodigger kept his silence, but a glance showed Gabriel his jaw muscles writhing.

"I had Deuel scout the lake," Gabriel replied. "About a week ago."

"You just up and flew, in front of him?" Catie asked. "Whew. I bet that was rough."

"Can you talk about me like I'm here?" Rodigger demanded, swiveling his gaze hard upon her.

"I was talking *to* you, silly," she replied. To his credit, he deflated a little. "You need to keep looking at people, even if you don't like what they're saying."

Gabriel smirked as he saw Rodigger's eyes go puppy-dog again. "It was definitely a surprise," Rod said.

Catie nodded with big eyes. "I can imagine. You probably haven't met—"

"Any," Rodigger interjected. "Any *behamien*. I had heard quite a bit, though."

"Like you said, everyone has," she agreed.

"Don't tell me you think what he believes is right?" Gabriel asked, turning his own fierce gaze upon her.

"Oh, what I think probably doesn't matter," Catie replied quickly. "We all create our world out of our thoughts, and you didn't give him much of a chance to think before smashing your fist into his world."

Rodigger's grin was silly as he looked at her. Gabriel frowned, stung, though she was right. He was too grumpy just now to admit it though.

"Of course, you should probably take some time to get to know Deuel for who he is," Catie continued easily. "Just in case you're wrong. Ho there!" she called, raising her hand toward a boat just landing itself on the shore.

There: his jaw muscles writhed again. Gabriel rolled his eyes and watched Catie approach the fishers.

"If you were a cave under the lake," she said as they neared the fishers, "where would you let people in?"

Grins split all their faces, but it seemed they were accustomed to Catie's methods. "How do you know I'd let you in?" the man at midships asked.

"Because I'm the sunniest girl in the Birnesath, Maf," she replied. "Also, you let people in before."

"If I existed."

"If you existed."

The men in the boat glanced at one another. "Whale fin?" one asked eventually.

"Yeah, or chopped grouper top," Maf said.

"Why those?" Gabriel asked. "Why not anywhere along the shore?"

"Because we assume you want to find it," said Maf. "And as you've already ridden all the way around the lake, you know a hole in the ground anywhere might be hard to spot."

"Where are these places?" Gabriel asked.

"There," chorused several of the men, pointing in opposite directions. Maf raised his hand playfully as if to strike them.

"Whale fin," he said, pointing one way. "Chopped top," the other direction.

"So, another week of searching," Gabriel said with a grunt.

"Unless you guess right the first time. Then it's only a few days."

"Whale fin is the cliff?" Deuel asked. Catie and the men in the boat nodded. Deuel glanced at Gabriel. "There."

Without word or waiting, Gabriel turned his horse toward the first direction. Deuel followed, then Rodigger. "Thanks, guys," Catie said with a wave, coming last.

"So long, sunrise," Maf replied with a sparkle in his eye.

8

TROUBLING WATERS

"I don't know why you make this sound so hard."
"Let us go speak with the God of All."
"Do we have to?"
"You do."

32 Thriman 1320 — Spring

It took them two days to reach the small cliff where they had rested while Deuel flew over the lake, and they spent that afternoon searching.

"It does almost seem like this would be a place to hide an entrance," Catie said.

"They hid the Berkarfor," Rodigger said sourly. "I'm sure they couldn't control where the entrance was. It's probably not even under the lake."

"Passet dem halta hinter laken, diese shulte cararven paken," Deuel said. "It is near this hill."

"Are you sure you interpreted all that correctly?" Gabriel asked with a grin.

"Wait, the hill?" Rodigger said, straightening. "It's not a hill, it's a cliff."

"It's half a hill," Gabriel offered.

"Does the verse say it's half a hill? And where did you find this, anyway?"

"A small book I recognized," Deuel replied. "In Stramfath. But when the Berkarfor were hidden, this was a hill. This side was washed away."

"By what? There's no river here." He saw Catie turning her head. "That lake is all the way over there," he said, cutting off what he knew she was going to point out. "There's no way it took out this hill, or made this cliff."

"Well, wait," Catie said, catching Deuel's attention. "If it didn't pull the soil all the way into the lake, wouldn't that mean we're standing on it, still?"

Deuel, Gabriel, and Catie all looked at one another. "So the entrance might have been buried," Gabriel said.

"And the lake wouldn't always have been over there," Catie added.

Rodigger stared at the dirt. "We could dig for days, and turn out to be wrong."

"Did anyone bring a shovel?" Catie asked.

There was silence as Rodigger's shoulders slumped even lower. "Cheer up, Rodigger," Gabriel said finally. "Turns out we can't dig for days."

A breeze arose, and Catie and Deuel both straightened, looking southward. "Oh, no," said Catie.

"Now what?" Rodigger asked, turning. Behind them, on the horizon but fast approaching, were piles of black clouds.

"Let's see how this cliff holds," Gabriel said, already leading his horse over to its base.

"If I know these types of storms," Catie said as they followed, "we might want to get comfortable."

"All day?" Rodigger asked, patting Gared's muzzle.

"If we're lucky," Catie replied. She reached into a saddle bag and pulled out six metal spikes, each as long as her forearm, a thick roll of canvas, and a wooden hammer. "The wind should blow most of the rain over us, but just in case," she said, handing a corner of the tarp to Deuel.

By the time the clouds rolled overhead they had a makeshift lean-to stretching over their heads from the side of the cliff. The rain pounded down around them, but as Catie predicted most of it fell beyond their shelter. Between their own body heat and the horses' it stayed warm, but the clouds brought night early.

The wind did not slack overhead, and they could hear it roaring over the top of the cliff. They were able to make a small fire with some fuel Catie had brought and heat a decent meal.

"Did you expect this?" Rodigger shouted over the storm. Catie shook her head, but smiled.

"I've been away some time," she said. "But I remembered. These are common in the spring, and you always want to be prepared when you go out."

"I didn't even think about the fact we wouldn't be near an inn," Rodigger said.

Catie shrugged. "I didn't travel much when I was little. Papa kept me close. But we did have our own little adventures not too far out of sight of Attelek."

"We didn't meet him," Rodigger said.

Catie's smile softened. "He's been gone a while."

"How did he—I mean, where did he…"

Catie's mouth said "I don't know" but Rodigger couldn't hear the words for the storm. She looked up. "He left when I was eight. Went out fishing one morning and didn't come back."

"Lost on the lake?" Rodigger asked.

"He didn't take his boat, and it was a calm day," Catie replied, her tone a little harsher on those points. "He was a fisher. No. He left, and no one told me why."

Some piece of Rodigger's mind knew he was on dangerous ground, that he shouldn't push his luck. That piece did not convince him. "And your mother?" he asked.

Catie glanced sharply at him. He hadn't meant for it to come out that way, and he was at least as surprised as she was at his almost accusatory tone. Miraculously, she let it pass. "She left four years later," she said simply.

Now Rodigger didn't regret his tone. "Why?" he demanded.

Catie's eyes squinted a little, and she looked down at their small fire. Again she spoke below the storm, but Rodigger could not read her lips. "What was that?" he asked.

She straightened and approached near him. She was his height, just a little shorter. With her shoulders square and her body erect, she was tameless as the cliff under which they huddled. Her eyes glinted, and Rodigger could barely meet her gaze. Just before he dropped his eyes, hers softened—but only slightly. "I said: 'you don't get to know that, yet.'" Then she was moving past him deeper into their shelter. As Rodigger turned to watch her, he noticed Deuel looking at her with an expression nearing curiosity. Rodigger wondered, too, why she felt the need to confront him in such a way, in front of the other two. Something to work on, perhaps.

"Come look at this," Gabriel said, standing just outside the entrance to the lean-to. Rodigger and Deuel both approached. Catie remained near her horse, stroking its neck.

"Look at the lake," Gabriel said with a brief gesture.

Rodigger watched. Rain pelted it. The wind made the rain fall unevenly, sweeping great braids of ripples across the surface, pebbling it. But nothing extraordinary, except that Gabriel and Deuel both watched it as if some great secret were being revealed.

"I don't see it," Rodigger said.

"Shocking," Gabriel muttered. Then, louder: "Look at the shoreline. Does it look higher to you?"

"I guess it does," Rodigger said vaguely. "Except right there..." he trailed off, gazing at it. Nothing in the contour indicated the shoreline would extend at a point directly in front of the cliff, and yet it did, almost thirty paces out into the lake and another twenty or thirty paces wide. "Why is it doing that?"

"The water is draining," Deuel replied.

Rodigger's shoulders slumped. "So it *is* buried?"

"Somewhere along that line, it would seem," Gabriel replied.

"We're going to have to dig *all that* out?" Rodigger gaped.

"Well hopefully not," Gabriel said brightly. He turned on Rodigger with a nearly evil grin. "But maybe."

"Good thing someone thought to bring spades," Catie said, startling Rodigger.

"I thought you said we didn't?"

Catie shook her head. "You need to start paying attention to what people say—what they *actually* say."

"You asked if anyone brought a shovel!" Rodigger said. "What am I supposed to think that means? Even Gabriel thought you meant that."

Catie shrugged. "And you were both wrong," she replied. "Notice how quiet Deuel is? He didn't assume what I meant."

Rodigger's eyes shot skyward briefly, and he glowered at nothing in particular. "Deuel's always quiet," he muttered.

"As soon as this storm lets up..." Gabriel cast his glance cloud-ward. "Hopefully in the morning, we'll see what we can dig up."

The first thing Rodigger noticed when he awoke was a great damp spot beneath his bedroll, and soaking into his pants. He blinked a few times, worriedly, then confirmed a small amount of rain had made its way down the cliff-face and through the seam at the top of the lean-to.

The second thing he noticed was a great chorus of birdsong that some recess of his mind knew occurred only on bright, sunny mornings. He picked his head up, gazing out of the shelter at dirt and grass aglow with yellow light.

He sat up, noticing he was alone in the tent. Had they really started without him? He didn't mind the sleep—and certainly couldn't be blamed if no one woke him—but he was surprised.

"About time," Gabriel said from behind him. He startled and turned. The fire was going, and everyone gathered around a skillet someone had rigged to suspend over the flames with a large stick. "You almost got breakfast for free," Gabriel continued, holding out a small kettle.

Rodigger shuffled out of his blankets, and out of the tent, then took the kettle from Gabriel. He stood for several moments in silence.

Gabriel squinted up at him. "Water," he said.

"Oh," Rodigger said, glancing down at the kettle. "Right." He stood for several more moments, glancing around for a spring of some sort.

"Rodigger," Gabriel said slowly.

"Hmm?"

Gabriel pointed without looking, and Rodigger followed his finger. He blinked, slow and hard, then moved toward the lake amid intentional silence from the others.

They breakfasted on sausages and small eggs, and Gabriel made tea. When the sun was a hand-span above the horizon they began digging test-pits. By the time the sun reached its zenith they had found a large rock beneath the sand and dirt that was a dark, almost satin black like faded coal. It took them another shift to find the crack that, when levered against, opened the rock like a door. Steps carved in the hole led down into blackness, though some small, faint sheen came from below as from a distant light.

"Torches, and weapons," Gabriel said after they had gazed into the cavern for some moments.

"Weapons?" Rodigger echoed. "To fight what, the darkness?"

"You *hope* that's all that's down there," Gabriel replied, already moving back to the lean-to. "But for something that's been hidden for centuries, it sure was easy to find."

"So we've been lucky," Rodigger said, following Gabriel only to continue to be heard, not to retrieve a weapon—in truth, he had none.

"Then it's about time for our luck to run out, eh?" Gabriel asked as he ducked inside. Catie was close behind him.

"No verse denied defenses," Deuel said quietly. "But none mentioned it. I would not worry."

"I'm worried he's going to hurt one of us," Rodigger lied. He didn't know why he did that, even with normal people. Lying to Deuel was as useless as a whittling knife on stone, and he knew it.

He heard a thin rustling noise, and looked up as Deuel snatched his staff out of the air. Gabriel was striding toward them, strange swords at his hips, still sheathed. But he had armbands on, now, of some sort—another rusted red band similar to the ones on the cuffs of the weapons, but one had a thin yellow stripe around its center like amber, the other a bright red stripe like ruby.

"Jewelry?" Rodigger asked, gesturing to the armbands.

"Don't worry about it," Gabriel said with vast indifference. "If we do find something down there, though, don't stand in front of me."

Catie emerged next with torches and handed out one apiece. With a brand from the cook-fire she lit them, then glanced at the three men. "I don't really have a weapon," she said finally. "So I'm not too hung up on ladies going first."

Gabriel turned and led the way. Deuel came next, then Rodigger and Catie. Rodigger gave one quick glance around the sunlit skies as he descended, hoping he would see them again soon.

It was a short flight of stairs till a hall opened before them. Though the path continued downward, it was a gentle slope, and a gutter of sorts ran along the left wall. Gravel lay strewn across the floor, washed and carried as far as it could be. Their footsteps crunched and squished as they walked, and the still air was filled with the mineral smell of cold, wet rock. Somewhere in the distance, droplets *plonked* as from a great height into a deep lake.

"A lake beneath a lake?" Gabriel asked as the sound grew louder.

"That verse would make even more sense," Catie offered, her voice hushed though she wasn't sure why.

Gradually as they descended, the tunnel began to curve this way and that, and the gleam from their torches was overtaken by some other light, a bluer light. Another sound rose as well. It took longer to notice it, because it sounded like their own breathing, except thicker and louder.

When the tunnel finally leveled off, the light was bright enough they could have extinguished their torches. They did not, unsure of what the light-source was. And the breathing, almost snuffling sound echoed up and down the hall. Rodigger scratched at his hip, wishing now that he had a knife of some sort—or perhaps a full-on broadsword.

They approached a sharp turn, and Gabriel had no sooner stepped around it than a piercing shriek sent him scrambling backward, suddenly out of breath. Rodigger winced as the echoes reverberated, pummeling his ears.

The shriek ceased. Gabriel stood braced against the wall, his eyes nearly wider than his mouth.

"What was that?" Rodigger demanded, a little too loudly. Another shriek came, not as piercing, but still alarming. Gabriel's eyes rolled, but he was silent.

"*Snehr-byor,*" Deuel said. He leaned his torch against the wall, and peered out from behind the corner. Rodigger gritted his teeth, but no shriek came. "He is walking away."

"Could we sneak up behind him?" Gabriel asked.

Deuel shrugged, and stepped out from behind the wall. He had no sooner disappeared around the bend when another shriek, louder this time, sent him sprinting back.

"By the God!" Rodigger shouted, pressing his hands hard against his ears. "What did you say it was?"

"It is *snehr...* Yeti," Deuel replied.

"It's no *kend* yeti," Gabriel snarled. "Yeti are myths. Myths that can be defeated in books. No one has ever written a story about killing a *snehr-byor,* because no one would believe it. The tale would never tell."

Rodigger twisted his mouth sideways, gazing at Gabriel out of the corner of his eyes. That sounded a bit extravagant. If the man didn't want to hunt down the Berkarfor, he could just say so. Rodigger moved to the corner, raising his eyebrows to ask permission from Deuel. The dragon-son gave him a glance, approval mixed with...mirth?

Rodigger rolled his eyes, then peered slowly around the corner. His body froze in place as his eyes grew steadily wider, and traveled upward. And upward, until massive yellow eyes glared back at him from hairy sockets, like snow-covered caverns in their own right. With a small, choked yelp Rodigger ducked behind the corner again.

"That thing is a house!" he whispered hoarsely. "It's a mountain! It's a chain of mountains with spires for teeth!"

"It must be something," Catie said from the rear. "That's the most descriptive I've ever heard you be."

"What are we going to do with this thing? This has to be the hiding place, so it has to be beyond him."

"Well," Gabriel said slowly, then drew a long sigh. "You're standing in front of me."

"What?"

"He said if we found anything to not stand in front of him," Catie said quietly, with a small smile.

Rodigger swallowed, then moved away from the corner. Gabriel approached, drawing his weapons from their sheaths. Rodigger's assessment had been correct: the blades were fixed to the underside of the wooden poles. Gabriel gripped the crossbar, and the cuffs fit around the bracelets he had put on his arms, snapping into place as he held them. The blades were the same rusty-looking metal as the other points of metal Rodigger had noticed. It was now that he also noticed it seemed too proper to actually be rust—its appearance was not an accident or a force of neglect, but as though the metal was supposed to look like that.

"Cretal," Deuel said quietly behind him, probably catching Rodigger's gaze as he caught everything else in life. "It channels the elements."

"He's using magic?" Rodigger hissed, grasping Deuel's arm as he forgot his distaste for the briefest of moments.

"No, not yet," Deuel replied in such a serious tone that Rodigger had no chance of finding it funny. Catie did not have that problem, and a smile briefly split her face.

"It's walking away again," Gabriel muttered. "Why does it keep doing that? It could fit back here to attack us. Might even be better for it if it did."

"Not better for us," Rodigger replied, aghast.

"My point is it's not acting the way it should be."

"So, it's easier to kill," Rodigger replied. "It probably hasn't fought anything in centuries. Lucky for us."

"Lucky for *us*," Gabriel emphasized, tossing an elbow toward Deuel. "You all don't have weapons, remember? Because danger doesn't exist anymore."

Rodigger said nothing, and Gabriel's gaze returned to his friend. "You ready?" he asked. Deuel's gaze answered him. Gabriel rolled his head once. "Then let's go."

He peered out, hesitated, then ran forward. The *snehr-byor* bellowed again bare moments after the two left, but they did not come scrambling back immediately. As the cry ceased, Catie's head came up. She darted forward to the corner and peered around it.

The *byor* stood staring at the two mercenaries, who were likewise motionless. It took a few deep breaths, then another wavering cry echoed through the chamber as it strode forward a few steps. Still the two held their ground. Again when the roar ceased, there was almost a hiccup as the *byor* drew a breath.

Gabriel's weapon came up, pointing at the beast. "Gabriel, wait!" Catie shouted, striding forward. Rodigger's eyes gaped as he watched her go.

Gabriel's weapon-point faltered, but he did not take his eyes of the *byor*. "Why am I waiting?" he asked as it stood, lips pulled back in a snarl as it panted at them.

"Look at it," she said, standing just behind the two men.

"I'm not looking at my fingernails, lass," he replied.

"No, I mean, look at *it,* not the *snehr-byor.*"

"You make no sense! What do you think—"

"It's not roaring anymore," she said. "It's not advancing. It's just looking at you. Look at it as if it were not a dangerous beast."

"Catie," Gabriel rumbled in warning.

"It's crying," Deuel said suddenly and quietly.

"It's trying to," Catie replied. "But I don't think it can."

The creature panted a few more times, staring at them with eyes that, in any other socket, would appear rimmed in red. Its chest and shoulders bristled at them, but every other muscle was limp, barely holding the creature upright.

"So what do we do, then?" Gabriel asked, his weapon already lowering.

"Let's back up a few steps and sit down," Catie said, leading the way. They all kept their eyes on the creature, but backed up a few paces and sat. Its snarl subsided, its upper body deflated, suddenly rendering it frail and weary. It turned and shuffled away across the cavern, glancing back at them only occasionally.

Rodigger approached quietly. "What by Oren happened there?" he hissed, keeping his eyes firmly on the far end of the cave as the *snehr-byor* disappeared down another passageway.

"Let's find out," Catie said as she rose. She entered the cave proper and looked up, her pace instantly slowing. "Oh, wow," she breathed.

"What is it?" Deuel asked, coming forward. Catie only pointed upward. Then they saw where the light was coming from.

They were underneath the lake, and the cavern ceiling was probably not far from the surface. Somehow the roof was clear, as though comprised of thin and remarkably pure quartz. Sunlight streaming through blue waters entered and rippled against the walls, bouncing off sparkling rock and lighting the way as far as it could. A school of fish went by above, their shadows slithering across the cavern floor.

A moaning wail from the passageway pulled their attention back. Catie led. The two mercenaries followed, weapons still drawn but held low. Rodigger remained gaping at the quartz roof and refracted light until he heard his companions' murmurs wafting from the hall.

"...wait here," Catie was whispering as he approached.

"Always 'wait'," Rodigger said in normal tones. "Glory waits for no one." He made to continue down the passage, but suddenly Catie was in front of him, her glittering eyes on his, her hand splayed on his chest and making its supple presence felt. He backed away a step before she could feel his heart's thrill. "Why?" he managed to demand, wanting desperately to show her he had worth without weapons.

"Respect," she said. He cocked an eyebrow, and she stepped aside so he could see down the passage to dimly lit cavern, where the *byor* hunched over another *byor* that lay utterly still on the ground.

"Is it dead?" he asked stupidly.

"Probably its mate," Catie said, her voice again in a whisper. "It doesn't want to kill us, it wants to grieve."

"It's a *snehr-byor*," Rodigger enunciated. He glanced at the mercenaries, but could tell instantly he did not have their support. "Oh, wow," he muttered. "The only one without weapons is the only one not afraid to use them."

With a snap, Gabriel disengaged his strange swords from his arms and held them out toward Rodigger. "Okay, then," he said, eyebrows up.

Rodigger's heart squeezed once. "No no," he said, holding up his hands in mock defense; "wouldn't want to interrupt the *byor's* grieving."

Gabriel snorted, but before he could reply, Catie hissed at them. Ahead, the *byor* had lifted its partner and had turned to face them. They stood gazing at one another for several long moments.

"Let's go back into the cave," Catie suggested, backing away slowly. The others followed—Rodigger wagging his head slowly—and as they moved the *byor* took cautious steps forward, keeping the same distance.

When they reached the cavern again, Catie gestured toward the back wall. The *byor* entered after them, pausing to glance sideways at where they stood motionless. It inclined its head toward Catie before moving to the center of the room and laying its partner on the ground. It knelt, back to them, and did not move. A low thrum echoed through the chamber. It took Rodigger several moments to realize it came from the *byor*. The thrum built and grew. Above the quartz, schools of fish paused. The thrum slid into notes, then split into many. Soon a chant grew that was also a song, and the *byor* weaved back and forth as it sang. Its hands danced and pressed upon the fur of its fallen partner in some pattern he could only half-see.

The *byor* went still as the song ended without fade or echo. Rodigger's eyes felt suddenly as if they had not blinked for long moments as his gaze locked onto the back of the *byor*. "Catie?" he whispered from the side of his mouth. When she didn't respond, his eyes darted sideways. She was no longer with them.

Before he could wonder, Gabriel gasped and Rodigger's eyes snapped forward. The *byor* had stood and turned to face them, gazing at them impassively. Rodigger registered that the dead *byor* was suddenly gone, and knew he should wonder about that. But all his attention was on the one still living.

It placed its fists on the ground and bent double as if to sniff the dirt at its feet—but it was bowing. It touched its forehead to the ground, then straightened and drew a deep sigh. As it exhaled, it evaporated suddenly as if into dust and drifted away.

"Ummm..."

"Oh, it wasn't real," Catie said, suddenly beside them again. "Here." She held up something wrapped in burlap, something in the shape of a goblet, but just out of anyone's reach. "And if you want to find the next one, you'll take me with you."

9

CONCERNING DEUEL

"See? That worked itself out."
"Teresh, there is more to do."
"I don't know what will convince him."
"That is why you must actually speak to him."

33 Thriman 1320 — Spring

"When did you know it wasn't real?" Rodigger asked, ignoring for the moment that Gabriel had taken the burlap bundle and began to unravel it.

"Whenever we arrived here just in time to see it mourn its dead," Catie replied. "Convenient, wasn't it?"

"I don't understand," Rodigger said.

"Shocking," Gabriel said. "Here. Is this it?" He held out the cup, finally diverting Rodigger's attention.

It was primarily silver, undimmed by centuries underground, with gold piping running a geometric pattern between gems of ruby and sapphire. It was not deep, or broad, but it was not meant for casual drinking, either. Rodigger paused as the refracted light from above ran across it, and a vision floated across his eyes of lifting the Berkarfor himself, accepting the draft.

Light and vision disappeared at once, and he nodded. "It is," he said. "Does it say where to find the next one?"

Catie held up a folded parchment, then quickly held it out of reach. "Were you listening, earlier? I found the first one, and I know how to find the second, and third, and fourth. But I'm not doing it from here."

"And how do you know we can't find the third and fourth without you?" Rodigger asked.

Catie's hand dropped, and she gazed at Gabriel. "Is he serious?" she asked.

"His jokes aren't as funny," Gabriel muttered.

"Just give us the note, okay?" Rodigger said, holding out his hand.

Catie looked at him several long moments, her smile widening. She shrugged, and put the parchment in his hand.

"See?" he said, glancing at the mercenaries as he unfolded the parchment. "Sometimes you just need to be forthright." He smiled, and read the words on the page. As Catie's smile peaked, his faded. "What the *houl* does this mean?" he asked finally.

"I can guarantee only Deuel will know," Catie replied. "Oh, and me."

"Oh, and you?" Rodigger asked scornfully. "And how does that work?"

"Because I'm very good, too," she replied.

As Gabriel took the parchment from Rodigger and read, Rodigger caught, briefly, Deuel looking at Catie with an odd expression on his face—if it was more fully developed, Rodigger might have called it curiosity. But he doubted the dragon-son lacked enough knowledge to even be curious anymore.

Gabriel was reading aloud:

"Cliffs squarely squat and mutter at the sky,
Angled angrily aground and never gaining high
Wanderers wend and waggle here, send and haggle here.

"Rainbows reach and ruin, dashed slap-dash at doors,
Wars wage and blare far beneath the floors,
Wendol ward the pass, guard the glass here."

"I may know where that is," Deuel said, the closest thing to uncertainty in his voice Rodigger had ever heard.

"So we don't need Catie?" Rodigger asked lightly, his mind buzzing with consternation for suggesting such a thing.

"We still want her," Deuel replied, his look again as if reading Rodigger's mind. "She sounds more confident than I am."

Gabriel looked at him. "Hnnn," he said. He re-folded the parchment and gave it to her. "Let's get back to Attelek. Then Catie will tell us where to go next."

But Attelek had not had a cliff or tarp to shelter it from the storm the previous day. As they neared, they could see every fifth building had a crew of townsfolk atop it, repairing roofs. Many homes in between had no crew though they still showed need of repair. Catie dodged between a few friends, speaking rapidly. It seemed no one was hurt, though Velta would not be making breakfast for a while: the roof above her stores had been hit early and everything inside drenched.

Forgetting about the three men for a while, though still keeping possession of the note, Catie ran to Grandmother's. Her house seemed undamaged. It was old, and had not survived so long by being frail. Catie went inside. Two other tired-looking men were in the kitchen, standing patiently by as Grandmother wrapped still-steaming bread in linen and placed the loaves in a basket.

"Welcome back, Caytaleane," Grandmother said, her voice clear though her eyes and hands were busy elsewhere.

"I'm going with the men to find the others," Catie said, knowing it was almost silly saying it in such a way, but knowing Tiamen and Arul would find it sillier if she said it plainly.

"I thought you might," Grandmother replied, glancing up with a smile. "It will be good for you, too. I think you will find much of what you're looking for."

"Are you sure you don't need help here?" Catie asked.

Grandmother glanced out the window, and straightened a little. "No, I think we will do fine," she said distantly.

Catie followed her gaze. Her brow furrowed at the scene unfolding outside. "I'll try to come back," she said absently, then left the building.

Rodigger and Deuel stood on the street, gazing upward as Gabriel positioned himself on a roof peak, helping a few of the men secure the topmost row of shingles. Catie approached, her gaze also on the mercenary.

"What's he doing up there?" she asked.

"Shingling," Gabriel called down. "You may have noticed a few houses around here need it."

"We need to go find..." Rodigger glanced around the street. "You know."

"Go ahead," Gabriel replied, leaning backward and handing a hammer to one behind him. "Throw me that rope before you leave?" he asked, pointing to a rope and bucket filled with more shingles and another hammer that was at their feet.

"Deuel, would you...?" Rodigger said, looking at the behamian.

But Deuel only gazed intently upward. "I think it will not help," he said finally.

"Try."

"Aloik," Deuel called softly.

Gabriel's jaw clenched, and he gazed downward. "Halm and Ro Thull are yours, again," he said quietly. He made a gesture with his left hand near his right shoulder. "Halm and Ro Thull are yours," he repeated.

Deuel surprised them all by gasping. He stood, his mouth open for several long moments. "You cannot..."

"Catie, would you throw me that rope, please?" Gabriel said angrily. "Staring at me while I'm trying to work. It's senseless for me to come all the way back down there..."

Catie bent over, grasped the end of the rope, and tossed it to the mercenary—or was he simply an old man, now? Gabriel pulled hand over hand till the bucket was close, then quickly tied it off at his waist.

"Thank you," he said. He turned his gaze back to Deuel for several moments, then up and across the plain toward the lake. "I'm tired," he said quietly. "A good day of honest work will do wonders, I can feel it. Maybe many days. It used to, before I started this, before I found and lost Tormina." His gaze lowered to nothing at his hip, then into the bucket. Without another word he pulled out a shingle and a few nails, and began hammering.

"Deuel," Rodigger said, almost pleading. "What is he doing?"

Deuel's mouth had closed, and his customary impassivity returned. "Shingling," he said, quickly fixing Rodigger with a stare that froze the young man's mouth open. "We will be on our way, where Catie leads us," he continued, turning to look at her, the question unformed but present.

"The other side of the Tevorbath," she replied.

"Very well."

"But what happened?" Rodigger said, trying to keep in the behamian's view as they moved toward their horses. "What is Halm and Ro Thull? What was this?" he mimicked the gesture, poorly, that Gabriel had made toward his right shoulder.

Deuel paused by his horse before mounting. "His weapons," he replied. "He is no longer my *aloik;* I am no longer his *skalderon.*"

"Oh," Catie said softly.

Deuel looked at Rodigger. "I am free."

Catie stopped one final time inside Grandmother's kitchen. The two men were gone out to distribute the warm loaves, and even Lucie was out helping in any ways she could. Catie felt a slight twinge of betrayal, leaving her home and friends when she had only just returned, when they needed all the help they could get. Even if Gabriel was staying behind.

But one look at Grandmother and she knew it would be okay. How many times had her presence engendered such peace? Catie hoped she could do the same for others, one day.

"We're leaving," she said.

Grandmother smiled, but there was still something in her eyes. A guarding, it seemed.

"What is it?" Catie asked, sitting down.

"Where do you go?" she asked.

"North of the Tevorbath to start," Catie replied. "From there...?" she trailed off with a shrug. "But I'll come back as soon as I can. I prom—"

Grandmother cut her off with a wave. "Make no such promise," she said quickly, her insistence surprising Catie, and hurting her.

"You don't want me to come back?"

"I want you to be who you were born to be, whom the God made you to be," Grandmother replied.

"I don't know what that is."

Grandmother's smile was pleasant, full of hope. "You will. This journey will teach you. Catie..." Her smile lessened.

Catie's was gone. "You never call me that," she said. Why was she talking so differently?

"Caytaleane," Grandmother said; "there is something you must know, before you leave. Your father did not die by drowning."

Catie sat quietly. She had all but known.

"Some men came from the northeast, came looking for your mother, to do her harm. Jular led them away, and died keeping them from her. We knew she would not be safe here, knew that you would not be safe with her. That is why she gave you to be Newmother, and left. It was not your fault. Nor, truly, hers."

The edges of Catie's vision swam in tears. "Do you know where she went?"

Grandmother took a deep breath, and blew an unsteady sigh. "North of the Tevorbath," she said. Her eyes fixed on Catie. "So many years ago, there is no knowing where she might have ended up, how she might have..." Grandmother twisted her hands together. "But there is more. I'm sorry I haven't told you yet, my Caytaleane, but your mother made me promise on oath to keep this secret until a day I deemed it absolutely necessary. Now, I believe you are leaving to never return and so I must. Please forgive us both, if you must. We did what we thought best."

"I always trust you, Grandmother," Catie said honestly. "You have wisdom far beyond my years."

Grandmother smiled genuinely. "Then I will not try to defend our decision to you. But you must know now: Kerlyn your mother came to us from the north when you were small, and Julan she met here."

Catie sat silently and still, comprehending. "So..."

"Julan helped raise you, and loved your mother," Grandmother continued. "But he did not give you birth."

Her breath left her for several moments. When she spoke, it came out a near-whisper. "Who did?"

"Kerlyn never told me, and as far as I knew she did not tell Julan either. But, as you journey north, perhaps you will find out. Perhaps, too, you will find healing for the hurt Roth has dealt you."

Catie pressed her lips together. "That is part of why I go..."

Grandmother's eyes cast down, and she shook her head. "Not that way. What has broken inside you is your trust—trust that you can love again."

Catie sat back. No, she definitely could not see herself loving someone else. "No one will ever compare to Dannid," she said. "You never met him, but he was..." She trailed off, seeing him in her mind's eye as they rode through the Dragonsbacks, wind through his hair as he laughed and told her his plans.

She blinked away the memory before it was too late.

Grandmother was looking at her with a guarded smile. "You felt joined to this man, Dannid?"

"We were married," Catie replied.

"That is not what I asked—Bolgad and Hathar are married, aren't they?"

Catie chuckled. "Yeah, well, Bolgad and Hathar—"

"Did you feel joined to Dannid? Did you feel almost as though you were one—not one single person, single-minded in everything—but as though you moved together?"

"We spent so much time together, in Sprativerg, through the mountains south, in Bokessin…" Catie paused. "I don't know how much closer we could have been."

Grandmother watched her closely. "I think, too, that one day you will know. True marriage is this: that the two are close-knit as one, united in purpose and heart."

"It sounds like I would have to give up who I am."

"Some, as he will have to give up some of who he is. Remember when Radolf painted his house?"

Catie wrinkled her nose. "That looked horrible," she said. "That's what marriage is?"

Grandmother laughed. "No, at least it is not meant to be. Do you remember how he made the color?"

"He mixed red and yellow dyes together."

"That is what marriage is: the red dye does not stop being red, nor the yellow, yellow; but together they add another hue to the myriad in the world. No orange will ever be like the orange Radolf made."

"Let's hope not," Catie replied with a smile.

They rode in silence much of that first day. It may have been a normal silence, if Gabriel had been present, but his absence made it awkward. Too awkward to break or pay much attention to.

The storm, though some days past, had made the road thick with mud, and travelers were scarce. Merchant trains did not exist. Rodigger paid for their beds, and they fell asleep to the sound of one another's breathing.

As the sun neared Noon the next day, the dragon-son cantered up to ride beside Catie, who led.

"You knew what it meant for Gabriel to give me my swords," he said, though his eyes stayed on the road ahead.

"Grandmother has told me some things about the behamien," she replied, her voice no louder than necessary.

"Why did she do that?"

Catie blinked, and frowned. "She has told me many things," she said finally, though creases appeared on her forehead as well.

"And your father left fourteen years ago?"

"Fifteen," she corrected automatically. She would untangle that situation later.

"That is a long time."

"For me, perhaps," she replied, and some of her creases disappeared.

Deuel glanced at her, now, and she felt his enjoyment of her joke. It reminded her, suddenly, that she didn't feel fear of him. Almost absurdly, she searched for it, tried to conjure it, but it did not come. And yet every other sense turned as if he were laughing openly, and she wanted to laugh with him, to smile, to recognize the outward signs that they had bonded, in some small way.

But her eyes told her he only looked at her. She tried to see the twinkling in his eyes, even, but they were the same cavernous yet not-empty pools they always were.

But then something else turned in her, as if the joke had recalled a painful memory or knowledge, and she felt a deep but slow-moving sadness—whether of the past or for the future, she could not tell. Before she could study it further Deuel looked away, and the feeling passed.

Like a thunderclap, she was back on the road, felt the warm spring day, heard the heavy hoofbeats, smelled the breeze carrying scents of horse-sweat, leather, and something like last winter's chill still oozing from the deep parts of the ground.

And Rodigger still maintaining his awkward silence.

"Have you ever been through the Tevorbath?" she called back.

Silence for several breaths, almost enough for her to think of repeating the question. "No," came the small reply.

"I haven't either, but I've heard the stories," she said. "Beautiful and bountiful beyond compare. And we should have pleasant weather by then."

Another silence, shorter this time. "It's a valley," he said. "How could it be beautiful?"

"Do you prefer standing on mountains?" she asked.

"No, I mean, it's land, it's just—space between two hills."

"Today is a beautiful day, isn't it?"

"It's not cold," he said.

"Rodigger, come on," she said, turning finally to look back and see if he was joking. His face was serious, and she gave a short sigh. "The weather is fantastic, it is not cold, it's even mildly warm, the sky is blue…"

"Okay, fine, yes! Compared with the days when it's cold and cloudy, today is beautiful. So compared with land that's flat and rocky, a valley is probably beautiful."

"Has he always been this pleasant to travel with?" she asked Deuel quietly.

Without looking at her, the dragon-son shook his head. "Well," he amended. "He is always this way toward me. I do not know why he would be this way toward you."

Catie chuckled. "Thank you for that," she said, smiling though she noticed he was not looking at her. She raised her voice a little. "It's an interesting point, though," she said. "That beauty only exists in comparison."

"Okay."

"Isn't that what you were saying?" she asked. She edged her voice with indignance. "You know, you could ride up here so I can talk to you instead of at you."

More silence. Catie shifted, letting a wrinkle work itself out of her pants that was chafing something awful. "That's okay," Rodigger said finally. "And I wasn't really thinking about it like that." A pause. "Here's where Gabriel would snort and say something about not being surprised."

"I don't snort very much," Catie replied, "or make assumptions. You're allowed to think about it however you want to."

"And that's where Gabriel would say he's surprised if I think at all."

Catie reined her horse up hard, so that Deuel was several strides ahead before he stopped. She turned to Rodigger. "Gabriel is not here," she said firmly, staring into Rodigger's eyes. "Not himself, or his attitude, or his thoughts. It's us. And quite frankly I'd appreciate losing the idea that I might think or feel the way he does."

Rodigger glanced quickly at Deuel, between blinks, but the dragon-son saw it.

"I am of the same mind," he said. "He is no longer my *aloik*. He has no say over my words or actions."

Rodigger managed to gaze at Deuel, this time. "Well, when he did, he must not have wanted you to speak very much."

As soon as he said it, Rodigger looked horrified, but Catie could feel Deuel's wry chuckle. "He did not hold as much sway over me as when he was younger," Deuel replied calmly. "As he grew older, I grew more silent, rather than say something he did not wish me to say."

"Oh," Rodigger replied. "Was he that bad?"

"I do not know what you mean by 'bad'," Deuel said as they continued riding. "It is the nature of the bond, it is amoral."

"I don't understand," Rodigger said, riding closer, but still behind them.

"You may be thinking of the relationship of a slave," Deuel said. "Masters may be kind or cruel in the eyes of some—though in the eyes of others, that bond, too, is whatever the master wishes. Behamien bond with humans for the sake of the bond, not for the sake of the human. A slave master is benefited by the slave," Deuel continued when Rodigger made a still-confused grunt. "And so he is above, the slave is subservient. As *skalderon* I am more like a student."

"Studying what?" Rodigger spluttered. "You know more than any of us, and you look like you know more than everyone."

"But I do not know what it means to be a human," Deuel replied, simply and quietly.

"So what?" Rodigger asked.

"One day, I hope to no longer be behamian. If I succeed," he continued, turning to look plainly at Rodigger. "I must not desire to kill you."

Rodigger did not get a good night's sleep until they were through the Skaldvath Mountains and nearing Sprativerg. Not that he was more comfortable with Deuel even at that point. He was simply too exhausted to care. Catie had looked thoughtful for a day, after Deuel's bizarre words, but had returned to her smiling, care-free self by the next morning. She trusted people too much, too quickly, he decided. Not a good quality, when they were setting out for lands where none of them had traveled before. Maybe he would talk to her before too long, about that.

It was exciting to think about, he had to admit—spending a life with Catie, helping her become a better person. She possessed many good qualities already, to be sure, enough to be a wife. But she was far from perfect. It pleased him that her looks did not distract him from her shortcomings, though her looks were certainly distracting enough. More than once he had imagined her standing before him on their wedding night, patient as he enjoyed the moment before stepping toward her...but that thought was never more frequent than the long talks they would have as he shaped her into the woman he knew she could be.

But then he was caught up in Sprativerg. The city was ripe for Roth's influence. Rodigger was there for only a day, tragically, but could feel the people crying out for purpose, for community. How he would have loved to take even a month to begin speaking to the people!

Instead, they rode out of the north gate the next morning, the peaks on the horizon a dark silhouette like the teeth of a great maw into which they rode, growing larger and descending upon them with each passing mile. At least those were far away, still, and not truly maleficent. Deuel's ever-presence loomed directly in front of him, and apparently desired to kill him unless he learned enough about what it meant to be human. What did that even mean?

Some of the comfort Rodigger had found over the past several days ebbed as he glanced at Halm and Ro Thull, Deuel's strange weapons, wrapped behind the dragon-son's saddle. Rodigger had been around soldiers since he was small, and had never seen weapons like those. And what were the bracelets that Gabriel had worn? He hadn't really seen them since then. And what kind of names were those? Halm, and Ro Thull. They sounded—

"What about them?" Catie asked as she rode between them.

Rodigger gaped at her. Had she somehow read his thoughts?

She turned and glanced at him. "You said 'Halm and Ro Thull'."

"Did I?" Rodigger asked as Deuel glanced at him.

Catie nodded with a grin. "Well, you muttered it, so I guess you might not have meant to say it out loud."

"Oh. I guess I'm just wondering..." What was he wondering? Was Deuel going to kill him with them? His shoulders sagged as he looked at nothing, at Gared's ears swiveling to the wind. "Do you know how to use them?" he heard himself say.

"Yes," Deuel replied. A smile flashed across Catie's face, and Deuel turned further to look at her. "It has been many years."

"Why did Gabriel have them?" Rodigger asked, coming to himself.

"The bond," Deuel replied. "A behamian gives his weapons to the *aloik* until he is free."

"Well, how long did Gabriel have them?" Catie asked.

"They were his when he was born," Deuel replied.

"I thought they were yours," Rodigger said.

"They were given to Gabriel by his father, as his father had given it to him," Deuel explained. "I first gave them to Gabriel's grandfather. It is the nature of the bond."

"For three generations?" Catie asked.

"At least."

"So, how long ago...?"

"One hundred years."

They rode in silence for some moments, a light, warm wind shifting in from the south as Catie and Rodigger both looked at the two weapons rocking behind Deuel's saddle.

"How old *are* they?" Rodigger asked first.

"They were made for me by the Kesten, in Burieng, for my eighth year."

The Kesten? Rodigger wondered. The name sounded familiar. Was it something Roth had told him, once? He couldn't remember.

"Why do you give up your weapons?" Catie asked.

"We must know vulnerability," Deuel replied, shifting in his saddle.

"For a hundred years?"

"For as long as it takes to understand it," Deuel replied. He drew a small sigh. "Gabriel did not return my weapons because I had learned it, but because he no longer wanted the responsibility of me. I do not know what this might mean."

"There's always someone stronger than you," Rodigger said with a firm nod. Roth had told him that since he was fourteen. "With or without weapons."

"Perhaps," Deuel said. "If I have a knife, and you have your sword, am I not inherently more vulnerable than if I have a sword? Unless I am the best knife-fighter and you are the worst swordsman."

"I suppose," Rodigger said.

"Tactics," Catie spoke up. "You might be smarter than him."

"The analogy breaks down quickly," Deuel said. Catie smiled again as if they shared a joke. "But let us maintain it for a moment: similar tactics, similar strength, similar ability, different weapons, different standing. Yes?"

They both nodded.

"Same swordsman against a dragon?"

There was a pause before Catie spoke up. "He better have an impressive sword."

"That is most often the case," Deuel replied gravely. "And others to help him. But if a dragon finds a man alone, he must understand vulnerability. Thus a *skalderon* may only have a small knife, one that does little harm."

"In case you want to kill them?" Rodigger muttered.

"Do you not want to kill me?" Deuel asked, almost lightly.

Rodigger glanced quickly at Catie's sharp gaze. "No," he said, hoping he chose the right tone from the myriad his mind desperately presented.

"You do not think the behamien should exist," Deuel said. "We are...an abomination."

"That doesn't mean...I mean, killing someone..."

"I exist," Deuel said, cutting him off as he stopped and turned his horse to face him. "The only way for me to not exist is to die. This is your reality, which you must accept. If you cannot, then your reality is *skef*."

Catie rode her horse between them, staring hard at Deuel—and there it was again, something like curiosity showing itself on Deuel's face, more pronounced than back in the cave, but still nowhere near normal human expression. But, of course, that made sense...

Rodigger swallowed as Catie's gaze swung to him, and his eyes cast downward. "Exactly," she said through gritted teeth. Rodigger's horse snuffled as the wind rose and shushed through the grasses. "I don't want to be facing whatever is guarding the next goblet, and worry about facing it alone. Do you?"

Assuming she was still looking at him, Rodigger said: "No."

More silence until Deuel said: "You are right."

"Then let's go."

Rodigger finally looked up as hooves thumped against the road. Catie and Deuel were already moving, so he nudged Gared forward. He had answered Catie honestly, but he already believed he *would* be facing the next guardian alone.

That night at the inn, at the top of a ridge in the Dragonsback Mountains, Catie watched Rodigger finally succumb to sleep two cots over. He had taken again to sleeping as far away from Deuel as possible without being completely rude, saying something about having a hard time falling asleep when he could hear people breathing. The wind roared outside, still from the south, but funneled up the passes from the broad Fallonvall.

Waiting a few more moments to verify his measured breathing, Catie finally turned over. "Deuel?" she whispered.

She felt him come alert before he answered, almost like turning and seeing someone looking at her. "Yes?" he said.

"Sometimes, when we're traveling—or, I guess, when we're talking, but not necessarily..." She wound to a stop, and gave a short sigh. "There are times when I feel like I know what you're feeling."

There was a pause, and the sense of his gaze became more acute. "Sometimes, a behamian will project his feelings, almost as if he were speaking them or showing them," he said.

Catie hesitated. It seemed like he didn't enjoy speaking about this. Something in his tone had changed, at least, and she wished she could see him in the darkness—not that being able to see him always did much good. "But do you control that?" she asked.

There was a much longer pause, and the sense now of intense scrutiny. "Not always," he said finally. "And once someone feels it, they are more keen to pick it up the next time."

Catie wavered for a few moments. "I used to be afraid of you," she said finally, not knowing where the topic would lead and being a little afraid of that, too. But she felt she must know, and so she took the first step.

"When?" he asked. He felt amused, now.

"Before I met you all," she said. "It was another reason I stayed ahead of you. I felt some sort of danger, from you. I mean, I didn't know it was you at first, until we were nearly at Getakenner. It's why I decided to finally face you, so I could try to see what I was afraid of."

"Are you afraid of me now?"

"No!" she said, her voice suddenly above a whisper. She brought it back down. "No, it stopped once we met."

"That is how it often happens," Deuel said. "I do not know if it is for our defense or yours that those feelings are foremost, until face to face with a behamian."

"It doesn't seem to have worn off Rodigger," Catie said wryly. She felt his sudden sadness, and her grin disappeared.

"His is a fear that nothing I do will erase," Deuel said, "because I did not create it. Only the one who planted the seed, or the one who continues to water it, can kill it."

"I'm sorry, Deuel," she said.

"He is many," he said simply, though still a little sadly.

Catie let out a small sigh. "And I'm sorry about that, too."

IO

TURNING TABLES

"That was not as difficult as I supposed."
"That, Teresh, is a lesson everyone needs to remember."
"Do you ever think sometimes they do very well without us?"
"No. Perhaps sometimes."

9 Halmfurtung 1320 — Spring

Early the next morning, they came to the place where the Balnathva River plunged over a cliff above them, falling away from the road to straddle a knife-like ridge two hundred feet below them. The right side of the ridge gathered a few springs, and continued southeast as the Tilvat, and filled the Agirbirt Lake. The left continued as the Balnathva to the Turidian Sea south of Bokessin.

"Just around the next bend," Catie said as they passed the falls.

"We're almost there, already?" Rodigger asked.

"Ha! Ahem. No," Catie said, covering her mouth briefly. "No, we're not even halfway yet, sorry."

"How far away is this place?"

"Well, we have to cross the Tevorbath, first."

"I thought you said it was just on the other side of that?" Rodigger said, swiping at a fly that buzzed near his ear.

"Well, not 'just'," she said. "And there's a whole lot of Andelen on the other side of the Tevorbath."

Rodigger groaned, shifted in his saddle, then was silent.

Soon the breadth of the Tevorbath came into view: 'The God's Feast' it had been named. A broad valley stretching as far as could be seen northward, bright green grass flowing from the banks of the Balnathva up the slopes until it turned into forest. Sheep floated on the hillsides like shadowed clouds, fallen from a sky almost perpetually blue. What true clouds formed at the head of the valley sat trapped by its walls, drifting slowly along and watering the land as evenly as a gardener. Below the herds of sheep, nearer the river, were great brown strips of newly-planted fields, whose crops would ripen as surely as the seasons changed. Out of this one valley came almost half of Andelen's food. In sacks, dried, or pickled, it shipped to far corners by endless streams of merchants and wagoners. The only way into the valley was to be born or married into it. Every farmer and shepherd who knew about it wanted his or her own plot, but for most it was only a dream.

For travelers, it was a place to be savored. Fair weather most days and guaranteed fresh food made it a favorite corridor, if one needed to traverse its length. News and entertainment ran aplenty. Since Sheppar's campaign thirty years ago, entertainment was more common than news, though travelers from the south often brought word of Roth's campaign, now.

The inns were almost always near-full, and one evening they took the last three beds there were. For a time, they enjoyed themselves as they traveled: Rodigger kept from insulting Deuel, though he still rode at the back. But the warm spring air and constant flow of travelers worked to cheer their spirits.

One day, about After-Noon, just two days after leaving Kendet's Vatenvilt nearly a third of the way through the valley, they came upon a herd of sheep milling on the road. Deuel and Catie glanced about, while Rodigger cursed and nudged his Therian forward as best he could.

"Where in all Oren is the shepherd?" Rodigger fumed.

"That's a very good question," Catie replied, standing in her stirrups and peering around the valley. She paused gazing eastward, shading her eyes. "It looks like the herd is coming across a bridge of some sort."

"Wouldn't it make sense for the road to continue following the west bank?" Rodigger asked, finally managing to bring his horse closer to his companions.

"It does," Catie said, sitting down again. "But the herds have to access the east side of the Tevorbath somehow, and it looks like they do it over there," she finished, pointing. "I think we should check it out."

"We should do no such thing," Rodigger exclaimed, kicking out slightly at a sheep who was taking a little too much interest in his pants leg. "We should continue north, to whatever destination you've concocted."

Catie glanced coolly at him. "I've reconsidered the words of the poem," she said. "I think what we're looking for is over there, across this little bridge. Maybe they're guarding it?" Without waiting for reply she urged Kelsie eastward.

They finally broke free of the milling herd and across a bridge wide enough for all three horses to cross abreast. Once over the river, Catie stood again, glancing along the hill sweeping up toward the far peaks of the Dragonsback. She paused suddenly, staring. "Over there!" she cried, spurring her mount forward.

As she drew near, the lumps she had seen resolved themselves into clothed shapes huddled in the grass. Catie stopped, her hand going to her mouth. When Rodigger finally came near enough to see, she wondered if he was stifling a retch as much as she needed to.

"By the God," he mumbled, turning away.

Catie swallowed a few times as she looked closer. The heads of both men were nearly detached. Their clothes were torn, and exposed flesh was lacerated and bloody. One man's leg lay a little separate from the rest of him.

"The sheep did not trample them," Deuel said beside her, his eyes scanning the wood-line near the base of the mountain walls. "This was done by weapons."

"Why would someone do that, though?" Catie said quietly. "They're shepherds!"

"Land dispute?" Rodigger said, still turned away.

"I don't think they're prone to carrying swords as a rule," Catie said. "Land disputes that end like this would happen in the moment, wouldn't they? Like, someone found them trespassing and the argument went badly. They would use what was at hand."

"We keep going until we find a farmhouse," Deuel said. "They will know."

"What if it's on the hillside, or in the trees somewhere?" Rodigger asked as Deuel pointed his horse back toward the road.

Deuel paused, gazing northward. "Smoke," he said finally, turning a little up the valley and nudging Rodan to a walk. Catie and Rodigger fell in behind, also looking up the road till they spotted the thin curl of gray on the horizon near the river.

"I guess it wouldn't make sense to be so far from water and trade," Catie muttered as Rodigger continued to ride beside her. She flashed him a calming smile, which he mirrored with little more enthusiasm.

As they neared, she could see a few chickens scratching around the side of the house, and a milk cow grazing further up the valley. But the farm itself was silent. Catie called out as they approached, to no answer. Deuel made one circuit of the outside. They saw little amiss, but the house was plainly deserted.

Catie took a deep breath. "Let's see what's inside, then," she said, almost muttering it. A hundred scenes went through her head of what they might find, and none of them did she want to see in person. As she approached the door, Deuel suddenly cut in front of her.

"I will look first," he said quietly, glancing quickly at Rodigger, who had hung back.

Catie cocked her head. "Why."

For a brief moment, Deuel's eyes flashed. "Because these are not my people," he said, before his eyes returned to the deep, calm pools she was used to.

She bowed her head, and took a step back. Deuel put a hand on the door. It was not barred. He slipped into the darkness inside, and Catie held her breath, waiting for the slightest noise.

Light flared in one of the windows as Deuel lit a lamp. Catie glanced between window and door as the light grew, then faded, then cast shadows. One of the chickens had made its way around to the front of the house and gabbled quietly. Kelsie snorted, and Catie glanced back at her, then at Rodigger.

"Come in," came Deuel's quiet voice.

Catie made a quick gesture to Rodigger, heard leather creaking, and entered the house.

It was not in wild disarray, as she thought it might be, but neither was it tidy. One wooden chair sat back on two legs against the wall, next to the fireplace whose fire was banked low. A table took up most of the center of the main room, and Deuel stood beside three other chairs gathered around it. There were several rude furnishings, but clearly only what was needed between sunset and sunrise. The rest of the day would have been spent outside the house.

"No one else here, at all?" Catie asked. Rodigger entered just then, and Deuel shook his head.

"But what is here?" Deuel asked.

"Not much," Rodigger said, glancing around. "There's barely a second room."

Deuel pointed silently at two doorways leading off the main room. Peering through the one closest, Catie could see a bed spread with wool blankets and a small wood-stove tucked in the corner, with its pipe bending through the stone wall.

"Is that a bedroom too?" Catie asked, pointing at the far doorway. Deuel nodded.

"Okay, so, one for each," Rodigger said with a shrug. "Wouldn't it be more odd if there weren't?"

Catie glanced around again, then at Deuel. "Four chairs," she said.

Deuel cocked an eyebrow briefly. Rodigger folded his arms. "Huh," he said. "So where are the other two? Figure they killed the ones we found?"

"I do not think so," Deuel said. "The second bedroom is far...nicer, than the first."

Catie's heart solidified. "Women?" she asked. Deuel nodded gravely, and Catie's breath escaped her.

"Well, that doesn't mean much," Rodigger said. "They might have done it, for some reason."

"Do you think it's more likely whoever killed the men took the women?" Catie asked.

"Oh," Rodigger said, his face falling. "Yeah, I guess so."

They were silent for a few moments. Catie's eyes continued to dart around the room, hoping for some sign of what had happened there. When that failed, her mind went to work.

"Where could they have taken them?" she asked aloud, though mostly to herself. "They couldn't stay on the roads, there's too many travelers. They can't take them to an inn—could they?"

"What inn would let them in?" Deuel asked.

"What inn poisons its guests and steals from them while they sleep?" Catie asked.

"Yeah!" Rodigger said.

"One that does not see many guests," Deuel replied calmly. "None like what we have seen so far in the Tevorbath."

"Exactly!" Catie exclaimed. "Surely they don't live completely on their own up here. They must go somewhere to get supplies they can't get from sheep, chickens, or cows."

"Like what?" Rodigger asked, glancing pointedly around the sparse room.

"Axes," Deuel said. "For firewood."

Rodigger drew a sigh. "It's more likely they replace their own broken handles, and sharpen their own axe-heads," he said. "It's a poor craftsman who can't fix his own tools."

"Clothes," Catie said. "I don't see much here for making textiles."

Deuel glanced down, then over at the second bedroom.

"Oh, come on," Catie said, her shoulders sagging. "Surely someone knew they were out here, or would know who they were, or would care that they're not here anymore! Besides me!" She could feel Deuel's gentle rebuke, but continued to stare at him unflinching.

In the silence, a whip cracked outside. Catie's eyes widened as she turned and bolted out the door. Deuel and Rodigger quickly followed.

"Hey!" she shouted as chickens scattered and Rodigger's Therian shied a little. There were two wagons, barely big enough to need their four wheels, hitched to a single horse apiece. The driver in the lead, his brown shirt pulled tight across his torso and collar hidden behind a great bushy beard, hauled back on the reins.

"What is it?" he asked as the second wagon came to a halt behind him, the similarly-dressed but thinner driver gazing at her with barely concealed annoyance.

"Do you come through here a lot?" she asked. "Do you know this area?"

"Sure, some," he replied. "We always do the run from Kendet's up the valley about halfway to Dagget's."

"Have the people here ever purchased anything from you?"

"Can't say they purchased it," the driver said with a broad grin. "S'there family owns Kendet's!"

"They do?"

"Sure! S'that strange to you?"

"No, but it complicates things," Catie said with a sigh. "We found the two men dead up the hill," she continued, gesturing away. "Killed. And we're guessing there are two women, who aren't here."

The bearded wagoner's face grew grave, and he turned and glanced at his partner, and a slow sigh turned into a rumble in his chest as he turned back to Catie. "And what were you all doing this way?" he asked in a low but meaningful tone.

Catie blinked. "We were heading northward," she said. "Sheep were blocking the road, and we wanted to see why."

"She wanted to see," Rodigger piped up. "I wanted to keep going."

"Where northward y'headed?"

"Tarver," Catie replied.

"Oh, is that where it is?" Rodigger asked.

As the bearded one turned to glance again at his partner, Catie turned slowly to Rodigger. "Do you have any idea how this looks?" she hissed. "Why would you try to make it worse?"

"Well we didn't do it!" Rodigger exclaimed.

"Why are you carrying weapons?" the younger one asked, his eyes finally finding their horses, and Deuel's weapons strapped to the back of the saddle. "Ain't been goblins and such for years."

Deuel took several strides forward, his gaze locking onto the young man's. "Those were given to me long before you were born," he said quietly. "Ask the eagle why its nest is still among the cliffs."

"Seems if you have 'em, you'd still use 'em," said the elder. But when Deuel's gaze shifted to him, he glanced quickly back to Catie.

"We didn't," she said evenly. "At least, not yet," she continued. The elder cocked an eyebrow. "Where could you hide four people around here?" she asked. "The women are missing, probably taken, and probably taken by more than one."

The elder paused a moment, rubbing his thumb on a rein. He glanced back at Deuel, then pointed ahead and to the east. "There's caves just inside the tree-line," he said. "Probably find a path. S'good storage places, keep things cool." He paused a moment, then looked Catie square in the eye. "You go find 'em. We'll head to the next inn. Bring 'em there. If we don't see you, believe we'll have everyone out looking for you. You try to go south, we'll send folks that way, too."

"You do not have to do that," Deuel said. "Stay here with them," he said to Catie and Rodigger. "I'll go alone."

"That might not be a good idea," said the elder. "If there's more'n you expect...ain't worth dying over."

"I will be fine," Deuel said. He strode over to his horse and pulled the sheathed weapons free, buckling them around his waist. He searched his saddlebags, pulling out two of the strange cuffs and sliding one each on his arms.

"Deuel," Catie said, watching him.

"What are your names?" he asked, ignoring her and looking at the wagoners.

"Eck," said the elder. He hooked a thumb toward the younger. "This is my son, Wallan."

"Eckuthan, do you believe in dragons?" Deuel asked.

Eck shifted a little. "How did you know the old name?" he asked.

"It is traditional," Deuel replied, gazing at him. "A dragon once flew the Tevorbath."

"Garedardan," Eck replied, almost a whisper.

"He ate what he wished, plundering herds, hopefully missing the shepherds as he flew—"

"No!" Eck cut in forcefully. "He kept those of the Tevorbath safe from raiding parties. We wouldn't have survived without 'im."

"I am glad you remember," Deuel said quietly. "I am Deuel." He threw back his cloak and leapt into the air.

The shock of their faces vanished as Deuel gained height. It always hurt, the first several thrusts after keeping his wings for so long immobile behind his cloak. It took some time for blood to fill the veins, for the muscles to remember they had movement. Maybe he was just getting old. Maybe he needed to fly more often.

As the land receded below him, he passed briefly above the peaks, saw outside the Tevorbath: to the east was brown and wide and desolate. The west was rimmed with trees around land that blurred the line to the sea. So much land to see, and this just one small portion of one small continent! Imaginings leapt briefly, unbidden, through his mind of the vastness of Rinc Na, or Cariste. Or Gintanos.

But he did not have time to enjoy the view. And he would fly north first, if he were free, to where the tip of the Dragonsback Mountains could not yet be seen. But that was not why he flew today.

He dropped, wings spread wide as cool air rushed over him. Between the conifers he could see a thin track, broken but extant, until it disappeared into rubble. He circled once. Nothing moved below. He carried himself to a point above the rocks, folded his wings, and dropped feet first. As he passed the tops of the trees, he flared his wings. With a great rustle his descent slowed, and he landed lightly on the rocks above the trail's end in a crouch. His wings returned beneath his cloak with a shiver.

Deuel sat for several moments, until a bird warbled nearby. He heard nothing else, saw no movement. He strode quietly to the edge of the rocks and peered down. It was indeed a cave. He continued to watch and listen. Then, as the wind dropped, he heard the careless metal ring of someone trying to be quiet and failing, followed by a sniffle.

Deuel calmly drew out Halm and Ro Thull, watching the cuffs snap over top the bracelets. He felt it almost instantly, that old connection. His right arm warmed slightly, the left felt suddenly unbreakable. Deuel took a steadying breath: he had not used these in decades. For a brief moment he tumbled around inside his head, recalling things he had not had to recall for three of Gabriel's generations. Then, as old friends, the names came back—smiling, hands outstretched in greeting, pints on the table behind them and an empty chair still saved for him in their circle.

Deuel stepped off the rocks, twisting as he fell to land facing the cave.

Two men stood in loose brown clothing, faces wrapped except their eyes and foreheads. Their hands went quickly to swords sheathed at their waists but Deuel was faster, Halm and Ro Thull swinging outward and slicing throats. The men fell gurgling as Deuel strode by. His irises switched quickly to the gloom, seeing everything in light grays.

Movement ahead, this in deep black. Something warm, blood flowing through its veins. A brief cry of alarm. Deuel pointed with his left blade.

"Binten."

Another cry, this one in fear, and rustling cloth as the man struggled against the stone that had swallowed his feet. Halm parried a frantic swing. Ro Thull thrust. Three.

A clack, and whizzing of feathered vanes. Deuel ducked right as the arrow sailed wide. A thrust with his wings carried him ten paces forward in an instant, both blades outstretched and sinking deeply into the fourth's torso.

The tunnel turned right, and Deuel paused at the corner. He could hear voices, quiet but frightened, giving orders. He recognized the syntax and cadence, but only some of the individual words. His veins chilled at the sound. *Why are they here?*

Footsteps, then, carefully edging closer. He glanced at Ro Thull, feeling the warmth pulsing in his arm, but he needed to know where the prisoners were before releasing such magic. Instead he bent his ears to the shuffling steps. There were three pairs, judging by the sounds. Two sounded closer to one another, but further back in the corridor, likely afraid. The third was closer.

He stepped out, wrapping one wing tightly around the first and pinning the man's arms to his side, useless. Three powerful strides brought him within reach of the other two, whose swords shook. He knocked them aside, razor edges of The Twins scoring and slicing. He unfurled his wing and thrust quickly, finishing the third.

Up ahead, light flared. His eyes adjusted again—greens this time for the cool rock, with lesser heat in yellow and great heat in red. Light or dark made no difference. Helpful in darkness lit by torches, it also helped him see someone in daylight at a far distance, when the need called for it.

He could see the two women huddled near a table, with only one left to guard them.

"Your men are all dead," Deuel said, his voice the deepest rumble he could make it. He spread his wings wide and fluttered them. That always seemed to unnerve men when he did that.

The yellow shape moved, roughly hauling one of the women to her feet. A thin line of green appeared at her throat—a knife, Deuel realized.

"I will kill her," the man said. She mewled, but Deuel was not sure of whom she was more afraid. He tucked his wings behind him again, looking at her and pushing compassion, and comfort.

"You will not die," he said, his voice calmer.

"That's not up to you," the man sneered. The knife, Deuel noticed, moved a shade further from the woman's throat.

It was a mistake. Ro Thull came up.

"Spearken."

The man shrieked, pushing the woman away as he swatted the air behind him. He danced, turning, the back of his cloak on fire. He faintly heard the rustle of leathery wings before one sharp pain bloomed in a kidney, a second in a lung.

Eck and Wallan's horses stood utterly still and calm. Rodigger fidgeted in the silence, and his Therian mimicked him. Catie stood beside Kelsie, rubbing her muzzle gently. Eck cleared his throat and spat, and his horse tossed its head twice, then was still again.

Catie drew a breath. "Didn't you say your horse's name was Gared?" Catie asked Rodigger.

"Yes, well...Roth said it was a good name."

"You didn't realize you had named it after a dead dragon?"

Rodigger only gazed at her, waiting for her derisive follow-up.

"Yer father didn't teach you that?" Eck asked, leaning back and squinting at Rodigger.

Rodigger scoffed. "No, he wasn't much for teaching. Nothing useful, anyway."

"Your mother?" Catie offered. Rodigger's glare answered her. "Just Roth, eh?"

"Roth expects something of me—expects me to make something of myself, not sit by and make something for everyone else while my family falls apart around my ears."

"What did he make, your father?"

Rodigger grimaced and looked away without answering. Catie glanced up the mountainside, looking for Deuel. She thought he would be back by now.

"He was a carpenter," Rodigger said, drawing her attention back to him. "He expected me to be one as well, even as mother lost more and more of her mind while he ignored it."

"Were you any good?"

"What difference does it make? I don't want it. I want what Roth wants for me: to be someone that people listen to, that they respect."

"Nothin' wrong with honest work," Eck growled.

Silence fell again. Catie watched Rodigger for a while, then turned to Kelsie, checking the saddle and bridle.

"I did like it," Rodigger said finally, quietly. He was looking at his hand, rubbing his thumb across his fingers. The hand dropped and he looked up. "But it doesn't matter. No carpenter ever wrote history. You know, you could—" he cut off suddenly, glancing quickly at Eck and Wallan. He took a step toward Catie and lowered his voice. "You could be written into history too. I could make that happen."

Catie arched an eyebrow. "Oh, could you?"

"Well, sure," Rodigger said, his eyes lighting up. "I mean, there's a few things we need to work on, but it shouldn't be too hard for you."

"Things we need to work on?" Catie asked, turning toward him.

"I mean, no one's perfect, so don't take it too hard," he replied. "And we can do one thing at a time."

"Oh, so, you mean there are things *I* need to work on?"

"Well, I mean, little things I've noticed since we've been together, that's—"

He cut off as a whistle echoed down from the slope. Catie turned, looking north and east: three figures were on their way down. Catie leapt aboard Kelsie, then gave a low whistle to Rodan, Deuel's horse. He followed her obediently as she made her way up the slope toward them.

The two women, both just a little older than Catie, did not look too much worse for wear. One had a small bruise on her cheekbone, and their hair was disheveled. But a frightened look only haunted their eyes, warring with relief when they glanced at Deuel and at Catie.

"Thank you," said the bruised one, reaching a hand out for Deuel's horse. Rodan tossed his head once, but a shush from Deuel calmed him. Catie dismounted, offering her hand to the other. "I'm Catie," she said. "You two should ride. I can walk."

"Priska," said the one without a bruise. Her voice still trembled, but the fear was leaving her face.

"Disceya," said the other. She paused beside Deuel's horse, looking down at the road below where Rodigger and the wagoners waited. "That's not Kielar down there," she said.

Priska, preparing to mount, stopped. "Nor is it Pyera." She turned to look at Catie, too closely for Catie to lie. "Where are they?"

Catie blinked. *You didn't have to watch him die,* she thought, before she could stop herself. *Be glad of that.* But they wouldn't be. And did it matter, really? She shook her head. They didn't know how their husbands had died, and that was something.

Priska and Disceya were both looking at her. Disceya's expression hardened. "I suspected as much," she murmured. She looked down, then at Deuel. "You did well," she said.

Tears had begun tracks down Priska's face, but she looked at Deuel too, and nodded some sort of thanks. Catie could feel nothing from him, and he did not return her glance.

"Eck and Wallan are down there," Catie said quietly. "Do you know them? They can take care of you, wherever you want to go."

"Yes, thank you," Disceya said, then pulled herself into the saddle. Catie touched Priska's elbow as the woman hesitated. Priska sniffed, then pulled herself up as well.

Rodigger had found some of his calm, at least, when the four of them returned. Catie glanced at him. He stood behind his Therian, and his gaze was restless.

"Hello, Priska," Eck said gently. "Disceya. Are you—did they—?" The women each shook their head. Eck's glinting eyes fell on Deuel. "Thank ya," he said with a nod. "S'good you were here, then." He glanced down at Deuel's sheathed blades and drew a breath. "Thought we were done with those," he said heavily. The women were dismounting, looking at their farmhouse though neither seemed eager to move toward it. "Almost can't imagine it, traveling with weapons again, havin' t'defend yourself."

Rodigger made some small noise, but few paid him any attention.

"What are we going to do?" Priska asked quietly. Eck glanced at her.

"Might be best to take you down to Kendet's," he said. "T'yer family."

"I know it sounds silly, almost, but what about our farm?" Priska asked, turning toward him. "What about the chickens, and cows, and...and the sheep?"

"We can't abandon it," Disceya said, more firmly, as she turned to face Eck as well.

"Y'might be able to find someone to take it over for you," Eck said, casting a quick, helpless glance at Catie and Deuel. "Animals will be fine for a few days, won't they? D'you really want to stay here tonight, anyway?"

"The inn toward Kendet's is too far, Eck," Disceya said. "Would you two stay with us tonight?"

"We can't be delayed," Rodigger spoke up.

Disceya glanced around, then back at Rodigger. "I didn't ask you to," she said.

"Well...right."

Catie's eyes narrowed at him, and his gaze fell. She turned back as Eck shrugged with a glance back at Wallan.

"I suppose we can, at that," he said. "But y'will go back to Kendet's?"

Disceya sighed. "I suppose we must, even if only for a time." She turned to Deuel and Catie. "Thank you, both. Would the God had brought you a little earlier..." She went silent, and her jaw tightened. Priska's head bowed, and Disceya went quickly to her.

Rodigger approached, subdued, as Eck and Wallan brought their wagons up closer to the house. "You've done well," Eck murmured as he pulled alongside the three. "We'll take care of them."

"Thank you," Catie said.

With quick handshakes around, Deuel, Catie, and Rodigger mounted and continued up the road toward the next inn.

They reached the inn shortly after night fell, and it was another one packed wall to wall. They managed a table in a far corner, though for a time no one spoke. Finally, Catie took a breath and leaned forward.

"What Eck said was right," she said. "About carrying weapons. It's been unnecessary for so long..."

"It may be worse than you think," Deuel said. "The men were nomads."

Catie's eyes widened. "From *Beltrath?*" she hissed. "What could they be doing here?"

"Sheppar should know about it."

Rodigger snorted. "What makes you think he would care?"

"What makes you think he wouldn't?" Catie shot back.

"He'll say Kendet's or Dagget's should handle it," Rodigger said. "He wants the Magiss' to handle everything, remember?"

"The 'vilts aren't set up to handle something like this, and they're too far away anyway," Catie said.

"Exactly."

Catie sighed, and gazed at Deuel. "Do you think they were on their own?" she asked.

"I cannot imagine nomads crossing that deep into the Tevorbath just to kidnap two farmwives," Deuel replied.

"How many were in the cave?" Catie said.

"Eight."

Rodigger's eyes went wide. "You managed against...?"

"We said he was very good," Catie said with a wry chuckle. *Eight?* she thought to herself, though. *And not a scratch on him.* "But, seriously, that is more than a simple raiding party."

"The nomads have not been seen outside Beltrath since long before the

Tevorbath became what it is," Deuel replied. "Nor has anyone been into Beltrath to see what is going on there. Something may be driving them out." He paused, then said again: "Sheppar should know about this."

Catie drew a deep breath, but Rodigger got there first. "We can't abandon the mission," he said firmly. "If a problem is growing, getting the Berkarfor to Roth will help more than getting a message to Sheppar."

"So you believe," Catie shot back.

"Did you notice the rule and order in the Fallonvall?" Rodigger asked.

Fire surged through Catie so fiercely her shoulders ached as she stared at Rodigger. Did he have any idea how Roth maintained that order? He had to have, so he simply didn't think about anyone who might have cared about who Roth killed. Her fingers tightened around the handle of her mug. One good bash, and maybe if she tore his eyes out, that smug look would leave his face.

As quickly as it came, the fire left. She blinked a few times, easing her cramped fingers. She glanced at Deuel, who was gazing intently at her. She took a few deep breaths, and a drink. She wished, briefly, that terror would come just so Rodigger could see he was wrong—but saving him from ignorance would not be worth the lives it would cost to accomplish it.

They would get a message to Sheppar somehow. They had to. The Tevorbath, the God's Feast, was no longer the haven it had been.

11

ANSWERS QUESTIONED

"I assume we cannot tell him."
"What they say about assumptions is not always true."
"So we wait?"
"Or you talk to the ones who have the knowledge."

16 Halmfurtung 1320 — Spring

A number of wagons lined the road by the time the three companions saddled their horses. The air was chill, but clear skies promised a warm day once the sun rose over the mountains.

"Wonder where they're headed," Rodigger muttered, glancing away from a heavily laden wagon pulled by only two donkeys.

"You should ask them," Catie replied. "They really shouldn't be driving those poor donkeys far."

"What difference does it make to me?" he asked, hunching a little and rubbing his left arm.

Catie shrugged. "You asked the question. I thought you actually wanted an answer. It's not like it's hard to ask someone a question, just because you've never met them before. I had more faith in you, Rodigger."

That straightened his back, and a considering eye fell upon the merchants. "Where are you taking those poor things?" he demanded suddenly.

Catie's eyes bulged momentarily as every eye in the caravan swung toward them, and she discovered a sudden itch on her nose that took her whole palm to scratch. *Say 'Balnath'* she thought to herself.

The sizable owners of the donkeys finally recognized Rodigger was looking at them. "What's it to you?" asked the slightly larger one, turning to face the companions more squarely.

"You've got a great big wagon and your great big selves, and only two donkeys to pull it all," Rodigger said, sitting even more upright in his saddle now. "If that cargo is any kind of important to whomever you're delivering it, I fear it will never reach them."

Oh, just say 'Balnath'. This plan was going quickly awry.

"This from a boy who brings a Therian into the mountains," snarled the smaller. "Or do you suppose this is the first time we've hauled a wagon?"

And Rodigger had no response. Catie could see it in his eyes. And she had led him into it.

"Many an animal can be treated cruelly for great lengths of time before it dies," Catie said. "And how do we know it isn't the first time those particular donkeys hauled that wagon?" *It's not like we'll be traveling with them anyway, if they end up hating us.*

It must have partially worked, because even the other wagoners were eyeing up these two, now, and they knew it. "How we run our business is our own!" said the fatter. "Who asked you to be inquisitors?"

"Roth Kamdellan cares for all of Andelen!" Rodigger announced loudly, and Catie could not stifle her groan. Rodigger didn't hear her. "As Andelian, you should care about doing a job well, not cheaply," he continued. "Would you like if another countryman sold you a product at the same cost when his own expense had been lessened? Would that not feel like being cheated? But on the backs of these pitiable creatures you cheat your fellow man!"

"We're going to Taferk!" the larger exploded. "You judgmental, self-righteous sheep-spawn! All three of you!"

Deuel glowered at him. "I said nothing."

"Well, two of you then," the man quailed. "What did you accost us for?"

The silence hung heavy, and Catie glanced up and down the line, keeping her head low. "Are any of you going to Balnath?" she asked only as loudly as she needed to be heard by the majority of them.

Rodigger turned quickly on her, the hurt flying out of his eyes. Catie tried to ignore him, looking instead at the row of wagoners who all gazed at her in varying amounts of dumbfound. She gave a small smile. "Anyone?"

But no one replied. A few eyebrows arched. All turned back to their wagons. Catie sighed, then spared a glance at Rodigger. His jaw shut, and he turned and rode away. Deuel followed him with his eyes, then looked back at Catie.

"I've had ideas that worked out a lot better," she said in a tiny voice.

"You would've had to," he rumbled.

She sighed. "Why doesn't Sheppar have patrols anymore?" she asked, nudging Kelsie after Rodigger.

"It's safe now," Deuel replied, following. "Rodigger would say it's because Sheppar does not care about the people."

"That can't be true," Catie said. "The man who rid the land of roaming beasts can't just suddenly not care."

Deuel shrugged. "It's safe now," he repeated, then glanced at her. "Does he need to care anymore?"

"He's still king, though."

"He's kinnig," Deuel corrected. "And what more does he owe this country, after such a campaign as he completed?"

"There's more to being king *or* kinnig than just solving one problem," Catie said.

"That was a very large problem," Deuel said. "Cannot the villages and cities solve the little problems?"

"And this new one?"

"This was unforeseen."

"Funny how so many of the big problems are unforeseen," Catie retorted. "You'd think, being that big, you could spot them a long way off."

"The problems become big because they are not handled when they are small," Deuel said. "A nomadic, non-allied collection of peoples on the other side of a great range of mountains is a small problem, but still a problem if they do not recognize your rule."

"So Sheppar's campaign should have included them?"

"Why do you think solving a problem means eradication?" Deuel asked, then shook his head. "I fear for Rodigger, then."

"Do you think they would have just recognized our rule if we asked them to? Do you think it would have kept those men still in the Wastes? Or would there be even more of them on this side of the 'Back?"

"Catie, we have no knowledge of why those men were here, we have no knowledge of what sent them out of Beltrath. That is what Sheppar will need to address first. They may need our aid."

Catie sighed. "So, first I need to understand Rodigger?"

"Rodigger is easy," Deuel replied. "He believes what Roth believes—and he likes you."

Catie stared at Deuel as he gazed levelly back at her.

"Do not look surprised," Deuel said. "That is why you got him to ask your question."

"That wasn't *why*," Catie said lamely. "I thought he would just cut me off if I tried to ask. And I thought men in general liked to please women."

"They do," Deuel replied. "But when you coax him, you make him think you like him as well."

Catie sighed. "Oh, no." She rode silently for several moments. "What happens when they find out they were wrong?"

"If you are very lucky, he thinks you hate him."

"If I'm lucky?" Catie repeated in an incredulous whisper. "What if I'm not lucky?"

"He believes you think he is a fool."

They stopped for lunch on the banks of the Balnathva as it swung close to the road. Though Rodigger did not sit far away, neither did he appear willing to talk. His eyes seemed lost in thought, and he did not notice—or flat out ignored—Catie's gaze as she tried to figure out how to approach him.

Perhaps I should just let him think. It would be good for him.

Goodness, I do think he is a fool.

Well, isn't he?

I don't know what's going on in his mind!

He probably doesn't either. Stop that!

Maybe he doesn't need to question everything; maybe he's happy with what he believes.

That is no excuse; happiness in stupidity is still stupidity. Cease this line of thinking right now!

I'm trying! I don't want to think he is a fool; we have too far to go yet for us to be at odds with each other.

You need to get him—

The thought broke off suddenly, and Catie blinked as if awakened. She glanced at Rodigger, noting his deep frown as he gazed at the river. She opened her mouth, but couldn't think of anything to say and closed it. And yet, there was something she needed to convince him of—some aspect of their plan? She couldn't imagine why, suddenly. Trusting him with their next step might mollify him. She paused. Deuel would keep her around, though she wasn't sure why. The behamian was interested in her—not in that way, she could tell, but something intrigued him. After that many centuries of life, it was surprising and more than a little heartwarming—if only she knew what it was. But Deuel was not her concern this moment.

"Rodigger," she said, before she could change her mind.

The only indication that he heard was a deepening of his frown.

"The riddle takes us to Kavlen, in the Nagrath Highlands," she said.

Deuel's gaze swung to her. Rodigger barely moved, though he stiffened.

"I wanted you two to know, just in case." She paused for a moment. "Not that I think anything will happen, but... We need to trust one another. We should look for the Grandmother when we get there, as we did in Attelek. She will remember the old legends better than anyone else."

"Have you ever been to Kavlen?" Deuel asked. Rodigger shifted. He was listening closer.

Catie shook her head. "I remember a story though," she said. "I hesitate to tell it, just because it's a little thin to be hanging all of the riddle on." Rodigger's gaze snapped to her, now. "I mean, I can't imagine another place like it, so it most likely is, but..." She paused and shrugged.

"I believe you are correct, though I did not make the connection immediately," Deuel said. "I have been to Kavlen, many years ago. It fits."

"Do you want to explain it, then?" Rodigger asked.

"Oh, I think the riddle does it justice," Catie replied with a smile. "Beyond that, you'll have to see it for yourself."

"You don't think I'll understand your description?" he asked.

"No, Rodigger, that's not it," Catie said. "I'm sorry I did that this morning. It was thoughtless, mean, and selfish. I just thought you would stop me if I asked if anyone was going—"

"I would have," Rodigger cut in. "If Sheppar can't control his own lands—or won't!—he shouldn't be in control of them."

"So those two shepherds deserved to die to prove a point?" Catie asked quietly.

"You give them too much import," Rodigger replied. "The point is made no matter who proves it. The point is reality."

"But if we can avoid more deaths by delivering a message—"

"He'll ignore it. It's too easy!" Rodigger said, lifting a hand. "He mounted his first campaign after hundreds of deaths, if not thousands. And that after the fortified inns were already built. Sheppar is a man of least required effort. He conducted his campaign because it was necessary. As soon as it was successful, he ceded responsibility back to whomever he could. He'll wait for others to respond to this new threat, and only involve himself after another several thousand deaths."

Catie opened her mouth, then closed it. Rodigger's gaze on her sharpened. He had the makings of a point. "We should still try," she said quietly. "If he ignores it, that's his responsibility. Ours is to call attention to it."

Rodigger's jaw clenched, and his eyes flicked to Deuel. "How fast..." The muttered words trailed away.

"Not fast enough," Deuel replied. "Once we were in Semmedor—"

"But by then we can probably send a messenger to him from there," Rodigger finished. He glanced back at Catie. "Is that good enough?"

"Y-yes, that's fine," she said. The nomads might still gain a foothold while they delayed. Rodigger probably knew that, knew the risk and took it anyway. But it was an improvement on his attitude toward her. "Thank you, Rodigger," she said.

He was, she decided, trying a little too hard to still look grumpy. She had him back. She swallowed, then. Best not to encourage him too much, though. But as she saw the glint in his eye behind the frown, she worried.

No, she was almost terrified. Swallowing again, she glanced at Deuel. His face, always still, looked hewn from rock as his eyes fixed on her. "Deuel," she croaked, but couldn't think what to say next. He shook his head slightly, his gaze still locked. The fear gave way to a brief moment of relief, and then anger—no, fury. Catie's eyes widened. Deuel shifted, and the fury subsided. But why was it there in the first place? A trace of fear returned, more purely hers this time. Where were these emotions coming from? Deuel? Why would he be frightened, then angry? Her eyes darted to Rodigger. Nothing the soldier had said should evoke this.

Another wave of peace washed over her, and her eyes went back to Deuel. He too seemed more at ease, though still not fully.

"What. Was—"

But Deuel's shaking head cut her off again. He would talk to her about it later.

Rodigger was looking at them warily. Catie forced a grin. "I thought I heard something," she said.

Rodigger grunted. "I thought I heard you say we needed to trust each other."

"Well, now it's your turn," she replied gently. "I'm not going to tell you everything about me right now, am I?"

Rodigger shrugged one shoulder. "I guess not."

Catie glanced up at the sun. "We should be on our way."

They agreed, packed, and set out for the next inn.

Catie was exhausted that night, and fell asleep quickly despite the questions racing through her head. It startled her, then, when she awoke in the darkness to a hand lying gently on her shoulder. Before she could draw a conscious breath the hand left, and she saw the dark shape of Deuel leaving the cot room. His profile lit briefly as he exited into the common room where the fire still glowed.

Catie turned her head. Rodigger had taken the next cot over, as the inn had been nearly as crowded as all the others. She managed to pick out his breathing among the myriad other snorts, rumbles, and snores: it was deep and even. She lifted her covers and slipped out, managing not to kick any of the chests on her way out.

Deuel had taken a table in the far corner, and sat facing the cot room door. Catie went to the hearth first and pushed the logs together, adding one more for good measure. It was not particularly cold, but neither was it comfortable. She went and sat at an angle to Deuel, so she too could keep an eye on the cot room.

"What was that?" she asked as soon as she sat.

"I told you those who can sense a behamian once, do so in increasing amounts."

"I figured that, because it felt like it was coming from you. At least," she amended, "the suppression of the initial feelings certainly came from you."

"The sense works both ways," Deuel said, placing his hands on the edge of the table, then rested his forearms. He looked like one who was uncomfortable trying to force a comfortable posture. "I can tell when you are sensing me, or sensing something that I also sense."

"Then what was that? Why did I feel fear and then anger?"

"Is that what you felt?" he asked, piercing her directly with his gaze this time.

Catie drew a breath. "I felt terror, and then fury. I felt utter emptiness, then I was suddenly filled beyond bursting. Why?" she asked, filling that single word with every bit of frustration, fear, and anger she could.

Deuel sat back. "I do not know," he said, then held up a hand as her eyes goggled. "That is a deeper question than you understand," he said quickly. "You felt something coming from Kaoleyn. Why you felt it, and why she felt it, is a mystery to me."

"Who is Kaoleyn?"

Deuel glanced at the cot room door, then away at nothing. Finally he drew a sigh and bowed his head. His arms left the table and went back to his side. Catie waited as he drew another deep breath and looked at her. "Kaoleyn is my mother," he said quietly. "In Burieng."

Catie could only stare at him for a few moments. "Kao—she—why did I feel something from—Burieng is so far away!" She glanced, along with Deuel, at the far door, then dropped her voice. "Well it is!"

"I know where it is," Deuel murmured, and she felt his amusement.

"Or did I just feel it through you?"

"Not at first," Deuel said, and she felt chagrin. "I only felt it after you did. But that sense is not limited by distance, only power."

Catie sat in silence for a moment. "That's why you're so reserved," she said finally. "If you were emotional, you would affect every behamian everywhere."

"Very good," Deuel said. "And I would affect everyone with the sense like you."

"Deuel, why do I have that sense? How does someone get it to begin with?"

"We do not know. Long ago only behamien and dragons had it. We suspect wyverns do as well, but that is difficult to prove."

"Why is it difficult to prove?"

"Because wyverns by nature are capricious, and do not have a language we understand," he replied. "Sometimes it seems they respond to our emotions, but it might be coincidence."

"Is it possible...I mean...am I..." She shrugged.

Deuel shook his head. "Do you remember when you were seven?" he asked.

"Of course."

"Did you live with a dragon?"

Catie smiled and shook her head.

"Behamien live with their dragon parent until they are eight, learning to speak and learning the ways of the people where they live before being sent into it."

"So why aren't you in Burieng? And how do you learn the language? I didn't think dragons could form words." She could feel his chuckle at her barrage of questions, and she smiled. "Sorry."

"Behamien are even less welcome in Burieng than in Rodigger's reality," Deuel said. "And we learn through our sense connection. You are right, dragons cannot speak human words. Everything we share with our parent is through that sense. But we can practice actual speech with our siblings."

"You've said a couple times about your 'parent'. Aren't there two?"

Deuel gazed at the cot room door for many long moments as if listening. Catie turned her head as well to listen, but she heard nothing. Finally Deuel turned back to her, and lowered his voice to just above a whisper. "Yes, there are two. But only two dragons may live on one continent. No one must know this!" His ferocity slammed into her and she could not breathe for a few moments. "I do not know why I trust you with this," he continued as she gaped at him, still breathless, still locked into his gaze as tightly as if bound by great chains. "Yet I do. Paolound—my father—is dead. One of his sons must replace him. I believe—" He cut off quickly, and as his gaze dropped Catie was released and took a deep breath. "I believe they are safe now," Deuel continued with less intensity. "But I believe someone tried to steal Kaoleyn's eggs today. That was her terror and her fury, for with Paolound gone and them stolen, our survival on Burieng, and perhaps the rest of Oren, was in great danger."

"I'm sorry, Deuel. When did he die?" Catie murmured.

He shook his head once, and she felt his turmoil. "I thought he died many years ago," he said. "But then suddenly he was not. He died again a few months ago, after we received our mission from Roth."

Catie's head snapped up. "What?"

Deuel gazed at her, and she knew he could feel her quivering. "This means something to you."

"It was late at night?" she pressed. "The night after you came to Akervet?"

"How did I know?" Rodigger mumbled from the doorway. Catie's wide gaze snapped from Deuel's intense look to Rodigger's groggy one. Rodigger shuffled in, moving toward the fire as Catie's thoughts railed against the injustice.

"Why are you awake?" she asked, unable to keep all of her frustration out of her voice.

Rodigger eyed her as he warmed himself in front of the fire. "Something woke me up," he said, his voice becoming clearer. "Having secret meetings now?"

"This has nothing to do with the mission," she replied, regaining control of her tone. *And everything to do with my life!* "We were almost done, anyway."

Rodigger waved her away. "I won't be able to get back to sleep now," he said. "It's amazing the racket sleeping people can make, when there's enough of them."

"I will try," Deuel said. Cate glared at him. *I won't!* she thought as loudly as she could. She could not tell if he sensed her as he stood. His glance as he began to leave said he did not—or he was very good at hiding that he had. As he moved past Rodigger, she sensed he wanted to put a hand on Rodigger's shoulder, but he made no motion.

After Deuel left, Rodigger turned and came to the table and sat. Catie only looked at him as his gaze stayed on the table. *This just gets better and better.*

"What do you think we'll face, in Kavlen?" he asked quietly.

He's frightened.

Catie took a deep breath, trying to wrench her thoughts from that night outside Akervet to the young man sitting in front of her. Had she witnessed, in some way, the death of Paolound? And why did that awaken something in her? Deuel said she could not be behamian, and yet he clearly showed surprise and interest in her ability to sense dragon-things.

Rodigger's eyes lifted from the table to hers, and she forced herself to look into them. His eyes did not look like ones who had seen death, or faced their own mortality—though perhaps they were, in some way, doing so now. But she also knew *fear* of pain or death was a far step removed from truly comprehending the *possibility* and nearness of death. He was still young. Or was she, perhaps, older than she should be? It felt like it.

"I do not know," she replied finally. "The riddle sounds as though there is some conflict going on. We might use that as a distraction."

"Conflict?" Rodigger asked. "I thought it just mentioned guards. You know..." He didn't speak it, but made some gesture.

"'Wars wage and blare far beneath the floors,'" Catie quoted. "The first goblet was underground. I assume the second will be, as well. Probably all of them will be."

"We three of us can't win a war," Rodigger said. "As good as Deuel supposedly is, so far we only know he faced eight men and lived." He paused under her appraisal. "Well, fine, eight is a lot. But he probably surprised them, and we don't know if he'll be able to again."

"We also don't know how many Wendol 'guard the glass' there," Catie offered. "It might only be two."

"That would be enough," Rodigger muttered. "They were the hardest for Sheppar's army to eradicate—and apparently they didn't even do a thorough job."

"Lucky for us, though, right?" Catie said. "If they had, we'd be short a goblet and wouldn't know where to look for the next one."

Rodigger shrugged. "Fair enough. But killing two Wen—It's not going to be easy."

"We didn't have the kill the *byor,* though, right?"

Rodigger blinked. "Right. But if they're guarding it..."

"The *byor* guarded, too, against those who would simply try to rush in and take the Berkarfor," Catie replied.

"So I guess I just have to trust you," Rodigger said with a wry grin.

"You need to trust yourself, as well," Catie said. "Take a moment to think—as small a moment as you want," she continued gently. "The world will probably not end because you take two breaths to consider something from a second angle. What you said earlier about Sheppar being a man of least effort—I like Sheppar, and I'm not convinced he is as bad as you say. But you gave me something to think about."

Rodigger's mouth twisted a little. "Roth told me that, first," he admitted. "So, Roth gave you something to think about."

Catie hoped her irritation didn't show on her face. How could he so willingly follow a man like Roth? After what he'd—

He probably wasn't there.

"Rodigger, were you at Bokessin with Roth last winter?"

Rodigger sighed, and a rueful grin flashed across his face. "No," he said. "I wanted to be. But Roth insisted it was better for me to stay in Akervet. Were you there?" he asked.

Catie nodded silently.

"Did you get to see him?" he asked, his tone as one who shared some awe-inspiring sight.

He had no idea what Roth had done there. She wished he had been there, to know who this man was he worshipped. Her heart cried out, and the words nearly left her mouth. But as she looked at the light in Rodigger's eyes, she wondered how dark they might go if that light left. Did disillusionment have to be so violent? Would it be better for knowledge to come swiftly? Or slowly? Would he even accept what she had to say? And if he did, would he allow her to continue, believing—rightfully—that she sought the goblets only for another opportunity at justice? If he still believed Roth was right, he would not. He seemed convinced, for whatever reason, that she had abandoned that hope. *Rodigger likes you* floated across her mind.

"Not really," she said, forcing her own rueful grin. "I had...other concerns that pulled me away after only seeing him briefly."

"That's a shame," Rodigger said, still smiling.

"It was," Catie agreed. She paused. Normally she didn't fear answers, and yet... "Rodigger, there was a time you thought I should be thrown deep into a hole, somewhere..." She trailed off with a quick glance.

"Oh." Rodigger shrugged. "Roth must have had his reasons for not doing that. And he never told me to stay away from you—just not to let you inside Akervet again."

They sat in silence for a few moments longer, Rodigger gazing at her, Catie looking toward the fire. She glanced back at him, finally.

"Okay," she said. "I think I'll try to get back to sleep, too. Good night, Rodigger." She stood, and his eyes followed her.

"Good night," he replied. "I'm going to stay out here for a little while longer."

She smiled, and left him to it.

12

FINDING WOUNDS

"I suppose you think that went well."
"You are improving."
"Small comfort."
"You want too much, Teresh."

17 Halmfurtung 1320 — Spring

"You know, maybe it wouldn't be a bad idea to start telling people about what happened," Rodigger mused as the sun cleared the mountains and scattered glinting jewels across the Balnathva River.

"No?" Catie asked.

"People should know there may be dangerous men around, and take steps to defend themselves."

Catie cocked an eyebrow at Deuel. He remained emotionless. "Well, should we wait for everyone to catch up, then?" she asked, nodding her head back down the road where the merchant convoys could barely be seen. Unburdened as the three companions were, they made better time up the road and daily left the more laden travelers behind.

Rodigger twisted briefly, then shook his head. "Oh, it's not that important. We'll see them at dinner tonight."

"But it might be safer for us and them to travel together," Catie said. "Like you say, we're all going to the same place."

Rodigger squinted at her as if trying to see if she were making fun of him. He rolled his shoulders. "I mean...we're probably fine. To keep going, I mean. Anyway, we can protect them from up here, too. They'd be more likely to attack the three of us. We could end up flushing them out."

"Sounds pleasant," Catie said. "Why don't you want to wait for them?"

"I said we'd ride with them tomorrow."

"Rodigger."

"Because I don't want to travel with a big group of people, okay?" he said, setting his Therian's ears swiveling.

Catie grinned slowly. "But you said we'd ride with them tomorrow."

"Tomorrow is further away than—" He jerked his head backward.

Now Catie laughed, but gently. "I didn't know you didn't like people. What about when we're staying at the inn? They've been packed since we came into the valley."

"Yeah, and I've hardly said two words the whole time," Rodigger said, settling down into his saddle. "And it's not that I don't like them, I'm just not comfortable talking."

"I thought you were supposed to be talking to people? Convincing them of the glory of the revolution?"

"And look how well that's turned out so far," Rodigger muttered.

"Well, you have to keep trying! No one gets it right the first...you know..." Rodigger glared as she looked at her fingers. She cleared her throat. "Bunch of times. So I'll be telling them about the nomads then?" she asked.

"Well, I can do that part. I *should* do that part, probably. Well, they might believe me more easily than you," he said when she shot him a look. "I mean, guys like these probably won't think you're trustworthy."

"Probably true," Catie said. "But then, if Deuel gives them a look or two, they'll believe probably anything."

"I wonder if you can do the same," Deuel replied.

Catie swallowed. Also probably true.

Rodigger glowered. "I'll tell them, that way neither of you have to glare at them for anything."

"I was only teasing, Rodigger," Catie said, though her heart wasn't in it.

"But you do *do* that," Rodigger replied. "How?"

She glanced up, frustration piling the words behind her teeth, but Rodigger was looking at Deuel. The words came out as silent breath as she glanced at the dragon-son.

"It is nothing I do," Deuel replied. "It is who I am."

"But you said she can do it too," Rodigger said. Catie sat up a little in her saddle. Was Rodigger about to ask her question for her? "So how does she do it?"

She settled back. Too advanced a question, then. She cocked an eyebrow at Deuel after he was silent for too long.

"Perhaps it is a trick of those most open and honest," he said finally. Catie's eyes widened and she looked away.

"Great," Rodigger said. "So I'm just closed and a liar?" he asked.

Deuel gazed at him a few moments, and Rodigger looked quickly away with a curse. Rodigger took a tighter grip on his reins, and urged his Therian forward ahead of them.

"Am I part behamian?" Catie asked quietly when Rodigger was out of earshot.

It was like a wall suddenly towered before her where there had been an open forest: infinite denial instead of obscured improbability. "No," Deuel replied. "Behamien do not mingle with humans."

"What happens if they try?"

"We die," Deuel said. "That," he continued with a meaningful glance at the seething young man ahead of them, "is an abomination. We only mate as dragons. It cannot happen any other way."

Rodigger cried out ahead of them. Deuel was racing forward as Catie only tried to see what was happening. Her eyes started toward Rodigger, but Deuel caught her attention as he pulled his blades free. He was alongside Rodigger when Catie finally nudged Kelsie into an unwilling trot. Deuel's right arm extended, and some word she didn't recognize came to her quietly. She yelped as a sharp, bright flash of blue and a low scream came from a stand of trees to their left.

Rodigger was staring at his arm, and as she neared Catie could see the darkening of the shirt sleeve on his forearm. "I was just brushing a fly away," he said slowly. "It kept getting stuck in my hair."

"You're okay," Catie said, coming alongside. She heard Deuel's voice again, but still jumped when a sound like small thunder cracked from the trees again. She called out: *"Leih par dak* you didn't get them yet?" But no answer came from Deuel.

"Catie!" Rodigger said, eyes goggling. "Did you just say that?"

"Let me look at it," she said. She took his hand and pulled his arm toward her. "Can you get Gared to stand still? Kelsie, easy." Hoof-beats diminished as Deuel left them. "Well, it's through the outside, not the center of your arm, which is probably actually—yeah, see how it's shaped?" The arrowhead resembled half a spade. "Usually you do that for fishing, with a line tied to the end so you can haul the fish back in. That's for really big fish though, pike or something, that would chew through a net. Rodigger, you're not looking."

"I got shot through the arm!" he said, still staring resolutely ahead.

"You're still lucky it didn't go through the middle...or through your head."

He whimpered.

"Sorry, I guess we don't need to think about that. Do you want me to take it out?"

This time his eyes moved, to stare at her wider than she knew his eyes could go. "Leave it in, please," he said in a whisper. His eyes crossed, focusing on the arrow. He fought back a retch and turned his eyes forward again.

"I meant did you want *Deuel* to take it out," she said. She saw his jaw muscles writhe. "Okay." She let go of his hand and gripped the arrowhead. With a mighty twist she broke the shaft, and Rodigger cried out again. Before he could make it worse, she pulled on the back of the arrow and yanked the whole thing free from his arm. His cry this time was deeper in his chest, and he swooned forward.

"Don't do that," she said, grasping his shoulder and hauling him upright again. "This is the best part of the whole event. Now we just bandage it and you heal. You already missed the best time to faint."

She heard hoofbeats, and glanced up quickly. Deuel was returning. "How many?" she asked.

"Only two," Deuel replied. He gestured to Rodigger. "He's bleeding."

"Right." Catie dug her free hand into a saddlebag and pulled free a rolled strip of cloth. "I guess we should wait for the convoy, now," she said. "Do you think your sleeve will go up?"

Rodigger nodded, pale, and tugged half-heartedly with his other hand.

"I'll get it," Catie said, tucking the roll under her leg and gently pulling his sleeve back. "Okay, hold that. Just a pair this time? Only watching the road, do you think? For another crossing?"

"And in the least inhabited portion of the Tevorbath," Deuel agreed. "We do not know how many may actually be here. But if they are ambushing small groups already, they are probably here in force."

"I hope those two women are okay," Catie said. "We didn't really leave them in a stronger position than they had been."

"We didn't know how bad it was, then," Rodigger murmured. Catie had the wound covered, and he was gazing at the bandage as she finished tying it off. Blooms of red still grew.

"He will probably need more than that," Deuel said gently.

"I was hoping he wouldn't," Catie muttered, rummaging through her saddlebag again. "Do you have—oh, the arrow shaft. Can you grab it for me?" She pointed with one hand as she twirled another roll of bandage, unwrapping it. As Deuel dismounted, she cut off a section, tucking the remainder under her leg. She tied the piece she'd torn off around Rodigger's bicep, leaving it loose. Deuel handed her the shaft and she ran it through, then began twisting. She watched the bandaged forearm. Rodigger groaned, but she did not stop until the blooms stopped growing. She used more bandage to secure the tourniquet, then drew a deep sigh.

"It'll stop you from bleeding out," she said, daring a glance at his face. His eyes were squeezed shut.

"It's incredible to think about how much this hurts," he said, gasping.

"Then don't think about it," she said, resting a hand on his shoulder and giving a small squeeze. She glanced at the sun, then down the road where the convoy behind them could still be faintly seen. By the time they arrived, they should loosen the tourniquet for a little. Hopefully someone in the convoy had tools a little better for handling such a wound.

"Do you want to scout to see if there's a larger force nearby?" Catie asked Deuel. "They surely wouldn't be far from water."

"They are nomads," Deuel said. "They know how to find water besides in rivers. But yes, I will before the convoy arrives. Keep him in the shade, and give him water."

"Should you leave us alone?" Rodigger asked, licking his lips. "You're the only one set up to defend us, right now."

"I will scout nearby first, and thoroughly," Deuel replied.

"Can you help me get him down, first?" Catie asked. As she nudged Kelsie away and dismounted, Deuel caught Rodigger as he slid out of his saddle and set him on his feet. They tied all the horses in the nearby trees, and Catie and Rodigger set themselves up at the base of a spruce, still in sight of the road.

"I will return," Deuel said. He took two long strides out of the woods, then leapt into the air. Catie gave a little shiver, and rolled her neck.

"I love watching him do that," she said.

Rodigger coughed, then braced his wounded arm. "I could do without it."

"Close your eyes, then," she retorted, then sucked on her lips. "You should rest," she said, gentler. "You haven't lost a lot of blood, but you're not in a good way."

"Thanks," he said. "I had noticed."

"I'm sorry, Rodigger, I don't mean to—"

"Yeah, but you do," he cut in, giving a little sigh. "Which means you must really think it, since that's what comes out when you don't have time to think about what you're going to say." He paused as she remained silent. "Right?"

Amazing, his ability to be perceptive at the worst times. A thousand responses came into her head, ways to defend herself, try to appease him—mostly lies. A light breeze rose, shushing through the pines. She felt it at her back, let it embrace her as she took a breath. "How much of what you say comes from Roth?" she asked finally.

Rodigger shrugged his right shoulder. "He's been my mentor. Probably most of what I say, at least about the sorts of things he talks about, is from him."

"What about what you think?"

"Why should I do that? Roth is right! If I disagree with him, I'm wrong. It doesn't matter how long I think about it, or what feels right or wrong to me."

"But, everything he says?" Catie asked. "No one has that many right answers."

"You said yourself the ideas I told you about Sheppar gave you something to consider. That came from Roth."

"Exactly! I'm *considering* it. I'm not sold on it. Especially without being able to talk to Sheppar about it, or anyone who knows him. You're making assumptions just on a few of his actions, without finding out what motivates him to act that way."

"No, that's fair. He's clearly doing a great job in securing this country," Rodigger said, lifting his wounded arm slightly.

"If he's made a mistake, then we tell him about it," Catie replied. "If he doesn't do anything after that, then we'll know he's not fit to run the country anymore."

"And if he does do something about it?"

"Then I get to tell you 'you were wrong,' and laugh at you," Catie replied.

"What about the Berkarfor?" Rodigger pressed. "You know what Roth wants them for. If you think Sheppar's doing such a great job, why do you want to see Roth succeed?"

"There's a great difference between gaining the goblets and succeeding," Catie replied.

Rodigger blinked a few times, his brows knitting. "Why are you helping us find these?"

"I needed something to do," Catie replied.

"No," Rodigger said, shaking his head. "No, no. This isn't just a distraction. This is way too dangerous to just do because you're bored."

"Well I didn't know it was going to be this dangerous," she said, gesturing to his bandage. "Did I? Couldn't know that."

"You want to get back to Roth, don't you? I'm not taking you. Once we find the last goblet, you're on your own. No! There is no—no! There is no way I'm taking you to see him. Why, so you can kill him? Or try to, again?"

"Calm down, already," Catie said, resting a hand on his good arm. "He said he wanted to see me try again, anyway. But no, that's not why I came along."

"Yeah right."

"I came because of Deuel."

Rodigger looked at her a few moments. "You two are as close as a groove joint, aren't you?"

She took her hand away. "I'm not sure what that is. Close as eel-skin?" she offered.

He stared where her hand had been. "What is eel skin close to?"

Catie opened her mouth, then shut it and squinted. "Its body?"

"Everything's skin is close to its body."

"Not a wrinkled lizard."

He looked up. "Well, it's still right there, I mean—"

"Rodigger..."

"You two are always talking about stuff! Always a little ahead or a little behind, heads together, sharing these little looks and expressions like you can read each other's minds."

Catie pursed her lips. *Probably shouldn't tell him—no.* "You know, if you tried to ride with us, we would either be forced to stop or turn to a gallop if we truly didn't want you around. Which might actually be funny," she said with a grin, "you chasing us down the road. We'd probably cover two inns a day."

Rodigger did not smile. "What's that supposed to mean?"

Catie looked at him seriously. "You always ride ahead, or fall behind, Rodigger, because Deuel makes you uncomfortable—maybe I do too, I don't know. But that's your choice, not ours."

"But...you know what he is," Rodigger said, his voice dropping to a whisper.

"Okay, let's say he is what you say he is, morally," Catie said. "And so to show your displeasure or disapproval, you ignore him, and get as much distance from him as you can. And let's say everyone who thinks the way you do, reacts the same way. Now Deuel is only surrounded by people who don't have a problem with who or what he is. If you think he can change, or you want him to change, or you *expect* him to change, how is the situation you've put him in going to do that? Or do you think he values your company *so* much he'll do whatever it takes to reconcile you to him, even by trying to ignore who he is?"

"I guess that's up to him," Rodigger said, gripping his left arm with his right.

Catie drew a sigh, and shook her head. "I think you don't care about Deuel, at least not as much as you care about your own piety. Whatever else you may say or think or believe, your goal is not the betterment of those around you, only the ability to say 'at least I'm not like them'."

"It's not like I'm the only way Deuel knows what he's doing is wrong," Rodigger returned. "He's been around a long time. I'm sure he's heard it before."

"A thousand drops of rain fill the bucket, Rodigger, but one makes it overflow." She peered south through the trees. She could hear, faintly, wheels clattering as they made their way up the sunbaked road. "Deuel better get back soon, that convoy is almost here."

As if in answer, Catie heard a footstep behind her, and she turned—but it was not Deuel. She leapt to her feet, already drawing the dagger from her boot as she yelped: "Rodigger!"

And then, before she could do anything else, Rodigger had leapt to his feet, drawing his own short blade from his boot, and with a sweep and a lunge both nomads fell to the earth. She gazed at him as he stared mutely over his work, both of their chests heaving.

"How long have you had that?" she asked quietly.

He looked at the blade, then quickly away. "Um, a while now. Why are they up to their ankles in mud?"

Catie looked, then looked again. They had fallen backward, knees bent, feet buried in what had to be a hands-breadth of mud.

"Magic," Deuel replied, striding down the hill toward them.

"Oh, thank the God," Catie said.

"What?" Rodigger asked Deuel.

"It was only supposed to hold them till I could reach you," Deuel replied, putting his blades away as he neared. "But you did well."

"You can use magic?" Rodigger asked.

Catie rolled her eyes, barely suppressing a sigh. Now he would hate Deuel for that, too. What a waste of a conversation.

"Halm and Ro Thull can," Deuel said. "You should clean your blade, and let us meet the convoy."

Without seeing if Rodigger would comply, Deuel untied his horse and moved toward the road. The lead wagon was nearly abreast of them, and he called out loudly with a raised arm.

Catie glared at Rodigger as she moved to Kelsie and untied her as well. "You're trying too hard," she said.

"No, he's making it very easy," Rodigger replied. "You're trying too hard to accept him."

"Fine, keep ignoring him," Catie spat. "Let me know how it works out."

"You should ignore him, too," Rodigger replied. "If everyone pushed him away, he would change. The human need for companionship is one of the strongest motivators."

"I suppose that comes from Roth, too?"

"What if it does?"

"Deuel's not human," Catie replied. "So your plan is flawed. Not to mention you will never get everyone to do what you want. In lieu of that, you might try my suggestion of actually caring about Deuel, and not yourself."

Are you coming?

Catie looked sharply toward the road, where Deuel stood beside the lead wagoner staring at her. *Did you just talk to me in my head?*

It was probably too far to see if he reacted, but she saw nothing, and felt nothing either. But it had sounded like him, at least a little. Maybe she had just suddenly become aware of how much time had passed. Maybe she was just tired of speaking to Rodigger. She led Kelsie through the trees without another word to him.

The merchants did have medicinal items. Catie cleaned and properly bandaged Rodigger's arm, still without speaking. The right glare, and he seemed to know what she expected of him. Probably he was smart enough, just didn't care to think ahead. It was a shame, really. He had just somewhat heroically saved her life, without regard for his pain, had done it out of apparent reflex. As if coming to her rescue was the deepest seed in his heart. But it didn't much matter when she knew his reaction would be far, far slower—petrified, probably even—if it had been Deuel in her place. Maybe that wasn't fair. How like life.

Once the story of Rodigger's wound was told, the merchants were more than happy to have some fighters—well, one at least—with them on the road north. They set out as the sun began to dip, with assurances they would reach the inn with some daylight left.

"Can either of you use weapons?" Deuel asked as they rode, now in the midst of the clattering wagon wheels and merchants' banter.

"I have been taught to use a sword, by Roth," Rodigger replied.

"I've used a bow for hunting," Catie said. "And I know my way around a Nagrath Dagger, if we can find one."

Rodigger smirked. "You think that will be useful against a sword?"

"If we find one, I'll show you," she replied sweetly.

"Why do you know that dagger?" Deuel asked quietly.

Her gaze darted to him. "My...father taught me before he left," she said uneasily. *He loved me like one.* "He wanted me to be able to take care of myself."

"Wasn't a very trusting man, was he?" said Rodigger.

"And yet here I am, in need of it," Catie replied, lofting an eyebrow.

They continued in silence, until Catie turned back to Deuel. "Where did those other two nomads come from?" she asked. "I thought you checked the area closest to us first."

"I did," Deuel replied, radiating regret. Catie gave him a forgiving grin, and he went on. "They are camped in a valley not far to the west."

Catie's grin faded. "They?" she echoed. "How many?"

"Too many," Deuel replied. "I do not know how they crossed the Tevorbath without being seen."

"Were you able to...?" She glanced at the back of his saddle, where his blades were sheathed.

"Too many," Deuel repeated.

"We're in a pretty remote area," Rodigger suggested. "If they crossed at night, who would see them?"

"And how did they cross the Balnathva?" Catie asked. "They would need a bridge—oh, no." Her eyes widened as she thought of Priska and Disceya. A glance at Deuel said he thought the same thing. "Maybe another sheep farm in the area," she said aloud, probably for Rodigger's benefit. She drew a deep breath. They would have done to it what the others did to Priska and Disceya. "But why would they risk it?" she wondered aloud. "There's nothing over there, is there?"

"We do not know why they are leaving the Wastes in the first place," Deuel replied.

"All the larger settlements are on the west side of the river, aren't they?" Rodigger asked. "I mean, they have been so far."

Catie nodded, her brow furrowed. "Well, outside of Ravverbit and Merneset, I think it's called. But Merneset is in the Wastes, so they don't need access to it. I wonder if there's a way to get news from there."

"Probably in Ravverbit," Deuel said.

Catie shook her head and sighed. "Plenty of answers to be had," she said. "And they're all a month away."

They continued in silence as the sun fell. When an orange smudge still lingered to the west, they could see lights far ahead on the road, marking the inn. But they had seen no farms or bridges across the river.

Around dinner, they discovered one of the merchants was carrying hunting bows bound primarily for Dagget's Vatenvilt. After dinner Catie purchased one. With Gabriel gone, Rodigger's funds were stretching even further.

"I'd like to practice, some," Catie murmured to Deuel when Rodigger was distracted by two merchants who were especially proud of Sheppar's kinnigship. Deuel followed her silently out of the inn.

In the stables, she found an empty sack draped over a stall and stuffed it with hay. While Deuel watched by torchlight she practiced until she could cluster three arrows in a hands-breadth from twenty-five paces. He stood silently nearby as she emptied the sack again

"Why do you not still have your father's Nagrath Dagger?" he asked suddenly, quietly.

Catie busied herself with inspecting some of the arrowheads. "I, uh, threw it into the lake," she said absently. She sighed and lowered the arrows, looking at Deuel. His gaze showed nothing in return. "Actually, he wasn't my father. He helped raise me, but..." She told him the rest, as Grandmother had told her before they left Attelek. "My mother, when she said she was leaving, said I would be able to take care of myself since he had taught me the Dagger. I guess I hoped she would stay if I lost it." She looked away for several long moments, then briefly shook her head, turned, and muttered gentle nothings to Kelsie. Finally she cleared her throat.

"How do your blades work?" she asked.

"You do not despise magic?" Deuel returned.

She shrugged. "I guess I should," she said with a brief glance. "I'm sure you've heard of things going on in Burieng because of it, too."

Deuel gazed at her for a few long moments. "I am not sure how *you* have, though," he said.

She turned back to face him now. "Oh, in Bokessin. I met a merchant who had recently come back from a voyage there."

"And yet you are curious."

"That's generally true," Catie replied with a small grin. "But you know how magic is, running around and doing all this damage by itself, with no one to control it."

Deuel appreciated her sarcasm. "You know how magic works."

"Some, just from being told why it's so wicked."

"Do you know there is a metal that has affinity to the elements? That can conduct it, like riverbanks conduct a river?"

Catie shook her head.

"It is called 'cretal'," Deuel continued. He pulled up a fold on his sleeve, revealing the bracelet underneath. It looked like rusted steel, but softer and clearer like rubies. Around the bracelet in a thin circle was a band of blue. He lifted the other sleeve. That bracelet had a band of red. "Water and fire," he said. "I have two others for wind and earth, but they are less versatile. Cretal also runs through the cuffs of Halm and Ro Thull, and through the rods and into the blade. The bracelets draw the magic and send it through to the blade."

"Why don't the blades have the magic in them? Because you would need four blades," she answered herself quickly. "Can you only do one spell each?"

Deuel shook his head. "I can speak a number of spells, and channel them through the blades. Some can be shot forth like an arrow, some remain on the blade until it strikes its target."

"So, who would win," Catie began.

"A magic-user," Deuel said quickly. She felt him smile. "If I were limited to using magic."

"You are otherwise very good, though," she said with a genuine smile. Something like a chuckle from him fluttered against her chest.

"I have my uses," he said.

"Deuel, how old are you?" she asked before she could stop herself. She instinctively reached up and began scratching Kelsie's forehead, her eyes boring into the mare's white star as she fought down the warmth surging into her face. After a few moments of silence, she glanced sideways.

Deuel was gone.

13

CHANGING MINDS

"They're almost there."
"Okay."
"Would this be a good time?"
"Better than most, I imagine."

24 Halmfurtung 1320 — Spring

They passed the days in peace as they approached Dagget's Vatenvilt. They noted only one crossing, a dilapidated but secure bridge across the Balnathva. There, too, the ground was torn by countless hooves. Catie was able to breathe a sigh of relief when the merchants told her that farm had been abandoned years before—no one to be killed, then, to be kept silent. With this viable crossing in place, the question remained of why they had also crossed further south, risking exposure and requiring such brutal murders to make it happen.

"And whether those two women made it out of there before anyone else came along," Catie added, rubbing her eyebrow. "They were probably trying to maneuver another group of soldiers across there, right? And why? What could they want?"

But no one could answer. The merchants had no dealings with the nomads, or with Merneset in the Wastes.

As the Vatenvilt wound into view, Catie hoped someone there might have news. It was not a large 'vilt, so close to Taferk, but for those heading south it was the last stop on the long road to Kendet's and Sprativerg. Many merchants would come from the north and turn around there, just as these merchants would turn back south when they left in the next few days.

The three companions went first to the Magiss. Rodigger's sword was easily purchased, but he scratched his head a few times at Catie's dagger.

"I know what they are," he said sourly. "We don't get much call for 'em. I could send you a hawk to Kostet's, maybe. He usually has stuff like that."

Catie cocked her head. "Where's Kostet's?"

"Just south of Agrend, corner of the Aug," he said.

Catie's eyebrows rose. "Could you send a message, instead of an order?"

The Magiss chuckled. "I can send one with an order: just a message is a waste of hawk, unless you pay me what I could make from a whole shipment floated down."

"No," Rodigger said loudly.

"I wouldn't, obviously," Catie said, rolling her eyes.

"No: no message," Rodigger replied. "He has to learn."

"Do you have something for me to write the message on?" Catie asked.

The Magiss shrugged and turned away. Catie followed as he went to his office.

"Hey!" Rodigger called after her, hurrying to catch up. "I said we could go see him eventually. I never said you could do this."

The Magiss glanced back at Rodigger, then raised an eyebrow at Catie. She shook her head. They went inside.

"Catie, I absolutely forbid it," Rodigger continued. "We can't let our job be interfered with by this!"

"Rodigger, you're an idiot," she said calmly.

The Magiss placed a parchment and quill at the edge of his desk and glanced at Rodigger. "Should I make you wait outside?" he asked.

As Catie bent and grasped the quill, Rodigger strode forward and seized her arm. She turned suddenly, pouring all her fury into her gaze, like she had never done before.

The blood left his face as his pupils dilated so wide his irises nearly disappeared. His hand on her arm trembled and she saw his legs shaking. In the last moment, she feard suddenly to see a spreading stain on his trousers.

The door crashed open. The Magiss protested as Deuel strode in, grabbed

Rodigger by the collar and dragged him out, never once looking at Catie.

When the door closed again, the quill in Catie's hand shook. She brought a hand to her mouth, trying to calm the corners and remember how to breathe.

"Seems like a right bugger," the Magiss said. "Ma'am?" he asked, noticing her trembling.

Her lungs opened, and she took a deep breath. "Sorry," she said, turning away for a moment. "He can be aggravating at times, but I probably went a little too far, there."

The Magiss snorted. "Seemed like he deserved it."

"No," Catie said, finally turning to the page. "No, he definitely did not."

She calmed herself enough to write a message, then rolled it and handed it to the Magiss. "It would be in everyone's interest if this made its way to Sheppar," she said. The Magiss started to grin, until he looked in her eyes. She broke contact as quickly as she could. "Something is going wrong, and he needs to know about it."

"Right," he said. "And do you want that dagger?"

She shook her head. "We don't have time to wait for it. I'll just have to get it from the source," she said with a smile.

The Magiss grinned and gave her a slight nod. "I'll get this out," he said.

She thanked him, and left. Deuel was waiting when she returned to the road. Rodigger was nowhere in sight.

"Wait here," Deuel said, striding quickly into the office. Catie stood, hands folded together. Deuel quickly reappeared.

"Walk with me," he said.

She swallowed. "Deuel, I know—"

But he had already continued past her. She followed, trying to keep her head high.

"No," he said finally, as the last inn dropped behind them. "You know, perhaps, because I have told you. But you do not understand."

"Understand what?" she pleaded. "I didn't mean to do it. And I promise I won't do it again. Deuel! You know how Rodigger can get, and he was worse than ever."

Deuel turned so suddenly, she halted by bumping into his chest. He grasped her shoulders and looked into her eyes. "I don't know what's happening with you," he said in a fierce whisper. "You can feel and radiate more than anyone should. Every dragon and behamian in all Oren felt your fury, just as they would have felt Kaoleyn's. They will not know why such anger is burning, and it is contagious, Catie. They will feel they are being threatened—first in Burieng, and now Andelen, and next...anywhere else it arises. And when behamien and dragons feel threatened, they behave just as humans do: they see danger everywhere, and feel hate everywhere. It is too late for you to never do it again! *I* know it was Rodigger, an utterly insignificant human being. But they will not. Our existence was tenuous when we were thriving. But now humans expand their settlements, and we cannot thrive."

Tears were running great tracks down Catie's face. "I'm sorry, Deuel," she mumbled through a sob. "I really, really didn't mean to."

Deuel drew a sigh, then held her close. "I know." One of his hands slid to the base of her neck, then across to her shoulder, pausing for a moment before sliding down her back and falling away.

"Do I have to explain anything to Rodigger?" she asked, her voice muffled against his chest.

"Yes," Deuel said. "But I believe you will have time to think about it."

"He's terrified of me."

He pressed a cheek against the top of her head. *He should be. Men like him are not worthy of you.*

Catie's sniffle stopped, but she stayed against his chest. *How do you do that?*

Deuel's head shifted a fraction. *All behamien can do that. The question, Catie, is how can you do that?*

I blame you. I couldn't do this before you came around.

Deuel shifted again, then held her at arm's length, gazing into her eyes. *There is probably more truth to that than you know.* "And we should not encourage your connection, I fear."

"Probably too late now, isn't it?"

"That is what I fear," he responded.

"What about Rodigger? Doesn't he have the sense, too? He understood my anger."

"No. He can understand when a dog is angry or happy, too."

"Thanks," Catie drawled, smiling to take the edge off.

"It has nothing to do with you," he replied. "It does not matter how clearly you speak if the person listening does not want to hear."

"Why do you think he's like that?"

"In Rodigger's case, he probably believed a lie and was, at some point, disillusioned," Deuel said, letting his hands finally slide from her shoulders.

"But he still does not trust himself to discern fact and fiction. So instead of deciding truth for himself, he found a person to trust and accepted everything they said. It was probably whoever exposed the first lie."

"But isn't he still risking belief in a lie?"

"Of course." Deuel drew a sigh. "But he has to believe something. Now he no longer risks disillusionment."

Catie hugged her arms. "I couldn't do that," she muttered.

"You believe truth is foundational, and can always be found—that lies will eventually be revealed and fall away."

Catie glanced away for several long moments. "If we keep looking for it, yes," she said finally. "Which means we have to keep questioning even what we think is right. Which is a lot of work, I guess."

She felt him snort. "Sometimes you humans think too much about effort and too little about consequences," he said. "It is a wonder the fortified inns were ever built."

Catie grinned ruefully. "Yes, Andelen is much safer now, with those inns. Safe even for nomads to cross the Tevorbath without resistance."

"Because the truth we believed was never again questioned," Deuel replied. He gazed northwest, where, eventually, Balnath Agrend lay. "Let us hope Sheppar still risks disillusionment."

Rodigger stood at the window in their room on the second floor of the inn, looking down the road as Catie and Deuel embraced. He swallowed hard. She had wanted to kill him—would have, if Deuel hadn't arrived and plucked him from death. Yet now he held her tenderly. Which was disgusting, really: she was twenty-three, he was three hundred? And behamian.

He both dreaded and longed to return to Roth. How could he face his mentor after so long in the presence of these two, allowing it to continue? But how much longer could he stand to be with them? If only he could trust solving the riddles of the next two Berkarfor.

He scratched at his bandaged arm as Catie and Deuel finally put some space between themselves. He wondered, briefly, what they were talking about. Probably better not to know. He could, possibly, ride out without them and get to the goblet first. Then if he couldn't solve it, they would catch up, he would apologize, and Catie would have to take him back because he was her link to Roth.

His scratching ceased. He would be rid of them, at least for a while—maybe forever. Catie would never even come close to Roth again. There was every chance for reward and almost no chance for failure.

But could he get a whole day ahead of them?

His arms dropped to his sides. There was a way. It would take even more forgiveness if he failed to decipher the riddle. But what choice would Catie have? And Deuel, he felt sure, would follow Catie. He watched as Deuel's hands slid down her arms and hesitantly drop away.

There was a way.

Rodigger lay awake with his eyes closed for what seemed like hours, waiting for Deuel to fall asleep. Something seemed to keep the...*it*...up, not tossing and turning, but breathing like he was awake. Once or twice, when Rodigger dared to glance over, he swore he could see Deuel blinking. Rodigger had never seen him blink in daylight, but he seemed to at night.

Finally, when there was surely no way the creature could be awake, he peeled the blankets off and sat up gingerly. He watched Deuel for a few moments, waited for the dragon-spawn to look at him or say something, then stood as quietly as he could. He picked up his boots and saddlebags, and with no shuffling footfalls made his way out the door. The lamps were trimmed low in the hallway, he was relieved to find, so there was no violent light to intrude into the room and wake the thing.

He glanced toward Catie's closed door and felt a twinge of guilt just as his forearm twinged with an awkward twist of the saddlebags. She had helped him, earlier, and had even been nice.

But then her blazing eyes and murderous intent flashed to mind. Rodigger's eyes narrowed, and he made his way out into the night.

Gared did not appreciate being woken, and made it known several times before he was saddled. Catie's and Deuel's Midlands, he was delighted to find, were steadfast animals who didn't complain about work no matter what the hour. They took bit and bridle without question, and thought nothing of being led out of the 'vilt without their masters. If they were going to be this cooperative, Rodigger began to wonder just where he should let them go.

Catie's eyes opened and she was awake, as if she had only blinked and the night had gone. The thoughts she had fallen asleep with were still with her. Only the sun coming through the window told her she had indeed slept.

Rodigger.

She wasn't sure what to think about having that man on her mind so much. She certainly would have liked to avoid it, but there he was—which, she realized, was just like him; making himself known no matter how much she didn't want to know.

You should wake up, now.

I thought we weren't going to encourage this?

Perhaps I just enjoy being lazy.

I find that hard to believe. Rodigger, perhaps, but not you.

Then this morning is full of events hard to believe.

Catie paused, brow furrowed, one foot in a boot, the other not. *What did he do?*

Will you control your emotions?

Her furrow smoothed, and she drew a breath. He got shot again—no, she might be sad or sympathetic, but not angry. He kept her letter from being sent? He sent a second letter? She sighed. He was capable of anything. *I have to find out sometime.*

He left in the night.

Catie closed her eyes. *Alone?*

For the most part.

Her eyes slitted open. For the most part? Who would he take with him? *Deuel, tell me he didn't...*

He did.

Catie's other foot thudded into the boot and she stood. *Where are you?*

Meet me in the common room.

When she arrived, she found the room mostly empty. Two sat at a table finishing their breakfast, one sat in a corner and seemed to have spent the night there. One serving girl sat behind the counter cleaning mugs. The keeper was nowhere to be seen.

Deuel entered, the sounds of the street waxing and waning behind the swinging door as daylight intruded, then retreated. Then it was dim and silent, with one bright square of sunlight through a window and dull lamplight, and occasional rubbing squeaks of the barmaid's rag in a mug. Catie drew a slow breath as she watched Deuel cross the room to a table away from the others. She sat, but still said nothing, listening to the stillness and enjoying the gloom, wishing they could cover the window and keep out the bright sun.

Deuel's eyes were intent on her, she realized. She returned the gaze and, after a few moments, seemed to surface from a deep lake.

"I guess I shouldn't have told him where we were going," she said.

"Perhaps." His gaze had not lost its intensity, but something in him, too, seemed to come back to the present. Catie wondered vaguely where they had both gone.

"Did he forget you can fly to him and catch him?"

"We still must retrieve the horses and bring them back here. He left most of the tack. He may let them drift after half a day, too."

"Kelsie will come back here on her own," Catie said firmly, putting her hands on the table in front of her.

"That may be worse, trailing her reins."

Catie cocked an eyebrow. "Kelsie can handle herself, I'm sure."

"You know her better. There is still the question of why he wants to delay us."

"Probably because I wanted to kill him yesterday," she said, and shrugged one shoulder. "He's already afraid of you. Now if he's afraid of me too...he's probably trying to escape."

"We might discuss if we should let him."

Catie sat in the stillness again. The sunlight was very bright, streaming through that window. It wasn't natural, putting windows in walls. If you built a cave, you must live in a cave.

"Why do you seek the Berkarfor, Catie?"

"To bring justice to Roth," she said absentmindedly. Silence. Stillness. Coolness. Caves were wonderful places, once you got used to them.

"Why do you need to bring justice to him?"

"He killed...someone," she said, barely conscious that she wasn't really paying attention anymore. "A lot of people, actually." There wasn't the stress and helter-skelter of life, in a cave. Just silence, stillness, coolness, and slow change.

"What would you do if you were free from bringing Roth to justice?" Deuel asked quietly.

Silence. Stillness. Coolness. Peace. That was it: complete and utter peace. No hurry, no fuss or bother.

But she couldn't. Kelsie was gone. She could walk. Walking wasn't the best. But it wasn't the worst. Or run. She was strong. Her hands clenched, her eyes bored into Deuel. "Balnath Agrend," she whispered, and wet her lips. And yet, when she said it, it wasn't right. It was a hollow resolve, a cave: firm and sturdy on the outside, empty on the inside. It would not fill her. But she had to get there! Run. She could run. She nearly stood up.

"Why there?" Deuel asked, his gaze boring back into hers.

"Silence. Stillness. Coolness. Peace," she heard herself saying. Why was she still sitting there? Why was he? He wanted to go too. He could fly. He could be there before she could, even if she were on horseback.

"Catie, you do not know what you're saying."

That was true. She didn't care. Walk. Run. Steal a horse. She had to get there. Her shoulders ached. She wished she could fly like Deuel!

Why?

Silence. Stillness. Coolness. Peace.

Was he keeping her there on purpose? He could get there first. He couldn't. She couldn't let him. Her jaw tightened, and her palms lay flat on the table.

"Catie."

She leapt up, her eyes afire. He *was* keeping her here! To get there first. She took a step away from the table. The room rocked and reeled. The floor became the wall and she leaned against it as the sun went suddenly black.

It was warm and soft, but still quiet. Blankets. And a bed. But quiet. Catie felt air drawing through her nose, and she breathed out a sigh. Her eyes opened and she saw the ceiling. A shadow in her periphery caught her attention: Deuel sat beside her, watching her.

"What happened?" she asked, her voice surprising her in strength and clarity.

"I think that answer will come when you answer my questions."

She looked at him, only blinking.

"When did your father die?"

"When I was very young," she said.

"Be specific."

"Late winter, 1305."

"Haschina," he suggested.

"I think so."

"Your mother left?"

"Haschina 33."

"That date means something to you," he noted.

"It means something to you, too."

"You can speak to me in your mind, and feel the emotions of dragons."

She looked at him long and silently. She could see the path of his mind, but it made no sense. She was not like him. For one thing, she didn't have wings. "Yes, but..."

"What is your earliest memory?"

She blinked. "That's not an easy question to answer."

"Try."

She closed her eyes, nestling back into the pillow. Grandmother's? It seemed like. Her baking in the kitchen, rolls or cookies. Grandmother made the best cookies. Catie was on the floor, playing with a doll? No, she was too high to be on the floor, because she dropped it and couldn't reach it. A chair? The floor seemed so far away, but she was reaching. Then Grandmother came over. No, she got down and got it. So she was old enough to get up and down from a chair. Then father came in to ask her to help, he'd just brought a deer.

Her eyes opened. Stillness. *No.* "Deuel, I don't know—" *Coolness.* She gritted her teeth against the thought.

"Try," he said again, his voice firm but his emotion calming.

"It seems like I'm too young for a clear memory, but old enough to help my father skin a deer," she said. "Which doesn't make sense."

"That's not it," he said. Now his emotion was firm and his voice calming.

"I don't want to pass out again," she said with a whimper.

"At least this time you won't hit the floor in front of other people," he said wryly.

"It's a little early to be drunk, isn't it?"

"A little."

"A cave," she said. "It kept running through my head, downstairs. Silence, stillness, coolness, peace. I thought you were trying to keep it from me, to reach the caves outside Balnath Agrend before me."

Deuel's brows furrowed—actually furrowed. She almost laughed, but the fact that her response troubled him that greatly stopped her. "What is it?" she asked.

The furrows disappeared. "The destination is correct," he said, "but not the early memory. Dragons—behamien—are not born or raised in caves."

"Well of course I'm not behamien," Catie replied. She flexed one of her shoulders forward. "No wings."

"I noticed. But you are *something,* Catie, something I've not seen before. Everything else fits, except the cave."

"But how? I thought you said I couldn't be anything like that?"

Deuel sighed. "You must forgive me that: it was an idea impressed...forcefully...upon us as children. No behamian I know would mate with a human, but behamien have mated with each other before becoming dragons. It was more frequent when we were many. Now it is greatly discouraged."

"But why?"

"Because we cannot change after giving birth in human form. I do not know why," he said as her mouth opened. "The teaching is that by so doing we are choosing our human forms over our dragon forms. In early times this was not seen as a bad thing. But as I said we are far from thriving, and behamien removed permanently from the pool threaten our survival."

"So my parents were behamien but I didn't know it? I don't remember my mother having wings either."

"No. If they were, you would be less advanced than you are." *We would not be able to speak like this, for one thing. Feeling my emotions, yes. But not complex communication.*

This doesn't seem that complex. We're just speaking.

You interpret what I'm saying because your mind knows Rinc Nain. If you spoke Cariste, or Isan, or Clanason, I could still speak to you this way and you would understand me. Because I am not speaking Rinc Nain, truly. And neither are you.

That seems very complicated.

I told you so.

"Oh, hush." *That doesn't help me know what I am.*

No, it does not. That may come later.

I'm not sure if I like that answer.

Good. It means you will keep seeking.

Catie paused and drew a breath. "Am I...do wyverns start as humans?"

Deuel gazed at her for several very long and uncomfortable moments. She wished, just this once, that he would let his emotions out just a little more than he did. Finally he took a deep breath. "I think we must assume they do," he said. "Perhaps that is why wyverns do not have arms. Yours will become wings, if you change."

She hadn't expected him to agree with her. Now that he did, there was nothing left to hold on to and she whirled away in the flood, an autumn leaf down a raging waterfall. Now more than ever she needed the silence, stillness, coolness, and peace. Especially the peace. But questions pounded down the door of her head, and fear and despair obliterated her heart.

"I don't want to be a wyvern," she managed to say.

Deuel was with her, holding her close and smoothing her hair. He had to know that made it worse. Well, it made her heart worse. So she allowed herself to cry that part out, clinging tightly to him and trying to gain some footing with her head. Questions could be answered. Emotions only did what they wanted.

"Do I have to change?" she asked, plucking up the first question that swirled through.

"No," he said. "I was committed to Gabriel the first time the Call came, and I stayed with him rather than answer it. It is...difficult, but with disciplined focus it can be done."

"Will you be able to help me?"

"Of course."

"So will I live a long time, too? As long as you?"

"I do not know. I think perhaps you have already lived longer than you realize."

There were more questions, awkward ones that she refused entrance into her conscious mind lest Deuel accidentally hear them. She drew a breath. Time to disengage. She squeezed once, then slowly sat back. He let her go, but continued looking at her. She didn't want to look at him, so she closed her eyes and rubbed them.

"I'm sorry," she said.

"I am sure you should have heard that from someone else, someone...wyvern," he added cautiously. "I know very little, but I will do what I can."

She smiled. "Thanks." With another deep, steadying breath she was able to look up at him. "So, what do we do now? About Rodigger."

Deuel paused. "Rodigger probably does not intend to keep our horses. I can go get them, or we can let them return alone. After that is up to you."

"We still need to retrieve the Berkarfor, "Catie replied. "You know Rodigger won't be able to, and it will make him more pliable if we don't punish him once we catch up. But I would like Kelsie back here sooner, especially with nomads strangely loose." Her eyes went wide at the thought. "You don't think they've already gotten her?"

Deuel shook his head. "Rodan and I have been together long enough, I would feel, faintly, if he were distressed. But I agree: we should not increase the chance. I will return as swiftly as possible."

14

CHANGING REASONS

"This one here, now."
"You can still change your mind."
"It is still a patriarchal society."
"We can be agents of change, Teresh."

25 Halmfurtung 1320 — Spring

R odigger glanced up, then backward. The sun had reached its height, and the Midlands still followed dutifully, their reins slack. He almost wished they would give him trouble, make him angry. But instead they kept pace kindly, gazing at him without a hint of consternation.

His mouth twisted, and he stared resolutely ahead. They would just see. He'd let them go tomorrow, get a really good head-start. He was already working on a story to tell at the inn as to why he had two extra horses, that's what he was doing! He certainly wasn't thinking about letting them go so soon.

One of them—Deuel's—whinnied shortly. When he glanced back, its head was up, eyes skyward.

Rodigger's Therian stopped just as his own heart did. Rodigger's eyes shot to the clouds as he searched for any faint but swiftly-moving specks against them. Of course Deuel would fly out to retrieve the horses! He was so stupid!

He threw down the reins as if they scalded him. Gared responded to the urgency of the motion, starting off at a trot before Rodigger gave him heel or command—and when the frantic command did finally leave Rodigger's lips they broke into a gallop.

He needed to be far, far away from those horses. He glanced back, saw them turning away and heading back down the road to the 'vilt.

Good horses, he thought, his nerves leaping about under his skin. *Get away, now.* He couldn't tell whether to laugh or to cry, so he muttered and let the wind sting his eyes.

Several miles passed below Gared's hooves before Rodigger finally eased back in the saddle. Gared snorted and blew, and shook his head as if knowing how close they might have come to a violent death. Up ahead, a convoy heading toward the 'vilt appeared. *Could have sold the horses to them,* he thought. But then, he might have been hunted down as a horse-thief. *No saying that still won't happen. But Catie and Deuel wouldn't do that, would they?*

Catie might.

Rodigger shivered. What had he done?

Survive.

Rodigger sniffled, but his jaw set. He did, didn't he? He recognized a threat, and acted boldly and without thought to personal comfort or safety to avert it. Wasn't Roth always talking about that? He knew when Roth was disappointed in him the most—the two times: when he didn't think the same way Roth did, and when he acted out of selfish comfort rather than strength and courage.

Well. He had just stolen a behamian's horse, and the horse of a woman who wanted to kill him, in order to leave them far behind and retrieve Roth's Berkarfor on his own.

And yet, something stifled his joy. He studied the approaching convoy as he tried to figure out what it was. It was the glance up the road that gave him the clue: usually he would see Catie, either directly in front of him or in close periphery. Now there was only brown road and green grass. He had previously managed a way to look near her, but not at her, and yet focus so she was all he saw. Despite her rage and her intent to kill him, his heart still reached out after her.

He cared for her, he realized, more deeply than he had ever cared for anyone before. He wanted to know more about her, where she had come from and where she was going. He could smell her, as he thought about her—slightly floral just after leaving a city, or more like the open plain if they'd been traveling a while. Like cold grass and clean air, and a little bit like sunshine, too.

He blinked. There was also the cusp of mystery. The breathless anticipation of being at the beginning of the story, not knowing how it would end, but knowing they two would be companions through it. It was the threshold of the open door, on the other side of which lay a life with her, the first step of a long adventure, wondering what each new step would bring. He wondered what it would be like to hold her hand, to kiss her, to...

But she was back in Dagget's, and he was here, and her horse closer to him than her. She would be forever a day behind, at least, if she did not just go to Sheppar as she wanted to. He might never see her again.

He gripped the reins tightly, taking deep breaths through his nose despite the horse-stink as he met the convoy and passed through it. The wagoners eyed him, most of them, but no one asked him a question. Because he was a lone traveler, and they were merchants or drivers—surely nothing held in common. He would have been a messenger, perhaps, or some Magiss' son out for a ride on a warm day.

Rodigger ground his teeth as the last wagon clattered past. Not one "hello" or "good day." No recognition they were all Andelian, and could exchange pleasantries along the road.

And no warning of bandits ahead—or whatever those marauders were. Yes, marauders would be a good word. Maybe not marauders, that sounded too concerted, too planned. Sneaks. Thieves, most likely. Thieves, they would be, little raiding parties from little nomadic bands from their little, pathetic deserts. Certainly nothing to be overly concerned about. And not worth killing someone over.

He did miss the sight of her, though.

Kelsie whinnied happily to see Catie again as night fell. Deuel handed her the halter as he swung off Rodan, and she quickly set about checking her Midland mare.

"She seemed well," Deuel said. "They were browsing, but alert. He did not run them hard."

"At least that," Catie said, still running her hands over the mare, for her own conscience and to show Kelsie she cared. She was barely even dusty.

They led their mounts to the stalls and prepared them for the night. "Have you decided for certain to continue pursuing the Berkarfor?" Deuel asked.

"I think so," she replied as she brushed Kelsie. When Deuel remained still, she paused. "Is there some reason I shouldn't?"

Deuel resumed brushing Rodan. "No, not for you."

"But there is one for you?"

The brush slowed, hesitated, then resumed. But Deuel said nothing.

"Deuel, you know I can sense your feelings," Catie said. She paused, too, stretching her shoulders before resuming the task.

"With Paolound gone, behamien will be going to their *veythya* to await—"

Catie cut him off. "Deuel, I don't know what that word is."

"*Veythya*. It is...to summon change...to become..." He trailed off this time.

"A dragon. And you should have joined them months ago," Catie said, feeling his uncertainty. "But even if you tried now, it might not matter?"

"So I should not try?" he asked quickly.

"Deuel, I just reminded you I can sense your feelings, and that's all I have to go by. I don't know how all that works."

He drew a breath. "Of course not. *Veythya* takes time, different time depending on many things, some unknown. But if several behamien enter it, and one comes out first, the rest will remain in their states until the next dragon dies—then their process resumes."

"So one might have already become a dragon?"

Deuel shook his head. "The Calling all behamien feel would cease. No, Paolound's successor has not yet been born."

"And you want to go enter your *veythya* in case your process is shorter."

"The first time the Call came in my lifetime was during Sheppar's campaign. Gabriel was young, and deeply involved. I could not leave him—I had not learned enough about humans anyway."

"In a hundred years, twenty made a difference?"

She felt him smile. "His family was *aloik,* but they were not my first *aloiken.* But yes, twenty years has made a difference. When this Call came at the start of another journey important to Gabriel, I thought again I could not answer it."

"Now, perhaps, you can," Catie finished, continuing to brush Kelsie, to keep from looking at the dragon-son.

Deuel stepped away from his horse. He looked at Catie for several moments, until she paused to glance at him. "The Berkarfor were important to Gabriel because he was paid for them. Your mission is important to you for...more human reasons, I sense."

Revenge? Catie wondered. That was probably more human, though she wasn't sure Deuel should learn too deeply about that. Maybe if she called it 'justice'—but usually, if one sought justice outside of the law, it was just called 'revenge' again. *I'm not sure if that's reason enough for you to deny who you are.*

"Not for the Berkarfor," Deuel said as she realized she sent that last thought to him. "You seek to find out who you are. I believe that answer will inform who I need to be."

"I thought I was a wyvern."

"That may be the vessel in which you reside. But it does not mean that's who you are."

"Oh," Catie said. "And what if you're wrong?"

Deuel hesitated, and she could feel his mournful sigh. "Then I will need to know even more what it means to be human," he said. "I believe this is the first time the Call has come twice to one generation. I cannot assume it will come again before I die—so if I miss this one as well, I may never know what it means to be a dragon."

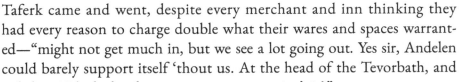

Taferk came and went, despite every merchant and inn thinking they had every reason to charge double what their wares and spaces warranted—"might not get much in, but we see a lot going out. Yes sir, Andelen could barely support itself 'thout us. At the head of the Tevorbath, and rightly so! It's the head as most necessary part, isn't it?"

At first Rodigger thought they finally had the right of it, seeing themselves as an integral part of a unified Andelen. By the third person he spoke to he realized they considered only themselves to be Andelen, and the rest of the country as babes on its teats. It was actually the fourth merchant who had used that exact phrase. Rodigger barely kept from shaking his head as he walked away, telling himself it wasn't just because he didn't have enough coin. There the road split, one arm heading west toward Fathistokset in the Rigarbod marsh, the other—the road Rodigger took—still north and slightly east toward Ravverbit.

As he rode one morning, Halmfurtung winding to a close as Spring settled in to stay, a wind came south through the canyon road to Ravverbit. On its eddies lay fragrances and spices which Rodigger had never smelled or sensed, and yet had some peculiar memory tucked in them too scant to blossom. When he tried to sniff deeper, he got mostly cool spring air that stung his nose and made his eyes water.

Ravverbit had only two man-made walls, one each to the south and north. To the east and west were the walls of the canyon, rising sheer and red till they gradually curved away, topped by spires that resembled stacked river-stones, and whatever rock *was* flat was gouged deep and rough—no cart or ballistae could traverse that terrain close enough to bring any destruction from above.

Not that the defenses were necessary, Rodigger noticed as he entered the streets: Ravverbit seemed to let anybody in who wished, without the need for violence. The spices grew thick and heavy, and now the peculiar memory was buried by overabundance. Men, women, and some children moved through the streets in both Andelian and Beltrath garb—and sometimes a weaver's nightmare of both. Simple homespun wool or cotton paired with light silks of every color including some, Rodigger was sure, didn't exist in the natural world. Horses and donkeys made way for taller, four-footed animals with long, U-shaped necks and two great hillocks on their backs, between which someone in even more layers of dazzlingly bright silk usually wallowed. He even heard some people speak in something other than Rinc Nain.

Vendors stalls were a similar hodgepodge of bright colors and strange scents and unusual wares. The shops, he was relieved to see, sold more typical fare—so at least the strange things were temporary. And, as he began to feel a little dizzy from the overwhelming assault on his senses, he realized the inns would likely be more standard fare as well. Unless there was some strange silk-swaddled creature pushing around rooms on wheels, he thought with a smirk—a smirk that caught the unblinking attention of one of the vendors. As the man glared at Rodigger, Rodigger couldn't help but stare back and let his smirk grow a little wider. What could the man do, attack him in broad daylight when he was clearly the interloper?

Distracted by the vendors and passersby in noticeable garb, Rodigger didn't see the man in dun and brown step away from a nearby building and follow after him.

He discovered the inns as he neared the center of town. He passed several where the noise of the common room might as well have not had a door between it and the street, and one or two others whose signs had script he did not recognize and images that did not evoke a sense of Andelen. Finally, at what seemed to be the precise center of the town, he found an inn that looked strangely familiar. As it was surrounded by the rest of the city, several moments passed before Rodigger realized it was a fortified inn, still there from when Ravverbit didn't yet exist. He smiled, and led his horse to the stable at the back, exactly where it belonged.

The evening passed quietly enough: Deuel didn't come swooping in and demand retribution for stealing his horse, and Catie didn't come running up demanding the same. The inn was well tended, but not well patronized. And by the second song of the sitting minstrel Rodigger thought he knew why. But it suited him anyway.

That night, several nightmares came to him, mostly of being shot with an arrow and men in strange clothing surrounding him. Once, the man changed into Catie just as the knife thrust forward, and her hate-filled eyes sparked with joy as she ripped open Rodigger's gut. In another, he defended himself, and watched the gleam in her eye fade as her own blood spilled. When he woke from that one, he wasn't sure which ending he preferred. But it was in that moment, as the early morning scents from the kitchen wafted into the cot-room, that he realized what fragrance it was he was remembering: it was the smell of those bandits, the thieves—what did he decide to call them?

What did it matter? The town reeked of those creatures! They were stealing across Andelen, killing some people and taking others, and shooting him with arrows. And now he was in the middle of them.

Slowly and quietly, he peeled off the blankets and reached down toward his locked chest. He cracked his knuckles on the lid, and in horror realized it was already open. He swallowed, his mind racing. Were they here, then? He turned his head slowly. The morning sun didn't come into the windows, now that there were buildings in the way, but there was light enough to see shadows and shapes, if they were there. But he saw nothing.

He got out of the bed, stepping quietly in his stocking feet. He checked the chest—his things were definitely gone. But his boots still lay at the side of the cot where he left them, so he picked those up and made his way into the common room.

One man was already there. Rodigger almost didn't see him, dressed in tan and brown clothing that fit more tightly than the flowing silks of the foreigners—Beltraths, they must be—and looked more utilitarian than the Andelian clothing. He was sitting behind a table on which lay Rodigger's things.

"I hoped you wouldn't sneak out the back," the man said, his accent such that he made 'd' sounds at every opportunity. For a brief moment Rodigger thought maybe the man had a cold. His hand strayed to his belt before he saw his knife lying front and center of his effects.

"It is a very nice knife," the man said, his eyes never leaving Rodigger's yet somehow seeing his every move. "But you should not have it back yet. Why are you alone?"

"Why, uh, why shouldn't I be alone?" Rodigger asked, working some of the sleeping thickness out of his throat.

"Because you were not alone one month ago."

"And you know this, how?" Rodigger's stomach—already a shriveled apple—tightened.

"I was told this by one who had seen this; do I need to convince you further?"

Rodigger shrugged, a motion intended for himself and the flurry of questions and fears running through his own mind. But it sufficed for the other man, as well.

"Where is the wingéd man?"

It took Rodigger a second to recognize the stress on the 'e', and he shrugged again.

"He has left you?"

"If I'm lucky," Rodigger muttered.

The man looked puzzled. "This is a strange thing."

One of the myriad questions finally popped out: "Who are you?" Rodigger asked. Blurted, really, though he didn't mean to.

"Sharéd Dusslin."

Now that one question had come out, the rest tumbled out behind it. "What are you doing here? What do you want? Why do you have my stuff? Why didn't you just talk to me when I woke up?"

Sharéd's gaze never wavered. "I am looking for the wingéd man. I want the wingéd man. I have your things because I will take you as well. And one does not speak to his captive. Normally."

Rodigger swallowed as his eyelids suddenly couldn't open as wide as he wanted them to. "What about now that the wingéd man isn't with me anymore?"

"Now I think you and I, we will spend much time together, and it could become boring if we do not speak."

And yet, Rodigger and Sharéd remained silent for a time—Sharéd's eyes relaxed but considering, Rodigger's eyes tight and thoughtless.

"Do we wait here—?"

"We wait for the wingéd man."

"His name is Deuel," Rodigger said.

Sharéd hissed, and the knife-point gouged the table. "He is the wingéd man and you will call him the wingéd man in my presence."

Silence again, for a time. Rodigger tried breathing, finding it noisy in the empty common room.

"Can I sit down?" he asked faintly.

Sharéd was silent. He began twirling the knife, point against the table and drilling mildly into it. Rodigger took the silence as acceptance and sat down. The bench scraping back and forth like the tolling of church bells without the echo—but just as loud and attention-arresting. The silence grew again.

But as the silence stretched on, Rodigger's mind began miraculously to move. "He might not come here," he said, as if there had been no break in the conversation.

The twirling stopped. "Why would he not do this?"

"Well, I stole his horse. He may not exactly give me another chance—or the one with him."

"The girl?" he asked, pronouncing it 'girrel'.

Rodigger nodded, trying to keep his lower lip from protruding just a little. "She'll probably be just fine with you keeping me captive."

"This is not to do," Sharéd replied. "Why are they your enemies?"

"Don't you know about the revolution?"

The twirling and silence resumed. Sharéd's eyes glinted as he studied Rodigger for some time. Finally, he said only: "yes."

"Oh. Well, they're on the other side."

"So of course they are your companions," he said drily.

"Well it wasn't my idea," Rodigger said, slouching a little.

"Where will they go, if not here?"

"We were headed to Kavlen. They may go straight there. Maybe not. But I think if you let me continue my mission, we'll definitely run into them again somewhere along the line."

"Why would they not go straight there? They have another mission?"

"Uh-mmm, no, I don't think so. Can't think of one," he said, shaking his head and forgetting to stop.

"You said 'maybe not' with some significance, I think," Sharéd replied. "Enough to assure me it would not matter if they did not."

Rodigger's voice started high and went low: "No! I just mean, I mean, you can't tell with those two. A wingéd man and someone who seems to want to please him more than those of their own kind? She wants to find, um, to continue the mission, with me, at least at the end. Dey—a—he, I mean, there's no telling what he wants." The shaking continued.

Sharéd's hand rested on the pommel of the knife, still driven point-down into the table, as he considered Rodigger sideways. "You are a very bad liar," he said, "and yet you tell some truth. What is this you seek at Kavlen?"

"Just something Roth sent me to do. Talk to the people there, try to gain some sympathizers." It helped that was partially true, as well.

"It has nothing to do with this?" Sharéd asked, raising his other hand: in it was the first Berkarfor.

Very few people could have resisted the urge to startle noticeably when one of their greatest secrets was revealed, and Rodigger was not one of those people. To his credit, he didn't say anything at first. But then the shaking head resumed, mute.

"It is a very nice cup," Sharéd said musingly, turning it over in his hand. "Perhaps I shall drink from it whenever we stop."

"I don't think that's a good idea," Rodigger said, his voice quivering.

"But surely it is not important? Why do you carry it?"

Rodigger shrugged. "Just something we found along the way. But it's very old, and we found it deep underground and it's probably been there forever. And I haven't washed it."

"That can be relieved."

"Wash something that old? I'd be afraid of damaging it myself. Which is why I haven't washed it yet. Obviously."

"I have said you are a bad liar, and yet you still try," Sharéd replied, setting the cup on the table and continuing to drill with the knife.

"I'm trying to practice," Rodigger replied in a rare attack of wit.

"You should have practiced long ago. But we will go to this Kavlen and wait for the wingéd man," Sharéd said, and then smiled. "And his friend."

The Beltrath's smile and last words stuck with Rodigger as they left Ravverbit, the infrequent silence that marked their conversation falling utterly now. Rodigger led, Sharéd close behind. His mount was clearly the purer physical specimen, and could give short chase if Rodigger tried to flee.

Fairly assured he was not going to die—and even feeling oddly safer, now that one of the thieves was his escort—Rodigger kept playing those words and that smile in his mind. The words could have meant one thing, which would mean Rodigger would be that much safer with one less person in Andelen who seemed to want him dead. Or the smile could have meant something else, in which case there would be one less person from Beltrath who potentially wanted him dead: there was no doubt in his mind that if Sharéd tried what that smile indicated, Catie would kill him, and probably have no trouble with it. Not that Sharéd seemed incompetent, but he probably wouldn't be ready for her. And yet...

"Sharéd, what do you want the wingéd man for?" Rodigger asked that night as the thief was binding his wrists and ankles.

"You will learn this when he comes," Sharéd replied with a few grunts as he made the knots tight.

"I mean, do you intend to kill him?" Rodigger tested the ropes. They were tight.

Sharéd sat back, studying Rodigger in the firelight. "Do you think I could?" he asked, almost as if wondering to himself. Rodigger's eyes strayed aside, then snapped back. Sharéd blinked. "I do not think this I could, if I wanted to."

"Then you definitely don't want to kill me?"

Sharéd's head cocked sideways. "Do you want me to? It is a long road to Kavlen, and you are not in the position to resist, right now."

Rodigger's eyes went wide as he tested the ropes again. Still tight. "What would you want to do that for?"

Sharéd stared into Rodigger's eyes. "Because you annoy me. Because you are a burden. Because you are not part of the plan." He shrugged. "The reasons are many."

The plan? Rodigger's mind began to turn, concocting reasons for wanting Deuel. It was difficult, since he wanted him for nothing, and more so after stealing his horse. But what plan could include such a creature? He tried to think like Roth, the best planner Rodigger knew.

He closed his eyes, and barely kept a curse behind his teeth. "Sharéd," he said quietly. "If you want to find the *winged* man, he is usually in the sky."

Sharéd's face went slack. "Why you did not say this earlier?" he asked flatly.

Rodigger glared at his captor. "Because you stole my things and made me think you were trying to kill me! Because it's *winged,* not win-*ged,* you wandering idiot! Now release me before I pelt you with all Roth's coin until it sticks in your skin and poisons you, and we find someone else to lead your people's part in this mission!"

15

TRUE COLORS

"I'm not sure how you manage this."
"Actively."
"It seems a difficult balance."
"Balance is easier if you are moving."

1 Fimman 1320 — Spring

Samdar glanced over the rolls of parchment in front of him with a sigh. *Join the kinnig's closest advisors and read all day.* Samdar knew Sheppar wanted to be a king for all people, not just the rich and powerful. But did he realize how many people wanted to write notes to him and tell him how to be a better—and sometimes worse—king because of that? *Rulers and people in authority should be unreachable* Samdar thought. Maybe not truly a good idea. But right now, when it was his job to read what had come for Sheppar's...edification...it was the best idea.

As he reached for the one to his farthest left—may as well approach it methodically—he noticed a piece of script on the side of another one closer to him. *I know that hand.*

He did: it was from Deuel. How many updates had Samdar read from Deuel during the campaign? Had tried not to read between the lines, but had been too close to the behamian not to see it—had known it would be there as soon as the order went out... Anyway. Deuel had never brought it up, so why should he?

Unless the dragon-son was bringing it up now. Samdar picked up the roll. It was addressed directly to him. And why wouldn't it be? He broke the seal and rolled it open.

It was a different script inside. Shakier. Someone who was not comfortable writing, but at least it was legible. As he read, his eyes first grew wide in amazement and horror, then narrowed in skepticism.

But at the end, there was Deuel's confirmation in his script. The report was true. A few details were added by Deuel concerning more accurate numbers...

By the God—and where? West of the Tevorbath?

The rest of the letters would wait. Sheppar needed to know about this immediately.

And yet, as Samdar stood quickly and threw on his cloak, he could imagine what the aging kinnig might say. *Maybe not if it was from Deuel. Surely Sheppar realizes how much he owed the behamien who had served him in the campaign.*

Samdar found the kinnig in the gardens. A few early tulips were blooming already, and buds were on many of the others, but it was certainly not yet the vision of a garden it would be. There was something hopeful about it, he realized as he approached. And he hoped Sheppar had one more season in him as well.

"My lord?" he called as he neared, also imagining Sheppar's response to *that*.

"Samdar, we have been together too long for that," he said. As was fore-told.

"That time has only reinforced the status," Samdar replied with a bow as Sheppar turned.

Sheppar's smile was easy, but mixed. "What is it?"

"I've received a very troubling letter from Deuel, my lord," he said. At Sheppar's dark grimace, he hurried on. "He's reporting movement in the Tevorbath, my lord. The Beltraths are coming out of the Waste in some very large numbers."

Sheppar stood motionless for a few moments. "What large numbers?" he asked finally.

"Deuel estimates five hundred in one encampment alone, that he saw."

"Five *hundred?* Does he say what they are doing?"

"He did not have time to investigate fully, my lord. He was unclear as to what, but something else has his attention right now. He reports that the nomads had not hesitated to kill anyone who observed their movements."

Sheppar closed his eyes. "The day is coming," he said softly. "I had hoped others would not pay my due."

"My lord?"

Sheppar's eyes opened. "You know as well as anyone else, we could not have done what we did in the campaign without making some enemies."

"I would have thought those enemies would have come from some-where...nearer by," Samdar replied, then pressed his lips together and dropped his head as he realized what he was saying.

Sheppar laid a hand on his shoulder. "So did I, old friend."

"My lord, what are we going to do about this incursion?"

Sheppar sighed. "Did the message come through one of the 'vilts?"

"It did, my lord."

"Then the magiss will need to handle it. It is their duty."

Samdar kept his sigh short. "My lord, the 'vilts are not made for that—you designed them! They are for trade only. And any of the villages or towns in the area have not had to stop an incursion in more than a generation. You've heard about Kavlen, how that village alone has changed. We cannot leave this to them."

"On the contrary, dear friend," Sheppar replied, moving along the paths of the garden as slowly as he spoke. "If what you say is true, then they need, more than anything else, to handle this incursion and learn from it, and stop relying on an old man to always come save them. It is the future."

"My lord, they may not have a future if we do not stop this."

Sheppar laughed hoarsely. "Five hundred Beltraths will not do so much devastation as that," he said. "Besides, they're probably coming for me and Balnath Agrend. It's been said: 'strike the head and kill the body.' Well, they can strike this head if they want. Why do you think I've been drawing back for the past twenty years?"

"You saw this coming? That long ago?"

"Samdar, I saw it coming when I made the decision. I knew I needed to strike, and then fade away. And when I'm gone, Andelen won't miss me." He paused his stride, looking out over the budding garden, nearly ready to explode in summer blooms. "No, each village and town will go on as it has.

Andelen may even be better for it, you know?" His deep blue eyes settled on Samdar, and the aide saw in them the glint of a man old and tired, yet victorious in a fruitful life ripening exactly as he'd meant it to.

But Samdar still only saw tenuous buds, nothing yet ready to pick. "And what about Roth's rebellion in the south?"

"Is there a rebellion in the south?" Sheppar asked, beginning his walk again. "I've heard a lot of Roth doing things on his own, of gaining support for ideas. But where's his army? Where is his power?"

"But if he does come—"

"Samdar, you still don't understand," Sheppar said with a chuckle. "Killing me will do nothing. Why do you think his ideas have stopped in the Fallonvall? After twenty years of great autonomy, all the towns in Andelen will not suddenly bow under Roth's yoke just because he talks to them about it. And any show of force he attempts will turn the people away, people too accustomed to keeping their blood in their veins, not letting it upon the ground for an idea. They will, however, let it out for the sake of protecting their future from Roth, or the Beltraths, or anyone else of violence—and they will do that without me, whether I'm living or dead."

"Yes, my lord," Samdar replied with a shallow sigh. He turned and started back through the garden paths.

"Samdar?" Sheppar called. He bent over a lily and breathed it in, then straightened. "Send letters to Kostet's and Fathistokset—and Merneset too, if you would. Find out what they know and what they don't." He grinned. "I would be there at Fathistokset to see how the Beltraths handle the Rigarbod, but..." He shook his head, and glanced at his aide. "Let them prepare themselves as they must."

"Yes, my lord," Samdar replied. It was more than he expected, at least. And, maybe his lord was right.

Summer neared, and for Rodigger and Sharéd, so did Kavlen.

Their pace had slowed since reaching the Nagrath Highlands, as the road curved and curled around rolling hills and bluffs, and sometimes went straight up the side of the less-steep mounds. Mostly it was sandy dirt and scrubby grass. But here and there rocks outcropped or broached the tan shocks, giving hint to the hard soul of the land underneath.

Then, between two hills and down in a sudden but broad valley, spread Kavlen. At this distance, there was something shimmery about it. The houses were not packed together like a proper town, but much of it seemed to be part of the land. Here and there chimneys stood up from the middles of small mounds, and thin tendrils of smoke went skyward. As they neared, it seemed to Rodigger that perhaps there had been jewels in the rock, and that the people here had carved the walls of their home from that rock and left smears of crystals.

But as they drew closer, he realized what it was he saw. Kavlen was largely carved from the hills. There were only a few standing houses or buildings, things two or three stories high and made of brick. For the rest, a face had been cut in the hillside, a door mounted, and he could only imagine rooms hollowed out inside. And every door of every house was a different shade than any of the others. It was a cacophony of colors, most of which he couldn't name: every shade of purple, green, red, yellow, orange, blue, brown—warm brown like roasted pecans and cedar and chestnut, not the brown of the grass everywhere else. There was a low stone wall surrounding the town, only about chest high, and every several paces, to Rodigger's horror, the sockets that would have been drilled to mount a palisade in time of war were instead filled with soil, and flowers grew inside them in another dizzying display of plants and color that he couldn't name.

What had the poem said? Something about rainbows, and being dashed slap-dash on doors. It fit better than he could have ever imagined. So, Catie hadn't lied, and now he was in the right place. The question was where to start looking.

They made their way to the inn—one of the tall, brick buildings, it had a door of a red hue that Rodigger had seen maybe once, in a sunset—and prepared their horses for the night before going inside. It was busy enough to mask guarded conversation without needing to shout.

"What is it we do now?" Sharéd asked. "We are going the wrong way, it seems. Balnath is west, you have brought us east."

"Where the *wingéd* man will come, we can be certain," Rodigger replied. "Now we find the Berkarfor, in case that mission gives us the greatest advantage. If not, we still have the first, and they'll have to come to us for the complete set. And we can deal with them then."

"Where is it we find this thing?"

"Underground," Rodigger replied with a smile. "At least, it was the last time. And the clue said it was hidden beneath the floors."

"So we dig up the floors?" Sharéd asked skeptically.

"No, not literally, it just means it's underground. Probably a cave we need to find."

"Where?"

Rodigger's mouth twisted. That was a good question. The keeper was on his way by, just then, and Rodigger snatched at his sleeve.

"Where might we find a cave?" he asked.

The keeper gazed at him blankly for several moments. "You know this town's name means 'Land of Caves' right?"

Rodigger's crest fell, and he swallowed. "How many, though? That haven't been made into homes." That might narrow it down, at least.

"A couple hundred. This place is lousy with 'em," he replied, glancing back and forth between the two. "It's the land—"

"Of caves, yeah, thanks," Rodigger interrupted with a sigh.

"Sorry pal. But if you want a home, we've got lots of options." The keeper shrugged, and went on his way.

Rodigger glared after him. Why on Oren would he want a home in this ridiculous place? And have to have the color of his door approved to make sure it didn't match anyone else's? He shook his head.

"So the first question comes back," Sharéd said off-handedly. "What do we do now?"

Rodigger set his jaw. "We'll start looking tomorrow. First thing."

"At these hundreds of caves?"

"No, not at hundreds of caves. At a lot of them," Rodigger replied, folding his arms. "Something will come to me. Something will be wrong, won't fit the riddle. I'll figure it out."

But after the fifth cave, nothing was coming to him. They paused for some water, and Rodigger tried to think as he sat on a rock in the sun.

"They're similar," he said finally. "We've been choosing caves at random, but they're similar, don't you think?"

"They are small," Sharéd replied, and took a drink of water. "Good for you, they do not take a day to explore."

"Yeah, they're small. And none of them go down. They're on one level, for the most part, right? If it's supposed to be below the town, it would have to be deeper." He capped his own water skin and stood.

"How does this help us?" Sharéd asked. "We have at least one hundred ninety-five more caves to search."

"Let's look at a few more—fifteen. Each: we'll split up. Let's see what they look like."

Sharéd said nothing, but they walked on. Rodigger's feet were getting sore. Very few of the cave floors were even, and he'd gotten used to riding.

By the tenth, something else was nagging at him. By twelve, he knew there was something obvious, staring him in the face—and it wasn't the town with its garish portals, he thought with a grimace as he exited the thirteenth. Fourteen and fifteen went by, and he stopped and waited for Sharéd as the sun topped its zenith and headed west.

As the Beltrath finally approached, Rodigger realized it *was* the garish portals staring him in the face.

"Every cave points away from the town," he said as Sharéd looked at him. "If it led 'under the floors' it would have to point at the town, or double back on itself."

"So we have spent half a day on this search, and now we must keep looking at caves that enter on the other side of the hills? They are hard enough to see sometimes when we look at them."

Rodigger chewed his lip. There had to be an easier way, a guide. They'd had one in Attelek—two, technically. "We need to find the Grandmother," he said. "She might know the old stories, and help us find it more easily."

The third person they asked knew who they were looking for, and, for the first time, the colored doors helped: "it's a little darker blue than the sky is right now"—and it was. Rodigger knocked. Apparently it was customary for Grandmothers to keep a young girl in the house to do odd jobs. This one looked about nine, hair in a single braid behind a heart-shaped face, and green linen summer dress over a strong frame. She narrowed her eyes when Rodigger introduced Sharéd, but apparently attendant-girls everywhere were also taught not to speak, and she brought them in without question.

This Grandmother appeared a bit younger than the one in Attelek. Her eyes, too, darted every now and again to Sharéd. "How may I help you?" she asked. Her voice, at least, was steadier than her gaze.

"Do you know of the Berkarfor?" Rodigger asked.

"I have told the story many times," she replied with a smile. "Do you seek a recitation?"

"We found the first under Agirbirt Lake," Rodigger said. He glanced sideways. "Well, I did. Sharéd joined me later. But a riddle came with it that spoke of Kavlen. It mentioned two Wendol who battle beneath the floors. So I believe it's underground, under Kavlen itself. But I don't know where."

"Have you looked in the caves?" Grandmother asked, with another fitful glance at the Beltrath.

"Some of them," Rodigger replied. "They all head away from town. I was hoping you might know something of the old stories to narrow our search."

Grandmother was silent for some time, glancing every now and again at Sharéd, at the young girl, outside, and back at Rodigger. "I'm sorry, young man," she said. "I'm afraid nothing jumps to mind. You may just have to keep looking. If they're as fantastic as the stories, I'm sure it's worth the search, though?" Her tone went up in suggestion. Rodigger sighed, and nodded.

"I suppose they are," he admitted.

"I am sorry I can't help," she said again. "Would you like something to eat?"

Rodigger waved her away. "No, thank you. We have a lot of work to get to."

As they left, Rodigger glanced at the lowering sun as it headed for the road that Catie and Deuel would ride in at any moment. No doubt they would come straight to the Grandmother, and when another group arrived looking for the Berkarfor, she would undoubtedly tell them of Rodigger and Sharéd's presence.

Rodigger muttered a curse under his breath.

"What is it?" Sharéd asked.

"We've unmasked ourselves, is all," Rodigger replied. "We shouldn't have gone to Grandmother, I think. She'll tell Catie and Deuel that we're here, and looking for the Berkarfor, and they'll find it first, and our advantage will be gone."

"I thought we were supposed to meet the wingéd man? I told you I wanted to."

"I'm just not sure how good an idea that is," Rodigger said. "Like I said, I don't know what kind of mood he'll be in—him or Catie—because I stole their horses."

"That is not my fault. I had the plan before you came. I should just follow the plan even though you came."

"Tell me this plan, then, and how I'm supposed to help," Rodigger said.

"Roth has not explained it to you?"

"Just that I was to meet you, what the key phrase was supposed to be, and that we would be working together. It doesn't involve the Berkarfor?"

"No."

Rodigger blinked. "Oh. Okay. So..." He raised his eyebrows expectantly.

Sharéd hesitated. "Without the wingéd man here..."

"Let me worry about that," Rodigger interrupted. "I've spent time with him. I may be able to help."

Sharéd glanced around the village. He took Rodigger by the arm and guided him away from the bustle of the main streets.

"We need to find the wingéd men—the ones not dragons yet," he said quietly.

"I thought it was just the one *winged* man," Rodigger said, emphasizing the proper pronunciation. He was weary of being reminded of how he had been made a fool.

"We need to know where they, ah, *veythya*—the *wingt* folk," he said, trying to mimic Rodigger's pronunciation and somehow using a 't' sound where he rarely did otherwise.

Rodigger shook his head a fraction. "Where they what?"

"*Veythya*—change into dragons."

"Why?"

"To take them prisoners."

Rodigger blinked, trying to imagine Deuel being taken prisoner. On the one hand, it was a pleasant sight. It just seemed a little too far-fetched. If he tried to imagine it, the wings fanned and Halm and Ro Thull... He closed his eyes and shook his head.

"I'm not sure Deuel can be taken prisoner," he said. "And if there are more like him at this place..."

"No, no," Sharéd waved his hands. "When they *veythya* they are like...worms in the cocoon. Not butterfly, not worm. Not awake. My people surround them, we get wingt folk—the ones not *veythya*—to break their *aloik* bonds and serve Roth."

Slowly, Rodigger's gaze dropped. Roth wanted to *use* the behamien? Something was wrong here. Well, Roth used Deuel because he had to—he had come with Gabriel as a set. Right?

He thought of the army, stalled at the northern end of the Fallonvall. Thought of this journey to acquire ancient goblets meant to transfer power to the one who drank from them. Thought of Gabriel abandoning the mission in Attelek—had that been part of the plan? Had Roth paid the mercenary to leave them, so that just he and Deuel would go on?

Rodigger shook his head. This was getting him nowhere. Only Roth could answer those questions, and he was far away. But surely Roth didn't know Deuel the way Rodigger did—didn't truly appreciate what Deuel was, what he represented. This plan wouldn't work. It might *work*, technically, but it wasn't a good plan. Rodigger's father, long ago, had taught him how to spot a bad plan: they didn't follow the rules. Plans that didn't follow the rules made for dilapidated houses.

"So where do they...change?" he asked. He didn't want to use what was probably a behamian word.

"We don't know," Sharéd replied. "Roth only told us where to hide, he would come to us. That is why we need—"

"Right." Rodigger cut him off with a raised hand. More answers that he probably couldn't find. He chewed his lip as the streams of passers-by flowed toward homes, or to the inn. The sun was low now, the shadows long. Darkness—and, at one time, danger—would be on them soon. People always sought shelter when they thought danger was near.

Not awake. People sought shelter when they slept. Surely the wingt folk would too? He liked that phrase, now: wingt folk—better than behamien. But the wingt folk had been around for a long time, maybe longer than inns. And people would have come to inns, people who might want to kill them. So they would need a different shelter. Shelter that had been around for a long time, and wasn't easily found.

"A cave?" Sharéd asked.

Rodigger's eyes flicked to the Beltrath. He really needed to stop muttering his thoughts aloud. Rodigger shook his head. Caves were perfect, but where? The ones here were too shallow; they were no hiding place, none of the forty-some they looked at today. There were several mountain ranges in Andelen—would they go to some other country to change? They could, but why would they? And he wouldn't be able to help if they did. No, they needed to be in Andelen somewhere.

The noise in the streets grew as more townsfolk met and greeted one another. Rodigger shook his head. He needed to figure this out before the clamor hindered his thinking.

What about the Dragonsbacks? It would make sense, they wanted to be dragons. But the road wound up from the south all the way through most of the 'Back, and the Tevorbath filled another part. So that left...

The Eye. And hadn't Gabriel and Deuel been in Agrend before Roth called them? It made sense they would be close to where Deuel needed to change. Rodigger drew a breath. Should he tell Roth? Most likely. Not that he was defying orders, but that, under current circumstances and what he knew of Deuel, hostages might not be the best idea.

"We'll send a hawk south in the morning," Rodigger said quietly, below the gabble. "I want to tell Roth what's happened the past several months—that my company has changed, and things may not be what he thinks they are. And then we go the Balnath Agrend with your people."

Sharéd cocked his head. "You know it is there?"

No. "Yes," Rodigger replied. "But in fairness to you, I'll tell you that our mission once we get there is going to change. I just wish we hadn't talked to the Grandmother. She's going to alert Catie and Deuel that we were here." He paused for a moment, then shook his head. *And the Berkarfor? Let Deuel and Catie go after them. If it works out, Roth will have everything he needs. And I'll be there to stop Catie from doing whatever it is she plans after handing all the power in Andelen to Roth.* "We'll try to be on the road tomorrow, early, and avoid those two. Where will we meet your people?"

"I do not know all your names. North of where there is water like jewels across a plain."

Rodigger thought for a moment. "Okay. And west of the Tevorbath?" Sharéd nodded. *If Roth told them to hide there, then he was probably on the right track with The Eye.* "Okay. We'll make for there as fast as we can."

"What are we doing when we get there?" Sharéd asked quietly.

"We're not going to use the behamien," Rodigger said. "We're going to kill them." And as the words left his mouth, he knew it was the right thing to do.

The next morning, Rodigger rose from several bad dreams with the vague sensation that he had awoken at some point during the night and saw Sharéd entering the room clothed and preparing to go to sleep. But the Beltrath lay now where he had the evening before—on the floor with barely a sheet. He had claimed the nights here were too warm. Rodigger didn't want to believe him, after hearing enough stories of how hot it was in the desert. But he didn't think about it much. By now he had gotten used to the strange habits of his strange companion, and strangely didn't care anymore.

After breakfast, he went to the message hall and sent the hawk to Roth in Akervet. When he came out, there was a loud procession making its way along the streets. Horns and long flutes sounded a slow and almost wailing song, it seemed to him. A knot of people in billowing white encircled some sort of bier, atop which lay a prone figure surrounded by white and yellow flowers. Behind the group, Rodigger recognized the braided young girl who walked with eyes downcast. He glanced again at the bier: it was the Grandmother, and she lay perfectly still as the bier rocked back and forth in the grasp of the swaying carriers.

People lined the street, touching their faces in some sort of reverent gesture as the procession passed. Rodigger swallowed hard. The hawk's clerk came up behind him, and moaned a sigh.

"I'd heard she passed in the night," he said, bringing his hand up flat, palm toward himself, and pressing the tip of his middle finger into his forehead. "Kierssa isn't ready—wasn't supposed to be." He paused and sighed again. "Times might be a little tough, without a Grandmother."

"I'm...I'm sorry," Rodigger said, glancing briefly at the clerk before striding quickly away, back to the inn.

"Sharéd, we need to leave immediately," he said when he entered. "The Grandmother has died. We might have been the last to see her."

"I heard," Sharéd said quietly. His things were already gathered and packed for the road. "Our fortune: she will not be able to alert the wingt man and the girl."

"Yes," Rodigger said, a little distantly. "Good fortune."

As the procession continued its winding path, Rodigger and Sharéd left Kavlen, heading west as quickly as practical.

Before they could see the town, Deuel and Catie heard the music. "That sounds sad," Catie said. "We should be careful."

"Very much," Deuel replied.

As they rounded the bend and Kavlen came into view, Catie knew she had been right about the Berkarfor. She had heard about the dazzling colors of the homes there, but it hadn't prepared her for the resplendent beauty of the place. It seemed odd, now, to come upon it with such a dirge echoing among the hills when the town itself seemed so vibrant and alive.

They passed the walls decked in tulips, marigolds, lilies, chrysanthemums, geraniums, irises, and dozens of other flowers she couldn't make out as the stone stretched away across and between the little hillocks. They rode down streets strangely deserted, but followed the music believing the townsfolk were probably gathered where it played.

A final turn, and they came upon the assembly. Up ahead, double stone doors opened into a hillside near the eastern edge of town—the only doors, it appeared, that were unpainted. They opened inward, and were lost in shadow but the very corners. It seemed the whole town was turned out, and arranged in a half-ring facing the cave. Beside the doors stood a young girl with a dark brown dress and her hair pulled into a single braid, her face lost in its own shadow as a bier was carried inside. A wizened man in white flowing cloak stood on the other side of the doors, chanting what sounded like a poem in an old tongue of Rinc Nain.

Deuel and Catie paused a respectful distance away; Rodan and Kelsie mimicked the quiet mood of their riders, settling themselves so as to not even dance a hoof. The poem went on as the bier was swallowed by the darkness. At a pause, the people raised their voices in a response. The man called again, and the people responded. He called a third time, and the people were silent.

That silence continued, until those who had carried the bier came out once more. The doors were pushed shut—none on the outside worked them, and they were clearly too heavy to swing shut on their own. Once they were visible in the light, Catie could see there had been carvings on the door, but time and weather had washed most of it away.

The crowd dispersed. A few startled when they saw the two riders, then canted their heads in acknowledgement of the respect the two had shown.

"Who was that?" Catie asked quietly as one of the folk came near.

"The Grandmother," she replied. "She died suddenly in the night."

Catie glanced at Deuel, her heart falling. "And the girl who stood outside?" she asked, dreading the answer.

"Kierssa," was the reply. "Far too young a Newmother. She'd only been in the Grandmother's home a few years." The woman shook her head. "I'd have more wisdom than that poor girl. Dark days indeed, for Kavlen."

"Yes," Catie said, breathlessly. "I'm very sorry. No village should be without a Grandmother."

The woman nodded thanks, and turned a glance back toward the stone doors. "She's in good company though," she said. "My own mother is in there, on the third floor. She and Grandmother had tea almost every day, near the end." The woman turned back and smiled at Catie through glistening eyes. "Now they can meet again every day until eternity."

"I'm sorry, there's that many rooms in there?" Catie asked.

"Oh yes, most of Kavlen is buried there," she replied. "It's the oldest and deepest of the caves, with many levels. Enough room for many generations to come."

"I had wondered about the doors, being without color," Catie said with a glance at Deuel. "It makes sense. Thank you. And, again, I'm sorry."

"Thank you, girl," the woman said, sketching a slight bow before walking away. After a few steps, she turned her head as if to glance back, her pace slowing, but she quickly shook her head, and continued.

Catie watched her a moment, then turned Kelsie toward Deuel. *Wars rage far beneath the floors,* she said. She felt his agreement.

"But how do we get in?" he asked.

Catie paused, shrugged, and looked again at the doors. They remained firmly shut.

16

ANGER HATE

"This is getting out of control."
"I think things are coming together quite nicely."
"You must not be looking."
"I look to the future, not the present."

14 Monzak 1320 — Spring

A violent knocking banished Roth's dreams, and he awoke clutching his blankets. There was no light in the room, so dawn had not yet arrived. Yet someone knocked, again.

"What is it?" he demanded. Not that they had been particularly pleasant dreams, but this was surely uncalled for.

"My lord, a message arrived. From Rodigger."

At this hour? "Give me a moment," he replied, pulling the blankets aside. He was not expecting a message, especially here in Vatenhal. And at night? Did the boy send an owl?

He pulled a robe around himself, then opened the door. "Give it to me. Bring the light," he added quickly. One of his guards entered, bearing a torch. "Here," Roth gestured, "get a taper, don't even think of trying to light—good. Thank you." He glanced quickly at the script and seal. It was from a message-hall in Kavlen—Kavlen! By the heavens, if his followers ever reached there...Surely this was good news, then.

He sat down, opened the scroll, and began reading. His eyes widened. "Worthless mercenary," he breathed. "And double worthless that boy! He was there to make sure the mission continued!" He kept reading. "Ah, I see. Well, at least that." The guard stood tentatively nearby.

Suddenly, Roth's hands were shaking. "The God curse that worthless, stupid boy!" he roared, smashing the parchment into a ball and slamming it repeatedly against the table. "What does he think he's doing?" he asked, shaking the crumpled message at the guard. "Ruining years of work and planning! Years!" He ripped the ball apart and cast the pieces across the room. He rose and paced, scratching his head with one hand and making fists with the other.

"Gabriel," Roth said suddenly, snapping his fingers as he turned toward his man. "Gabriel may not care about the Ber- the, uh, goblets, but he'll care about the behamien." He sat down again, taking fresh parchment and a quill. "Send this immediately," he said, scrawling frantically. "Get it to Gabriel in Attelek, and prepare our horses—perhaps ten men." He held the scroll toward the guard, then snatched it back and melted wax for a seal. "Leave our colors. You do not ride with Roth Kamdellan, but with Durla Fest, merchant lord." He held the scroll out again, now sealed. The guard received it smoothly. "We ride for Balnath Agrend to stop a disaster."

Catie sat looking at Deuel. Deuel watched the door.

She hadn't realized how empty the common room of an inn got, in the middle of the day in a village where everyone worked. Usually she was busy herself—or, lately, she was traveling from one destination to the next. It was their fifth day in Kavlen, and she liked it.

She had thought about how to get into the catacombs to try to find the Berkarfor, but not as often or as hard as she probably should have. Maybe she would have found it by now, and they would be on their way to the next. Maybe that was why she tried not to think so hard about it.

But then there was Deuel. He never said anything, but of course she could feel him: he thought they wasted time for no reason, that Catie was clever enough to have figured out a solution by now.

"Why don't you try to think of something then?" she asked suddenly.

Deuel's gaze turned to her. "I do not know humans as well as you do, especially as it concerns death," he said. "I would think your race would be far more accustomed to it, as often as it occurs. And yet you seem to hold it more in awe than any other creature for whom death is a natural cycle."

"Oh." They would be sensitive, most likely, to someone wanting to explore their dead. Even Catie was a little nonplussed by the idea. Maybe that was why she didn't think too hard about it.

She sighed. No. She liked it here, and didn't want to leave just yet. She was singing and playing her Tamis flute again, to supply them after Rodigger had taken all the coin. She was connecting with people, again, making them laugh, and *care*.

She felt a tension in her head, almost a headache but not quite. That had happened a few times since arriving in Kavlen, and she didn't know why. She looked again at Deuel. She was sure he felt it too, though of course he hid it.

She took a deep breath to calm herself. The keeper had opened a window to the warm spring air, and she could hear birds, the faint wash of the wind through some leafy plant—and raised voices. Someone was arguing. That had happened a few times, too. In the middle of one of her songs only two nights ago, two men had suddenly stood up shouting at one another about some argument that had seemed an old hate long buried. Their wives had appeared, it seemed in order to take them each home, and instead ended up joining the argument. Finally the keeper had them all tossed out. But Catie hadn't been able to restore the mood to the common room the rest of that night.

The raised voices outside died down. Deuel gazed at her. "There was much in the riddle about anger, war, and hate," he said, reading her feelings again. "It would not surprise me if the battle the Wendol fight makes its way to the townsfolk's consciousness." He paused as she returned his gaze, conflicted herself. "You know we must face the Wendol and find the goblet," he said gently.

"Then we need to talk to Kierssa," she replied with a resigned sigh. "As Grandmother's heir, she would be allowed to visit the sepulcher, with an escort of her choosing."

It took them some time to find her. She would not be left alone, and so she was handed from house to house until a way of succession was decided. Once they found the family she was staying with, it took greater effort to convince the wife to allow them to talk to the young girl aside.

"Hi Kierssa, my name is Catie," she said gently. "This is Deuel. We saw the end of Grandmother's funeral when we arrived in Kavlen. I spent some time with my Grandmother, in Attelek, too. I was not to succeed her. Still, I can imagine some of what you're going through."

"Did you disappoint everyone, too?" Kierssa asked.

Catie sat back. "They're not disappointed in you, Kierssa," she said. "They may be disappointed, but it's not your fault."

Kierssa's lips compressed, and she said nothing.

"Please understand, this is very hard for me to talk to you about," Catie continued. "Like I said, I was very much like you at one time. But we are in desperate need. Will you help us, if you can? If you can't, that's okay though," she added hurriedly.

Kierssa let out a small sigh, but nodded.

"Kierssa, Deuel and I need to get into the crypts for a little bit," Catie said. "Would you take us into them? They'll let you."

"Why?"

Catie leaned forward, her gaze wary but determined. "Kierssa," she said in a near-whisper. "Did Grandmother ever talk to you about the Berkarfor?"

Kierssa's eyes went wide and she leaned back. "No, I don't know anything about them. She never taught me anything about them."

"Okay, it's okay," Catie said hurriedly.

She knows, Deuel thought.

I know, but she's terrified. It'll do no good to press her about it, and we don't need to, anyway. "We were sent to find them, and we're certain one of them is in there."

"I don't think it is," Kierssa said. "I don't want to go in there."

"Is something bad in there?" Catie asked.

"No, dead people aren't bad, they're just—but I don't want to. Find some other way, if you have to."

Catie sat back again for a moment. "Kierssa, have you ever seen people suddenly start arguing, for no clear reason? Or fighting?"

Kierssa glanced from Catie to Deuel and back. "Sometimes," she said. "I just thought people were like that, though."

Catie grinned and gave her head a brief shake. "Not usually. Deuel and I both believe the things down there guarding the Berkarfor might be causing people to act that way."

"I'm sure they don't mean to," she said.

"Sometimes things happen even if people don't mean it to," Catie said with a gentle smile. "You know?" Kierssa looked about to cry, but she nodded her head. "If we go down there," Catie continued, "we might be able to get it to stop."

Kierssa's voice became a hoarse whisper. "I don't want to go down there," she said.

Catie blinked, and smiled again. "It's okay. You don't have to," she said. *Something is wrong,* she thought to Deuel. *She should be sad, of course, but she feels more guilty than seems right. We shouldn't force her.*

Then we still need to find a way down there.

I'll think of something. "I understand, Kierssa," she said. "I'm sorry for your loss. And remember, it's not your fault."

Kierssa didn't reply, only turned and left. Catie thanked the family, and she and Deuel returned to the inn.

After dinner, while they were still in the common room, the woman who had told them about Grandmother entered and approached their table. Her gaze was on Catie, except for one glance and smile for Deuel.

"I'm sorry," she said when she stood over them. "But you've been on my mind a fair bit of the day. I thought maybe you were familiar to me. My name is Wendeya." She held out her hand.

"I'm Catie," she said. "This is Deuel. I'm sorry, I don't think I recognize you."

She shook their hands. "It was some time ago, you were probably only a little girl. Which is why I didn't think...well really, I don't think it was you."

Catie smiled uncertainly. "Then..."

"Was your mother named Kerlyn?"

Catie's heart froze in her chest. Her mouth worked soundlessly for some moments. "Um, yes."

A smile bloomed on Wendeya's face. "I thought so! How is she? Is she well? I haven't seen her...well, not since she left, I guess." She sat down next to Catie and folded her hands on the table.

Catie continued to stare at her, mouth agape. "I...I don't know. I mean, she left me fifteen years ago. No, it was for my sake—oh...well." She laughed nervously as Wendeya's expression changed dramatically. "It wasn't like that. Someone was after her, and she knew I wouldn't be safe with her so she left me to be Newmother in Attelek."

"Oh," Wendeya said, clearly wanting to believe. "I didn't think—she didn't seem the type, I wouldn't have thought. So you haven't seen her? I guess not, you just said so. Hmm." She smiled and nodded, looking at her hands.

Deuel's glittering eyes went from Wendeya to Catie.

"Did she say...how long did she stay here?" Catie asked.

Wendeya brightened. "Oh, she was here for, I don't know, a few years I think? She was...I think she liked it here. She helped around town a lot. Actually helped with all the flowers!" She gestured a circumference. "On the walls?"

"Oh! Those were really beautiful," Catie said with a small laugh. "She...really, my mom did that?"

Wendeya nodded. "Mmm! She had...I think she had a little shop, for a while. Sold it to Timan...or, left it to him. They left very quickly, actually." She cleared her throat.

Catie blinked. "They?"

"Um, it was after she had been here for a year—two years?—A man came to town. You know, he reminded me of you a little!" she said, pointing at Deuel. "Isn't that funny? That's probably why it awakened my memory so much. Why, you two...Well, they got along, let's say that." She laughed a few peals, then seemed to remember they were talking about Catie's mother and stopped. "It was all..." She made a smoothing gesture. "I mean, he was a very good man. He was in town almost a year before they were really seen together. Things seemed to be going really well for them." Her head was bobbing again, but her eyes were distant.

"But then they left?"

She focused again. "Yeah. Just, almost in the middle of the night. They left a signed paper, leaving her shop to Timan—oh, her hand was very distinctive. Eight of us verified it with letters she had written to us. And then they were gone."

"Do you know where they went?"

"I'm afraid not. We didn't have a roving watch, so no one really saw her leave. A few saw her sort of packing, and that man was with her. Oh, what was his name? Legule? Ledorn? Le-something. Very nice, just...unobtrusive. Sometimes it's worse if someone's name comes too easily to mind, right? But..." She shook her head and shrugged. "We don't know where they went. I'm sorry. I had hoped you would tell me more than I would tell you. I'm so sorry."

"No, it's..." Catie paused with a wave, and smiled. "Not your fault."

Wendeya stood, smiling and in a sort of hunch that maybe was supposed to be another bow. "I'm sorry. Good night. I'm...sorry." She turned and left.

Catie swallowed, and looked at Deuel. His fathomless pools gazed back at her. In them, somehow, she found comfort and smiled. "Well, then," she said, and couldn't help but laugh. It trailed off too quickly, though, as she drew a breath and muttered: "how about that," as her eyes unfocused.

Later that night, Catie awoke with a start.

Anger. Hate. Fear.

She sat up, and felt in her mind for Deuel. It wasn't coming from him, and didn't seem to be coming through him, as Kaoleyn's feelings had before. But it was strong, far stronger than the feelings had ever been before in Kavlen.

"We need to go down there. Now," Deuel said, and Catie yelped in surprise.

"Would you use your thoughts when its dark and quiet? And when you're not supposed to be in my room?" she demanded.

"I'm sorry. But you know it's true."

"I know it's true, I just don't know how."

"You may have to convince the guard."

"Deuel, it's not that it'll be guarded," Catie said. "It's that it's sacred."

"So is peace," he replied. "And with anger that strong, it will not be peaceful here for long."

Catie sighed. Of course he was right. Already dogs were barking a storm, and at least one owner was trying to match his hound's volume. "Okay, let's go," she said.

As soon as they stepped outside, she saw a figure walking toward them. Despite the gloom of the night, she recognized Kierssa.

"What are you doing here?" Catie asked in surprise.

"You're right," Kierssa said. "Things happen when we don't want them to, and it's not our fault, not always."

"What are you talking about?"

"Please, can we just go to the shrine?" Kierssa asked. Catie nodded, and let the young girl lead the way.

As they approached, the guard called out: "Kierssa? That you? Who's with you?"

"Just some friends," she called back. Both of their voices were competing with the dogs' now. "I needed to put something in Grandmother's alcove, and they agreed to escort me."

Catie tried to emanate peacefulness, but also a hint of danger. It may have been unnecessary, but the guard rang a little bell. In short order one of the doors swung open, and they entered.

"You know, once we get down here, we're not sure how to get to where the goblet is," Catie whispered as they made their way down the halls.

"I think I do," Kierssa replied quietly, with a tiny glance backward.

"Did Grandmother talk to you about it?" Catie asked.

Kierssa's head shook. "She had a drawer she told me never to look into," she said softly.

Catie smiled. "My Grandmother had one of those, too," she said. "I think Grandmothers tell us that so we'll find exactly what they want us to."

Kierssa's head bowed, then straightened again. Catie could feel her smile, and yet there was still that deep sadness that felt deeper than it should have been. Catie hoped Kierssa would let it out soon. She knew it would need to be.

Lanterns lined the walls of dressed stone that arched overhead high enough for Deuel to walk upright. Every several paces, a doorway opened off to the side, and casks were tucked in alcoves in the walls in great rooms. On the floor of each room was a unique mosaic—Catie thought perhaps it related to the family interred there. Soon she began recognizing the exact hues of some of the doors in the village, and gave her head a satisfied nod.

They descended the floors quickly. There seemed room for five or seven families on each. Kierssa led them through even the third floor, past what Catie was sure was Grandmother's tomb. Finally, on the fifth floor, Kierssa turned into one of the rooms. The walls here were lined with alcoves too—all empty. "Grandmother said once this was for a family yet to come," she said.

Catie glanced at Deuel, who glanced at the floor. The mosaic here contained depictions of cups, and a white bear-like creature whose head more closely resembled an ape of some sort. *Wendol,* Deuel thought.

Isn't that a little obvious?

Only if you've found the first Berkarfor.

Catie turned to Kierssa. "How do we get in?" she asked.

Kierssa turned to the alcoves, pointing to each one across a row and counting to herself. "Eight, nine, ten: one, two three..." Now counting down the column. She stepped forward, reached inside...

And a *thunk,* and a door off to the side swung open. Catie and Deuel turned swiftly to face the opening. Growling could be heard echoing up from the dark hole. Catie was keenly aware of how light she was: no weapon weighed down a scabbard. Deuel alone had Halm and Ro Thull for whatever they found down there.

We didn't need them last time, though, came his thought. Catie took a breath.

"Here," Kierssa said, holding out a lantern. "I'll be here when you get back."

"Thank you," Catie said. "If you decide you want to leave, though, we'll be able to find our way back."

Kierssa did not reply. Catie turned toward Deuel again, and he led the way into the dark door.

His lean shadow speared through the globe of light cast by the lantern as they descended a flight of stairs. Catie's shadow climbed back up the stairs, reaching for the receding rectangle of light at the top. The growling and...barking, it almost sounded like—but more like a human barking than a dog—grew louder, and seemed to echo longer the closer they approached.

They reached a landing. After a short hall, the path turned and descended again. At the bottom of this flight they could see a strange light again, not blue like the first time, but a warm brown. The hall at the bottom was lined with lanterns, but these were encased in an earthy shell, as if someone had managed to take a slice of rock thin enough to allow light to come through. They did not flicker as if a flame were behind the panes, but emitted a steady glow.

Catie set her lantern down. As the light shifted, Deuel glanced back at her. "I still don't necessarily want them to know we're coming," she said, feeling a little foolish, and fairly certain it showed through her smile.

But Deuel only nodded, and continued to lead the way. Ahead, the hall let out into another large cavern. Here, again, a ceiling that matched the style of lanterns along the hall soared overhead with the same steady glow emanating down. It illuminated two Wendol standing a few paces apart, fierce gazes locked upon one another, as they growled and barked at each other. Talons were out and arms held wide as if ready to leap.

Behind them, tucked in an alcove similar to the tombs above, sat a leather bag about the size of a goblet.

"Do you think it's as simple as walking past them and taking it?" Catie asked.

Deuel's gaze swung slowly to face her, and she shrugged.

"It was just a suggestion," she said. "I notice you're not going for your swords, though."

"Neither are they," he replied.

Her gaze snapped to them, and saw they too had turned to look at her and Deuel. She looked in their eyes, seeing there the spark of something more than mere animal. Likely because they weren't real.

Were they? They still felt real. It had been real anger—

ANGER!

Catie blinked and looked at Deuel. He shook his head. It had come from them, not him.

Angerhate.

Catie blinked again. Those emotions had come almost on top of one another. *But why anger and hate?*

Painjustice. The Wendol turned and snarled at one another.

Both of their feelings are coming through at the same time, she thought to Deuel. *I think they're trying to tell us what's wrong.*

Try something else, he suggested.

Why pain?

SelfishpunishmenthateANGER!

The Wendol faced each other again with growling, barking, and gestures coming close to tearing each other with gleaming ebony talons.

"Deuel, we need to separate them somehow," she said. "We aren't going to get anything out of them like this."

In a swift motion, Deuel drew Halm and Ro Thull and strode toward the Wendol, emanating authority and pushing respect and reverence toward the beasts. When they finally turned toward him, his wings punched sideways, spreading to the utmost of their glorious length. He pointed a blade at each of the Wendol, gesturing them apart.

Still growling, one Wendol moved left, while the other positioned itself directly in front of the alcove with the goblet. That made sense, and Catie didn't really care at this point, as long as she could separate them and find out what was wrong.

Deuel turned to face her, keeping sideways glances on the separated Wendol. *Go ahead.*

She turned her gaze on the left Wendol—she called him "Vensi" in her mind, and the other would be "Skald"—and said: *why pain?*

Selfish.

Quickly she looked at Skald. *Why punishment?*

Selfish.

"Great. They're both selfish," Catie muttered. Deuel tried to hide his amusement behind his authority.

Why selfish?

Pain, said Vensi, a hand near his stomach. *Lack,* with a gesture at his mouth.

Hungry? she tried, imagining the feeling of being hungry.

Vensi looked at her a moment. *Hungry. Satisfaction,* Vensi continued, holding up a hand. *Satisfaction,* he said again, shaking the hand. He brought up his other hand, made a grasping motion, then held it toward Skald. *Steal!*

More growling and barking, until Deuel glared at each of them in turn.

Why steal? she asked Skald.

Selfish, Skald said with a glare at Vensi. *Hungry,* he said, putting a hand near his stomach as well. But then he raised his hand as Vensi had done, shaking his head: *lack.*

"One of them had food and the other didn't, but they were both hungry. But surely this hasn't been going on for centuries, right?" she asked. "Or however long the Berkarfor have been hidden."

"It doesn't make sense," Deuel agreed.

She turned to Vensi. *Divide, share,* she tried to project.

Vensi looked at her blankly. *Not ask.*

"Well their vocabulary is improving," Catie said with a grin. *Ask share?* she sent to Skald.

Vensi growled before Skald could answer. *Not equal. Take more* he said with a sideways glance at Skald.

Her glance flitted from Vensi to Skald. *Why take more?* she asked Skald.

Skald's glance darted sideways, then down. *Hate* came softly. *Always anger. Always...sad...not satisfied. Always punishment.*

Vensi's head turned to Skald. *Always anger,* he said, gesturing to the other Wendol. *Always need, always sad.* He put a hand on his chest. *Never enough.*

Anger, Skald said, with a low growl.

Hate, Vensi muttered in response.

Pain, Catie pushed at the both of them.

They looked at her. *Painpain.* They paused, and looked at each other. *Sadsad.* They turned and faced each other fully.

Deuel sheathed Halm and Ro Thull, and folded his wings back under his cloak. He took several steps away and turned again to face them. After several moments of looking at each other, the Wendol turned to face the two companions. Their images shimmered, thinned, almost like a reflection on glass. The two images slid toward each other, joined, and became as one Wendol, solid again as they had looked before.

They seem to be back in harmony, Deuel thought.

Then the image bowed, and shattered into sparkling dust. "They had me going there, for a moment," Catie said as Deuel stepped forward and took the bag from the alcove. "I wonder why they aren't real?"

"Because they would be dead, and not able to guard anything, by now," Deuel replied, handing her the leather pouch. She untied the top, and pulled out the Berkarfor. This one was porcelain, perfectly smooth to her touch, with colors dyed in brilliant, unfaded hues in patterns she had never before seen. No chip or crack was evident. It was flawless in every respect she could think of.

Inside was another rolled parchment. She pulled it out, glanced over it, and handed it to Deuel. "It's not in Rinc Nain," she said.

He looked over it. "It is," he said. "But an older form."

"Oh, right," Catie said. She drew a deep breath. "So, where are we off to next?"

Deuel lowered the parchment, his gaze shifting by degrees to look at her. "Ethfirlaf," he said suddenly. He glanced at the parchment again, and nodded. "Freckled bark and shadowed spark," he said.

"Emerson tree, and..." she trailed off.

"I am not sure," Deuel replied. "But I have heard several times, long ago, of the shadowed sparks in Ethfirlaf."

"I hope you're right," Catie said, turning back for the stairs. "I mean, I'd be surprised if you're not, of course." Deuel said nothing as they walked. "It just...seems too easy," Catie said.

"Only if you have someone nearby who reads older Rinc Nain."

"And someone who can communicate their feelings through thought," she realized. She paused to look at him. "The Berkarfor are supposed to be found by either a behamian or a...wyvern."

"It would seem so."

"I feel like that should be significant."

But nothing came to mind. They shrugged at each other and fell silent.

When they reached the upper chamber, they found Kierssa had gone. "I guess she got tired of waiting," Catie said.

"You did say we could find our own way out."

They wound their way up through the floors. On the third, Catie stopped suddenly as she heard sniffling. She glanced in, and saw Kierssa near Grandmother's alcove.

"Kierssa? It's okay, honey," Catie said, coming in and kneeling beside the young girl. Deuel remained in the doorway.

"Are you leaving?" Kierssa asked, wiping a sleeve across her nose.

"Yes, we'll leave first thing tomorrow," she replied.

"So they're real?" She glanced at Catie and saw the goblet in her hand. "Where's the next one?"

"Ethfirlaf, it sounds—Kierssa?"

Kierssa turned swiftly, her eyes wide, and she pressed back against the bier. "I didn't mean to," she gasped. Then, desperately, she repeated: "I didn't mean to!"

"Didn't mean to, what?" Catie asked.

"He just asked where the Berkarfor was, but I promise I didn't know! Grandmother never told me!"

"Who asked?"

"The man who...who killed Grandmother," Kierssa said.

Catie's eyes went wide. Deuel's boots sounded across the floor and he knelt beside Kierssa, projecting a strange and heady mix of peace, safety, and imminent, terrible justice. "Tell us what happened," Catie said, trying to mimic Deuel's emotions for Kierssa's benefit.

"Before you came, two men came to Grandmother, looking for the Berkarfor," Kierssa said. "Grandmother didn't want to tell them, she said she didn't know anything about them except the stories. I had been in her secret drawer so I knew she knew. But she didn't want to say, so I was quiet too."

Catie smiled. "That's very good, Kierssa," she said. "Never speak of something unless Grandmother does first."

Tears started coming again. "I didn't, even when the one man came back later that night," she said. "I woke up and heard them talking in the other room. Grandmother sounded scared, so I stayed in bed. He kept asking where the next Berkarfor was, but she wouldn't tell him. Then there was a lot of noise, scraping and shaking and it sounded like Grandmother was kicking." Kierssa began crying again. Catie reached out and gripped her shoulder.

"It's okay, Kierssa, you're safe now. Did you get out of bed?"

"Y-yes," she said. "I wanted to see what was happening. I went into the room, and Grandmother was on the floor and wasn't moving. The man was there, the second one who was quiet when they were together. He looked at me and asked me if I knew where it was. He said he would do the same to me if I didn't tell him." She looked up earnestly. "But I really didn't know! I just wanted him far away, so I said Ethfirlaf because I knew it was far away. And then he left."

"Kierssa," Catie said, her stomach turning cold. "What were their names, the two men looking for these?"

"The one who did most of the talking said he was Rodigger," she replied. "The second had a strange name. He didn't look like Rodigger, he had dark hair, more like...yours," she said, looking at Deuel. "But he didn't look like you," she went on quickly.

"Did he look like he spent a lot of time in the sun?" Catie asked, thinking of the nomads they encountered on their way through the Tevorbath. The gloom she felt at learning Rodigger was involved felt more like the beginnings of fear from Deuel—which made her even more afraid.

Kierssa's nod affirmed Catie's suspicion. Deuel's grip became tighter on her arm.

"Kierssa," he said. "It's very important you remember the second man's name," he said.

Deuel, Catie said gently, but he ignored her.

"It was... 'Sha' -something...Sharéd—that's what Rodigger said."

Deuel released her, and terror washed over Catie from him. "Deuel, what is it?" she asked, her own voice shaking. What could terrify Deuel?

"Sharéd Dusslin?" Deuel asked, his voice barely above a whisper.

Kierssa nodded shakily. "I think so."

"Are you sure they went to Ethfirlaf?" he asked. His voice was calm, in complete contradiction to the emotions she felt whirling from him.

"I don't know," Kierssa replied, appearing on the edge of tears again. "I told him that's where it was, and I never saw them again."

"Thank you, Kierssa," Deuel replied, standing. "You've been a very brave girl. I do not know your custom of titling Grandmothers, but if bravery is important, you will be a very good one."

"Th-thank you," Kierssa replied, turning to look again at Grandmother's alcove.

Catie stood as well. "Will you be okay?" she asked as Deuel exited the room.

Kierssa nodded, wiping her nose again and sniffling. "I'll go back to Wendeya's soon," she said. "She's watching me now. I just want to be alone with Grandmother for a little bit longer. I'm sorry I didn't..." She trailed off.

"Kierssa, you did very well," Catie said. "I don't think I would have handled it as well as you did, in the same situation."

Kierssa smiled, though her eyes still shimmered. "Thanks."

"Okay," Catie said, patting the girl's head.

We must go, now!

Coming, Catie said hurriedly. She found Deuel just outside. "What is it?" she asked, his fear returning to her again.

"We have to get to Ethfirlaf," Deuel said, striding quickly toward the stairs to the next floor. "I should have recognized those Beltraths we found in the Tevorbath. If it is Sharéd, if he's here..."

"Who is Sharéd? How do you know him? Deuel, please slow down, my legs aren't as long as yours."

Deuel sighed. "During Sheppar's campaign, he decided he wanted to get rid of the dragons too, because people were afraid of them."

"Eck wasn't."

"Most people were. But it was late in the campaign and he didn't want to lose more men getting rid of them." Deuel was silent for a time. "So he forced the few soldiers with *skalderon* to deal with it, thinking the behamien would kill a dragon if ordered to by their *aloik*."

"But you might be murdering your own parents!" Catie said, aghast. She had never thought Sheppar capable of such a thing.

"It had been a long campaign," Deuel replied. "He just wanted it to be done. In some ways I understand. But no," he continued, shaking his head, "none of us would kill a dragon, even if our *aloik* told us to."

"But, the dragon is gone. Garedardan isn't in the Tevorbath anymore."

"You are right, Garedardan isn't in the Tevorbath anymore," Deuel stopped, and faced her. "He's in the Wastes."

"But..."

"A dragon accustomed to the fertility of the Tevorbath does not easily move to the Wastes," Deuel said. "We found an oasis—one held by Dusslin's tribe. But it was not big enough to support both."

"Deuel..."

"I am not proud of it," Deuel replied. "I have wanted to go and make it right more than once. But the bond of *aloik* was strong enough to prevent that. We forced Dusslin's tribe to move. It was all but a death sentence to them, in the Wastes. I thought, by now, they *had* died." He paused, shook his head, and turned away. They continued on. "But now he's alive, and he's outside the Wastes with a force of over five hundred men. And with Rodigger, who might hate behamien more than Sharéd, even with less reason, and maybe involved somehow with Roth..." He trailed off as they approached the door to Kavlen. "There is no way to look at this that does not make me fear for the behamien on Andelen, and for Garedardan in the Wastes." He paused again, and sighed. "If we don't find Rodigger and Sharéd quickly," he said, glancing at Catie, "I have to find the others and warn them."

Catie skipped a step. "You..." *You'll leave me?* she managed to keep to herself. Of course he would: wouldn't she, if Attelek were in danger? Besides, everyone else had. She pushed that emotion aside. "You should," she said instead. "You should fly up the road. They have five days' head start." *Because I got distracted and wanted to settle down here, with...*

Deuel shook his head. "I will stay with you for a little while longer," he said. "There is little they can do on the road to Ethfirlaf." He drew a heavy sigh. "And I..." He stopped, his eyes glittering as he looked at her.

But he said nothing else, and they returned to the inn for the night.

17

MEMORY SPARKS

"Will you tell me one day what it is you see?"
"We each see things differently, Teresh. You must learn what you see."
"I see chaos."
"Then start with that."

15 Monzak 1320 — Spring

Gabriel awoke to someone knocking on his door.

He blinked, trying not to count the areas of his body that were sore. He had thought that, as a mercenary, he had kept decently limber. The 'simple' life here in Attelek had taught him differently. Yesterday had been his first foray into fishing.

"Gabriel?" came a young voice. At that age, he could never figure out what gender they were. In this town, it seemed not to matter as much as elsewhere. *Maybe that's why Catie turned out the way she did.*

Gabriel grunted. A strange thought, even if it were true. "Coming," he called, surprised at how tired and gravelly his voice sounded. He cleared his throat a few times as he rose and threw on a rough shirt and plain trousers.

"What is it?" he asked, opening the door. It was a boy. Tyafor? Maybe his little brother. He held a small scroll out in front of him.

"This came for you, sir," the boy said.

Gabriel stared at it for several moments before remembering he was supposed to take it and read it, at least at some point. "Oh," he managed, finally. "Thanks."

He held it as the boy smiled uncertainly and left. He continued to look at it, remembering when he had held a similar small scroll with a similar seal in Balnath Agrend. No, not similar. The seal was identical. Several thoughts flashed through his mind of how the mission might have gone awry, how Rodigger and Deuel and Catie might have ended up.

I want to leave that behind. Why couldn't they continue on their own? Rodigger had all the coin anyway, he could have returned my share to Roth.

It's been months. Too many things might have happened in such a rapidly-changing world.

Gabriel sighed, closed the door, and broke the seal. As he read, his gloom and despair settled even deeper. *I wanted to leave this behind.*

You know you can't. Deuel needs your help.

The letter says Roth wants my help.

That is not for him to decide. That is for you.

And how will I do that?

Get to Balnath Agrend first. Take it from there.

Gabriel re-rolled the scroll and tossed it into the embers from last night's fire. Then he began packing his saddle bags for a long journey.

Catie lay in her bed that morning with no desire to get up. To get up would mean to get back on the road, and quite frankly she was tired of traveling. To get up would mean chasing after things she was losing faith in:

A boy who would never grow into a man if he never left Roth's apron-strings.

The barest chance of some sort of delayed justice or revenge.

Possibly the success of the rebellion.

In bed, under a layer of blankets, eyes closed, she didn't have to choose. Each moment that passed was another moment not following a choice she didn't like.

But it would be worse. She never was one to avoid a choice, or to sit and make no choice. She took the time to think, to reason, to ask questions. Sometimes she went on instinct. But she always made a choice.

She thought of the Berkarfor. Everyone wanted her to find them: Roth, for his own power. Rodigger, to see his hero win. Deuel? Well, Deuel didn't anymore. He wanted her to figure who she was, though probably now without him.

And yet, who she was had brought her here, hadn't it? Her sense that first night, when Paolound died, had told her she would return home, but not stay. And when they had come to her village, she knew without being asked that their mission was why she would not stay home, that she was to go with them. What was it about those goblets, though? Why were they hidden, guarded supposedly—though, so far, they hadn't been truly guarded.

Except they never would have gotten past if they had tried to just fight the creatures. A real *byor* Deuel likely could have handled, with Gabriel's help. But that one hadn't been real. And clearly Deuel could have handled the Wendol if they had been real, too. But they weren't. They were magic of some sort—an illusion. So if not to physically guard the goblets, they had been there for...what?

Catie rolled over. The Berkarfor weren't there to be taken, they were there to be pursued. Just something to get the pursuer to encounter the guardians and interact with them.

But what might happen if she didn't act the way she was supposed to? What if she did outright attack the next one? She contemplated several scenarios. Most ended with her dying, blown to dust the way the guardians were. But she would never try such a thing. She felt victorious approaching the guardians the way she had been, trying to understand them and work through whatever problem they presented.

What she did not know, and could not begin to guess, was what would happen once she had all four Berkarfor. And she wanted to find out.

She sat up, and took a breath. And what about Deuel? She didn't want him to go off alone. Well, she didn't want to go off by herself, if she needed to be honest. She could follow him afterward.

But, after what? She still needed to decide what her own plan was.

Deuel thought his fate was somehow tied with yours. What if it's the other way around?

So I abandon Dannid's justice and pursue my own future?

No one said those were mutually exclusive.

Catie slouched a little in bed. Was that it, then? Let Deuel go if they couldn't find that *boy* and his Beltrath friend. Find the last Berkarfor. Then try to find Deuel again. But would he tell her where he was going?

If I were a dragon-son, where would I go to change?

Change happens first in the eye.

Catie held her breath. Had that last thought come from Deuel? She didn't recall pushing that one. She reached out gently, trying to sense him. She pulled back with a faint yelp: he was awake, and she was surprised she could actually tell. But he wasn't aware of her.

Are you ready to leave yet? he asked suddenly, causing her to yelp a little louder this time.

Can you warn a girl before you do that?

Last time you told me to use my thoughts. How exactly would you like me to get your attention?

Last time you were IN MY ROOM. Try standing outside and knocking, and calling softly, like normal people!

There was silence. So the first thought had not come from him. But what did it mean? The eye? Whose eye? What eye? A dragon's?

Catie stood, reaching for her clothes. A dragon's eye. Of course there would be hidden caves all through that region, plenty of places for behamien to go away from prying eyes. All she had to do was find two more centuries-hidden goblets guarded by magically-created creatures, and then travel across the country and find a hidden cave outside Balnath Agrend.

How hard could that be?

As the days passed on their road eastward, Catie kept waiting for Deuel to leave. She could feel him getting more concerned: at every inn they asked, none of the keepers could remember anyone like Rodigger or a Beltrath, especially traveling together. At first, Deuel reasoned that the inns were large, numerous, and busy with traders going between Ostflir and Agrend. Two individuals could easily slip through unnoticed, especially if they were trying. But by the end of the week he had begun flying ahead while Catie kept the horses, trying to spot them unaware on the road.

At Finstaff, early in the night, there came a soft knocking on Catie's door.

She blinked, reached out and sensed Deuel, and smiled.

"Come in," she said. "That was perfect," she continued as he entered. "Do it like that from now—" But she could tell from his expression that would be the last time he would need to get her attention. At least, he believed that was so.

"They are not on the road," he said. "Whatever happened, they have chosen not to go to Ethfirlaf. I can only think, after what they did in Kavlen, they have abandoned the Berkarfor. And what we know of Rodigger and Sharéd, it is likely they are pursuing the behamien."

"How would they know where to find them? *I* don't even know."

"Because Roth knows many ancient things that were supposed to have been lost," Deuel replied. "And there are only two roads out of Kavlen. I do not know how, but they know."

"I want you to go, Deuel, I do," Catie said, then paused a moment. "I'm asking this for your advice, not to try to make you stay: what if I need someone in Ethfirlaf? Or wherever the next Berkarfor is supposed to be hidden? What if I can't figure out the next riddle?"

"You are resourceful, Catie," Deuel replied, a spark of respect in his eyes. "You will find a way, as you always have."

"And what about after? You said you wanted to see who I was, that you felt it would help you understand humans better. How do I find you again?"

Deuel looked at her a long moment. "I cannot be sure you will need to," he replied finally. "If I enter the change, or if Rodigger and Sharéd get there first..." He trailed off. She felt his smile. "You must focus on your journey, Catie. If you are meant to find me, you will. I must focus on my journey."

Catie grinned sadly. "Are you leaving tonight?"

"I am."

"But, I mean, where will you stay?" Then, she wasn't sure why, but she just noticed he did not have on his customary thick cloak, and what he wore clearly showed his wings.

He must have seen the recognition in her eyes, for he nodded solemnly. "I have, for so long, kept hidden who I was," he said. "I have given Rodan to a respected hostler. If I need him again, I will come for him. But from now on, I fly."

Catie nodded, pleased with that choice, at least.

Two days after they parted, she could no longer sense him in her thoughts.

She continued north and east, trying to get used to Deuel's absence. Kelsie soon stopped shifting when Catie did, thinking they were turning when Catie only wanted to make some comment to the dragon-son.

She talked to caravaners on their way inland, talked to innkeepers, played her Tamis flute for guests, and sang songs. And for moments she was happy. But eventually the day would end, she would lie in her bed, and reach out for Deuel's awareness. And find nothing. They had never shared less than a cot-room, never shared a bed. And yet that connection, that ability to talk without speaking had created a space that—now bereft—was a void that no mere conversation could fill.

She tried enjoying the road. It wound through the Brithelt Forest, a landscape of towering trees and fern-carpeted hillsides. Little streams trickled through nearly every valley, and with summer upon them the birds of the deep forest made song heard nowhere else. Her respect for the Tamis flute increased, and she studied their music to create her own melodies for the inns at night.

From a map she had studied at the inn just inside the border of the Brithelt Forest, she knew one day that she was nearing Tarkusnaab. She started earlier in the morning, pushed Kelsie a little harder through the day, and continued riding later than she otherwise might have. Tarkusnaab was the halfway point to Ethfirlaf, and she was ready for this journey to be over and to find Deuel again.

Torches ahead, blearing through her half-closed eyes, alerted her to her arrival at the hilltop village. Stifling a yawn, she guided Kelsie along the roads without thinking. Tarkus was not a large village, just enough to have a fair share of cross-streets. She passed several, then turned her mare right. Past another few buildings, then left.

And she was lost. She blinked at a house-front, its windows dark, looking for the swinging sign announcing the inn and not seeing it. Kelsie sat patiently while Catie turned a few times.

"It was here," she said. "It was..." She trailed off, nudging Kelsie to the next cross-street and glancing down it both ways. "There's the forge," she said aloud, where a banked fire still sent a diffuse orange glow onto the street. "Past is the tannery." A riffle of wind and she could almost smell it. She turned the other way, noting the signboards for potter, woodcarver, candlemaker, seamstress—but there was no inn.

Suddenly, she sat back and blinked. *I've never been to Tarkusnaab,* she realized. *How am I supposed to know where the inn is?*

But as she turned and looked each way, and back the way she came, she felt it was too familiar. Not familiar like it reminded her of Attelek—the trees weren't so thick there, and emerson trees did not exist beside Agirbirt. More like, if she took away that house, that one, maybe a few others, it would fit the image perfectly in her mind. Except where the inn was supposed to be.

It was slightly different, yet it's exactly the same. I've been here—but when?

Grandmother had said my mother brought me to Attelek when I was small. She didn't say how small.

She turned Kelsie back down the road, retracing the steps that brought her there. She recognized more of the houses, knew the miller had lived in that one, that the watermill was past the west end of town at a natural waterfall.

But as far back as she could remember, she had been in her parents' house, then Grandmother's after that.

And yet, somewhere, there was Tarkusnaab.

She finally found the inn—left, not right—but the building appeared newer than some of the village, as most of the ones on this street also did. And it was bigger, she thought.

She put Kelsie in a stall, settling her for the night before going inside.

The common room was empty and quiet. A cat lay on the bar. It snapped its head up as she passed, purred, and laid back down.

"I hope there's no nocturnal mice," she said wryly.

"What's that?" called a voice on the other side of a door behind the bar.

"Sorry I'm late," Catie replied, her voice at half-volume.

The door swung open, and a middle-aged, thin woman with dark hair in wisps from beneath a hastily-donned bonnet stood in the doorway. "You aren't kidding," she replied. She glanced down at the sleeping cat and clicked her tongue. "Get five, ten patrons in here with their drinks, she's everywhere at once," she said, gesturing. "Five, ten mice are around, she's fast asleep. I suspect you need a room?"

"If you have one," Catie replied.

"Two coin a night. Breakfast and dinner is extra. I'm Scearon."

"Catie," she replied. She dug in her purse and pulled out the proper coin.

"I'll just be the night. Maybe breakfast."

"Whatever you need, my dear," Scearon replied, taking the coin. "Rooms are in the back."

"Um, do you mind?" Catie asked, as she was about to turn to leave. "Has the inn always been here?"

Scearon blinked. "No. It used to be other side of the village," she replied.

Catie nodded. "I had thought so."

A smile crept onto Scearon's face. "Did you indeed? You talk like you remember the old place."

Catie smiled tentatively. "I thought I did," she said slowly.

"Ha!" Scearon laughed. "Then I'll need your secret. It hasn't been there since my grandmother kept it. So you're...fifty?"

Catie managed a chuckle. "Must have been somewhere else, then," she said as lightly as she could. *Why do I have a memory from over fifty years ago?*

I think perhaps you have lived longer than you realize, Deuel had said, once. "Is there a Grandmother here?"

"Surely," Scearon replied. "Couple houses down from where the inn used to be. Got witch hazel out front."

"Thanks," Catie said with a smile.

As she lay in bed, she realized she and Deuel hadn't spoken about her strange abilities and memories, and what they might mean, for some time. Now it was staring her in the face again. And she couldn't talk to the dragon-son about it. *How am I supposed to figure out what it means to be a wyvern if the only person who seemed to know is heading to the other side of the country?*

The void in her heart—far from healing with time—grew larger.

The next morning, she found the house easily enough. She paused out front, looking at the windows, the doors, the gambrel roof—familiar in shape, if not color. She closed her eyes, trying to remember. All she could summon was a vague notion, and that might have been from trying too hard. She blinked, walked up, and knocked.

The Newmother answered, gazing at her silently, eyes and hair black and skin whiter than her linen dress. She turned and led the way into the house, pausing only to hold a hand toward the Grandmother before padding off.

"Hi," Catie said with a small wave.

Grandmother gazed at her, brown eyes considering. She was a thin woman, yellowed skin sunken against vein and bone. Gray hair was pulled tight into a braid. Her dress matched the Newmother's, though iller-fitting. When her inspection of Catie seemed complete, the barest of smiles finally touched her thin lips. "Hello," was all she said.

"I seek your wisdom," Catie continued, clasping her hands in front of her and inclining her head a notch to appear demure.

It didn't seem to help Grandmother's mood. "I assumed."

Catie took a measured breath, listening. The house was silent, empty: a dust mote falling through the air. None of the sounds of morning made it in, and the room was windowless and lit only by candles.

She hesitated. "Do you...remember me?" She looked up.

A deep frown. It seemed more comfortable. "A name might help."

"Catie," she said. "Caytaleane."

Grandmother's sniff seemed to echo, her shuffling steps shook the house. "Named after your mother? I was only Newmother at the time."

"Kerlyn?"

The shuffling stopped. "No. Caytaleane. Kerlyn was her sister."

The emptiness of the house loomed around her. "I don't understand..." She faltered.

The shuffling resumed, and suddenly Grandmother was in front of her, gripping her chin and gazing into her eyes. Grandmother's shoulders relaxed as she took a breath. "Well, then," she sighed as she took a step back. "You're not what you appear, are you?"

Catie shrugged. "I guess not. You do know me?"

Grandmother shuffled toward a chair, beckoning Catie. "You're taller, and you look a little older." She grunted as she sat. "But you've done better by far than I have. Better than I've ever seen. But," she continued with a tired smile, "I have heard of such things, even here in the Knob."

"What things?"

"Women who don't age," Grandmother replied, her eyes sparking just a little. "Well, you aged, that's plain. But the fact you don't remember it?" She shrugged.

"Why don't they age? Why don't I remember?"

"And why do you say Kerlyn was your mother?"

"She said she was—she *was*. She raised me in Attelek, with my father."

Who had not been her father. She set her jaw a moment before changing tack. "You said 'one of my sisters.' Were there more?"

"Five of you showed up, one day. We thought you were lost. You certainly didn't talk much, except to say you were sisters and give us your names. Strange by far, you were—off in a clutch talking to each other low and quiet. And not in Rinc Nain, at least not a lot. Sometimes, when I tried to sneak up and listen you all went quiet, but by your looks back and forth I always wondered if you were somehow still communicating."

We probably were. "How long were we here?"

"A few months, I think. Then you left by twos, except the last. She stayed around a little longer and avoided all our questions. Seemed she wasn't sure what to do, on her own. Finally one morning she was gone too. But you weren't here long enough for us to notice you as one who doesn't age." Grandmother leaned back into the chair. "Why they don't age, I've never heard, or why you don't remember. I've never seen any like you since."

"Do you know anything about wyverns?" Catie asked.

Grandmother sat still for several long breaths. "No, I don't," she said finally. "Like miniature dragons, though? Wings instead of arms? Why do you ask?"

"I'm not sure," Catie said with a smile. "I'm just wondering if I am one."

The sparkle in Grandmother's eye only made it to one corner of her mouth. "Well if that's your secret," she said, "I'll let you keep it."

She rode for Ethfirlaf the next morning. Every building was where she remembered it, but the road outside of Tarkus was completely unfamiliar. Now that she thought about it, the road in had been unfamiliar as well. Somehow, she had been in Tarkusnaab long enough to memorize where nearly everything had been, but could not remember one step outside of it.

Kelsie plodded on as Catie rode in a daze, calling up alternating memories of a cave, and Tarkusnaab, and trying to see around them. The cave was still more sense than visual: the cool, the peace, the silence and stillness. And Tarkusnaab was much more visual than sense. She remembered where each of the buildings were, remembered a fair number of people who were probably all now dead—that didn't help her contemplative daze. But she couldn't remember what it *felt* like to live there. Couldn't remember knowing any of the people, just where they lived and what they did. And she reached out to sense Deuel countless times before she realized she was doing it.

As she neared Ethfirlaf, she began to see the pockets of clearings. Most of northern Andelen got its lumber from the region. Deep within the Brithelt, the idea of running out of trees was absurd, and so they were harvested almost constantly, with wagons heading south along the road every day laden with either raw logs, logs stripped of bark and smoothed, or cut lumber—a wheeled stream delivering every type of wood to Balnath Agrend, to Ostflir, to Taferk. Ironwood, oak, maple, chestnut, hickory, ash, mahogany, emerson—a lean tree of tough fibers useful for anything from archer's bows to Tamis flutes and lute necks, depending on how it was prepared. Sycamores in the valleys and firs on the heights.

And, somewhere outside the village, a Berkarfor.

Catie pulled out the slip of parchment Deuel had given her, reading over the riddle. It was much shorter than the other one. One line, it seemed, for the general location: Ethfirlaf. One line for the specific location, but she would have to ask where to find 'shadowed spark.' And one for what she should expect to find there, guarding the goblet. Given what she had faced so far, this sounded rather tame: wolves. And not necessarily a very large pack. But a white wolf would be involved somehow.

The inn at Ethfirlaf was very near the southern entrance. There were scattered patrons in this one—benefit of arriving at a decent hour, she chided herself. But though she sang that night, she was uncertain about pulling out the Tamis flute here, where she was fairly sure it had been created.

When she had finished, and had some dinner, she mentioned the shadowed spark to the keeper. He looked at her warily.

"I don't remember seeing you here before," he said slowly.

She shook her head with a smile. "Just arrived," she replied.

"And you want to know where our rarest resource is," he said.

Her smiled slipped. *Resource?* "Yeah, I guess I do."

He returned a thin smile, said nothing, and moved to the next table.

Well, it's a spark, right? And a figurative one, probably. Should be visible. Maybe more so at night.

The moon is nearly gone, though. Tough to see where I'm going in the dark.

It might not be as hard as you think. Deuel sees pretty well in the dark, doesn't he?

What does that have to do with me?

Try it.

As Catie went out into the night, she felt as though her vision...rippled. Was it a trick of her mind, or just that she paid attention now? The watch roved with torches, but Ethfirlaf was not quite large enough to boast lit streets. And yet, as she made her way through town she saw details just as clearly as if they were. Maybe when she exited the town and was under tree canopy...

She suddenly remembered Kavlen, that she had been able to recognize Kierssa even in the dark of night. She looked up: the sky was overcast. No starlight, no sliver of moonlight. Yet she could see.

She could see at night, like Deuel. Sense the feelings of dragons, like Deuel. Project feelings and thoughts, like Deuel. Would being a wyvern be so different from being a dragon? Apparently he would not be able to communicate with her anymore, would not understand her speech if she changed. Neither would she understand him, if he changed. Just basic emotions—or so it seemed. What if they both changed?

She sighed and shook her head. Questions she would not be able to simply puzzle out the answers for. Time to start looking for a 'spark' somewhere in the middle of the largest forest in Andelen. Perhaps by the time she found it, she would know why she could see in the dark as clearly if it were a full moon.

By the end of the third night, she had walked wide circles north, east, and south of Ethfirlaf, and found nothing. She would wake sometime before dinner, sing for a shift or two, eat, and head off into the woods until nearly Morning. She felt she walked far enough to be just outside what should be associated with Ethfirlaf—though, except for the road south where the region of Tarkusnaab lay, any land elsewhere could only really be considered 'outside Ethfirlaf,' but she tried not to think about that.

She had to look west tonight before she could truly start losing hope. But it was summer, and nights were short. Maybe she should wait until winter when she would have fistfuls of night-shifts to walk in the endless woods.

She forced a smile, and began to hum one of the songs that the patrons here preferred the most—'Hatchlings in the Dale' they called it. She thought she had created it after hearing the birdsongs in the woods on the ride into town. But, then, probably a lot of folks had heard the same birdsong, so it shouldn't have surprised her that someone had put words to it as well.

The west side of Ethfirlaf, unlike the other quarters, had a carpet largely of fern, quieting her steps. The previous nights' walks had been through accumulated dead leaves and twigs crackling and crunching underfoot. Every few steps, she could glance to her right and see a wavering torchlight in the direction of Ethfirlaf, peering between the maze of trunks. After Night-Fall, the insects of the forest went to sleep, and there was left only the barest *shush*-ing of ferns against her boots. Even the wind was calm, and the trees themselves seemed to settle in for the night.

So it didn't surprise her as much as it may otherwise have to see a wolf, ahead and to her left, slinking in between the trunks of oak and maple. It was not looking at her, but only ahead to where it was going. She paused mid-stride to watch it, and continued once it had put her firmly behind its tail.

If there are to be wolves guarding the goblet, she thought, *it makes sense this one would lead me to the others.*

Perhaps a quarter-shift later proved her right. Ahead, a pack of wolves had gathered in the night, looking for all the world like people gathered for a speech and awaiting the head speaker. Mother wolves tended bickering cubs. The males conversed about the days' business, or tended their mates. A few apparently un-mated wolves tried to look momentarily busy but relationally available. Catie put a hand to her mouth, keeping in a chuckle. She could even see Rodigger, sitting next to an important wolf and acting as though the importance was shared, though he was a little bedraggled and didn't appear too bright.

Catie sobered. She hadn't thought about Rodigger in some time, she had been so caught up with Deuel leaving and her continuing the job alone. Of course, she hadn't really thought of it as a job from Roth in so long either. She shook her head, returning her attention to what was going on ahead.

She noticed, then, a large stump in the middle of the pack that seemed to be alight with fire. And just as she noticed it, a massive wolf, snowy white, leapt out of the darkness and onto the top of it. As if a whip-crack signal, all the rest of the wolves' gazes came immediately to attend who was clearly their leader.

Catie's brows knit. Likely, then, the Berkarfor was hidden in the stump, or was somehow connected to it. She continued to watch the pack. They made no sounds, but as the white wolf glanced around those gathered she felt he was somehow imparting something to them all.

The last two times, the 'guardians' needed us to react to them in a certain way, to solve some issue or let one sort itself out, before they would leave and give us access to the goblet. So what is supposed to be going on here?

Catie stood and watched until her legs began to stiffen. But nothing up ahead changed. If it was a speech, it was an interminable one. She saw, occasionally, one of the other wolves shift. Snow-white would gaze at it and shift a little, and they would seem to go back and forth for a time. Then another would shift, and snow-white would turn to it.

Perplexed, Catie reached out, trying to sense any feelings or thoughts coming from the wolves—but there was nothing there. She took a few steps closer, quietly, and tried again. But still there was nothing. Maybe a faint sense of an almost tangible vastness, but that might have just been her.

Catie frowned. Standing still seemed to be accomplishing nothing. Maybe these guardians required her to walk up on them before something else would happen. She took several more steps, until her foot finally landed on a rare twig that broke beneath her weight.

Snow-white's head snapped up and it stood, hackles raised and a deep growl echoing through the night. The entire pack turned and assumed a similar position. A few circled to her flanks.

Maybe this goblet requires courage? she thought—hoped. She stood firm, gazing into Snow-white's eyes and pushing calm and curiosity. But the wolf on the stump took no notice. It raised its head and let out a deep, long howl. The wolves on the flanks leapt suddenly toward her.

She paused for a brief moment. *I think this Berkarfor requires me to run!* she thought. True to her thoughts she turned and bolted for Ethfirlaf.

The soft ferns were a trap, now, snagging her feet as she dodged between trunks. She could see the flickering watch's lights ahead, so impossibly far away. Growling and barking closed in behind her. The ferns seemed not to hinder her pursuers.

"Help!" she shouted into the night, hoping the guards would hear. She ducked beneath a branch, and around a trunk. A wolf launched sideways, its snapping jaws just missing her arm. She wished she had brought a weapon of some sort. The wolf landed to her right-front, turned, and leapt again. But its feet slipped, and it fell short. She twisted around another tree. She could see a few buildings, now.

"Help me!" she cried again. Something hit her back and knocked her flat. She twisted quickly, elbow out, knocking the wolf's head sideways just before its jaws lunged for her neck. She brought a knee up swiftly, and the wolf pitched behind her. But a second was right behind it, eyes shining and teeth dripping. She gripped the fur of its throat, arm stiff. It twisted its head, trying to bite her arm.

Another appeared beside her, and fangs sunk deep into her left shoulder as she screamed. She tried to bring up her left arm to keep that one away, but her muscles refused to work. The wolf wrenched and tugged as she cried. She couldn't let go with her right hand, for it would allow that one to finally reach the prize of her throat. She tried to bring a knee up, but the wolf skittered sideways.

It yelped, suddenly, releasing her arms as a halberd's point drove it to the ground. The wolf in her right hand twisted to get away. A sword came for that one, and she released it just quickly enough to keep her flesh away from the blade.

She sucked in ragged breaths, her eyes squeezed shut as fire consumed her shoulder. A torch lit her eyelids, and a voice called out to her. But she was not yet ready to answer questions.

18

HEALING WOUNDS

"That wasn't my fault."
"You cannot retract that claim, if she grows from this."
"Are they on their way yet? Perhaps they can help her."
"You still do not realize her potential, do you?"

4 Savimon 1320 — Summer

Catie awoke the following morning, but did not open her eyes. Someone would be there looking at her. They would ask how she was, if she was okay. And she didn't want to fake a smile and lie through it.

She had refused to watch or speak as the doctor sewed up her wounds. Fortunately, around so many woodcutting saws and axes, the doctor here was familiar with cut and torn flesh. Her shoulder in the morning actually felt better than she thought it would. So, in a way, she would not be completely lying. But she knew that wouldn't pass a Grandmother's scruple.

Her first real test since being on her own again, and she had failed—miserably. Had to run for help, and almost didn't get it. They had asked how she had come across the wolves, and the only explanation she could give them made her seem like more of an idiot, some empty-headed girl who only worried about clothing and hair and whether or not she was beautiful, and had no business being on her own in a sawmill town.

The room, though, was silent. So here she was, alone. Everyone had abandoned her yet again, because they had more important things to attend to. Gabriel had chosen life in her village. Rodigger, his own hate for Deuel. And Deuel? At least Dannid hadn't had a choice: Roth took him from her. Deuel, who shared thoughts and feelings, who had seemed to care about who she was and what was happening to her—of his own freewill had left her because his own desires were more important.

Part of her knew that wasn't fair, but it was a far smaller part of her than the part that felt alone and incapable. She shouldn't have been surprised: she was a woman. A girl. Rodigger had known she wasn't capable, and had only retreated from her when she tried to assert otherwise. But until that point, he had seemed interested in her. Maybe he hadn't abandoned her, she had pushed him away with her delusions of competence. Maybe if she'd felt a little less capable, Deuel would still be here, too. And if she'd felt a little less capable, she wouldn't be in this bed in the aftermath of a wolf attack with stitching in her arm. Stitching done, by the way, by a man. A *capable* man.

And so she stayed in bed with her eyes closed, waiting for someone more capable to feed her and tell her it was okay, that it wasn't her fault because she shouldn't truly expect to be successful anyway, that she should just stay in bed and get her rest. One day she could go back home with a caravan filled with capable people. She could get married back there, and have children, and do all the things in life that were expected of her. Nothing difficult, things people were okay with her doing, as a woman. A girl.

But no one came to feed her. She peeked once, and no food was by her bed. There was a pitcher of water, but no glass. Dangerous, probably, for her to try to get her own drink or feed herself. Better wait for someone to come.

The shifts dragged by. She blinked her eyes open wide and glared at the ceiling. She glanced again, managed to raise herself up a little. There was definitely nothing to drink from except the pitcher. Where *was* everybody? She cocked an ear, but she heard no sounds outside the door.

She managed to rasp a faint "hello?"—her throat was so dry!—but no one answered. She needed a drink. This was ridiculous. She rolled to a sitting position on the edge of the bed, still glancing toward the door. She flexed her shoulder. It hurt, and she couldn't move her arm easily, but it moved. She stared at the pitcher, rose, and walked over to it, and took a sloppy drink from its wide mouth.

The water was so *cool!* She had never tasted water so pure and cool. She raised the pitcher again, not caring as water spilled off the sides of her mouth and onto her shirt. She paused to breathe through her nose when she needed to, but drank half the pitcher in one shot. Well, maybe a third of it, with the rest of a half spilling down her front. Even that was refreshing.

She took a deep breath, and sighed. The house sat on the edge of town, and the Brithelt Forest stretched away outside the window. It was Evening, at least: orange eve-light lit the trees and ferns in sporadic shafts that flickered in a breeze. And when the dancing leaves parted just right, a thin beam made its way to her eye. Her window faced west, toward last night's debacle.

Why had the wolves acted that way? The white wolf fit the riddle. The 'shadowed spark' was evidently some sort of glowing lichen, and had been there. What had changed? *Should* she have simply stood her ground?

Or was she meant to find the location only by the wolf and the lichen, but approach in daylight? Should she try to find out?

I thought you weren't capable?

Catie snorted. Capable of fighting wolves by herself? Who was? She had misunderstood. A failing, perhaps, but one she could repair. Maybe if more people weren't afraid to misunderstand, they would admit when they did, and move on to understanding instead of straining violently to cling to their misunderstanding as truth.

Like you misunderstand Gabriel, Rodigger, and Deuel?

Let them pursue their own desires. Deuel, she knew, did what was right. At least, what she would do if faced with the same fear. Gabriel, too. Rodigger? No, he was one who clung to misunderstanding, and she would never be like him. She couldn't force him to change, but neither could she think he did what was right, what could set him free to become the man he might be capable of being.

And Roth?

She paused. The Wendol in Kavlen fought and argued because each had been hurt by the other. Did Roth, too, fight and argue because he had been hurt? Did he simply hide that hurt under anger and hate, because it was easier than admitting the hurt? She didn't know—couldn't know unless she could talk to him.

And she couldn't talk to him without bringing him the Berkarfor. If she did that, then maybe he would listen to her.

She drew another deep breath. Time, then, to put her theory to the test.

But first, she wanted a bit more information on wolves. Just to be safe.

The keeper glanced up as she entered, looked her up and down.

"You don't look too much worse," he said. "How do you feel?"

"Foolish," she replied.

The keeper chuckled. "Thrad said you did okay, for having two wolves at you," he said. "Said he couldn't imagine facing more than one, and that without a blade."

"Tell him I don't recommend it," she replied with a smile. "Speaking of which, where might one get a blade around here?"

"Going sawin'?" he returned with a grin.

"Actually I was hoping to find a Nagrath dagger," she said.

The keeper had the good sense to look in her eye before laughing, and didn't. He acknowledged her sincerity with a respectful frown. "Seems—most often—folks that know how to use one of those don't look much the part," he said. "Kiel'll have one. Two shops up from the south sawmill." He paused to wipe a mug and place it under the counter. "Going hunting for the wolves that got you?"

"I assumed the two that got me were killed by the watch," Catie replied. "And I don't hunt things I don't understand." *Except Berkarfor.* "Much."

"Smart lass. You might ask Eidemon," he said, gesturing with another mug toward a patron Catie hadn't noticed. A quick glance told her he was old and wore thick pelts, even in summer.

"Does he know the ones around here?" she asked, glancing again at gnarled fingers and thin russet hair that looked only slightly better-kept than Gabriel's had been.

"I don't know. Newer in town, only showed up a month or so ago," the keeper replied. "Not sure what he does with himself either. But you don't get a coat like that without learning a thing or two."

"Oh?" She looked again, recognizing now the thick wolf pelts. As if sensing their conversation, the man named Eidemon looked at them. He frowned. Catie looked back at the keeper. "Thanks," she said. "I'll see what he has to say."

She put on her most reassuring smile as she walked toward him. His frown only deepened as he looked her up and down, but he said nothing.

"Hi, my name's Catie," she said as she neared. "The keeper told me to talk to you about the wolves around Ethfirlaf."

"Catie, eh?" he said, his visage relaxing a little. "You almost look familiar to me. At least your outfit does. Do I know you from somewhere?"

Catie shrugged. "I don't think so. And I'm from a long way from here."

"And what would bring a young girl like you a long way from home?"

She smiled, a spark in her eyes. "The wolves of Ethfirlaf," she replied.

"I told a mercenary friend of mine, once, that folks needed to learn what dangerous beasts was, and what wasn't," Eidemon replied, his face stern. "I think you need to learn the same lesson."

"What do you think did this?" she asked, gesturing to her shoulder.

"Your stupidity," he replied swiftly. He turned his gaze resolutely down and ate.

Catie regarded him for a moment, then sat down. He still refused to look up. "You care about them," she said finally. He paused a moment to swallow, and take a drink. His gaze softened, but still did not rise. "And your coat," she said, glancing at the many hides. "Found them left to rot?"

"A wolf doesn't deserve that," he rumbled, his words still not wanting to leave his mouth.

"I saw a pack of them, led apparently by a white wolf," she said. "They were intelligent, self-controlled, and respectful." She paused to let a wry grin surface. "I'm afraid I may have snuck up on them."

"I doubt that, lass," Eidemon said, his eyes finally coming to meet hers. "There's nothing can sneak up on a white wolf. She would have known you were there."

"She certainly seemed surprised. She was holding some sort of—council, it seemed like, with the other wolves."

Eidemon gazed at her, seeing if she was making fun. But her walnut eyes were honest. "Most would find that hard to believe," he said.

"Most don't care about wolves," she replied.

"Why do you?"

"I think they protect something that I'm looking for," she said, leaning closer as she lowered her voice. "I tried to get it last night, but the wolves were there. I need to know how to get past them to get at it."

He looked at her, then glanced around the room. "I've been away a long time," he said, his voice also quiet, but firm. "But I know they don't want strangers finding what I think you're looking for."

Catie considered him a few moments, then smiled. "Oh, no. I've already found the 'shadowed spark'—"

"It's called gnotglow," Eidemon said.

She cocked her head. "But it does glow," she said.

Eidemon chuckled. "No, *gnot* glow," he repeated, enunciating. "It means 'night glow.' I think the name used to be *nochtglow*, but..."

"Oh. Well, you can keep all that. I'm looking for something a little older and a lot more rare."

"How rare?"

"There are only four of them."

Eidemon whistled. "That is rare. Why do you want them?"

Catie couldn't help but laugh a little. "Because I'm the sunniest girl in Andelen," she replied. Eidemon cocked an eyebrow. She shook her head. "Never mind. I'm just trying to understand wolves, so if there's a way to get around them, I can do it."

"I would find it strange that the wolves are there all the time," Eidemon replied with a shrug. "Just go when they're not there."

Catie drew a breath. "I'm not sure these are normal wolves," she said. *Even though they acted like it last night.* "And I don't want to wait until tomorrow morning. Would you come with me, this time? Then you'll get to see what I'm looking for," she offered.

Eidemon took a last bite, his gaze considering her as he chewed. "Why do you think that will make a difference?"

"What will?"

"Me coming with you."

Catie shrugged. "Because you know them, or it seems like you do," she said. "I tried understanding them last night, and it didn't work."

"They're just animals. You can understand a mountain, but that doesn't make it easier to climb."

"But taking someone with you that knows how to cross the mountain can keep you from dying," Catie replied.

Eidemon smiled. "I'll go with you," he said. "But I think you might do just fine on your own."

They rose. Catie watched as he threw his cloak over his shoulders. When he turned back, she managed to put on a smile. She *had* seen him before, long ago in Aresmak. She couldn't help but wonder if his mercenary friend had been Gabriel. *That would be a coincidence for the ages,* she thought as she led the way out of the inn. Even if that weren't the case, he had lived here, but had also lived in the south, and she could not know how he felt about Roth or Sheppar. Either way, he might misinterpret her seeking out the Berkarfor—want her either to give them to Roth, though she intended no such thing, or not want her to, even though she intended no such thing.

The further I go, the more I step right in it.

Give him a chance.

Without a weapon of some sort. And with an injured shoulder.

He is weaponless too. And you don't want to approach a wolf with a bared blade. They don't understand that.

Catie sighed, heading west. The sawdust smell of the mills gave way to the paler scent of leaf and wood, both living and decaying. Breezes today were light. She looked around the darkening wood, suddenly unsure if she could find her way back. She had roved a circle last night, starting from the south, and she couldn't quite remember how long she had followed the wolf before reaching the council.

But Eidemon was beside her, making no comment. Surely if she was going the wrong way, he would say something. He glanced at her, and something in his look confirmed it.

"You know a lot more than you let on, don't you?" she asked, her voice hushed, though the sawing and felling of trees by lumberjacks using the last of the daylight was loud enough to mask it.

"No," he replied, eyes twinkling for a moment before going flat again.

Caution to the wind. "Do you know what I'm looking for?"

"No," he said again, with the same brief twinkle.

"But you know why I'm looking for it."

Eidemon was silent, his eyes roving through the trees. "I once heard someone in a green hood speak out against a powerful person, in the presence of his followers. I thought they were stupid." His roving eyes came to rest on her. "But I also thought it was a man. There's your wolf," he said, flicking his eyes forward.

Catie looked up, seeing the wolf paused in mid-stride as it regarded the two of them. The sounds told her the lumberjacks were in far off other-reaches, almost as if they knew to stay away from this place. Which made sense, if they were so protective of their gnotglow.

The wolf considered both of them for a moment before continuing on its way. Eidemon followed, and Catie followed him. The wolf would pass behind a tree, stop to see if they still followed, and continue on.

Then, as they entered a nearly silent part of the woods and night fell, the white wolf appeared, sitting on the same gnotglow-covered tree stump.

You came back.

Catie blinked in surprise. *You* can *talk to me? Why didn't you do that last night?*

You didn't ask, you only pushed. And I didn't know you. But I knew if you returned unarmed, you were to be trusted. I didn't imagine you would bring The Hunter with you.

Catie swallowed. *I didn't know he was a hunter. I'm sorry.*

The white wolf's mouth opened in what seemed to be a smile. *He doesn't hunt us. He hunts with us.*

Is he...I mean, I've read stories...

Too many stories. No, he is human, which is why he looks at the both of us with such curiosity.

Catie glanced quickly. Eidemon indeed looked perplexedly between the two of them, as if realizing there was a conversation going on that he could not hear.

And why can I talk to you?

White's mouth closed, and her head cocked. *If you do not know, I do not believe I am to tell you.*

Because I'm a wyvern?

White glanced her over, and Catie felt amusement coming from her. *You do not have wings, scales, or claws. No, I do not think you are wyvern.*

That's not what I meant.

A low growl came from the wolf. *Are you abandoning, then, what you came out here for? What your shoulder was torn for? What two of my sons died for?*

Catie's gaze dropped. *I'm sorry,* she said again. *I didn't want them to be killed—not really.*

White settled herself a little. *They were not supposed to. But they did not do exactly what they were told. Even wolf younglings are often wise only in their own eyes.*

We are almost always wise only in our own eyes, Catie replied. *I'm out here because someone sent me who thinks he is wise. Maybe I'm only here because I think I am wiser.*

And why is that?

Catie sighed. *I think, because Roth attacks Sheppar because he believes he is right to; but Sheppar, in doing what he thinks is right, attacks no one. Violence may sometimes need to be met with violence. But I don't understand meeting peace with violence.*

Then you have learned something that many animals know, White replied. *And for that, I will teach you what no one else knows. Come to me, and look in the hollow of this stump.*

Catie hesitated, then walked forward. The white wolf, she realized as she drew nearer, was *massive,* even recognizing she was elevated on a stump. Had Catie seen her running through the forest, she might have feared for her life. But now, Catie glanced down as she drew near, looking only for the hollow White had spoken of, and not at the great shaggy beast towering over her.

At the base, directly below the great wolf, was a dark hole a little bigger around than Catie's fist, black in the middle of the effusive gnotglow that lit the stump as if it were on fire. She glanced at White, then back down.

Inside.

Catie knelt down as White watched. Reaching inside, she felt only earth. Her fingers searched, and she worked her arm farther in, until...

There. She felt the round hardness of the goblet, though the surface was rough. Found the stem and gripped, and pulled it from the stump. In the light of the lichen, she saw the cloth wrapped around the cup, and removed it. This was carved from Tiger's Eye, polished smooth with crystalline white lines between the brown and refracting even the faint orange glow of the lichen. Inside its cup was the rolled parchment she expected.

She looked again at White. *Thank you,* she said, bowing her head.

White bowed her own. *Thank you,* she replied. Catie felt her amusement again. *Now I can go back to a normal life, without protecting this stump for all time.* With that, the great wolf turned and bounded away. As she faded from the light of the gnotglow, Catie could see the rest of the pack detach from the trees where they had hidden, and follow.

Catie unrolled the parchment, reading it in glow-light as Eidemon approached.

"Why do you bother?" he asked. "Even with the lichen it's too dark."

She glanced quickly at him, then back down. She could read it clearly enough. She just couldn't understand it:

"Where a man could starve surrounded by food;
another die of thirst surrounded by water;

below, there mirrors the dancing rings;
the line is drawn between the kings:
the urchin and the otter."

Eidemon looked at her, eyebrows raised. "You have to figure out where that is to find the fourth?"

"This one is harder than the rest," she admitted, frowning at the parchment.

"You sure you read it right?"

"I can see pretty well, Eidemon," she said.

"And speak to wolves, if I'm not mistaken."

"It seems so." Catie rolled up the parchment, the words still etched into her mind's eye, and tucked it into the goblet. She took a breath. "I wish Deuel was here," she said, turning toward Ethfirlaf with a glance at Eidemon.

"Is this what Roth sent those three out to get?"

She nodded.

"I don't understand Gabriel leaving his mission," he said as they walked back to town. "How many years I've known him, he's always finished the job."

"And Deuel was probably always with him, right?"

Eidemon cocked an eyebrow. "Do you mean they're not?"

Catie shook her head. "Gabriel is in Attelek. Deuel is headed to Balnath." She stopped suddenly, not sure if she should have mentioned *exactly* where Deuel was going.

"Off to see the Kinnig, is he?" The old wolf man chuckled. "I suppose it was about time."

"You knew about that, then?"

"Gabriel and I served together, back then," Eidemon said. "Not always side-by-side, but we kept up. I got to know Deuel pretty well, too, and if he's headed to Balnath to see Sheppar..." Eidemon shrugged. "Do you plan to join him there, once you've found the fourth?" he asked suddenly.

Catie bit her lip, her gaze on the ground in front of her. "I think, if I can," she replied quietly. "He may need my help."

Eidemon stopped, casting a glance toward Ethfirlaf before leaning in close to her. "How much help do you think he'll need?" he asked.

Catie hesitated. She knew Deuel didn't want everyone to know what was near there—wasn't sure *she* was supposed to know. But if Eidemon knew him, and Gabriel, if they had been close, at all? "I think there is a very serious threat against Sheppar," she said. "Deuel may get caught up in it. That's all."

Eidemon's eyes searched hers for several long moments. Finally, he nodded. "You do well," he said. "That is a very close secret, one which I've kept for years as well." He paused, his eyes growing distant. He straightened, and focused. "The ocean," he said, with a smile.

Catie blinked. "What?"

"Where a man can die of thirst, surrounded by water."

She looked at him and drew a deep breath. "Well, that makes it easy," she said, easing her tone with a grin. "Anything else?"

Eidemon shook his head. "Never much cared for the ocean, so I didn't visit it much. You'll be okay. It's probably in a port, not just out in the middle of the water. Try Ostflir, it's closest."

Catie groaned a chuckle. "Thanks," she said. "It's probably in Satost, to teach me patience."

He laughed, and she laughed too as they continued into Ethfirlaf.

19

LIGHT SONG

"I hope I'm not being too obvious."
"You must learn by doing."
"I'm not sure that helps."
"We guide them, Teresh, not each other."

5 Savimon 1320 — Summer

Rodigger shifted in his saddle, trying to not cast another glance at Sharéd. They were in another of their long silences—days long, this one. Sharéd spoke, certainly, but only to innkeepers, and only when Rodigger refused to. They exchanged few words.

It didn't help, either, they were on the exact same road they had traveled to get here. If he had to spend another month in northern Andelen, they might have gone through the Brithelt, just to see it. But no, Sharéd always wanted to make time. Rodigger shuddered to think what would happen when his Therian reached the mountains.

"Are all your people gathered here already?" he asked, striking upon another idea.

Sharéd glanced at him, almost startled he had spoken, then looked away. "Enough."

"Are more supposed to be coming, though?" he pressed.

"They might."

Rodigger could tell the Beltrath was getting testy. "I just mean, I mean, better more than enough, than less, right? Can we be sure these behamien will be easy to take?"

"If they are in *veythya*—"

"But what if they're not? I think we should get everyone ready, and keep training until some more come," Rodigger said in his best Roth voice. "Really go after their stronghold in force."

Sharéd said nothing as they continued to ride. Rodigger thought he saw a shadow move quickly in the corner of his eye. But as he turned to look, Sharéd's stare distracted him. "What?" he asked.

"Why delay now? A week ago you were..." He gestured a flapping motion with his hand. "*Pamdras.* Now..." He sneered and went silent.

"The mountains are difficult, Sharéd," Rodigger replied. "They might be able to watch us approach from a hundred different directions."

"What do then suggest?" Sharéd asked, facing forward again.

"We approach from a hundred different directions," Rodigger replied with a grin. "We should send out some scouts, first, and find where they hide. Then bring our troops up through as many avenues as possible, until the last possible moment."

Sharéd sniffed. He reached down and took a water skin, uncapping it and drinking a few sips. When he capped it again, he glanced quickly at Rodigger. "I think this is a good plan," he murmured.

Rodigger smiled. He thought it was a good plan, too.

Catie rode out of Ethfirlaf, saddlebags repacked for another week on the road. That would get her back to Finstaff. Then it was the longer road east to Ostflir, the great port of northern Andelen. Anything from overseas making its way to Balnath Agrend, and almost everything leaving Andelen for the Clanaso Islands and eastward, went through that port. It was a broad ocean between the continent and the Islands, and she hoped somewhere in that expanse of water to find a cup. She almost never could believe the tasks she set up for herself.

And yet, as she glanced down, she remembered that she had already found three goblets that had remained hidden for centuries. It was not the first time they had been hunted. In fact, they had been hunted enough that most were convinced the Berkarfor were legends—for surely nothing hidden could be so hard to find. It almost didn't bother her that she had lost one to Rodigger. He would be easier to find than a cave hidden beneath a lake, right?

And yet here she was, loathing the long journey to Ostflir for the last one. How many before her would have done backflips of joy for finding three of what everyone said didn't exist? To have faced down a *snehr-byor,* two Wendol, a massive white wolf... She wondered what waited ahead of her. The riddle didn't quite say. Unless it was a massive otter that would break her over whatever it meant by 'urchin.' No matter the guardian, history suggested she would overcome that, too. And she had her dagger, now. *Saferd* might have been a better word—longer than a dagger but smaller than a short sword, with saw teeth along the back edge from tip to about half-way back, and a hook for sword-breaking. It was called a Nagrath dagger because, according to legend, no one could survive the Nagrath Highlands with anything small-er. Her father had taught her to use it because it was wieldy from a young age, almost as if he had known he would leave before she was old enough to be taught by him on a true sword. She remembered asking Grandmother about that, long ago. But Grandmother had only smiled a sorrowful smile and said sometimes folks knew, without knowing.

Catie picked up her reins and clicked Kelsie into a fast trot. It was a beautiful day for riding through the trees, and she intended to enjoy it.

As the month closed, Catie found herself atop a small knoll, finally looking down the long road into Ostflir below. After so long on the road and at inns, the size of the port surprised her. Tall square buildings crowded the wharf, spreading out and up a broad bowl like sheep bedding down for the night. Great arms of land, bristling with more shops and homes, held the flat, gray-watered bay in a loose embrace. Far out on the points, barely visible at this distance, were look-out towers. Beyond that lay green, unsettled ocean, and a ship full of sails making its way in.

The breeze gusted, overflowing with salt and spices and animal and people smells, and, fainter, the cry of barterers and a white bird she didn't recognize.

Clattering wagons and lowing oxen, eager for rest, passed her by on their way into town.

As she gazed between land, sea, and sky, she thought she might actually prefer looking for the last Berkarfor on the sea, rather than in Ostflir. One of those ancients could easily have stuck it in someone's house, and it would never be found by someone actively looking for it.

She pulled out the parchment—it had become a daily habit since Hyalendel—and looked over it again, then up at Ostflir. *Where a man could starve surrounded by food. An expensive inn?* She grinned. Probably not that. Somewhere food was visible, but not attainable. She glanced down again. What if two lines referred to the same place? *Surrounded by inaccessible food and water...fish, and saltwater.* As she gazed out over the vista, her grin faded. If it was actually in the sea, she could swim, she knew that. But what was she supposed to do, dive down over and over again until she found it? More likely it would be so dark she wouldn't be able to see it. But then, strange lights attended every other Berkarfor: blue light in Agirbirt, brown light in Kavlen, orange light in Ethfirlaf. Maybe light wouldn't be a problem, but a clue.

She would still need to breathe, somehow. And she would need to know where to dive. For now, the sun was failing behind her. She tucked the parchment away and began riding for town. *The line is drawn between the kings: the urchin and the otter.* So, she would find a boat to take her out into the ocean until she saw an urchin and an otter, dive down between them, there would be some magical light, and a goblet. And a guardian, of some sort. Then she would travel back across Andelen, find Deuel, and...then...do something else with her life.

Simple. It was always so simple.

She found an inn, and sat in the common room trying to overhear conversations. Each goblet also was tied to the history of its hiding place, and she assumed Ostflir would be no different. But most of the people here were foreigners, only passing through, and most of the conversation seemed to surround trade and trading routes. She finished her dinner—fish, of course; there was abundant supply just on the horizon—and went to bed. Staying at one inn would probably not serve her well.

The next morning she went out to the docks. Clouds hung low and threatened a drizzle that never quite formed, but always seemed like it did. Even the birds—seagulls, someone told her with a grimace—didn't seem to want to go into the air today, bouncing in their fast-footed walk and peering at the interlopers who carried boxes and bundles and sacks and jars and hopes for a brighter future.

Well, most of the interlopers seemed to carry those hopes. As After-Noon came, Catie began to discern another group of people. These went about the docks quiet, reserved, undistracted, usually in light linens and heavy-soled sandals, and deep tans. Fishers. Men whose home would be Ostflir. Men who would have their own boats.

"Excuse me," she said to one with a beard as white as foam and more wrinkles on his face than Agirbirt on a windy day; "My name's Catie. I might need a boat ride one day. Soon," she added hurriedly as his face scrunched in puzzlement. "Would there be a boat I could pay to ride out on, just for a day?"

"Will it stop me fishin'?"

Catie thought a moment. "Not necessarily, but I would need to go to a specific spot."

"Which spot?"

Another thought. "Between the kings?" she said.

A grin split his face. "Lots of those, dearie." He gestured a hand loosely indicating the waters behind him. "Magiss a hunnerd years ago set up kings at every compass of the bay."

She craned her head, looking along the wharf wherever a ship didn't block her view. She could see the statues, now, standing at the ends of prominent piers and gazing across the water at one another. At least it meant she shouldn't need to leave the bay.

"What's an urchin?" she asked.

"Sea urchin?"

She shrugged. "Sure."

"Spiny things, 'bout yea big. You hungry?"

She shook her head. "Not really. You can eat them?"

"You can. Not very filling, so they ain't cheap usually. And they're harder and harder to find, anymore. Otters always seem to get 'em."

"In the bay?" Simple. It was always so simple.

The fisher laughed. "Not anymore, too many ships chased 'em out, I think. Further down the coast, though. Is that where you want to go? See you some otters?"

She smiled faintly: not that simple. "No, I don't think so. I'm not sure yet.

But I'll come find you whenever I'm sure. What's your name?"

"Pag," he said. "If you get here early enough, I'm usually at Gart's dock, that way," he said, gesturing.

"Perfect. Thanks," she said with a smile. "Oh! How much will you want, if I want you to take me somewhere you can't fish?"

"A day's catch brings me twenty, thirty coin, most days."

"Oh," she said, managing to keep her hand from straying to her coin purse. "Thanks. Hopefully I'll see you again soon."

She returned to town, to a different inn this time: Fishers and Crowns, it named itself. It was closer to the docks, where Catie hoped sailors who lived in Ostflir might patronize on their way home at night. After paying for her room and dinner, she tucked her purse away and pulled out her flute.

In Ostflir, it became apparent, patrons paid the musician directly, instead of through the keeper. Also in Ostflir, people were tighter with their coin than in most of the villages where she had tried this before. She played everything she could think of, as lively as she could manage. But as Evening wore on she still had only a few glints in the cloak she had placed on the floor to catch the thrown coins—the first few had bounced away and into untold recesses of the room before she thought of putting something down to catch them.

Finally, late at night when the patrons were sufficiently drunk, one shouted out: "play one we know, already!"

"What would you like?" she asked. He laughed lewdly, joined quickly by the others equally drunk as he. "What song!" she groaned over their racket.

The first drunk glanced around, an evil light coming to his eyes. "Liebast!" he said suddenly, and the laughter started again. "Sing the one about Liebast!" The others quickly joined him, hoisting their mugs.

"Ho hey! Liebast!"

They began singing, then, a shanty about someone named Liebast, apparently known for his exploits with women. Catie sighed, looking toward the keeper. He was talking aside to a man with a lute-case on his back, and presumably a lute inside the case. They both glanced at Catie, then to each other and nodded.

Catie glanced back to the patrons. She didn't know the song—happily, she thought—but she hadn't made nearly enough yet. Fortunately, it was a shanty, and she had already picked up the tune.

She raised her Tamis flute and joined in, following the melody with the deep reed and highlighting the jokes with peeps and whistles on the short reed. The patrons howled with laughter, and a few more coins arced her way.

At first she tried to ignore the words, suggestive as they were, but the more she tried to anticipate the wordplay, the more she had to pay attention.

Liebast had been a king of Andelen, apparently, who sired an untold and untellable number of children as he copulated his way through the breadth of Ostflir to the ocean. There he died, drowned in ecstasy, beer, and seawater, so worn out from his activities that he couldn't keep his head up for breath or women as the tide came in. Though history named him one of the greatest kings, and elevated him to the very pinnacle of the heights of Ostflir, true natives knew him—as the song ended—as a man "so prickled out from ten days of nights, that he lives in paradise *kal-fites.*"

Catie smiled faintly as the laughter galed over her. She had no idea what the last term meant, but they seemed to think it was hilarious. She glanced down at her cloak. There were enough shiny bits gleaming in the folds to last her, so she gave the stage to the lutist, gathered up her things, and went to her room.

She went again to the docks the next morning, hoping to find something on the statues of the kings, or maybe pick up more conversation about Ostflir itself that might help. Down in the heart of things, the incessant noises common to the sea seemed to fade into the background. The sailors shouting, feet running along the wooden piers, the various creaking and thumping of boats that rocked together, avian cries—all became part of a music so prolonged it faded as if into silence. Catie focused instead on making her way to each dock, studying the plinths and statues for some sort of resemblance to the riddle-poem.

As Noon approached, she saw another great ship as she wandered, coming into the bay through the watchtowers. This one looked a little different, somehow. More aged, perhaps, and the cut and number of its sails were different from what filled the rest of the wharf.

Smaller boats went out to greet it, and guided it toward the dock where she stood. She realized it might get very busy very soon, but she hadn't made it to the king standing at the end yet, so she backed as hard as she could against a stack of boxes and tried to stay out of the way. Dock-men moved past her, preparing to receive the ship. She startled as something slippery brushed past: it reminded her of a fish, a little, or maybe a frog except it was upright and only a little shorter than her. It wore only a loincloth, and a band of blue wire on its left arm. It seemed to move a little less surely than the others on the dock, and kept its head down. She wondered what it was, but didn't have the time to ask as the ship drew nearer, catching her attention again.

Sailors scrambled through the rigging, drawing sail and letting the oared boats move their ship. A few folk gathered along the rail: apparently a cargo ship that also took passengers—she had seen it before, but it was uncommon. Most of the passengers lining the rail were not Rinc Nain. They had black or brown or yellow-white hair—she had no idea what nation had yellow-white hair. Lots of strange things to see in an international port, she thought absently. There were two, though, that were Rinc Nain: a lady, it appeared by her rich blue dress and posture. And her attendant, though the poor man was missing his left arm below the bicep.

Ropes leapt from the side, and dock-men hurried to tie off the ship. Gangplanks ran out, and the passengers offloaded first. Catie kept her eyes on the two Rinc Nain, watching as they descended but didn't seem to know where to go. The lady spotted Catie and approached.

"Do you know where we might stay for a night? And we'll need horses."

Catie smiled. "I'm sorry, I'm new here too. Well, newer. Just don't stay at Fishers and Crowns, lady. I don't think you'll appreciate it there."

The pair smiled, and glanced at each other as if sharing a joke. "I'm not a lady," she said. "But I thank you for your advice."

They turned and moved away, their heads together in conversation that looked closer than a lady and her attendant. Catie wondered what the joke had been. Maybe she was called a lady despite her protests for the entire journey from whatever port she had come from. Catie smiled as she remembered Geezer's words.

"Ready to go yet?" came a familiar voice. Catie turned, and glanced down toward the water. Pag sat in his boat gently rocking, squinting up at her. He had been one of those guiding the ship in.

"I thought you were only a fisher?" she asked.

"I take what comes," he said. "They were headed my way, and it's easy coin. Where to?"

Catie grimaced. "I still don't know," she replied. "And even if I did know, I'm not sure I can get to it."

Pag continued to squint. "But you know it's by boat."

"Well, it might be in the water. Deep, in the water."

"And you can't swim?"

"No, I can. I grew up in a small fishing village on a lake."

Pag drew a breath. "I've been on easier fishing trips than trying to get answers from you, girl," he said. "You know you need to get somewhere on a boat, but you don't know where. You know you might need to swim, and you can, but you can't. No wonder you young kids never get anything done."

"It's a very long, very complicated story," Catie said. "And the answers might bring more questions than they solve."

"Well, you dodged that net," Pag growled. "It's a large bay. Get in, and you can tell me all about it while I row."

Catie blinked. Why not. She squatted onto the dock and sat, then lowered herself into his boat. He seemed to eye her praisingly as she kept the rocking to a minimum. "I said I grew up in a fishing village," she said as she sat down.

Pag said nothing, but pushed them off with the oar and slipped it into the lock in one smooth motion. He pulled them away. Catie unlocked the tiller, looped her arm over it, and steered as a smile came to her face. It had been some time since she'd been on the water, and she had forgotten how it felt.

As he pulled, he began muttering a song in time. Catie cocked her head. "What language is that?" she asked. It wasn't Rinc Nain.

"Old Clansmen," he said. "I guess we picked it up on our way through those islands, and some of it stuck."

"And what does *kal-fites* mean?" she asked.

Pag chuckled. "Again with the sea urchins?"

Catie stared hard at him. "Which one is King Liebast?" she asked, gesturing to the statues.

"Ah, him. Poor man never had a chance. Well, most folks coming into port don't even know their kings, so I guess it doesn't matter. He's the one on the left," he said, jerking his head toward the twin arms making the mouth of the bay.

"Who's on the right?"

"King Tareddor. Longer ago than Liebast. Swam the bay around in one go, because someone said he couldn't."

"So he was a good swimmer?"

"Could you swim around this?" Pag asked with raised eyebrows.

Catie's head swiveled. She didn't even want to *walk* around it. "As good as an otter?"

Pag frowned. "Now you mention it, they did call him The Otter. How about that?"

"Yeah," Catie said, glancing toward the watchtowers, on which stood The Urchin and The Otter. "How about that."

"That's where you want to go?" he asked.

Catie nodded, adjusting the tiller. It was still a broad mouth, even if you drew a line between it. That left one more line: *below, there mirrors the dancing rings.* Somewhere along that line, she hoped, would be something of an image of dancing rings.

Pag rowed her along the line, then patiently across again. But she saw no rings, and certainly no dancing. She sighed, looking out to sea. The sun was high overhead. It was a clear, hot day, and though she did the least work, she was beginning to sweat. And it was lunch time. *Surrounded by food,* she thought, and looked down into the water again. It would be supremely foolish to just start diving down, hoping to see something under the waves.

"Are there any sunken ships down there?" she asked.

"Probably," Pag said. "This harbor mouth looks wide, but come at it in the night, in a storm, maybe one of the watchtowers' lights has snuffed out?" He shrugged.

"But none you know of for certain," she said.

Pag shook his head, resting on his oars. They sat without speaking. The locks clicked and groaned as the boat rocked. The waves slurped against the side of the boat. But it was otherwise a sort of silence, as if the world waited for her to solve the riddle.

"I'm hungry," she muttered at length. She rarely could think while she was hungry, and she had been growing tired of the silence, too.

"You didn't bring anything?" Pag asked. Her gaze was so close on the water she didn't see the sparkle in his eyes.

"I didn't know I'd be out here right now," she replied, a little snappier than she had meant to.

"Here," he said. "I always bring extra." He held out a cloth wrapping. She sat up and looked at him warily.

"Fish?" she asked. She'd had more than she thought was enough, the past few days in Ostflir.

"Imagine it's chicken," he said, giving the wrap a quick shake.

She took it. "Thanks," she said, pulling back the layers. It did look like chicken, but it smelled...fishier. "What is it?"

Pag held a finger to his lips, and leaned forward with the same finger held pointing upward. "It's seagull," he whispered.

Catie glanced up. Gulls were circling overhead, their cries blending with the rest of the music so she had forgotten they were there. She smiled. Most people would be so concerned with the food so obviously below them, they wouldn't think there might be food above.

Her smile froze. Surrounded by food. Music meant dancing, and circles were like rings. She glanced away. The gulls swooped above the boat, but not above the water anywhere else. She looked down into the boat, expecting to see the Berkarfor there, maybe dredged up in a net and forgotten.

"I told you to imagine it was chicken," Pag said defensively.

"No, it's..." she trailed off, looking down into the water. How deep was it, here? Deep enough to let ships pass. Too deep to dive?

"Going in?" he asked, beginning to understand.

"I think so," she said, trying to calm her breath. She needed to relax, if she wanted to hold it for any length of time. But something held her back, seemed to tell her the goblet wasn't there.

Below, there mirrors the dancing rings.

Mirrors weren't the object, they reflected the object. Below mirrored above. She looked up, squinting as the sun dazzled her with its brilliant white.

Blue light. Brown light. Orange light...white light?

She blinked, sitting back a little. What did the colors mean? Why would white come after orange?

It wasn't the color. It was the light shining through: water, earth, fire...and air.

She shaded her eyes and looked up again. The gulls still circled, still cried, but something wasn't right. They weren't looking for food, weren't landing on the water or flying away. They were just there—had seemed to be there without warning. And they were definitely too high to grab.

She reached out, trying to sense their little bird brains. Maybe she needed to communicate with them, like she did the other guardians. But it was as if nothing was there. Not that there wasn't something to communicate with, but literally as if the gulls didn't exist. Like she was imagining things.

To come this close, and yet seem so far, to have spent so many months searching, solving puzzles, learning, growing, sympathizing, forcing herself far, far outside the places she felt comfortable. Allowing herself the concept of forgiving Roth, of letting go of what happened, because she wanted to be *better*—better than she was yesterday, and better tomorrow than she was today. And to reach this point, and be stuck yet again? What was it all for? Catie sighed. She truly believed the Berkarfor were to be sought, not acquired. But how was she to know if she had actually found it, unless she saw it? She needed to know. She needed to see it. If only she could bring the birds down closer. Call them, somehow.

Catie pulled out her Tamis flute almost reverently. She looked up at the gulls, and began to play like the birds in Ethfirlaf, in the Brithelt. After all, Tamis had created the flute to attract the birds back to the devastated forest. Maybe she could use it to attract the seagulls lower.

She listened to their cries, tried to mimic them but more soothingly. Still they circled, not looking, not even seeming to exist except Pag had seen them, too. She continued playing, trying to ignore Pag's look as if she were losing her mind. She knew that what she sought was there, and didn't care how she looked trying to attain it. It had to be there. Right?

After a few more moments, just as her hopes splintered, one of the gulls swooped lower, drawn by the music. It came down, wings spread, landing perfectly on the gunwale, its eyes piercing Catie's.

On its back it carried a goblet of a crystal so clear it seemed invisible but for the occasional swirl of rainbow light across its surface, or the refracted sparkles reflecting off the water's surface as if it were encrusted with a thousand diamonds. Lowering the flute, she reached out, and grasped it.

Blinding white light struck her. Or, it seemed like it should have been blinding, but it didn't hurt—it seemed rather to heal. It seeped into her like water into a cloth, spreading along every fiber, into every corner of her mind, soul, and body. It flashed, *becoming* her mind, soul, and body. She drifted away, above Ostflir, above Andelen. She could see the Clanaso Islands like dots, Gintanos farther south like a god's smoke-pipe. The Pal Isans. Rinc Na like a two-headed beast. Carist south like tussling kittens. She could see the breadth of Oren, stars, great clusters of stars, thin clouds of brilliant green and red and orange with more stars in them—drawing further and further back until even those seemed tiny and insignificant. And then there was only the great ponderous bulk of time, shrinking and wrapping and crumpling up until a thousand years ago was yesterday, and two thousand years into the future was only tomorrow.

She paused there in utter stillness. She would have fainted except for the brilliant light becoming her and keeping her together. The great expanse of world and stars and clouds and time began drawing a breath, slowly, as if fearing that too sharp an intake would shatter everything. A hum grew, the beginning of a note of music too sweet to release. She wanted desperately for that note to release, to sound across the world and across time, knowing it would begin the purest melody ever created. The bow was on the string; the hairs drew across it in anticipation.

But the bow lacked sufficient hairs to vibrate the string. The note could not be made. To strike now would be to destroy everything with a pitch-less keen. In the stillness she knew the light that had become her had created her first, could shape her into an adjoining hair. That when enough others joined her and the time was fulfilled, they could start the note that would start the tune. But she had to let herself be shaped, drawn tight, and pressed hard against the other strings. As she imagined the note that might be sounded, realized her wildest imaginations did not even equal the fourth part of the hum she heard now, she yearned for it. Begged for it. Pleaded for the chance to be part of the making of the melody.

The drawing breath ceased. The note retreated from the cusp, and Catie fell from the stillness. Great thin clouds, and stars, and continents, and Andelen, and Ostflir, and Pag's boat, and the 34th day of Savimon rushed toward her.

Suddenly she held the goblet. The seagull and the light were gone. And Pag looked at her closely as she wept without restraint.

20

THREADS GATHERING

"I didn't know they could do that."
"She is definitely the first to do it while alive."
"What does that mean?"
"...I'm not sure."

1 Fulmatung 1320 — Summer

C atie sat on her bed, trying to remember yesterday. She knew it had felt real, as if she had truly been there, had seen Oren and stars as if from an unfathomable height. Now, reaching back in her memory, it felt more like remembering a dream. Which, truly, made more sense.

The Berkarfor were real, though. She had three of them arranged on her trunk. They could have hidden them in houses, nondescript as they were, just clay, wood, and steel. She thought for a moment the first had been silver, wondered what it looked like now. She hadn't looked at any of them that closely lately. Maybe that had been the steel one. No, that was the one she had just found. A mirror, like the riddle had said. Wood from a stump, clay from a cave. Just cups. Perhaps someone would have thrown them away, if not hidden.

She sighed, scratching an itch on her foot. She still wanted to find Deuel.

The thought, innocent as it had seemed, surged through her. She needed to find him. There were things to be done—too many things. Deuel, Roth, Sheppar, Rodigger, Gabriel: so many people she knew, so many that needed to join the song.

But even as she considered them, she felt it wasn't right. She needed to go...somewhere. But why? She paused, one leg swung off the bed. She didn't know. It was the same sense she had gotten in the grass outside Akervet. There had been a voice, she thought, while time was unfolding and uncrinkling and flattening back out to normal and depositing her into yesterday again. What had it said? She closed her eyes, trying to remember the dream. *Remember the Ekllar?* And yet, it was not her who heard it, it was someone in the future. Was she going to say it to someone? What was an Ekllar?

There had been another memory too, one she did not try so hard to remember. A memory of wyverns in the sky, of her flying with them. She was not settled on that life, just yet. There seemed too much to do, first.

She shook her head. Maybe something had been in the seagull she ate. She stood and pulled on her shirt. When her head came out the top, she saw the goblets arranged on the trunk. No. It had been real, and it had something to do with seeking—not finding; seeking—the Berkarfor.

And now she needed to find Deuel, and then go...somewhere. Time was...she almost thought *of the essence,* but time was not the master. She would move with purpose, not impatience. *I have a purpose.* She smiled with a mix of joy and duty. She had a purpose, and she would fulfill it. Whatever it was.

As she rode out under blue skies, she passed a convoy on its way down Great Merchant Road. The sun was rising clear of the watchtowers, the two kings, light filling the harbor.

"Are you following us?" a pleasant voice asked.

Catie startled forward, a quick denial on her lips that never left. It was the lady and her attendant from the ship.

"Oh, no!" she said brightly. "I'm just leaving the same time as you, I guess."

The lady—woman—smiled. "So are a lot of people, it seems."

"Well, a lot of cargo comes into Andelen through here."

"I've been cargo for far too long now," the woman said. "It could have been made a little faster a trip," she added, with a sidelong glance at her attendant-companion.

"If I had known it would be so hard for you to give up, I would have left you to it," the man replied. Though his voice rumbled, Catie could tell he wasn't in earnest. She felt like playing along anyway.

"Seems like men never leave women to it," she said lightly. "We always have to give things up for a man's demand."

"Oh I didn't do it for him," the woman said, her voice now sincere, and low. She took a breath and smiled. "He just happened to be right, this time."

"My name's Catie," she said. "If we're going to be traveling a while."

"Sarah," said the woman.

"Geoffrey."

"What brings you to Andelen?"

"A friend asked me to come," Sarah said. "Geoffrey decided to come with me."

"I'm sorry, I was trying to figure out if he was your attendant, or someone," Catie said.

"Just a long-time and very good companion," Sarah replied. "We've been through a lot together."

"Oh." Catie managed to hold her smile in place. "I had one of those, not too long ago."

Sarah's smile faded. "I'm so sorry. What happened?"

"Oh, that sounded bad! He's alive, I think. I'm pretty sure. He's..." She trailed off and laughed. "He's very good."

Sarah looked at her with an arched eyebrow and chuckled. "Is he indeed?"

"He just had something he needed to do, east. In Balnath."

"Are you headed there to meet back with him?"

"I hope so. I'll have to find him, though."

"Then perhaps we *will* be traveling together a while," Sarah said. "We're headed there as well."

"With the convoy?" Catie asked.

"Well, it's been some time since I've been here," Sarah replied. "Unless Geoffrey remembers the country better, I'd like to stay with people who know it."

Geoffrey shook his head. "I did not explore very much," he replied. "When I was here, I was mostly concerned with heading south."

"Well, I'll be taking a different road when we get to Corsred," Catie said. "The convoy will head down Gathering Road—there's more to trade along the way, and it follows the water. But there's a faster route for riders on Forest Highland Road toward Mihrlandhen we could take, if you're interested."

Sarah glanced at Geoffrey, who shrugged and nodded. "We've been awhile at sea," Sarah said. "It might be well to make up some time. We're not sure how quickly Sheppar needed me to come."

Catie's eyes went wide as Sarah's mouth went thin. "Shep—" Catie cut herself off, glancing at the wagoners they rode among. She eased Kelsie a little closer. "Your 'friend' is the kinnig of Andelen?" she whispered fiercely.

Sarah sighed. Geoffrey rolled his eyes and gazed at her expectantly. Playfully. "Not exactly," she replied quietly. "One of the rulers in Burieng is, and I am his friend. He asked me to come and see what I could do."

"What can you do?" Catie's hand went to her mouth. "I'm sorry, that sounded mean."

Sarah laughed. "I understand. When I was asked, I had...other abilities. Now?" She shrugged. "Geoffrey and I have been through a lot. We might be able to give him counsel."

Catie sat back. "He probably needed it more, about a year ago." She glanced between the two companions. "Is that what you gave up? Your wind magic?"

Sarah glanced at her, a new light in her eyes. "It was. How did you know?"

"I guessed. Wind magic would have helped you sail here faster, you're wearing a blue cloak like I imagined a wind-user would, and you look..." Catie trailed off, but was plainly looking at her face.

"I'm a little older than Geoffrey," Sarah affirmed. "Maybe you'll be able to give counsel to Sheppar as well."

Catie gave a thin smile. "Could be," she said. "I've been through a lot, too."

Sheppar glanced up from the lilies as Samdar approached, a scroll clutched in the aide's hand. It was the third, and the latest, so it must have come from Merneset. If he was honest, he was a little more than curious about the relationships between the peoples represented there. Even twenty years ago, at the height of tensions, it was commendable that a Rinc Nain town within the Wastes managed to survive. If this recent incursion was in retaliation for the campaign, he would have thought Merneset would have been the first to go.

"Yes, Samdar?" he asked.

"It's from Lukens," he said. "Captain of the guard there after Jochavel retired last year. They've had no problems, have not seen any marked increase or decrease in gate passes to Beltraths. Prices on the streets are a little higher than normal, but there's rumors that a few of the springs have failed, and maybe some sort of blight on goats."

"So he believes everything is fine," Sheppar asked. Samdar nodded. Sheppar sighed. "How old is Lukens?" he asked.

"Oh, his father served with you in your campaign, my lord," Samdar replied. "He was a good man. Led the 4th Heavy in the Tevorbath."

"Ah yes, General Lukens," Sheppar said, smiling at his lilies. "I thought the name sounded familiar. His son's a good man?"

"I haven't heard any bad reports, my lord."

"Hmm. Beltraths in Merneset are charging more, and their water is scarcer in a land already made scarcer by us. They probably don't have milk, and less meat, because their goats are dying. And Guard Captain Lukens—son of General Lukens who helped drive Garedardan, whom many people worshipped, out of the Tevorbath—Captain Lukens doesn't perceive there to be a problem." Sheppar bent down and breathed deep of the rich, sticky scent of the lilies.

"Um, my lord..." Samdar began, spreading a hand wide.

Sheppar stood. "Send a message back to relieve Captain Lukens at once. Order patrols around Balnath Agrend, and especially into the Dragon's Eye itself. And send one detachment to Kostet's." He paused and squinted up at the sky. "And please request Fathistokset, Taferk, Ravverbit, Semmedor, and Narpont keep a look-out, would you?" He glanced at Samdar, a gleam in his eye that had faded almost twenty years ago. "The Beltraths are coming, if they're not already here, and we are going to help protect the behamien the way they helped protect us."

"Yes, my lord," Samdar said, bowing low.

"West!" Roth hissed. "We're going west, Stethen, because we cannot have five hundred..." He broke off quickly, glancing around the still-crowded market. "Five hundred *kettles* sitting in town," he finished in a moderately lower tone. He shook his head. "Do you know there was a time I enjoyed the catch-phrases and speaking in riddles? Especially when teaching that worthless, stupid boy who now threatens to ruin everything!" He pounded his thigh with a fist. "I hate catch-phrases and riddles. I should have taught the boy plain so he would not *wreck it all* in some ridiculous attempt at piety. I cannot remember what I saw in him. If there was anything before, it is gone now. And if there is still breath in him when I catch up to him, I'll make sure that's gone as well! I told them to make camp west of Fathistokset, far out into the plains where they would not be easily found, until I could come to them and tell them where all the little hiding places were, in the Eye. So, do you understand why we're going there now?"

"Of course, sir," Stethen replied. "I misunderstood. I thought Durla was our cover, and it was all we needed."

Roth glared at him. "Durla is not a large enough cover for *five hundred kettles*. Durla could not cover *ten* kettles this far west of where kettles are made."

"I'm sorry, sir," Stethen said.

"This is why Durla can rarely come out of the Fallonvall," Roth continued to seethe as they rode out of town. They had brought a few wagons north with them, and had them sitting outside of town also as cover. Supposedly, that's how Durla Fest preferred doing business. "Because Durla is surrounded by very sorry people."

"Yes sir," Stethen replied tiredly, letting Roth ride up to the wagons ahead of him. There was a time—it was a while ago, now—that Steth had admired Roth, admired what he stood for and proclaimed. Then Roth had started to change. A few months ago, the change had become severe and pronounced. Close as he was to the man, Steth still did not know what happened. It was almost overnight, Roth had suddenly begun violent temper swings. The army was falling apart around him. The southern villages had started slipping away, returning to their own ideas and lives. Maybe that was it. Suddenly, Steth couldn't remember which had come first.

Whatever Roth hoped to find and accomplish here, Steth wasn't sure it would be in time. Lately, he wasn't sure he *wanted* it to be in time.

Gabriel entered Taferk, tired and sore.

It had been a long ride through the Tevorbath, as it always was. At least there had been a few days he was able to push to a second inn, and made the ride a little shorter. Now, he felt it in his muscles. Usually, he had only felt it in his conscience.

It was not that long ago, by his reckoning, that he could catch at least one glimpse of Garedardan on any given ride through the valley. A great, black-scaled dragon, Gared had always jealously protected the Feast, and kept a keen eye on it. Gabriel suspected that, as behamien, Garedardan had lived in the Tevorbath, had somehow had a closer connection to it than it being simply his nest.

It had taken a lot of persuasion to get him to leave, more than Gabriel was strictly comfortable with. Harder still to find a place in the Wastes, and convince him to stay there. Deuel had been helpful in that: flying at height, he had been able to see the glint farther off where the sun struck water. Deuel had been able to fly to it and scout, to see who protected the oasis and whether it was large enough—of course, he had the dragon's eye for it. And it had been Deuel, with a little prompting from Gabriel, who had talked the great, magnificent dragon into seeing it for himself.

The rest had been relatively painless. Except now, spending days and days riding through the valley, looking for the great, graceful blackness, constantly remembering it wasn't there, remembering where it was instead.

Still, it was like riding a saddle for a long day. It ached and pinched in the evening, but given enough time the pain was eventually forgotten. At least, until you had another long day in the saddle. That's what he told himself as he lowered himself to the ground with a grunt, and handed the reins to the young boy who waited with outstretched hand.

The clouds below him passed, and Deuel could see the peaks and sharp valleys of the Dragon's Eye. From this height, it truly resembled an eye, a circle of peaks near the center as pupil and iris, great valleys stretching away east to west giving the illusion of a lidded ball, the foothills themselves the lids.

It was also easy, from this height, to see where the caves lay. From the ground, he knew, the valleys forced most on foot or hoof to traverse right by the place of *veythya*. But from here?

He pitched forward and folded his wings, a stooping falcon in man-size plummeting from the blue skies. He hurtled past the highest peak before snapping his wings open, muscles straining to slow him down. He banked, circled, rose, and landed on a stone porch before a great black opening. To the right, jagged rocks like stairs led to the valley floor. He shuddered his wings—they were trying to fall asleep after the sudden release of strain—unsheathed Halm and Ro Thull, and entered the cave.

His eyes adjusted quickly. There appeared to be no danger, no one hiding. He had passed Rodigger and Sharéd still on the road sometime back, he was fairly certain. He had known that didn't mean Sharéd's men might not have already scouted and found the cave. But everything appeared as it should have.

He drew a breath and walked deeper inside. There would be many rooms. Each dragon-son was to have his own, if he needed it, to have space to grow. With one sense testing for residual Calling—even if another had already entered *veythya*, the Calling might persist, as growing times varied—and another sense reaching out for sentient life, he quietly entered the next room.

He stopped. Lying on a shelf against the back wall, was a behamian. His gray wings were folded around himself and had already hardened into a chrysalis. Deuel stood at the entrance, angling Ro Thull to catch the light of the cave opening and reflect it into the room. It shone through the semi-translucent wings and onto the face of the behamian underneath.

Deuel's breath caught. He knew he might recognize him, but this—this was still unexpected.

Rodigger entered the camp with Sharéd, eyes wide as he looked at the gathered tents. They were low, and situated in the surrounding terrain so that he hadn't seen them till they had come around a low hillock. Even now, the further they wound into the camp, the more he could see them stretching away.

"This is five hundred of you?" he asked.

"More have come," Sharéd replied, without looking around. "Perhaps delay is not needed."

Rodigger glanced around, and behind him, then shook his head. "No, I agree. But we still need to scout the Eye to find where they are staying, before we move in."

"Roth does not know this location?"

Rodigger pursed his lips. Probably Roth did know that. But if Sharéd didn't, and Rodigger himself didn't, that meant Roth or a messenger was on their way with that information, and might convince Sharéd to stick to the original plan when they arrived.

"We should already be in position, though. If we can," Rodigger said. "And since we'll be waiting, we can spend that time scouting. Here." Rodigger dismounted his Therian, scuffing the ground to clear the grass. It took him longer than he wanted, and he began to feel foolish continuing to kick the ground, but he was committed by then. More Beltraths gathered around, glancing between their leader and Rodigger.

"Keff ka duuli geyrda dana shah?" asked one of those gathered. Intent on the ground, Rodigger missed Sharéd's half-smile and shake of the head in response.

Finally he had a space of dirt large enough to draw a map, and knelt. He pulled out his dagger. "Balnath Agrend," he said, sticking the point in. "Dragon's Eye," he continued, tracing a line. "Us. I want scouts, four teams of four, going into the Eye, dividing it in quadrants. I want our forces split into four groups and camped here, here, here, and here," he continued, pointing to each side of the Eye as he went. "When one scouting team finds where the behamien are, each member returns to the four camps and leads everyone in."

"Might I suggest the scout teams are larger?" Sharéd asked, gesturing. Rodigger looked up. "Dangerous things in the mountains, not good for one man to walk alone."

"Sure, fine," Rodigger said, glancing back down. "Whatever size you think is appropriate—but divisible by four, so equal teams can go to each camp."

"And the other three scouting teams?"

Rodigger shook his head. "We'll have to count them a loss. Besides, the behamien may have more than one lair, so it will be better for my purposes—our purposes, rather, if they keep looking and make sure there's nothing there. Once one lair is cleared, the camps return to their original position, until all scouting teams have reported back."

"Good," Sharéd replied with a nod. Despite being contrary to Roth's original message, it was a good plan that allowed Sharéd his justice. Most of it.

"If we find the wingt man," he continued with a significant nod at Rodigger, "he is left for me. I must meet with him alive."

Rodigger glanced at his hen-scratched map for a moment, then nodded.

Catie shifted in the bed, rolling onto her side with a sigh. Twisting her neck, she could see through the window the half-moon over Mihrlandhen. The night was past its zenith and headed toward morning.

For months—most of her travels, really—her shoulder blades had not ached like they did in the Fallonvall. Now, suddenly, they decided to keep her awake again.

It was no use. Even on her side, they still bunched and hurt. It wasn't stress. Traveling with Sarah, if anything, relieved her stress. Geoffrey was not even that bad, considering he was nothing like either Gabriel or Deuel, and especially not like Rodigger.

She eased herself upright. Sarah was on the next bed, breathing deep and evenly, but she doubted it would take much to awaken the former sorceress. Catie slid on her pants gently, pulled her shirt over her head but only snugged the laces at her neck a little, picked up her boots, and stole into the hallway. There she tied the laces and tugged on her boots, creeping past Geoffrey's door before walking normally to the end of the hall, and entering the common room.

She was eager to find Deuel, to be rid of the Berkarfor if she could, though she knew it would do Roth nothing to hold them. She opened the door and stepped out into the cool night air. Autumn was definitely approaching, now. She began walking toward the forests around the edge of town.

She was a little concerned with how she might find Deuel, and what, if any, predicament he might be in. She couldn't imagine many. The dragon-son was certainly capable of handling himself. She wasn't sure what Rodigger might have planned, but didn't think it could be much. But that wasn't why her shoulder blades hurt.

She entered the woods proper, outside the edge of town. She still gave a brief shudder as her vision rippled, despite slowly getting accustomed to the uncontrollable shift. Here as in Ethfirlaf, she could tell her vision was better than the moonlight should have allowed. It had not been like that in the

Fallonvall, or even out of it that she could remember. Not until Kavlen. But then, until Kavlen, she had not been outside at night that often either.

She breathed deep, drinking in the smell of the forest—of growing, woodland things. She could hear, faintly, the trickling of a small stream over rocks. She moved toward the sound, picking out the fold of ground where she knew she would find it.

The shadows gathered in the valley, and even here her sight was not perfect. Here and there the moonlight glinted off the water like scales of a fish rolling in shallow water as it pursued its prey. She breathed again, expecting the cool, liquid smell of the stream.

But something else was there. It took her a moment to realize she was not alone in her mind. There was a presence, mammoth and ancient, between her and the stream—that the glint was not from something *like* scales, they actually *were* scales. And for a moment, she was terrified.

Then she saw the eyes, all warmth and sunlight and inviting like flames from an unexpected campfire on a freezing night. And then her terror was replaced by the kind of joyous surprise that only fits in a void left by banished fear.

Who are you? she asked; the 'dragon' part was obvious.

I am Lamendaretha.

I am Catie—Caytaleane, she corrected, remembering the old ways. *Did you summon me out here?*

In part. The rest was you. And Deuel.

You've heard from him? Is he okay?

He has reached the Eye. But so, I fear, have many others.

Catie took a step forward. *Is he in grave danger?*

It is likely. He is strong, but he is only one.

True. But what can just the two of us do?

More than you can believe, Lamendaretha said with an enigmatic smile. *For one, you understand humans better than our son.*

I thought he was Kaoleyn's son?

Lamend chuckled. *The sons are more concerned with parents than parents are with sons. While he was in Burieng, he was Paolound's, and Kaoleyn's who gave him birth. Here he is mine and Garedardan's.*

I think Garedardan needs to return from the Wastes, Catie thought. *The danger Deuel is in is because of that.*

That is yet to be decided. For now, you must go to him. Lamendaretha's head snaked forward a little, and she breathed on Catie. As Catie drew the warm air into her lungs, it seemed her sense of the dragon heightened. *You will now be able to sense Deuel more keenly,* she said. *The Eye is formed to keep the unlearned lost. Take this, as well.* Suddenly, images flashed through Catie's mind of great valleys and passes and peaks and a cave. She blinked rapidly. When it was done, she could not recall the images to mind.

I think I've forgotten them already, she said with some alarm.

You will remember when you see it. Lamend's nostrils suddenly flared, and she looked up. *One comes.*

Catie's head whipped around as someone crested the rise behind her. She thought she recognized the form—Geoffrey perhaps? Yes. His left arm.

It's one of my companions, she said.

He smells of death.

Catie turned back. *I'm sure he's not that dirty.*

Lamend's head dipped. *He has killed,* she clarified. *Dragon.*

"Geoffrey, I'm here," Catie called as she stood. "It's okay. This is Lamen-daretha, she protects the Brithelt."

"Well that is gratifying to hear," he replied. "I was not prepared to die just yet."

Tell him to put his weapon away, Lamend said with disgust.

"Geoffrey, your sword?"

"Right." He sheathed it quickly. "What are you doing out here?"

"I wanted to go for a walk," Catie said. "My shoulders were sore and I couldn't sleep." *Why are my shoulder blades sore so often?*

Deuel desires veythya, Lamend replied. *It is how his Calling affects you. But only when he dwells on it too much.*

"Did you kill Paolound?" she asked Geoffrey as he drew near.

He skipped a step, glanced between the two, and bowed his head slightly. "The second time, we did—four of us did. Sarah and I and two other companions. We did not know his spirit was being controlled by another."

"Controlled?" Catie asked, the same time as Lamend. *I could sense something was wrong,* the dragon continued. *I have never heard of this, though.*

"Yes, a mage in Burieng, Lasserain. He had killed Paolound some fifteen years ago, revived him with Life magic—" he paused as Lamend snorted her anger "—and Lasserain's spirit was able to manipulate the dragon to attack us."

"Is he—this mage—is that why you left Burieng?"

Is he still free to make war against dragons?

"We left after we killed him," Geoffrey replied. "Haydren, another of our companions, was able to fight and kill him this autumn."

Catie blinked. "Geoffrey, it's not autumn yet."

He paused. "Of course, I forget how far south Burieng is. It would have been your spring—the end of Halmfurtung."

"Paolound is avenged, then," Catie relayed from Lamend to Geoffrey. "She is grateful. She wants to know if there is anything she can do for you."

"We each had our reasons for what we did," Geoffrey replied. "The reward was in the success."

Catie cocked an eyebrow at Lamend, feeling her joy welling up. *What is it?* Catie asked.

Ask him to remain still, and to trust me, she said. *Tell him that some of the rules that humans are meant to abide by have not been emplaced on dragons.*

Catie relayed the message. Geoffrey held still as Lamend approached. Her great green head, sparkling like a thousand emeralds, bowed toward Geoffrey. The light behind her eyes grew till they pierced the night. As she breathed, her tongue flicked out, touching the stump of his arm, and he gasped as if sunk suddenly into cold water.

The lights in her eyes dimmed as Lamend retreated.

"She says to rest," Catie said, watching the dragon settle herself once more into the valley stream. "And then to hurry toward the end of our journey."

"Very well," he said quietly, his glances between his arm and the dragon.

As they walked back toward town, Geoffrey kept glancing down at his arm. "It's cold," he would mutter. "Her breath and tongue were warm, but this feels cold."

Catie was able to make her way into bed without waking Sarah. The next morning, she awoke to a terrific pounding on the door. She and Sarah both leapt up, throwing on their clothes quickly.

"What *is* it, by all things?" Sarah demanded as she opened the door. She stopped, her hand flying to her mouth.

Geoffrey stood outside, holding up both hands, his left arm completely restored.

21

ARRIVES TEN

"Things are about to get very complicated."
"They have been for some time."
"And the Islands?"
"Difficult to say."

10 Nuamon 1320 — Summer

After helping Geoffrey explain to Sarah what happened—several times—Catie spent the rest of the morning riding in relative silence. The two companions rode ahead, Sarah holding Geoffrey's restored hand as they spoke only by touch and glance. She was happy to see them that way. The love they had for each other was plain, even from the back. And she could not imagine losing something that significant and then receiving it back in such a manner. After all, she never actually had Deuel.

It wasn't the same, and she knew it, but it didn't help. Lamend's breath on her had changed something. Even now she could sense Deuel, though nascent and distant. But even if he rode beside her, would it be any different? He would always be behamien, and she would always be not. And what kind of relationships would wyverns have? Could she have if she could choose not to become one? Dannid had been fun, had been exciting. But he was a pale spark next to what Deuel had been able to offer her—*had given* her, right before he went away so she would have to chase him down again. Half of her screamed to dig in her heels and make Kelsie fly. The other half wanted to turn and run the other way, to pursue what the wretched, incomparable Berkarfor had shown her. Either prospect was exhilarating and impossible to even dream of, and yet she would have to pick only one. If only Deuel had been a terrible person, like Rodigger.

Autumn approached as inexorably as the Dragon's Eye, and by the time they left the Brithelt it had arrived. Another week, and the mountains themselves rose pale and gray on the horizon. The road ran obliquely to meet the corner, the Eye Fold—thus, Agrend.

One day's ride from the great capital city, Catie rose in her stirrups and gazed south at the mountains. It may have just been a trick of the morning sun...

No, it was the pass. As she gazed at it, she realized that even Kelsie would struggle on those slopes.

"What is it?" Sarah asked.

"I need to go into the mountains," Catie said. "I don't think Kelsie will make it through, though." She glanced back at the two. "Would you mind taking her with you to Balnath Agrend? I'll come back and find her when I'm done."

"Sure," Sarah said with a quick glance at Geoffrey. "Do you need anything?"

"I should just need a small pack," she replied, reining Kelsie to a stop and dismounting. She repacked the saddlebags as Kelsie and the others watched, moved her Nagrath dagger to her hip. Then she went to Kelsie's muzzle.

"Be nice to them," she said with a grin. Kelsie was always on best behavior. "I'll see you again in a few days. And thank you, both," she said with a smile for the other two.

"Be careful," Sarah replied. "We'll leave a message with the tower guards, to let you know where to find us. It was a pleasure riding with you."

"You too." She gave Kelsie one last rub, and turned for the mountains as Geoffrey and Sarah continued down the road.

It had been some time since Catie walked, and she'd forgotten how much slower things got closer. As the sun continued west toward the horizon, she entered the foothills—sharp, rugged hillocks here, as if long ago the mountains had punched through the surface of the land and showered great blocky boulders on the plain.

Darkness approached. She reached out for Deuel, but instead of finding his deep presence she felt a hundred small ones—several hundred, even. She paused, feeling deeper: they were men, banded together, and not too far away.

She continued forward quietly and carefully, keeping below the hills as much as possible. She wanted to get as far along as possible, and with her improved night vision decided to continue after it got dark.

She reached the base of the pass. The ground veered suddenly upward, not too steep to climb but steep enough that if she fell she likely wouldn't stop until she hit the bottom. Craning her neck, she thought she could discern a little shelf about fifty paces up or so. She took a deep breath and began to climb.

Using her hands to grip little tussocks of grass, she managed to reach the shelf. It cut back maybe two paces before the hill went up again. She paused to catch her breath, and looked down.

Below her and to the northeast, she saw faint glows as of coal-fires, kept low. But if that were so, it would mean at least two hundred fifty men—probably more if they cut down the number of fires, which she would have done if she were trying to remain hidden. She glanced along the shelf, but saw that it disappeared precipitously only a few paces that direction. She looked up again. Maybe she would see more from up higher.

She continued climbing as the moon rose, full and silver, lighting up the night for her like morning. The pitch grew less steep, until she could walk almost completely upright. She paused and looked down once more, chest heaving. Whoever they were, they hid themselves well. Even now she could only barely make out that there were, indeed, several hundred men, fires, and tents pitched below. Surely it was Rodigger and Sharéd's army, coming after Deuel and the behamien.

The sight gave her new energy, and she pressed on into the night until she had reached the summit and scrambled a few hundred paces down the other side. The valley below ran east to west, with another ridge directly in front of her. She looked back and forth. East was the way to go.

Her legs were on fire, and her knees didn't want to stay in one position. But Deuel was in danger, and might not know it. She reached out again, probing deeper into the interior of the Eye.

He was there! No longer a wisp, but solid and real as if she could reach out and grasp his arm, feel his flesh and bone beneath her hand. She closed her eyes and sighed. How would she ever see him face to face and leave him again?

She took a few breaths, turning her mind toward the great vastness she vaguely remembered from her dream in Ostflir. It *was* real. It was *real. It* was real. She had been there, had seen worlds and stars as small as sand. She was part of that, now.

She reached out again. *Danger,* she sent. Somehow she knew that anything more wouldn't translate. She felt him respond.

Catie?

I'm coming.

She continued scrambling down the slope. It was so much easier on this side. A few times she was able to just sit and slide. But the Eye was large, and she knew it would be another day or more before she would find him. Yet, somehow, she wanted to keep going, as if she could reach his cave any moment now. She continued up the valley, looking for the next pass to register in her memory as the moon climbed.

It was long after nightfall when Sarah and Geoffrey were finally ushered into Sheppar's study. The room was small, with a few plain wooden chairs and desks littered with papers, some loose and some in tight stacks. Sheppar sat back in one of the chairs, scanning a document by the light of the forlorn candles that emitted almost as much black smoke as flame. He had undone a few of the top buttons on his cloak, revealing a dirty-white tunic underneath.

"Twenty years since I gave them authority," he said as the steward shut the doors on his way out. "You would think they would know by now what help I give, and what I don't."

"But you still read their messages," Sarah replied.

Sheppar glanced over the top of the parchment. "Sometimes they're right. Have a seat, please. It hurts my neck to look up at people."

"Thank you," Sarah replied. She moved a small stack of papers off one chair and arranged her dress as she sat. Geoffrey took another nearby. "You do not have aides to read them for you?"

Sheppar barked a laugh. "They don't usually know what help I give either. It doesn't matter," he said, putting the parchment down and sniffing. "It gives me something to do. Sorry for not seeing you more formally, but by this time of night formality is usually tired and looking for a bed to sleep in, too. What can I do for you?"

"Earl Durdamon sends his regards," Sarah replied with a smile, "and his regrets: with recent events in Burieng he was quite busy. But he asked if I could come and offer my services."

Sheppar gazed at her blankly for several long moments. "Services for what?"

Sarah glanced at Geoffrey, then back. "I believe he said you were facing a rebellion."

"Oh, that," Sheppar said, leaning back with a wave of his hand. "I *thought* it was too prescient for the Beltrath incursion, no matter how much Durdamon knows. Well, I hope you have other business in Andelen, because the rebellion is nothing—Roth getting upset and talking to too many people."

"We had heard he controlled the Fallonvall. That seems like a large portion of Andelen to simply be dismissed."

"Well if he controls it, it's because the people want him to control it," Sheppar replied. "If that's what the people want, they shall have it. And he hasn't moved outside the 'vall in almost five years. I assume it is because he can't."

"And the Beltrath incursion you mentioned? They are from the east, right?"

"That matter is all but concluded, before you even arrived." Sheppar shrugged. "I'm sorry, but Durdamon worries too much." Sheppar's eyes slid to Geoffrey, then back. Whatever had been in his glance, Sarah did not understand it.

But it seemed Geoffrey did understand. "My kinnig," he said, leaning forward. "Durdamon knew something—you know he knew something. And for good or ill he sent Sarah as his emissary. I asked to come along, but she is the one you should be talking to, not I."

Sarah managed to keep her composure as Sheppar sighed. "Very well," he said. "I'm still not sure how much harm there is in him, but I've been hearing...troubling things, out of the south. There was sent from Roth some time ago a mercenary group looking for four goblets of legend."

"The Berkarfor?" Sarah asked with a raised eyebrow. At Sheppar's sharp glance, she smiled. "I had heard something about them a number of years ago when I lived in Andelen for a short time."

"Yes, well. Those. I'm not as worried about the goblets themselves as what it signals from Roth. He always had been a little over-eager for power, but to chase such a legend is absurd even for him."

"You know him?" Sarah asked.

Sheppar frowned. "You are intelligent, at least. Yes, he was one of my—no, he *was* my top general during the campaign twenty years ago. I relied on him for so much of the success. But then it was he who championed killing Gared. And he never quite forgave me for being so hesitant about the whole thing. Then, once I began handing control over to the magiss'..." Sheppar shook his head. "He resigned within the year. Said the people of Andelen owed us for their safety, and we should exact as much as we could from them. I think he believed that was the whole point of the campaign—not that we did it *for* the people. I don't know to this day how he missed that, but..." He shook his head again. "I suppose I missed it in him, too."

"And why do the Beltraths invade?" Sarah asked.

"I sent some of our troops into the Wastes, trying to do an especially good job of keeping Andelen safe—Rinc Nain Andelen, anyway. After I made them kill the dragon, the same people who wanted Garedardan dead, including Roth, wanted all threats pushed away from Merneset. It required far more violence than I had wanted. But I also wanted it done with, and quickly. So I don't blame them, those who wanted it done. I wanted it done as well."

"We're not here to weigh in on that," Sarah said. "But with the incursion coming so close to the mission for the Berkarfor—are they related?"

"I doubt—"

Sheppar was cut off by a knock at the door. He looked up. "Come in," he said. "Ah, General Piembry. News from the patrols?"

"Yes, my lord," he said with a bow. "The patrol south reported: they discovered a Beltrath camp between here and Kostet's, approximately two hundred fifty men. We suffered approximately ten percent casualties, but we took most of them."

"And the rest?"

"They fled east my lord. My men pursued them as far as they could, but they quickly disappeared into the Eye. We broke off at that point and continued south, to garrison the 'vilt."

"Very good. Thank you, General."

"Sir," Piembry saluted, and exited.

Sheppar sighed, then glanced at Sarah. "You see? All taken care of."

"But something else troubles you."

Sheppar was silent for some moments. "I would have preferred they didn't enter the Dragon's Eye," he said quietly. "It's too easy to..." He trailed off, then closed his eyes for a moment. "I think that will be all for tonight," he said finally, looking up again. "I will take care of a few things in the morning. Please come see me again after lunch, and we'll discuss how you might help me."

"Thank you, my lord," Sarah said, standing. Geoffrey echoed her words and actions, and made for the door. Sheppar stood as they exited. Sarah paused, glancing back as Sheppar stood over one of the candles, studying it wearily. As it guttered, he took a shallow breath and blew it out, then bowed and shook his head. "Too easy," he muttered again.

Sarah shut the door and followed Geoffrey down the hallway.

Where are you?

Catie glanced up. He was far closer now than he had been. Was his cave so near? She gazed at the mountains, at every detail of the peaks, and sent it to Deuel. *There are men—Rodigger's men in the walls outside the Eye,* she said.

She paused, waiting for the response, but nothing came. Hesitantly she started forward again, her boots crunching on the stone that frequently breached the surface. She took a breath and shook her head. Surely he had heard her.

A wind rose in the west, rustling through the trees behind her. Except, there hadn't been trees. She turned quickly just as Deuel landed, his wings folding with a few shakes.

"Hi," she said. Her brain at this moment would only allow her a few letters at a time.

"Come with me," he said.

Anywhere, she managed to keep to herself.

He stepped forward and picked her up very suddenly, and she gasped as her arms went reflexively around his neck. "What are you—?"

She broke off with another gasp as his wings unfurled and shot them into the air. "What about the soldiers?" she shouted as the air whipped past them.

Who? he asked with amusement.

Well it's not like I'm used to this! she retorted, swallowing as she looked at the ground now far below, and then the peaks still far above them. *The soldiers. Rodigger and Sharéd have their forces outside the Eye.*

Very well. We'll stay below the peaks a little bit.

Are you sure you can carry me? she asked.

I surely won't drop you. You could hold on a little less tight, though.

Sorry, she said, loosening her arms. Deuel rotated his neck a few times, then suddenly pitched right and up, taking them swiftly over a saddle of the mountains. Catie's stomach, though, stayed for a moment in the valley behind them.

She swallowed, and rested her head against his shoulder. The beat of his heart and wings lulled her. She closed her eyes and let her momentum shift as it needed to. She wasn't sure how long they flew, and she wasn't entirely sure she stayed awake the whole time, though she couldn't imagine how she would have let herself sleep at a time like that.

Eventually, though, he was in her mind again. *Get ready to run a little bit.*

Um, what?

I'm going to let you down quickly. I may be more tired than I realized.

Oh. Okay.

She opened her eyes, seeing now that they were headed toward a cave opening halfway up on of the cliffs. She let her gaze wander. They had to be near the middle of the Eye. Suddenly, movement in the valley to the south caught her eye.

Deuel, she said.

I see him. It's too late, now. I'm going to let your legs down. I'll be right behind you, so keep running.

Have you ever done this bef— she cut off suddenly as her legs dangled in mid-air. She took a few deep breaths through her nose, tried to poise herself as the cave approached. When his wings flared, she slipped a little and his clutch choked her throat. Then she was falling. She flailed her arms as she tried to right herself. Her feet slammed into the ground and she ran, smacking her palms against the hard stone to keep from sprawling flat.

But she did it. She kept running, hearing Deuel's feet behind her. Finally she slowed and stopped, her heart racing as she was panting.

Are you okay?

Her palms burned, but she felt fine. There was a faint light from further in. *Do you have a fire?* she asked, a little alarmed, but also a little cold.

She felt his amusement. *Yes, you may warm yourself.*

She continued into the next room, then stopped as she looked at the wall.

Yes, Deuel said, coming in behind her. *That is what our chrysalis looks like.*

Do you...is it... She trailed off, glancing from the hibernating form to Deuel.

Yes, he said, and she could feel a somberness she didn't understand. *It is my brother.*

She reached out and put a hand on his shoulder. "Is that...isn't that good?" But then she thought of herself as she watched Sarah and Geoffrey, seeing what they had that she could no longer be happy with. "I know you wanted it, too."

But Deuel shook his head. He pulled a stick from the fire and held the flame closer to the head. It was still clearly human, but had also changed dramatically. The dimensions and form were almost canine, she thought, if dogs had smooth, reptilian skin instead of fur.

"I don't..."

"He's becoming wyvern," Deuel replied, his gaze locked onto Catie.

She knew her gaze spoke volumes; Deuel's did not. "But if he is behamian," she wondered, "what does that mean?"

Deuel was silent for several moments, and only the crackling of the flame broke the silence. "I don't know," he said finally. "We were raised together, taught together. But I have not seen him for over two hundred years. I do not know what may have happened to him during that time. I did not even know he was in Andelen."

Catie winced as he gave evidence of his true age, but turned her mind quickly onto the...wyvern...before her. She wanted to help, but she didn't know wyverns even existed until she had met Deuel. She was sure she had never heard any stories about them.

But she had heard plenty of stories about dragons. Deuel's brother, then, was likely to be buried into anonymity, an unknown race that even those who could communicate with their minds couldn't understand, according to Deuel. "So this is what I will become?"

"I cannot be so sure, anymore. It would seem wyvern and dragon are not as different as I thought."

Her chest heaved as she drew a sigh. "I do know. The guardian of the third goblet told me I was. And then... It's a very long story, but I have some sort of future memory of me flying with a whole group of wyverns. But I don't know if I can..." She shook her head as he stared blankly at her, as if he didn't know where her thoughts were going. "I thought, when you left... Have you changed your mind already?"

"You do not understand the effect of the Call. And now to be here, and see this... To be so close. Would you prefer I deny it? Are you sure you can stop from being a wyvern? If you had this 'future-memory' then am I to remain as I am while you become what you are?"

"I'm not certain that's what it was! Deuel, I don't know anything about this. I don't..." Her lips pressed together. "I don't know how you feel about this. You never talked about your brothers very much. You know more than me about wyverns and dragons and behamien and I don't even know why I can sense you and talk to animals and dragons, but I thought—"

"When did you talk to a dragon?"

"We met Lamendaretha in the Brithelt," she said. "She gave me the ability to sense you at longer distances, and showed me how to get here." Deuel went still. "What?"

"This...this..."

"This is where I come in!" said a new voice behind them.

Catie whirled, her dagger flying from its sheath. Deuel took a few steps sideways to stand out from behind her as Roth entered the chamber.

"How perfect!" he said, holding his arms wide. "I have a behamian and the woman who had better have my Berkarfor, all gathered together in one place."

"You'll have to—" She cut off as four soldiers entered behind Roth, arraying themselves in a line behind him.

"I'll have to what?" he growled. "I paid out good money for those goblets and you *will have to* give them to me—I wouldn't do that!" he said, pointing at Deuel. Catie glanced at him, saw his hands going for Halm and Ro Thull where they leaned against the back of the cave. One of the soldiers approached, sword held in front. He made it until one hand rested on the pommel of Ro Thull before Deuel swiped the out-stretched sword aside, grabbed the soldier by his throat, and flipped him backwards.

A bow creaked, and Catie looked up again to see the arrow aimed unwaveringly at Deuel's chest. The soldier on the floor groaned as he climbed to his feet. Roth chuckled.

"I didn't tell you to do that either," he said to the soldier. "What *idiot* would get that close to a behamian? But no matter. Unless this behamian is immune to arrows, he won't do that again."

"Do not touch that which isn't yours, again," Deuel said.

"He's really, very good," Catie said, still staring down her blade at Roth. "I wouldn't be surprised if he is immune to arrows—or at the very least able to swipe them out of the air with a wing."

"Possibly true," Roth agreed with a smile. "Still, might not want to risk it, just in case you're wrong. Besides, all you have to do is give me what I know you have, and we'll all be on our way."

"I don't think it's that simple," Catie replied.

"Let me try," Roth replied, taking a step forward. "First, you get that knife *out of my face!*"

She lowered it a little, in surprise if nothing else. Roth had been so controlled last time she met him.

"Next, you give me the goblets which I assume are in that bag. Then I leave, and take the country back for myself." He smiled, arms wide again. "What did I miss?"

"First, I only have three of them. You'll have to talk to Rodigger to get the fourth."

Roth waved his hand. "That child would give me his throat if I asked him."

"More importantly," Catie continued, "I don't think the Berkarfor do what you think they do," she said. "I was with them for the finding of each one, and...it's hard to explain."

"Fortunately, you don't have to, little *girl,*" Roth sneered. "I've read more about the Berkarfor than you've read about everything. But we needn't have this little argument here. Instead, you just give me the goblets, and let me worry about what I know and what you don't."

"And you'll leave the behamien alone?"

"Of course I will. They were...just in case," Roth said, his smile returning.

"Catie," one of the soldiers said. She glanced at him, her brows furrowing, then going wide in recognition.

Roth turned on him slowly. "It was you, wasn't it?" he said. His fist lashed out. The soldier ducked, his out-flung arm striking the bowman. With a cry the bowman twisted, tried to catch his balance, and released the string. Catie shouted a warning. Roth roared anger and pain as the arrow embedded deep into his thigh.

"You imbecile!" he roared, collapsing onto the ground. "I'll kill you all! Get me to my horse this instant! Get me a sage! A wizard! Not you, conniving, usurping, witch-spawn! Stay with them or I'll gut you and everyone you love! Bring me my Berkarfor or I'll gut your Grandmother like I gutted your husband! Put me down until she gives them to me. Kill the behamien if she doesn't!"

As Roth continued to curse and splutter, Catie shook her head at how far gone this man was over something he didn't understand. He had only read about them, made them in his mind to be something they weren't, and went mad with desire. She suddenly was not sure if it would help him more to keep them, or show them to him. If seeing them would shatter his expectation, destroy him, let him heal—or if he would continue to see them as he thought they were, try to wield them in a way they weren't designed, to who knew what end.

Before she could decide, she heard the tramp of many feet outside the cave, and she shuddered.

"No one move!" came a voice, this one far more familiar, though marked with greater authority than Catie had ever heard him muster. She quickly understood why. Behind Rodigger came ten or fifteen men armed with drawn blades, and it sounded as if even more were gathered outside.

"How dare you!" Roth shouted. "Do you even understand—"

"More than you know!" Rodigger said overtop of him. "To think I believed in you and what you *said* you stood for. And here you are making *treaties* with these...these..." He turned and looked at Deuel, his eyes sparking with hatred. His gaze turned to Catie, softening a little into a sort of regret, though it turned her stomach. Then the gaze slid to the wall behind them.

A torrent of emotions washed across that gaze, then: betrayal, hate, disgust, violence, a tinge of fear that was quickly squashed as he strode forward with a growl that became a roar. Catie wanted to step in front of him, but something in her chest vibrated, something that knew Rodigger was not himself.

"Rodigger," she managed weakly. He did not even hesitate. He passed her, and his hand jerked swiftly.

"Rodigger!"

"You—!"

"No!"

The last from Deuel, who leapt in too late. Rodigger, fueled by rage, kept Deuel away long enough to drive the blade home, in between the translucent wings. The wyvern inside shuddered and shook, squirming away from the steel as blood ran out and filled the chrysalis. Its mouth opened wide in soundless, writhing screams, then finally went still.

Deuel stared at his brother, dead in the cocoon. Three Beltraths came forward, blades outstretched to protect Rodigger, who backed away a few steps with a mixed look of horrified triumph on his face. Catie stared at Deuel, feeling the swirl of emotions coming from him and blending with her own.

"This is only the beginning," Rodigger whispered fiercely. "My men and I are going to continue through these caves and dispatch with every filthy vermin we find—starting," he continued with outstretched finger, "with you. And then," he pointed at Catie, "with those who sympathize with them."

"The wingt man is Sharéd's!" one of the Beltraths said, glancing at Rodigger.

"Sharéd isn't here!" Rodigger spat back. "He hasn't lived day in and day out beside this...thing! You'll tell him you couldn't help it, that Deuel attacked you."

"I do not serve you," the Beltrath replied, turning to face Rodigger.

Catie lashed out, catching the second Beltrath's sword in her dagger and wrenching it from his grasp. Deuel leapt forward, taking down the third.

More came forward. Roth's soldiers joined in, assuming Roth would be taken as well by someone entering who did not know who was who.

Rodigger tried to skirt around it all, parrying with a small sword as best he could as he pressed against the wall of the cave, edging toward the entrance. Catie pursued, but more nomads came in from outside.

Deuel came around behind her, Halm and Ro Thull ringing. He hadn't had on the bracelets to lend magic to the fight, but he was very good with just the blades. The shadows dancing from the fire confused the Beltraths. Deuel's and Catie's skill and advantage of being on the other side of a small opening kept them from surging in the numbers they hoped.

Suddenly a hand grabbed Catie's foot and pulled. She fell with a shout. Roth laughed, kicking her with his good leg. Stars exploded in her vision, and her ears rang. She rolled away from him, losing track of the fight for a moment. One of his soldiers, nearby, stabbed downward. She squeezed her eyes shut, and heard a terrific ringing right in front of her nose. When she looked up, she saw the soldier she recognized crashing a fist into the one that had tried to kill her, knocking him senseless.

There was a prolonged shout from outside, and Deuel was back in the room. Catie rolled to her feet, miraculously still hanging onto her dagger. Her ears still rang, though the pitch had changed. She came in beside Deuel, drawing some of the Beltraths away.

Suddenly she heard growling, and men shouting, but their speech was not Rinc Nain so she didn't understand what was being said. The fighting in front of her slacked.

What's happening?

I think there is another force outside.

She managed to reach the arm of the soldier in front of her, slicing it. He yelped and backed out of the cave, leaving her, Deuel, Roth, and the other soldier. She glanced around. The other three in Roth's entourage had fallen.

"I'll go out and see," she said. She exited the cave into pre-dawn light. The mountains hid the sun but the sky was already turning blue. She turned on the cliff, looking down the stairway as the backs of a few more Beltraths receded.

In the valley below, a pack of wolves were loose among the remaining fighters. The men were huddled together, trying to keep a circle, but the wolves too easily dodged blades and got inside. As she watched, suddenly Catie grinned.

"It's Eidemon!" she shouted back into the cave. "He's brought wolves with him! That innkeeper said he knew something about them!"

Below, the Beltraths were breaking, running southward as if trying to get out of the mountains. But there was a steep climb ahead of them, which surely the wolves could ascend more easily—

As her eyes continued upward, Catie frowned. "Eidemon!" she shouted suddenly. "Bring them up here!"

She pointed, where at the top of the ridge a new force of Beltraths were forming and preparing to descend. Eidemon glanced where she pointed, then at her with a nod. A few whistles and shouted commands in a language she didn't recognize, and the wolves and Eidemon were making their way up the natural staircase.

"It won't be perfect," she said when he neared the top, panting twice as hard as his wolves. "But it'll be more defensible than the open valley."

"I thank you," he managed. The wolves looked between the two.

Thank you, and be welcome, she said. A few cocked their heads, and seemed to nod in respect.

"Deuel's inside, as well as Roth," she said. "We seem to be holding him for now."

"Well, let's go," he said. Catie nodded, glancing again at the south ridge top. There were another several hundred men gathering as though waiting for those fleeing to bring them news on the forces they faced. In her mind's eye, Catie could see them laughing with their superior numbers.

"I'm not sure we'll be able to hold them," she said as she came into the cave. "Or outlast them, if they simply sit outside and wait."

"I'm bleeding," Roth said, petulant now that he held the lower hand.

"You could tie it off," Catie replied. "Or let someone do it for you. You're not going very far."

"Of course I could," he said, veritably spitting at her feet. "Those are my Beltraths out there. They're not going to kill me if I tried to leave."

"You *did* bring them out?" Catie asked. "Why?"

"I needed to get out of the Fallonvall. I needed Sheppar to take me seriously."

"Why not use the troops you already had?" Catie asked.

I think I can guess, Deuel muttered wryly.

"Because I'm the last one," said the soldier.

"You be silent!" Roth roared.

"Or what? There never was an army," the soldier went on.

"There never...then, how? Why?"

"He had heard the story of a lieutenant in Burieng overthrowing an entire province on the rumor that he had an army poised to strike. A long time ago, during the Age of War. Roth thought he would try it here. The problem was, the Province back then was united under a common heritage. Andelen isn't."

"It could have worked!" Roth spat. "If Sheppar hadn't demanded that everyone be different, everyone worry only about themselves and no one else—he should have united them instead of letting them divide."

"Like you did?" Eidemon interjected. "By force?"

Those soldiers will be here any moment, Deuel said. *We either need to let him go, or begin preparing.*

I say we let him go.

And the Berkarfor?

"I tried persuasion," Roth replied. "I tried it for years. People were too stubborn and too selfish. With the threat of the Beltraths, and the power of the Berkarfor, they would have loved to follow me. I could have given them the world they didn't know they needed."

Catie took a breath to cut in, then paused. Something was changing, she could feel it. At the edge of her consciousness was something vaguely familiar, but fresh. "I'm inclined to let you return to wherever you need to go to get help for your leg," Catie said, finally. "I'll keep the Berkarfor for now, and give them to you later."

"Absolutely not!" Roth said. "You're going to die here, and I'll never see them."

"Then I'll hide them in here. You can come back after we're dead and retrieve them."

Roth glared at her. She raised her eyebrows, waiting for his decision. "Fine," he muttered finally. "I'll go to the 'vilt, south—just in case you manage somehow to make it out of this alive. But don't think I'll request it of the Beltraths. They can have you and your...*friend*."

"Thank you. Steth, wasn't it?" she asked, turning to the soldier.

He smiled. "I'm pleased you remember," he said.

"It's been a long road since you brought me Kelsie," Catie replied, smiling. "Help him south, will you? And keep an eye on him until I get there?"

"Are you sure you will?"

"I've made it this far," she said with a shrug.

"Why aren't we keeping him as hostage?" Eidemon asked. "We could use him to barter with the Beltraths."

"Oh, I don't think we'll need to," Catie replied. "And I'd rather he didn't die just yet, actually."

With Steth's help, Roth got to his feet. They had been able to stop the bleeding, and had trimmed the arrow down to a nub just long enough for the surgeon to grasp, when that time came. As he hobbled out of the cave, he laughed.

"Something must be working in my favor," Catie heard him cackling to Steth. "Here I have my turncoat soldier helping me away from a lunatic of a woman, too silly to dispatch her enemies when she has the chance."

"I'm not sure I disagree with him," Eidemon said in a low growl. The wolves were laying down and resting, but now they looked toward the mouth of the cave expectantly.

"Would you mind helping me get these bodies out of here?" Catie asked. She went to the nearest one and picked him up under his armpits.

Eidemon turned to Deuel, keeping his voice low. "*Has* she gone mad?"

Deuel only looked at him, then went to the next body and picked it up. Eidemon watched him go. When he turned back, his wolves only looked at him. Muttering under his breath, he grasped one near him by the collar and began to pull.

"They're still at the bottom of the valley," Catie said from the cliff. *Would you mind helping too?*

After a pause, the wolves got to their feet as well, and began dragging the dead out of the cave. Eidemon glared at them, then at Catie.

"Would you kindly mind telling me what we're doing this for?" he asked.

"They'll want to honor their dead," she replied, entering the cave for the next fallen soldier. "I thought we could do the same."

"And you think they won't still kill us after they've honored them?" Eidemon said. "They may not, you. But they'll still be furious with Deuel."

Catie paused, cocking her head as if listening for something. "No, they won't kill us," she said finally. "But we should still hurry. Make sure to leave the entrance clear," she added, dragging out the next one.

The procession continued until all the Beltraths were laid out to the side of the cliff, near the stairs, just as the living Beltraths reached the bottom and began their ascent. "Back inside," Catie said, swinging her arms in a herding motion. Eidemon glanced down the cliff-side, then at her.

"You must know something I don't," he muttered.

She smiled. "Oh, I do. Stay just inside, and stay calm." *Everyone in the cave is friendly.*

Eidemon obeyed, looking outside. Shortly there came a light whistling, like wind among the crags. A sudden flap, as from a massive bird, and his eyes doubled in size as Garedardan, shepherd of the Tevorbath, exile to the Beltrath Wastes, settled on the cliff outside and waited for the soldiers below.

22

DEPARTS FIVE

"Seems to be nearly finished."
"There is yet one more thing to do."
"But have I done well?"
"As I said you would."

30 Nuamon 1320 — Autumn

As the Beltraths reached the top of the climb, they froze. Catie stood next to Gared, her hand on his shoulder. "Take your dead," she said. "Garedardan is leaving the Wastes. Roth has abandoned his purpose," she continued, gesturing with her free hand to where Steth and Roth were making their way out of the Eye below. "There is no need to decimate your people further."

They paused, looking at one another. Finally one turned back to Catie. "What about the wingéd man?" he asked.

"He is not your enemy. It was not his fault alone that Garedardan was put where he was. Punishment is coming to those who were truly responsible for that decision. As I said, no more of your people should die because of this thing. But know that *this* place is sacred, and critical..." She trailed off, realizing what she was saying. "I'm sorry," she said, bowing her head. "I know your oasis was sacred too, and critical to your survival. And I know nothing can replace having that taken from you for a generation. But nothing, not even killing a dragon and his children, can return that time to you."

"But their death is safety for our children's children," their leader replied.

"They were a tool," Catie said. "Used by others to hurt you. Roth tried to use them as well—and you—to hurt his own people. Would you have Andelians come again to your land to destroy you, because Roth promised you vengeance in return for your destruction on this land? Would you have them seek to kill all Beltraths for the safety of their children's children? Or would you ask their forgiveness for acting because of how someone made you feel, instead of what was peaceful?"

"You ask this as you stand beside our enemy, in front of our dead? You ask us for peace?"

"I ask you to think of your children's children. When they hear about how many died in order to kill two or three; when they hear that you had a choice to depart from the path of your past onto a new road, and you didn't take it; that they do not have a grandfather because he sought vengeance for *his* father—will they care? Or will they see the children with grandfathers, and only feel the lack? Nothing done before now has been right. Your choice now is to start down the road of what *is* right. You may not be able to forget the past. But if we are ever to leave this cycle of war, you have to forgive the past."

"You do not know what you ask."

"My husband was killed by that man," she said, gesturing again to the dwindling form of Roth. "He tried to kill me. And yet he goes, still living. And I will do nothing to kill him. I only ask you to do as I have done—to make your decision not from bitterness at the past but in hope for the future. Please take your dead, and honor them. And then return home and honor the living by *going on* living."

Go inside, Gared said. *You have said enough, and they will make their decision. But they will not be presided over by a Rinc Nain Andelian.*

Catie bowed to them, and turned. It was only then she noticed, at the back of the group, a young man standing a little taller, and who had seen far less sun. *I wondered where he had gotten to,* she thought. She went into the cave, wondering if Rodigger had thrown his lot completely in with the Beltraths.

"I think you did well," Eidemon said as she entered. "I hope you did, anyway. I'd like to be on my way."

"I'm going to explore more of the caves," she replied tiredly. *Have you looked for any others in here?*

No, Deuel replied, similarly weary. He stood beside his brother, again. The blood had run out of the chrysalis and stained the wall, puddling on the floor and adding a metallic smell to the wet stone. She paused beside him.

I'm sorry, Deuel, she said, resting her cheek against his shoulder. *I guess I have to hope you won't seek revenge, either.*

It is a difficult position, he agreed. *So is mine. He was my brother, whom I have not seen. I mourn his death, but I do not need fear for our race. I think that would make it worse. But I cannot say it makes it better.*

I know, she said. She embraced him from behind, and he reached up and put a hand on her arm as they stood silently for several long moments.

Thank you, Caytaleane, he said finally. *Go, see if anyone else has entered* veythya.

Okay, she said. *I'll be back. Garedardan, have they decided?*

They are gathering their dead. I will come in shortly—we must trust them to keep their word.

Thank you. Catie turned to the dark opening leading deeper into the caves, wondering how much her vision could adjust.

It rippled, but she still struggled in the dim gray. The next room was empty, and she could make out a long, winding path to the third, but few details. She entered, and everything settled into a haze. Halfway across the floor, a shape on the wall to her left caught her eye. She squinted, then took a few steps forward. There was definitely one there, but it was different from Deuel's brother. The chrysalis seemed...fuller. But then, as the dragon grew, she realized it would have to. She took another step closer...

And gasped. Drawing closer to the changing form, her sight brightened, confirming what she saw. There were two bodies inside, curled back-to-front as if cuddling. She didn't recognize the face of the form in the back, but in the front, her body melding with the form behind, was Catie's mother.

Deuel, could you come here please?

Garedardan is coming as well, he replied.

She waited, shaking a little, as she heard footsteps—small and large—coming down the tunnel. When they entered, she felt a love coming from Garedardan that she hadn't felt in a very long time.

"I don't understand," she said, somehow knowing Gared did.

Lamend told me about you, about your meeting in the Brithelt. Knowing it might come to this point, we agreed to tell you some things that normally are not told.

"Why is my mother here?"

She is actually your older sister. You two spent a number of years growing up in the Brithelt. A great number of years.

"Why don't I remember being there?" Catie asked.

It was a long time ago, Caytaleane. And, you are supposed to forget.

"What am I supposed to forget?"

That you are behamona.

Catie's eyes went wide, unsure if that meant what she thought it meant. *Behamona?*

Dragon-daughter.

She sat down. She couldn't help it. *But I don't have wings,* she thought faintly.

You are female, Garedardan replied, still chuckling but also as if appalled. *Females do not have wings.*

Why didn't Deuel tell me? She looked at him. He was only a little less surprised than her.

I didn't know, Deuel said. *I only realized a few moments ago that you were not wyvern, but indeed dragon-kind, when you said you had spoken to Lamend. I knew only dragon-kind could do more than sense the emotions of dragons. I still don't understand how.*

Garedardan glanced between them, his eyes kind. *It is for behamien to forget they are human. It is for behamona to forget they are dragon. In this is balance. Deuel has probably never considered the fact that all his siblings were brothers.*

His expression told all.

There is an age where your memory begins to fail. It is this age you are sent out among humans, to be raised with them, and to believe you are one of them for a time. It was Bahamut's way of ensuring compassion.

"Did my...sister know, then? Or find out?"

When several of Sharéd's tribe came seeking revenge, and the man you called father died defending you both.

Catie pressed her lips together, hoping a similar walling-off took place in her mind. Perhaps her sister had done what she thought best, but wouldn't she have been able to help Catie as she got older? Help her understand what had been going on with her?

Your Grandmother did that, whispered a thought that was not from Deuel or Gared.

Had she? It was not custom to let a Newmother wander off into the world, as she had been allowed to do. Had Grandmother let Catie leave in hopes that she might figure things out better than staying in Attelek? Catie thought back to their conversations when she had returned to her village, had started preparing to leave with Gabriel, Deuel, and Rodigger. She knew that was exactly what Grandmother had done.

Deuel glanced from Catie's sister to Gared. *What about wyverns?*

Wyverns are born when a dragon-child enters veythya alone. There is not enough flesh and bone in one child to grow into dragon. But for you, Deuel, understand this: do not think of wyvern as 'not-dragon'; they are wyvern. They are not defined by what they lack. There is much that wyvern can—and do—that dragon cannot, and do not. Their story in this age is yet to be understood. One day it shall be told. Spare yourself shame on that day by honoring them now.

Catie shook her head. "I still don't understand why this knowledge is hidden. Why not tell the children that, to become dragon, they must enter veythya with a mate?"

It seemed as though Garedardan smiled. *And shall I also tell you that you will marry someone with dark hair, so that you look past all those with light hair? Ages ago, too many dragons entered veythya with a mate because they knew they must. Within a few years, those dragons died of inner torment because their two halves were at war with one another. Only those who truly love—who are willing to sacrifice themselves to see the other become who they were made to be—will survive as dragon.*

"I still..."

Paolound has died. A male dragon must be born to replace him, Garedardan replied. *Were it the other way—had Kaoleyn died—Ledogar must be willing to live as female dragon to replace her. Some of Kerlyn's traits will survive, as they must to make the dragon complete, as I carry in me many of the things that made my wife who she was. But to the world, I appear as male. To the world, Lamendaretha is female, though it took a complete male to make her as well. What we appear to be on the outside is dictated by the needs of the world, and the time in which we are born out of veythya. But what we are on the inside will always contain parts of both.*

"So, if Deuel wanted to become dragon..." Catie broke off, and her face went red. From Deuel she felt very little emotion. From Gared she felt rolling laughter.

This is why Lamend and I decided to give you some knowledge that is not normally given at this early time. Deuel would be with you, gladly—he has demonstrated that, as you have demonstrated you would take him. Gared paused for another chuckle. *But Lamend and I both believe dragon-kind will be best served if you wait until a female must be replaced.*

Catie's hand went to her mouth, and she closed her eyes. *I'm sorry. I've just been on my own for so long, I had to...I'm used to making decisions for myself, and acting on them.*

Do not be ashamed about this, Gared said. *Among humans, perhaps, Deuel should be ashamed for acting as what they perceive is 'not-man'—but that is only because male is considered supreme, and female as always lacking. Deuel is himself; you are yourself. What you each may lack in your character has nothing to do with your sex, but because you are young and still selfish. There are times where you still do not look beyond yourself, or this age, to understand and do what the Great Harmony requires.*

Is the Great Harmony... Catie trailed off, and tried to call up the memory from Ostflir. Garedardan's gaze sharpened.

Even I have not been allowed to see that much, he replied. *The God has blessed you, Caytaleane. But for what purpose I do not know.*

I have spent more time with her than you, Deuel said, his gaze much softer. *I have seen her prepared to do whatever was necessary, despite risk or lack of understanding, than anyone. If the God has some great purpose for her, his guidance would not be wasted.*

Gared glanced between them. *And does he guide you, Caytaleane of Brithelt?*

Catie considered for a long moment. The memory of the Ekllar, that strange future-memory—but she also knew it was not meant to guide her. Beyond her plan of finding Roth again...

Maybe that was enough. She had promised to bring him the Berkarfor. Perhaps after she kept that promise, her next step would become clear. "I will find Roth," she said. "After that, I do not know."

I will take you to him, Garedardan said. *Deuel should see to the honors of his brother. After, I will bring her back?* He said it as a question, looking at Deuel.

That will be fine, he replied.

A memory exploded in her mind. "Oh, Rodigger has the first Berkarfor, though!"

"Was he one of the dead?"

"No, I saw him outside."

I saw him as well, Gared said. *If he was carrying it, he hid it well.*

What do you mean?

Let us return to the first chamber.

They walked through, and when they reached the room they found that Eidemon and his wolves had already departed. Catie's gaze swept the room, lighting quickly on a small pack near where the fight had begun.

"Is that his?" she asked, trotting forward. She retrieved it, and peered inside.

She pulled out an iron goblet. *I don't understand,* she said. *I know when we found these they were very exquisite, some of the finest craftsmanship...*

Charmed, Gared said. Deuel broke his gaze from his brother's corpse to look at the great black dragon. *There is an ancient dragon-charm on all the Berkarfor to make them appear more valuable than they are.*

"Usually when you want to hide something, you make it appear common," Catie said.

You also put real guardians around them, to prevent anyone from taking them, Garedardan replied. *Everything about the Berkarfor are designed to frustrate the plans of those who would take them for easy power, and only truly bless those who retrieve them realizing the important thing is who you become in the journey, not what you get out of the pursuit. You see them for what they are because they hold no power over you, Catie.*

"So, Roth?"

It will be as it should, Gared replied. *Whatever his intentions with these goblets, we must let him make his decisions, and abide by the consequences.*

Deuel returned to tend to his brother, and as Catie and Garedardan continued outside they found the Beltraths were gone too. The sun was well over the mountains, then, and a hawk circled below for prey. Taking a deep breath, Catie climbed Gared's offered foreleg and onto his back.

He won't have gone far, Catie said.

I know. I can see them.

You all are very good, she said with a laugh. *I keep forgetting that.*

You are very good, as well, Gared replied as he dropped off the cliff and soared out across the valley. *But I think you've never believed that.*

Who me? The sunniest behamona in Andelen? she asked, and they both laughed.

Roth and Steth stopped as Gared's shadow swooped over them, craning their necks. He settled in the valley ahead of them, and Catie dismounted.

"Let me down!" Roth shouted. "She brought them to me—miracle of heaven! Get me on the ground!"

Catie strode forward as Steth struggled to comply. Though he cried out several times, Roth finally made it to the ground, and lay down.

"Bring them! We don't have much time!" he said hoarsely, laying a hand on the tourniquet Steth had applied. "You do have them?"

Catie shook her head slightly as she held the bag out in front of her. As he gazed inside it, she knew Roth wasn't seeing them as they were, but as what he expected them to be—knew by the glint in his eye and light in his face, that he was seeing the jeweled, sparkling Berkarfor. She feared for what he was about to do.

"What order did you find them in?" he demanded, pulling them out. Catie gestured to and numbered them each.

"Perfect! Excellent!" He took the first cup, undid the tourniquet, and began filling the goblet with his blood.

Nothing prepared her for that. "What are you doing?" she demanded, taking a step back.

"The legends say, to gain the power, you must drink blood from the Berkarfor—there is life in the blood! Life, with new power." He began filling the second goblet.

"I don't think that's how they work—I *know* that's not how they work," Catie said, taking the step forward again. "Roth, you must listen to me!"

"No!" he shouted. "I know what you think—you who would see me die! *And* you!" he said with an accusing glare at Steth. "You are working together, I know you are, and I will deal with both of you when I am done." He let his blood into the third goblet.

"Roth, I don't care anymore," Catie said. "I've given up on that. But I have actually made the effort to find the goblets, and I can assure you the finding is the most important part."

"*You* found them? Ha! You would never have begun looking if I hadn't found out they existed to begin with." The fourth went near his leg and blood stained the cup. "I am certain I had the harder task."

Gared, help me stop him.

They are said to grant great power, Gared replied. *He may be right.*

"You know he's not," she said, turning to face the dragon fully. "You know this will kill him."

He will not be stopped. Whether this way, or some other, he will kill himself. Do you see?

Catie whirled. Roth had already downed the first goblet. She stepped toward him. He snarled blood at her, lashing out with surprising strength, a small dagger in his other hand. She jerked backward, too slowly, as blood oozed from the small cut.

Steth came forward, pulling her away from Roth as he slurped down the second goblet.

"Please, stop it," she said, tears coming to her eyes, and not entirely from the fire in her arm.

Roth laughed, more blood spraying from his throat, before lifting the third. Catie buried her head in Steth's shoulder. *Why do we do this?*

Because we believe we have the ability to judge for ourselves.

Roth drew a deep breath and smiled, setting down the fourth goblet. "Now, it is time," he said. He tilted his head back, spread his arms, waited for the power to infuse him. "No one will ever know anyone as great as Roth Kamdellan."

Catie drew a breath, looked at Roth, almost hoped he *would* receive whatever power he thought he would.

But instead he became pale. He shook feebly, as if with chills, and his lips turned blue. His eyes widened in disbelief and horror. He bent forward suddenly, vomiting. Shaking and gasping, he fell backward, his breathing in swift gasps as his limbs twitched.

"No...can't...be..."

Catie looked at him more intently as he tried to speak between coughs. His eyes locked onto hers, and rage filled them. "You...did..." He coughed again, his body writhing. His head snapped backward, he arched away from the ground as he twitched.

Suddenly he went slack. His voice, when he spoke, was deeper. *"The way south is open,"* he said, as though confiding in someone else, someone Catie couldn't see. *"After centuries..."*

Coughing wracked him again. He cut off in the middle of a wheeze, frozen as if unable to draw strength to inhale. He stayed like that, heels and fingernails wrenching at the ground, as all the color left him, and seemed as if his flesh withered in on itself.

Catie drew a shaky breath, and pushed herself away from Steth. She glanced at him, could tell by his expression that he hadn't heard Roth's last words.

"He never was himself, lately," Steth said, also sighing. "When I first followed him, it seemed he had a wonderful vision for Andelen. Probably most of us felt the same way. But ever since this spring..." Steth trailed off, shaking his head. "Something changed. He was almost always angry. The more time went on, the more he would fall into fits, like you saw him today. I guess I assumed it would be the end of him soon. How is your arm?"

"Oh, it's fine," she said, waving him away. Her sleeve was stained, but no fresh blood was evident. "Can you do something for me? Go to Agrend and let Sheppar know what happened? I need to get back to Deuel."

"Of course," Steth replied. He stepped away, but did not turn. "It was good to see you again," he said. "However briefly."

"You too," she said with a smile. "It was your fault," she continued lightly. "If you hadn't brought me Kelsie..."

"That was a long time ago," he said with a dismissive wave. "I wouldn't presume there weren't a great many things you've overcome since then. I will bury Roth. He probably still deserves that. And I will deliver your message. Fare well, Catie."

"You too, Steth," she said. She turned and climbed onto Garedardan, waving one last time as the dragon leapt into the air.

Did you hear him? she asked as they winged toward the cave once more. *'The way south is open, after centuries'?*

It sounds like Gintanos, Gared replied. *Cariste landed there long ago, but have stayed north of the mountains, believing it was impossible to make their way south. Perhaps they have found a way.*

I think that is where I am to go, Catie said slowly. *The next step.*

And Deuel?

He will have to make his decision, first.

"You could perhaps head south," Sheppar said, gesturing on the map as if he had not suggested it three other times earlier in the conversation.

"My lord, the Beltraths here suggest Roth may be here," Sarah replied—also as if she had not used the same rebuttal at least twice. "By the time we travel all the way south, learn this for certain, and come all the way north again—"

"I have said that Roth is not the concern," Sheppar said, seating himself. "The state of the settlements in the Fallonvall *is*. We must know how much sway he holds, because removing him from that power may not be enough. If he is here, it is because he has the Berkarfor already, and is preparing an attack of some sort against Agrend. If we make him a martyr, then the rebellion will not die. But if you go south, you might undermine his support there—cut out the heart, instead of removing the head."

Sarah drew a breath, then glanced at Geoffrey. That actually made some sense. The problem was cutting out the heart before the head struck off Andelen's head. "How fast can we get down there, though?"

"The fastest route would be by boat," Sheppar said. "There is a private port, to the west. They would be suspicious of people traveling south on foot, anyway. If your ship docks at Satflir, you can say you are from Burieng."

"Are you up for another boat ride?" Sarah asked with a twinkle in her eye.

"Of course, lady," Geoffrey replied.

She glowered at him playfully as a knock sounded on the door.

"Come," Sheppar said. When Samdar entered, he smiled. "Ah, Samdar, perfect timing. These two need to go by boat to Satflir."

"My I ask my lord's purpose?" Samdar asked, also smiling. "It does not regard the rebellion, does it?"

"Why shouldn't it?" Sheppar asked.

"Roth is dead," Samdar replied. "A messenger came with it a few moments ago."

"What happened?"

"Apparently the Berkarfor are not what we believed them to be. Roth drank his own blood from them, and died."

"Oh! Well, then..." Sheppar glanced at Sarah and Geoffrey, his smile tinged with a little sadness. "I'm sorry you came all the way here," he said.

Geoffrey glanced down at his arm. "I'm not," he said quietly. Sarah gripped his hand, smiling as well.

"This is such sudden good tidings. What will you do now, though?" Sheppar asked. "I still might have a use for an advisor—two advisors," he amended quickly, smiling at Samdar, who appeared properly concerned.

"Carist?" Sarah asked, glancing at Geoffrey. "I left my father on bad terms. I hoped to make it up to him."

"Rinc Na, first," Geoffrey replied. "I have work to do there." He shrugged. "And we might find Haydren."

Sarah smiled, and nodded. "Did the messenger mention anyone named Catie?" she asked Samdar.

Samdar cocked his head, shaking it. "No, but I could ask him."

"She is supposed to meet us here. We'll find out then."

"Very well," Samdar said with a bow.

Garedardan landed with Catie, on the cliff outside the cave. Catie drew an unsteady breath, wondering if Deuel had decided. She almost wished he had not, that he would go with her. She had to follow her decision, she knew that. But, thinking of the time in the Brithelt away from Deuel, she did not enjoy the idea of leaving him again. She knew, deep inside, she would if she had to.

Sometimes, that felt worse.

She walked into the cave. *Deuel?* she asked.

I am here, he said. She could sense nothing from his words as to what he might be feeling.

She walked in. Deuel's brother was no longer on the shelf. There was a cairn in the room, now, beside which Deuel stood, head bowed. She walked up to him, placing her hand on his shoulder, keeping silence as he did.

Deuel drew a breath, and turned toward her. *Do you know what you must do?*

I know where I must go, she said. *I don't know why, yet.*

That is enough.

The silence stretched on as Catie waited for him to indicate his decision, if he had one, knowing that her previous hope was too much to ask for. "And you?" she asked finally.

"How have you made your decision?" he asked instead.

"Deuel..." She glared at him. He waited patiently for her. *Gared can tell you,* she said finally. *If you don't want to trust me.*

I want to make sure we can decide separately from each other, Deuel replied.

That you can follow the plan for your life, even if it means leaving me.

"We did that already," she said, taking a step back. "Remember? You came here, and I kept searching for the Berkarfor? I would never keep you from doing what you felt you needed to do, Deuel, and I know you would never keep me from it either."

"I am sorry," he replied, and she felt that he meant it. "I had not thought...I did not think what it would mean for you to go on alone. I knew only that I had to come here. I'm sorry."

"Well, Roth killed Dannid, and I forgave him, so..." Her mouth quirked into a smile.

"I remember another brother of mine, Berygal, went east, when we left Kaoleyn's nest," Deuel said. "I had thought to find him, and tell him about...Marethal," he said, glancing at the cairn.

Catie pressed her lips together to keep the ridiculous smile she felt inside from showing. "How far east?" she asked.

"I believe he went to Gintanos," Deuel said, his eyes searching hers. She knew he could sense it, but didn't care. "He always liked the cold. And you?"

"Something happened as Roth was dying. He mentioned the way south was opened after centuries," she said.

Deuel gazed at her for several moments. "Gintanos," he said. "The way south through the mountains."

The smile started to seep through her determination.

"We will have to be content to spend a lot of time together, then," he said, stepping closer to her. Her smile disappeared as she looked into his eyes.

He pulled her close, wrapped his wings around her to hold her even closer, bent down, and kissed her.

Rodigger lay resting in the sun as it crested the mountains. His Therian stood nearby, reins loose. He wondered, briefly, how Gared would make it out of the Eye. Their trip in had not been easy, even with the scouts to guide them. The Therian was just not made for steep, loose trails.

It had hurt, seeing Catie with those creatures—Deuel, and the one wrapped in its own wings, sickly and gray, and with that *face*. He didn't understand how such a pretty girl could stand that close to something like that. He had really hoped to carry her out of there, to save her from her own delusion. But, here he was instead, fearing for his life again.

There wasn't much left. The Beltraths didn't want him, obviously, even though he was sure he could have made a fine leader. Under Sharéd, of course. He would have been obedient to Sharéd, if he'd had to.

Too late now. His best hope was that Deuel, in a rage, would come and drive Halm and Ro Thull through his heart. It wouldn't have been a surprise, or any less painful.

After all their traveling together, he didn't understand how Catie could have turned the way she did. He coughed. He had never seen this coming—any of it.

A shadow passed over him. Here comes Deuel now, he thought. Come to finish me off. The shadow passed again, and he looked up to see a winged shape circling slowly. It wasn't Deuel, it was too small.

The vulture landed just out of his reach, looking at him. Another shadow passed. Another vulture circling lower.

Rodigger coughed again, looked at the Beltrath arrow pointing skyward from his chest, then again at the pair of vultures. They wouldn't have long to wait.

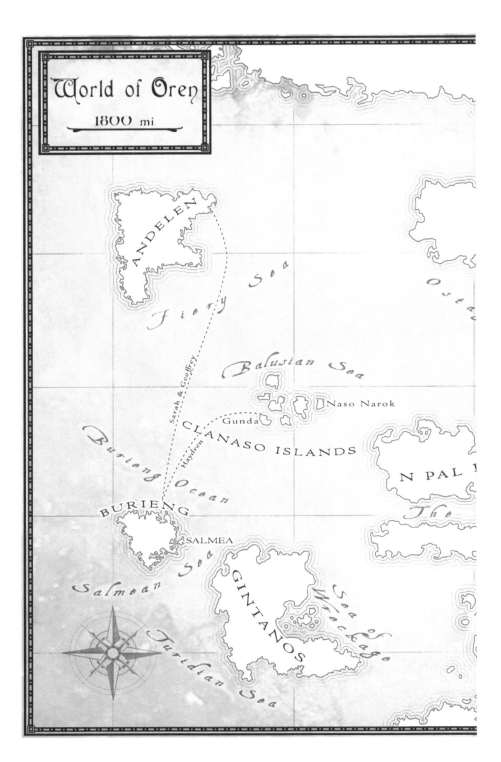

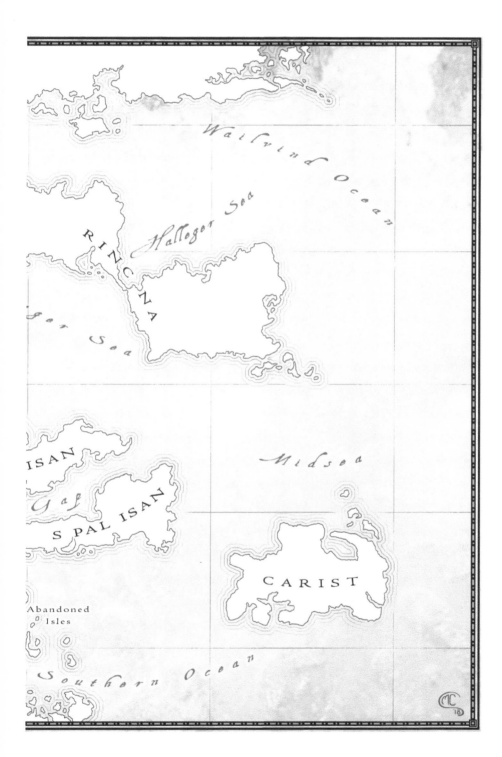

Author's Note on Calendar

I provide here a brief description of the history of Oren, its Ages, and Calendars.

As conquerors, Oren history is told mostly by the countries of Rinc Na and Carist, and the Ages and Times as they understand them are assumed.

The First Age, the Black Age (B.A.), is an unknown age. Some few documents remain in fragments, and there are none who know when it began or how the world looked when it did. Every culture's Creation Myths are guesses at this Age, but little more.

The Second Age, the Magic Age (M.A.), is defined and known as the year when magic was first discovered in Carist, and began to be taught by those who used it best. From start to finish numbers 1,095 years as the knowledge and use of magic grew exponentially. Discoveries were made by many great men and women, daring souls who spoke a language they did not know or understand, and many died in the pursuit. The Age ended with the terrible conclusion of the Wizard War, or War of Magics, that had wrought so much devastation to the lands it touched.

The Third Age, the Age of Discovery (A.D.), began as Cariste and Rinc Nain began to pick up the pieces and embark on a new pursuit: that of sailing to all parts of the existing world. Over the succeeding 2,060 years these two competing countries settled all the known world, either living with or displacing native peoples on the Pal Isans, the Clanaso Islands, Andelen, and Burieng. Cariste found none living on Gintanos at first, though in the current Age that is soon to change drastically (the first hints of this can be found in *The First to Forgive,* and will come to full fruition in *Sacrificing All Pain*). The Age ended when the settlers on eastern Burieng sent a missive to Carist declaring their autonomy from that home country, and was the first stroke in the most tumultuous age of history.

The Fourth Age, the Age of War (D.W., or During the War) was not a time of constant strife, though strife indeed pervaded every year. In Burieng, Cariste and Rinc Nain fought over the country and were overthrown suddenly by the native Endolin under King Burieng. News of rebellion against the home countries of Rinc Na and Carist spread, and each country in turn declared and fought for their own autonomy from the lands where they had originated. After 896 years all was settled once more, and with only minor exceptions the countries look now as they did then.

Finally, the current Age, after the eight continents solidified, (A.E., or After the Eight). A common calendar was formulated and agreed upon by all Rinc Nain and Cariste, and eventually by the natives as they conducted business with those two peoples. The calendar was conceived and developed by the Rinc Nain, though only those people know it as "the Rinc Nain calendar." It consists of 400 days across 11 months of varying lengths. It begins with **Haschina** (named from legend), on the Winter Solstice in Rinc Na and countries north of the equator; or the first day of Summer in southern latitudes. It continues with **Mantaver** (Month Two), **Thriman** (Third Month), **Halmfurtung** (Half Four Moon, as four Full Moons have come and gone), **Fimman** (Fifth Month), **Monzak** (Month Six), **Savimon** (Seventh Month), **Fulmatung** (Full Eight Moon), **Nuamon** (Ninth Month), **Tetsamon** (Tenth Month), and **Elfumon** (Eleventh Month).

ACKNOWLEDGEMENTS

Time again to remember all who made this thing possible:

My Alphas and Betas, for their eager anticipation of drafts, and critical early opinions.

The Faith Family Writer's Group, and their gentle, sensitive opinions as they ruthlessly erase all my semicolons.

New to the game, cartographer extraordinaire, Soraya and her AMAZING work on my maps.

My cover artist, Abigail, and her continued passion and excellence in making my books look good enough to judge by their covers.

And, of course, my wife and family for continued support and devotion.

Oh, and Baby Bear, now grown into a Buddy Dude, who came into the world last autumn and helped me wake up early—though he usually preferred I feed him than work on this book.

About the Author

Daniel Dydek is a multi-genre author with his sweeping epic fantasy series The Triumvirs, and his supernatural suspense series, Spirit Wind, has already garnered two Finalist awards from Realm Makers. Besides writing, he also enjoys a personal relationship with Jesus Christ, mountain biking, reading, coffee shops, book stores, and Durango Colorado. He lives in Canton Ohio with his wife and son and two cats.

Support for the Author

First, thank you for reading this story on whichever medium you chose—Kindle, KU, or paperback. Your support means dreams come true! If you loved the story, there are a lot of ways to continue supporting the author FOR FREE. Here's a few:

1. Subscribe to the newsletter on danieldydek.com

2. Tell your friends!

3. Leave a review on Goodreads, Amazon, Barnes & Noble, or on your social media. (This is probably the greatest support of all, because we love hearing what people enjoyed about the book! Plus, you know, algorithms...)

4. Request your local library to get a copy

All these things help promote the books, and encourage the author to keep writing stories you'll love!

—The Beorn Publishing Team

The Triumvirs epic fantasy series

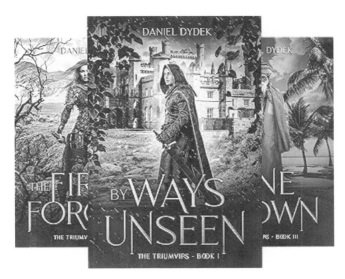

Centuries ago, the world of Oren was ravaged by uncontrolled magic during the Wizards War. In the wake of such devastation and evil, the God of All took three wizards and established for them a Room, of darkness and consciousness, and placed before them a great table whose appearance is of translucent slate, through which they might call up visions of the lands, entering when needed. Few even know these former wizards exist, and their work will always be credited to brave men and women of the world who were faithful in their obedience.

These wizards' task is keeping the peace, of prompting action against the forces of evil. They answer still to the God of All, but retain autonomy. He named them The Triumvirate, and over the centuries twenty-two Triumvirs have guided Oren through wars, famines, pestilences, and the rising and falling of countless empires.

Now, in this current Age of men, will come their most difficult battle.

Amazon search: The Triumvirs Dydek

Spirit Wind Christian suspense series

Cursed with left-handedness, then cursed with fire.

Except the fire seems to comfort, to strengthen, to speak wisdom. Wisdom like:

"The wind bloweth where it listeth, and thou hearest the sound thereof, but canst not tell whence it cometh, and whither it goeth: so is every one that is born of the Spirit."

And so Rae-Anna is borne on itinerant winds, never knowing what danger she'll be asked to face. But she knows this: it will always be demonic. And she will never be alone.

Amazon search: Spirit Wind Dydek

Made in United States
Troutdale, OR
12/04/2024

25852346R00195